PROCLAIMED A HERO MARCUS ARRIUS IS OFFERED COMMAND OF THE PRAETORIAN GUARD IN ROME BUT INSTEAD CHOOSES DUTY ON HADRIAN'S WALL AS FAR FROM ROME AS HE CAN GET.

"By the gods, I had no idea there would be this many." Arrius looked at General Gallius. "Did you know anything about this before we came here?"

"Commander Turbo told me to expect some resistance as we approached Beth Thera, but I did not expect the entire Jewish Army. We will need Jupiter's help this day for certain. What do you estimate their strength to be?"

"Possibly 20-25 thousand, perhaps more behind those hills." Arrius now understood the intense expression on Turbo's face when he said farewell three days ago. "General, I believe it was not intended for you to know more than you were told. We are the sacrificial goat staked out as Turbo's bait."

Marcus Arrius is the senior centurion of the ill-fated XXII Legion, Deiotariana, serving in Judaea during the second century Roman Empire. Focused on duty and his men to the exclusion of all else, Arrius is a loyal, battle-tested soldier. Following Hadrian's brutal suppression of the second Jewish revolt in Judaea in 135 CE, his core belief in Rome begins to erode without fully understanding why. For his exploits in Judaea, he is decorated and given his choice of assignments in Rome including command of the Praetorian Guard. His request for duty on Hadrian's Wall instead surprises both the generals and Arrius himself. It will be Ilya, a beautiful native woman in Britannia, who will become the catalyst for understanding why he chose command of an obscure frontier fort instead of fame and fortune in Rome.

"Preston Holtry sets a new standard for the historical novel with *Arrius–Sacramentum*, which takes place in the second century Roman Empire. Mr. Holtry masterfully weaves a fictional tapestry rich in authenticity and detail and places within a set of characters that fit perfectly into the context and manage to transcend it. As a result, readers will fully share the characters' experiences and emotions, while being transported to another place and time. A stunning piece of historical fiction."—*Hank Luce, author of* A Darkness in the Pines.

"Holtry shows a deep knowledge of both the Roman Army and the campaigns they fought. It follows Centurion Arrius from Britannia to Judea and then back to Britannia where he leaves the life of the legion to command a mixed cohort of auxilia. The style reminds me of Simon Scarrow. The first in a trilogy, I can see this book addicting readers."—*Griff Hosker, author of the Norman Genesis series, The Anarchy series and Sword of Cartimandua series.*

"*Arrius-Sacramentum* is an intense and beautifully written story. Holtry skillfully transports readers to the outer reaches of the Roman Empire through a warrior facing dangerous enemies, even within his own ranks. Meticulously researched, the strength of this novel lies in the depth of the characters and the vivid imagery of ancient times. Holtry established himself as a master storyteller in his first series, and he hits a homerun in the first installment of the *Arrius* trilogy."—*Steve Brigman, author of The Orphan Train.*

"With Preston Holtry's Morgan Westphal mystery series, we find through extensive research the creation of well-crafted plots, realistic characters, and detailed scenes, creating fast paced stories. Jumping back in time, Preston has done it again with *Arrius-Sacramentum*. A man on his way up the ranks in the Roman Legion shows he's more than a blind follower but uses his brains and initiative, sometimes to his own detriment. Join him in Britannia near Hadrian's Wall, travel through the Middle East and the war with Judaea, and back to Britannia where he commands his own forces.— "*A great read--can't wait for the sequel. Randall Krzak, author of The Kurdish Connection .*"

ARRIUS
VOLUME I
SACRAMENTUM (OATH)
Preston Holtry

Moonshine Cove Publishing, LLC
Abbeville, South Carolina U.S.A.

FIRST MOONSHINE COVE EDITION JULY 2017

ISBN: 978-1-945181-16-0
Library of Congress Control Number: 2017945635
Copyright © 2017 by Preston Holtry

Front cover design by Cynthia Guare, back cover design by Moonshine Cove staff.

For Allyn, Anthony, Gary and all other centurions who have seen the face of war

About The Author

Preston Holtry is the author of the Morgan Westphal period mystery series and the ARRIUS trilogy. He has a BA degree in English from  the Virginia Military Institute and a graduate degree from Boston University. A career army officer, he served twice in Vietnam in addition to a variety of other infantry and intelligence-related assignments in Germany, England, and the United States. Retired from the army with the rank of colonel, he lives with his wife, Judith, in Oro Valley, Arizona with much of his time now spent writing the next novel. Holtry is the author of four published mystery novels set in the Southwest during the period 1915-17 featuring the private detective Morgan Westphal.

Read more about his interests and writing approach at his website: http://www.presholtry.webs.com.

Acknowledgment

I deeply appreciate the efforts of my wife, Judy, Bruce Filer, and Don Ayers, D, Ed, for the time they spent giving editorial counsel and trolling for the infernal typos that lie in wait, hidden from the author but inevitably noticed by the reader. My thanks to Clarence Alford for permission to use his painting Legionaries Marching to Camp for the jacket design. Finally, and not least, my thanks to Moonshine Cove for constructive criticism, the patience to deal with an author who doesn't always get it right and, most of all, for giving Marcus Arrius a chance to tell his story.

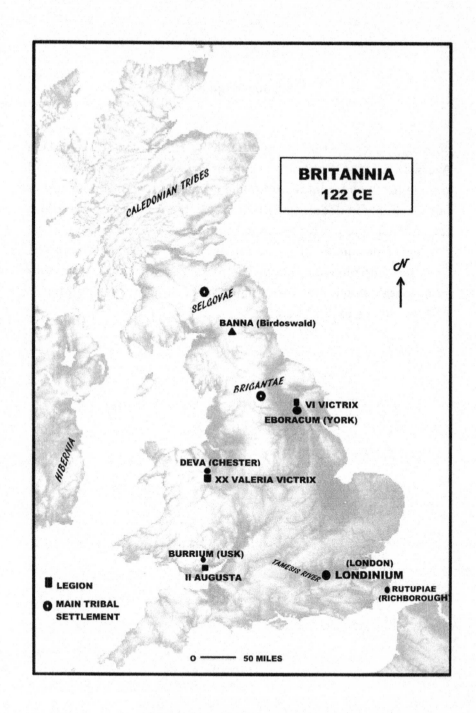

Map of Britannia 122 CE

Principal Characters

The Romans

Attius Cato Varro, Camp Praefectus of Legion XXII, *Deiotariana*

Decrius, an optio in the First Cohort and by birth a Brigantian tribesman

Marcello Aculineous, a replacement centurion assigned to the First Cohort

Marcus Junius Arrius, Commander of the First Cohort and *primus pilus* of Legion XXII *Deiotariana*; subsequent *praefectus* of an independent command on the northern Britannian frontier

Marius Strabo, a senior centurion in Legion XXII, *Deiotariana*

Metellus Caecilia Gallius, general and commander of Legion XXII, *Deiotariana*,

Philos, Arrius's former slave, mentor and closest friend

Publius Aelius Hadrianus (Hadrian), Roman Emperor

Rufus, a common legionary, later promoted to *optio*

Tiberius Querinius, *Tribunis Laticlavus*, senior tribune of Legion XXII, *Deiotariana*, and a senator designate

Vitellius Turbo, one of Hadrian's senior generals in Judaea

The Jews

Shimeon ben Kosiba, known as Bar Kokhba or Son of the Star, principal leader of the second Jewish revolt

Eleazar, a tribal chief and principal lieutenant to Bar Kokhba

Sarah, confidant and mistress of Bar Kokhba

Foreword

When Hadrian was proclaimed Caesar in 117 CE., the Roman Empire was at its zenith, but there were already noticeable fissures caused by native populations discontented with Roman occupation. The latter was particularly true in Germania, Judaea and Britannia. As William Shakespeare is so often quoted, *past is prologue*; therefore, I will leave it to Hadrian in the prologue to explain the challenges facing the Roman Empire when we first meet Marcus Junius Arrius.

The bibliography lists the references from which I drew either inspiration or fact for a better understanding of the Romans, Jews and Brythonic Tribes. I want to acknowledge the scholarly works of two authors, whom I found to be especially helpful in understanding the Roman Army. Graham Webster's *Roman Imperial Army of the First and Second Centuries A.D.* offers detailed insights on every aspect of Roman military life including descriptions of armor, weapons, clothing, food, customs and religious beliefs. Edward N. Luttwak's *The Grand Strategy of the Roman Empire from the First Century A.D. to the Third* provided a much-appreciated background regarding Roman organization, imperial strategy, tactics, mobility and so much more. I created the maps for Judaea and Britannia from terrain maps obtained off the internet from maps-for-free.com.

Since the novel is focused on the Roman Army, it might be helpful to the reader to know something about the Roman legion, its size, organization and the role of the centurion. The imperial legion in the second century CE. had an assigned strength of about 5000 legionaries organized in ten cohorts. The first cohort consisted of five centuries with each century having an assigned strength of 160 legionaries. The first cohort with 800 legionaries was nearly double in size to each of the other nine cohorts. The first cohort was commanded by the *primus pilus* (first file, although some historians translate the term as first spear), the senior centurion and fourth in command of a legion. The five centurions of the first cohort were called the *primi ordines* and enjoyed great prestige and privilege; an assignment to the first cohort was coveted and a sign of advancement. The other nine cohorts each totaling 480 legionaries were organized into six 80-man centuries also commanded by a centurion. The basic unit of a century was the 8-man *contubernium* in which the legionaries shared a tent, shared rations and represented a close-knit bond considered to be the cohesive backbone of the legion.

The centurions were expected to be at the cutting edge of the battle leading by example and frequently stepping forward to personally engage an enemy in individual combat. Thus, the casualty rate among centurions was incredibly high. The prestige and financial incentives were commensurate with the risk a centurion faced. The duties and responsibilities of the primus pilus were considerably greater than that of the other centurions. By tradition the position was held for only one year after which transfer as primus pilus to another legion was possible. Just as likely, it was a significant step to promotion to procurator in the civil service or as *a praefectus castrorum* (third in command of the legion ranking below the senior tribune). After leaving the position of primus pilus, a centurion would be customarily addressed as *primi pilatus* in recognition of his previous position. The rank of senior centurion elevated the beneficiary to equestrian status which equated to the upper middle class in Roman society. The term equestrian was figurative rather than literal and connoted sufficient wealth to be able to afford a horse, an important distinction in a class-oriented society. Once a primus pilus completed his tour, he could be reappointed to the position, be reassigned to another legion in a similar position, leave for duties outside the legion in a civil post or simply retire.

Although *Arrius* is a novel, I believe it is important to maintain fidelity to historical events, ancient customs and the military tactics of the period; however, typical of those who write historical fiction, I occasionally rearranged things a bit to support the plot. In the historical notes at the end of the novel are brief comments for the discerning reader to separate fact from fiction.

PH, Oro Valley, AZ

Arrius Vol I

Sacramentum

Prologue
Britannia, 122 CE.

Aulus Platorius Nepos, governor of Britannia, watched Hadrian standing at the edge of the escarpment wearing a faded cloak and a worn cuirass, one hand resting on the hilt of his *gladius*, the ivory-inlaid sword hilt that was one of the few exceptions to vanity Hadrian otherwise avoided. The short beard he wore that flouted the clean-shaven Roman style was another exception to his otherwise austere persona. Cultivated in the Greek style, the beard was not a popular masculine feature at a time when a clean-shaven appearance was the norm. Hadrian was in the habit of unconsciously tugging on his beard when he was deep in thought, as he was now while looking north at the distant horizon.

In the valley below, Nepos heard the muted sounds of tent stakes being hammered in the ground, the whinnying and braying of the cavalry horses and baggage mules and the low murmur of nearly five thousand legionaries of the VI Legion, *Victrix,* preparing the night encampment. Occasionally above the hum could be heard the shouted invective uttered by centurions clearly dissatisfied with something not being done fast enough or not being accomplished in the way the Roman Army always did things. Out of earshot of the emperor, a tribune standing near Nepos recognized one of the voices and commented in low tones on how fortunate it was not to be a ranker serving under Centurion Trevinius Lavinius. Silently, Nepos agreed. His mind began to drift to other things; consequently, he didn't at first hear Hadrian call his name until a louder more insistent tone conveyed imperial impatience.

"Nepos, Titurius, attend me."

Nepos hurried forward. Behind him, he heard the footsteps and muted rattle of metal accouterments as the legion commander moved quickly to obey. The two men took position in front of Hadrian and waited for the emperor to speak.

"I suppose you've wondered why we've been traveling around the countryside the past several weeks in such miserable weather, but I assure you there has been a purpose."

Nepos said, "Why, Caesar, I hardly noticed the weather."

"My dear Nepos, the misery of slogging through this most inhospitable part of the empire would have been justified if only to bring you out of the comparative comfort of *Londinium*."

General Titurius was unable to suppress a chuckle.

"Caesar, as it's my profound duty to serve your every wish, I am content to have pleased you, which alone is sufficient to give purpose to my life here in Britannia."

Hadrian laughed. "My dear Nepos. It's no wonder you've been successful in the Senate. Too bad I need your administrative abilities here, or you would be able to shore up the Senate's lack of enthusiasm for my policies. I'm certain your departure from Britannia for Rome would be a reluctant one; therefore, rest assured we shall keep you here."

With effort, Nepos did not let his disappointment show.

"Trajan expressed concerns over the continued expansion of the empire and our decreasing capability to defend what we've conquered. His defeat in Parthia and the loss of most of the lands he gained at considerable cost more than suggests we've reached our limit and capacity to advance beyond the frontiers we now control. I include Britannia in that assessment. In short, we are perilously close to the breaking point. We are no longer able with confidence to resist simultaneous encroachment on multiple points along our frontiers should such attempts be made — and they surely will be made. I've already given orders to draw back from some of the eastern provinces to a more realistic and defensible frontier." Facing north, Hadrian spread his arms. "This will be our northern frontier in Britannia. From here stretching east to west is the second narrowest section of the island that offers both a logical and defensible location. Notice the commanding view of the terrain to the north and look how that small river curves from west to south forming a spur. A fort here would also control any bridge built across the river." Hadrian paused then pointed downhill. "I should think down there is where a bridge should be built."

The legion commander coughed. "Caesar, we already have considerable influence over the Caledonian tribes north of here since Agricola smashed their fighting capability at Mons Graupius," referring to the decisive battle establishing Roman dominance fought in the distant highland foothills nearly forty years before. "Why do we need to consider reducing our area of influence?"

"General, influence is not the same as control. The defeat of the Caledonians at Mons Graupius was a long time ago, and we no longer occupy the Caledonian mountains as Agricola did for a brief period. Do you honestly believe the results of one battle are enough to convince a new generation of Caledonians to maintain the status quo? The reality is we need more than that to give Rome a reason to sleep soundly at night. Titurius, you've been in command of the Sixth Legion for over two years. In that time, how many patrols have you sent to the highland foothills?"

"Perhaps a dozen, possibly fewer."

"How many of those patrols engaged the Caledonians?"

"All of them, Caesar."

"I'm sure your legionaries of the Sixth Legion acquitted themselves superbly. My point, however, is not to question the valor or the eagerness of your legionaries to fight the barbarian but simply to emphasize there is no love for Rome in the far north. Mons Graupius only increased the hatred the northern tribes have for Rome. Agricola had one advantage we no longer enjoy. The Caledonians did not know how the Roman Army fights much less how well it fights even when vastly outnumbered as was the case at Mons Graupius. More importantly, Agricola had nearly six legions, twice what we now have in Britannia."

His curiosity now overcoming his physical discomfort, Nepos said, "Caesar, I'm unclear on just what it is you are proposing we should do here in Britannia. Are we to evacuate our forts and discontinue patrols between here and the mountains to the north? Do you intend we go no farther than where we are now standing?"

"In part, you are correct. We will certainly have to limit the extent our patrols will go consistent with maintaining vigilance in the region to prevent being surprised. Although vigilance is one thing, provocation is another. I want to make it clear that our intent is to preserve a status quo and refrain from conveying any purpose to seek or to establish anything but a commercial relationship with the Caledonian tribes. As far as fixed installations, these will have to be limited and should not reach any farther north than we are able to support from where we now stand. To further define this demarcation, we shall construct a wall from east to west that will bisect Britannia and better define the frontier and separate us from the barbarians."

Nepos and Titurius remained silent, each attempting to interpret and understand the vision Hadrian had just defined. Noting their mute reaction, Hadrian continued. "I will leave the precise dimensions to you both, but let me be very clear that you understand the kind of barrier I have in mind. I don't want some small thing a man can piss over. I want something on a grand scale, one tall enough, large enough to symbolize the power and grandeur of Rome."

"But, Caesar, such an undertaking will take years to construct," General Titurius said.

"We shall require more than our current strength in Britannia to accomplish what you've directed," Nepos said.

Turning first to Nepos, Hadrian's reply was harsh and biting. "You may conscript as much local tribal labor as you can afford to buy within the resources now available here in Britannia. There is an incentive for you to begin work immediately *before* I levy the legions you now have for additional legionaries to reinforce more unsettled provinces than Britannia."

Still struck by the grandiose scale of Hadrian's vision, the two men nodded, intimidated by the sheer scope and magnitude of the undertaking while concealing their personal reservations for both the need and the practical considerations involving such a vast undertaking.

Hadrian turned away and pointed north to a small settlement in the distance. "Titurius, what tribe is represented in that village?"

"Caesar, the village is part of the Selgovae Tribe."

Hadrian then gestured to the south near where the legion was encamped. "What about the one over there — is that also Selgovan?"

"I believe not, Caesar. If I'm not mistaken, the village belongs to the Brigantes Tribe. I understand the tribes north of here do not get along with the southern tribes."

"I believe you indicated it was a Selgovan-led ambush that unwisely engaged your cavalry two days ago." Hadrian referred to the brief skirmish a flank patrol experienced that resulted in the death of several legionaries and the capture of two prisoners. Following a brief interrogation, both prisoners had been summarily executed.

"The prisoners so indicated, Caesar."

"Well, we shall have to ensure our Brigantians living south of the wall embrace the idea they are better off serving Rome peacefully than asserting any tribal interests. We can't very well tolerate having the enemy behind us, can we? They must be subjugated or annihilated. General Titurius, I'll leave it to you to determine which it will be."

Marcus Junius Arrius stepped back and regarded his efforts with a critical eye. As the legion's standard bearer, the safekeeping of the eagle standard was his responsibility including ensuring it did not topple over during a rain-soaked night. He took hold of the long staff once more and pushed it even further into the soggy ground. The wind was biting, and the leaden sky continued to deliver more than a hint of either rain or snow, possibly both before dawn. He wanted to make doubly certain the standard was securely implanted no matter how hard the wind blew or how much more it rained.

He was a large man, one of the tallest legionaries in the legion. Of course, that was a major reason he'd been selected for the honor of carrying the standard and wearing the distinctive leopard skin covering his helmet. Soon after taking command of the legion in Germania, General Titurius had noticed the tall sergeant marching in the first cohort where the largest legionaries were assigned and directed that he be reassigned to the headquarters staff.

The eagle standard, positioned as it always was in the vanguard during battle, frequently made the life of a standard bearer a short one because of its weight and the fact both hands were required to carry it. The standard bearer did not have the benefit of a protective shield; consequently, he was completely dependent on the legionaries nearby to protect him even as the entire legion depended on the standard bearer to ensure the eagle did not fall into enemy hands. Better the standard bearer died protecting it than he should survive its loss. It took a stalwart individual both strong and brave to survive the assignment, but there was an incentive in the possibility of an appointment to the centurionate. General Titurius had made an oblique reference to such an appointment several weeks ago. Arrius had only served twelve years since taking the *sacramentum*, the oath every recruit must take when he became a Roman soldier, and if selected, he would be among the youngest centurions in the Roman Army.

Arrius paused and looked up at the escarpment above. He saw the group of officers near the signal tower still conferring about things he had no knowledge of and at that very moment, less interest in. He was too far away to distinguish individual features. He identified General Titurius by his distinctive helmet plume, and the blocky figure was Governor Nepos. The emperor was easiest to spot for he stood nearly a head taller than the rest and, as usual, without a helmet. Hadrian had spoken to him occasionally in passing during the past several weeks, and Arrius had formed a favorable opinion of the man. At times, he acted more like a legionary than a man who one day the senate would proclaim a god as was the custom following the death of an emperor. At least he looked more like a god, robust and healthy, compared to some of the past emperors whose statues were on prominent display throughout the empire.

"Arrius!" He did not have to turn around to recognize the deep voice of Trevinius Lavinius, the *primus pilus*, and senior centurion in the legion. Gray-bearded and cadaverous, Lavinius had made his life miserable when he'd first been posted to the first cohort. In time, Arrius realized the extra duty and discipline he was subjected to was the centurion's way of ensuring he might one day be ready for something better than standing in the ranks.

Arrius came to attention. "Yes, Primus Pilus!"

"I'm told your appointment to the centurionate will be signed tonight. Look surprised when the general calls for you. This will be your last night to care for the eagle. The ceremony will be at first light tomorrow. The emperor himself will be there and intends to honor you as well so best get some of that muck off you."

Arrius could hardly believe his ears. When the sun came up tomorrow, if it came up, he'd be entitled to wear the distinctive transverse crest on his helmet signifying the rank of centurion.

"Well, what have you to say?"

"I owe my good fortune to you, for without the approval of the legion's primus pilus, I would not even be considered."

Lavinius shrugged off the thanks, but Arrius knew they had been well received. "Are you ready to hand over the standard?"

"I am, but there will be regrets." Arrius looked up at the gold eagle.

Lavinius noted the look. "Is it the eagle you hate to part with or the privileges that go with being a member of the legion commander's personal staff?"

"Aye, some of both. When I carry the standard, I feel as if I'm carrying Rome — that I've been given the honor of protecting Rome itself."

"Have a care you don't get too carried away with such thoughts. You'll find out in time, as I have, the metal bird on top of that pole is just that and nothing more."

Arrius was taken aback at the cynical words bordering on sacrilege. The eagle was esteemed in the Roman Army nearly to the same extent as the gods were venerated and with virtually the same reverence. He looked around anxiously to see if anyone else had overheard the remark. Aware of the younger man's discomfort, Lavinius clapped him on the shoulder. "Relax, Arrius, the priests are too busy pawing through the guts of a goat to see if the sun will show itself again to pay attention to an old centurion goosing tradition and religious blather. One day if you remain in the legions, as I expect you will, you'll likely go far, probably farther than I have. Your promotion to centurion is coming ten years before mine did. At some point, you'll begin to realize the symbols you revere today in the end are only symbols. Generals will use you, Rome will use you and when it's all over, the only thing you'll have left is a handful of medals on a cuirass sitting on a shelf. That and a small patch of land given to you in a place you never wanted to go much less wanted to live."

What struck Arrius was the matter-of-fact way Lavinius spoke and without a trace of bitterness. "Surely you don't mean what you say. There's glory and honor in what we do."

"I grant you that, and I hold without it there would be no point in serving at all. It's only the trappings and the false promises I condemn. You're asking yourself now what does it all mean if I speak thus. I'll tell you what makes it all worthwhile, it's them," pointing toward the legionaries preparing the night's marching camp. "Most of them are the misbegotten offspring of fathers they never knew, others were one step away from being sentenced to the galleys and the rest had no other option than the army for getting a decent meal. As bad as they are, they would give their lives without hesitation for the other seven men in their *contuberinium*. Treat them half-way decent, and they'll do the same for you."

Arrius was bewildered by the centurion's comments. He knew Lavinius's tenure as senior centurion had nearly run its course. There was already speculation he was leaving the army, but Lavinius had yet to confirm it. He sought to change the subject and steer the sobering conversation in another direction. Pointing to the higher ground where Hadrian stood, Arrius asked, "Primus Pilus, do you know what they're doing up there?"

"I've no idea, but with Hadrian it probably has something to do with another building project. I'll wager it's a monument, most likely one of those fancy arches he's so fond of. I wouldn't be surprised if the Sixth Legion will be building something soon."

Arrius looked away and resolved to leave Britannia at the first opportunity. For his initial duty as a centurion, he didn't relish the idea of supervising a work detail on some meaningless monument in the middle of nowhere. He had every intention of going to Parthia as soon as possible where the opportunities for fighting and advancement were far better than here in Britannia. He looked up first at the escarpment and then the village nearby. "Does this village have a name?"

"I'm told it's called Banna because of the spur the river makes." Lavinius stalked off to continue his inspection of the night camp.

Arrius remained where he was watching the ridgeline above. He saw the emperor and senior officials mount their horses and slowly make their way toward the river bottom below. He couldn't shake the feeling there was something about this place that had significance for him. It would be many years before he would have occasion to see Banna again and much longer still to understand what Lavinius had been trying to tell him.

"Victory in war does not depend entirely upon numbers or mere courage; only skill and discipline will ensure it."—Flavius Vegetius Renatus; *De Ri Militari, Book I,* 390 CE

PART I

JUDAEA

134-135 CE

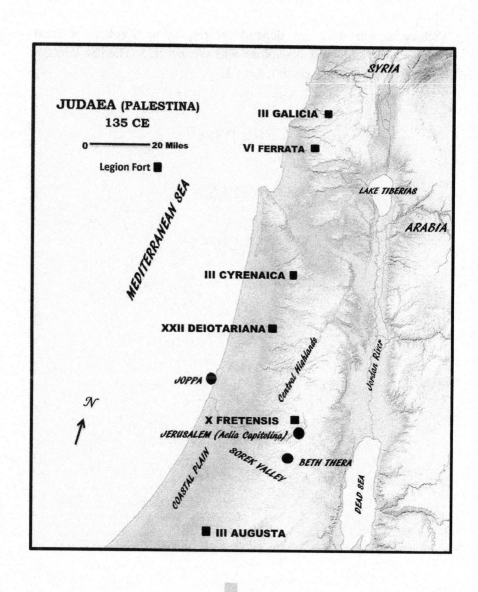

JUDAEA (PALESTINA)
135 CE

0 ——————— 20 Miles

Legion Fort ■

SYRIA

III GALICIA ■

VI FERRATA ■

LAKE TIBERIAS

ARABIA

MEDITERRANEAN SEA

III CYRENAICA ■

XXII DEIOTARIANA ■

JOPPA ●

N

Central Highlands

Jordan River

X FRETENSIS ■
JERUSALEM (Aelia Capitolina) ●

COASTAL PLAIN

SOREK VALLEY

● BETH THERA

DEAD SEA

■ III AUGUSTA

Chapter 1
14 years later

It was nothing he saw that bothered Marcus Arrius, the primus pilus of Legion XXII, *Deiotariana*. It was what he didn't see that bothered him. The usual small birds flitting among the bushes were absent as were the goats so common to the region that seemed to thrive, at least in his opinion, on a nearly barren landscape. Even the small rodent-like ground squirrels usually darting from rock to rock were nowhere to be seen. He had the prickly feeling they were being watched.

If size was not enough to set him apart from most Roman soldiers, the scar that extended down his right cheek to his chin added further to an already intimidating appearance. Before the Parthian cavalry sword had nearly ended his life ten years before, women considered him pleasing to look at; the scar now repelled most except for those who overlooked the disfigurement when he paid for their time.

Senses now fully alert, Arrius forgot about the soreness in his limbs accumulated over the past seven days, the sweat stinging his eyes and the dryness in his mouth. He surveyed the narrow canyon to his front and on the flanks for anything that stood out from the natural surroundings. The rolling hills with rocky outcroppings and occasional sparse groves of olive trees provided excellent opportunities for a Jewish ambush. He took notice of the ever-narrowing canyon and wondered if his calculated gamble to encourage the enemy to attack had become a prelude to disaster. He looked behind him at the dust-caked men marching three abreast in four columns weaving through the curving pass like four large caterpillars. The legionaries in the outside ranks carried their heavy shields bearing the distinctive eagle and lighting bolts facing outside to stop the volley of arrows expected at any moment. His jaw tightened when he considered the cohort should have numbered eight hundred as it had when the legion departed from Alexandria nearly a year ago. Since then, battle casualties, sickness and desertion had reduced the cohort's numbers as well as those of the legion. Just as problematic were the endless work details the legion commander seemed never to tire of. As a result, now little more than five hundred legionaries marched behind him.

He turned and spoke quietly to the centurion walking several paces behind. "Strabo, tell them to stay alert and get ready, the canyon is narrowing. If we're to see any Jews this day, it will be soon."

Arrius heard Strabo warning the legionaries behind him. Moments later came the blast of a ram's horn. The sudden shouts and arrows raining down from the surrounding rocks were almost a relief. It was always the waiting before an engagement that was the most difficult to tolerate, not the fighting. As he reached down to draw his sword, he felt a sharp pain in his left forearm where an arrow glancing off his leather cuirass had left a bloody but otherwise superficial wound.

He turned to join the formation behind him as the columns began closing ranks to form the *testudo*. The tortoise formation with the outside files holding their shields positioned outside and the inner files lifting their shields above their heads was designed to protect the column from the arrows and rocks raining down. Already the fusillade had claimed a few victims. The battle noise reverberated off the canyon walls, a cacophony of high-pitched yells, the screams of the wounded, the twang of arrow strings and the drum-like sound of rocks bouncing off the shields. Arrius knew the Jews would soon swarm down from the rocks to follow-up the arrow volley with a quick ground attack. At least he hoped that would be the case for this would be the opportunity to take the initiative. Then it would be the time to employ the kind of synchronized, close-in fighting for which the Roman Army was noted and the reason he'd risked entering the canyon in the first place.

He sensed the volume of arrows and missiles begin to taper off. Shaggy-bearded men in short, threadbare robes with cloths tied around their foreheads emerged from the cover of the surrounding rocks and converged from all sides. This was the moment for which he'd been waiting. He turned and shouted the order to form fighting ranks. The attacking force was larger than he anticipated, prompting him to wonder if boldness may have outweighed discretion. Jewish tactics favored the ambush instead of pursuing large-scale engagements that dictated looking for more risky methods to encourage the enemy to engage.

The first volley of spears brought down the front rank of Jews like sheaves of wheat, but the attack did not falter. The second rank of legionaries stepped forward and hurled their spears. He admired the Jewish tenacity and resolve. There was time to launch another volley of spears before the initial wave of Jews crashed into the legionary shields with a thunderous boom. The first warrior to reach him was careless enough to raise his sword for a downward stroke; Arrius took advantage of the young man's mistake and thrust his sword into the man's belly before engaging two more warriors whose skills were characterized more by exuberance than technique.

For the next several minutes, Arrius was conscious only of parry and thrust and the immediate press around him. During a brief lull, he quickly surveyed the progress of the battle. Although satisfied his casualties so far appeared light in comparison to what his men were inflicting, he realized the Jewish assault was taking a toll. The Jews were acquitting themselves with unusual aggressiveness and more skill than in previous engagements. It was also evident the enemy showed no sign of breaking off the attack in comparison to more recent engagements. He wondered how long the assault would continue then began to worry after hearing the drawn-out notes of a ram's horn, and a second Jewish wave began running toward them.

Above the canyon on top of a rocky outcrop, a tall man of middle age with gray streaks in his beard observed the battle unfolding below with clinical detachment. Shimeon ben Kosiba saw the precision by which the Romans resisted being defeated by an overwhelmingly numerical force. The current battle was not going as well as he had hoped.

He was no longer called Shimeon ben Kosiba except by the very few who were closest to him. At the urging of Rabbi Akiva, he'd adopted the name Bar Kokhba which meant *Son of the Star*. As the most important religious figure in Judaea, the rabbi had linked the coincidental observation of a new and bright star to add a mystical dimension to his claim Shimeon ben Kosiba was the new messiah, the chosen leader of the uprising. It was a shameless association with a Jewish prophecy not unlike the one preceding the birth of Jesus of Nazareth over a hundred years before. At first, ben Kosiba considered the affectation merely an astute move to unify support from a widespread and just as widely-differing Jewish population. Eventually he became almost convinced he really was the chosen instrument to end Roman occupation. Of late, he began to discourage the name Bar Kokhba, preferring to use his given name instead as losses continued to mount. He gave a sigh of bitter resignation and turned to the younger man standing next to him.

"Eleazar, even with our considerable advantage in numbers and our choice of the battlefield, the Romans still prevail, may God curse them and their sons for seven generations. I hate them beyond all reason, and yet I can't help but admire their fighting ability."

Eleazar was one of several prominent tribal chiefs in the larger Jewish community and one who had become the de facto principal lieutenant to Shimeon. It was also Eleazar who had been instrumental in helping to galvanize the disparate political factions and religious differences to achieve consensus among a people who were generally mistrustful of all who were not within the family or the village unit. In that sense, Eleazar complemented ben Kosiba by being more practical and honest in his assessment of how the rebellion in general was progressing.

"I admire nothing about the Romans." Eleazar spit to one side to emphasize the point. "Considering the number of our men lying on the ground in comparison to Roman casualties, we can ill afford such losses."

"I admit things have not gone as well as I hoped, but even in a less than successful outcome such as this, we can still learn how to defeat them in the next battle. Look how some of our men are virtually standing idle in the back unable to engage the Romans because of insufficient room to maneuver. See how the Romans form close ranks quickly and with precision to counter our arrow and missile attack only to expand in attack formation to meet our charge. These are techniques we must learn and use while finding better ways to attack their formations. We are still a rabble lacking in the basic concept of fighting as a unit. Instead, we attack them as so many individuals, each bent on personal glory and fueled by hatred alone. Numbers alone are not enough. We must fight more with our heads than our hearts. You must give them their due; Roman discipline and organization are superb."

"The only due I want to give a Roman is the point of my sword, starting with the large bastard with the white crest on his helmet." Eleazar pointed to Arrius's conspicuous figure below.

"Unlike us, the centurion is a professional soldier. He fights because that is what he does and what he is paid to do, and when the fighting here in Judaea is over, he will leave. We, on the other hand, are fighting for a homeland and something more than a handful of sestercii."

Eleazar gave a regretful sigh and said as much to himself as to ben Kosiba, "It's unfortunate we don't have enough shekels, for if we did, perhaps we could buy soldiers like them to fight for us. Even better, simply pay Hadrian to leave us in peace."

Ben Kosiba stood up. "It's time to back away from this and admit the Romans have outmatched us again. Somehow, we must find a better way to fight them."

The mournful notes of the ram's horn sounding the withdrawal followed the two men as they turned and began to make their way back to the Jewish camp.

His lungs heaving with the exertion of the battle, rivulets of sweat running down his back and chest under the hot leather cuirass, Arrius heard the ram's horn sound again and dreaded what it might signal. He wasn't certain how much longer they would be able to withstand a sustained attack. He was relieved when the Jews began withdrawing, dragging their dead and wounded with them.

Arrius beckoned to Strabo to join him. Smaller in stature and younger, Marius Strabo was the cohort's *princeps*, the centurion next in seniority in the legion and one of his closest friends.

"Marius, post men in the rocks above just in case they get the idea to come back then get me a head count. I want to know our losses as soon as possible. Kill any Jews too badly wounded to take with us."

"They're hardly worth the trouble, Marcus. I've heard the market for Jewish slaves in Rome is way down."

"We'll use them to help carry our dead back to the fort. What happens to them after that is up to General Gallius."

Arrius moved among the legionaries assessing the extent of their casualties and wondered if he was getting too old for this. Maybe it was past time to think more about his long-term future than the next battle including the once unthinkable but now lingering question was it time to leave the army. He'd never given much thought before to what life outside the legions might be like if he simply left. Ever since his early days as a young recruit, he'd assumed one day he would be left face down in the dust, the victim of aging reflexes and a faceless enemy who happened to be younger and faster than he was. Now that he had managed to beat the odds, he was beginning to consider if there was anything else he might do with the years left to him. He thought it was the current campaign that was causing him to dwell on thoughts that would never have occurred to him before coming to Judaea. He knew it wasn't because he harbored any sympathy for the Jews, a people he neither understood nor had any inclination to do so. On the contrary, he shared the prevailing Roman belief the Jews were an ungrateful lot and completely unappreciative of the benefits of serving Rome. His introspection ended when Strabo arrived accompanied by the three other centurions and the senior *optiones*.

"Marcus, we've 38 dead and 72 wounded," Strabo reported a few minutes later. "Many of the wounded will likely not last before we get back to the wagons, and I fear more will never make it back to the fort."

"All right, it's worse than I'd feared but not as bad as it could have been." He saw one of the centurions examining his shoulder where an arrow still protruded. "Queros, it looks as if you've picked up a souvenir to remind you of this day's work."

"It's nothing, Primus Pilus, a scratch hardly worth talking about. By Jupiter's balls, I've been stuck worse in more than one whorehouse."

"I expect that's true enough," Strabo said. "You need to quit thinking every whore you meet wants it from you for free just because you think you have the biggest cock in the legion."

Assuming a more serious expression, Arrius said, "Attend to the wounded as best you can. I want to get back to the baggage carts before dark."

Except for Strabo, the centurions and optiones quickly left to carry out his orders. Arrius gratefully removed his helmet and ran a hand through his close-cropped hair that was beginning to show more than a trace of gray.

"We were lucky today. If the Jews had been more tenacious, the outcome might have been different."

"We fight better than they do."

"True, but it's another pointless battle that changes nothing, more legionary's dead and even more Jews." Arrius noted Strabo's perplexed expression. "Marius, have you ever wondered why we do this?"

"What do you mean?"

"Why we decided to become legionaries. Was it because we didn't know enough to choose another life?"

"Does it matter? We're here, and it serves no purpose to wonder about it now."

"I suppose that's true. Did you know I considered staying in Alexandria?"

"What the hell for? I can't believe you would consider turning down another opportunity to be primus pilus even if it meant serving a second-rate legion in a shithole like this."

"You're right about the *Deiotariana*, although the legion has come a long way since you and I gave our oath to it. I was thinking of a woman I met in Alexandria. Her name was Min-nefret; she didn't seem to mind about this." He pointed to the scar. "I might have stayed if she had asked me, but she didn't."

"Why did you expect her to ask you instead of just deciding to stay?"

Arrius shook his head and looked away. Thinking there wasn't going to be an answer, Strabo started to leave only to stop when Arrius said softly, "By the gods, Marius, I didn't know then, and I still don't. I think I was more relieved than disappointed she didn't."

"You think too much, Marcus. Besides, what kind of life is there outside the legions?"

Arrius watched the centurion walk away and thought perhaps Strabo was right.

Chapter 2

The weary column approached the village which had continued to grow since the legion had established its main encampment nearby. The village appeared almost overnight with tents and temporary structures constructed of clay and wattle. In a comparatively short time, temporary structures were replaced with the more permanent stone and mud-brick architecture characteristic of the region. The thriving community now occupied most of the once barren plain.

The village contained every conceivable venture designed to part a legionary from his pay dominated as it was by the proliferation of taverns and brothels catering to the more prosaic needs of the military camp. There were also other shops and vendors who made money from the Roman occupation by supplying the camp with equipment repair services, foodstuffs, animal fodder and anything else the legion needed. Arrius found it ironic that many of the villagers from their dress appeared to be Jewish, and yet, at least superficially, they seemed to have no aversion to supporting the Romans. He suspected the reality was that many of those merchants so openly friendly in the daytime were at night serving the Jewish cause, a reality that privately he was unable to condemn.

Despite their fatigue, the men began to straighten up and march more briskly at the urging of the optiones. Arrius felt his own tired body reaching for the last reservoir of energy as he, too, quickened his step. It would never do for the first cohort to slouch into camp like some spiritless rabble no matter how tired they were.

The legion's main camp almost a mile farther on conformed to the traditional layout of a legionary camp located anywhere in the empire whether in permanent garrison or on the march. Standard configuration was mandated even if building materials differed according to local conditions. Uniform design was dictated for practical reasons. On the march, it facilitated quick establishment and occupation when every legionnaire knew exactly where the streets, parade field, headquarters, legionary tents, latrines, stables and officer quarters were located even on the darkest of nights. A common design also expedited defense in the event of an attack at night. Confusion was minimized by ensuring the legionaries did not stumble around in unfamiliar surroundings while moving to their assigned positions on the ramparts.

Arrius noted work had been accelerated on the *Porta Principalis Dextra*, the east gate they were about to enter that would soon match the gates recently completed at each of the other three walls. The gateway was already covered in preparation for finishing the platform over the two archways; a work detail was in the process of positioning stone blocks in a crenellated pattern on the rampart. A pair of massive wooden doors reinforced with iron studs was set in each archway. One door remained open to allow visitors access to the camp under the watchful gaze of two sentries dressed in full armor. The alertness of the guards was made more so by the stern-faced optio standing in the doorway of the guard house located just inside the arch.

The double-arched gate was centered on the exterior wall. An eight-foot deep, V-shaped ditch in front of the outer wall added more height to the wall extending nearly 450 feet on either side of the archway. The external walls did not join in a right angle but were rounded to reduce the vulnerability of the more traditional square corners. Similar platforms were located halfway between the gates and the end platforms and accommodated the smaller spring-fired *carro-ballistae* or *scorpiones* that could send a bolt long as a man's arm out to 900 feet. Elevated platforms at each rounded corner provided positions to mount the *ballistae*, catapults that, depending on their size, launched either heavy stones or light arrow-bolts. The parapet on the inside walls was gained by stairways located inside each gate and to the rear of each ballista platform. The interior walls to the inside parapet were sloped to allow faster access to the ramparts in the event of an attack.

Arrius had questioned the wisdom and the need to continue the aggressive building program initiated by Gallius. With a legion now so reduced in strength, he wondered how they would be able to defend the fortress against a determined attack if one ever materialized. He knew as tired as his men were, they would get no favors from Gallius, who would expect all but the seriously wounded to be on the morning fatigue duty to continue the building program.

The roads leading into the camp from each gate intersected in the center and were sufficiently wide for the legionaries to assemble for inspection or in preparation for field duty. To one side where the roads intersected stood the *principia*, a complex of stone buildings and tents arranged to form a central courtyard where the legion headquarters, administrative offices and supply buildings were located. A small elevated platform with an altar to one side near the headquarters building was used by the priests for ceremonial sacrifices or on rare occasions when the legion commander wished to address the assembled legion. Slightly smaller and adjacent to the headquarters and the only other stone building in the principia was General Gallius's private quarters. Opposite the headquarters complex were the tents of the tribunes and those of the *primi ordines*, the five centurions of the first cohort and the senior centurion from each of the other nine cohorts.

As primus pilus, Arrius's tent was larger than those of the other senior centurions and nearly equal in size to those occupied by the four remaining tribunes; there was open space remaining for two additional tribunes, but the probability of receiving any officer replacements to round out the full complement of six tribunes remained highly unlikely and not justified until when, if ever, the legion achieved full strength. Behind the tribune and senior centurion quarters were the smaller tents of the cohorts arrayed in long parallel lines with narrow streets in between. The tents were made of leather and large enough to accommodate an eight-man contubernium. Around the inside of the walls were the various storage tents, bathhouses, workshops for equipment repair and altars variously dedicated to popular Roman deities. The horse and mule corrals including the blacksmith forges were situated at the opposite ends of the camp where the latrines were located.

As he led the column through the shadowed archway past the saluting guards, Arrius heard his name called.

"Hail, Marcus Arrius, how goes the war?" boomed the voice of Attius Varro as he tapped the shaft of a Jewish arrow against his leg, an affectation Arrius assumed had been adopted when Varro gave up the centurion's *vitis*, the vine stick which was the signature mark of a centurion. The aging but capable *praefectus castrorum* was the camp prefect responsible for overseeing the operation of the camp including training, logistics and medical support. A former primus pilus, Varro was the third most senior officer in the legion and next in command of the legion after the senior tribune.

Genial face wreathed in a smile, Varro said, "You look like dried mule shit. I saw the dust from atop the wall, and from the direction, I thought it might be your patrol."

Arrius liked the portly soldier who, despite a benign face and jovial manner, had earned over a dozen awards during his nearly forty years of legionary service. His military record was already legendary. Varro was even more respected for his unwillingness to extol his own accomplishments, an uncommon practice in a society that tended to over-indulge in self-aggrandizement. Arrius had seen Varro wear his parade armor on only one occasion; the *phalerae*, his numerous awards, were in such number the underlying breastplate was hardly visible. Varro might have been mistaken for a common ranker except for his age and the calm manner of projecting his authority without the need to proclaim or demand it from those subordinate to him. He was grateful to Varro for acting as a buffer between him and Gallius by frequently intervening to reduce the friction and tension between him and the legion commander that threatened the effectiveness of the legion.

Arrius stepped away from the column and stood next to Varro as his men filed past. "Attius, I suspect I feel worse than I look, but nothing a bath, a shave, decent food and maybe a soft woman wouldn't fix — soft is the important part, beauty a secondary consideration." Then after a moment's reflection, he said, "Perhaps no consideration at all."

Varro laughed. "I remember the feeling even if the inclination is now more often thought than deed. By the gods, I can remember as a ranker standing in line for hours waiting for my turn at one of the camp whores after coming back from the field. After your turn, you just got back in line, and by the time it took to get back to the head of the line, the short gladius had already grown sharp again."

"Maybe you need to go on patrol the next time we go back out; it might do more for you than reliving old memories, and it might trim off some of that extra padding under your belt as well."

"Not so fast. I'm more than ready to leave the field work to you young cocks. I wouldn't want to get in the way or steal the glory." Then assuming a more serious and quiet manner, Varro asked, "How was it?

I see the carts are full so it looks as if you found a few Jews, or they found you."

Arrius briefly summarized the less than successful results of the patrol. "Frankly, Attius, I'm not sure what we're doing is accomplishing anything. We're killing a lot of them, but they're doing the same to us."

The aging officer looked sharply at Arrius. "Have a care when and where you voice such sentiments although I share your view more than you might think. If Gallius heard such talk, he'd have you on charges for sedition. He still believes we're defending the bastions of Rome against the rabid barbarian. By the way, he's waiting for your report. I suggest you get cleaned up and report to him."

Arrius cursed, and Varro held up a hand to quell the now familiar tirade about to follow. "Easy, don't go over there ready to kick him in the balls. It wouldn't take much for Gallius to finish you with the stroke of a pen."

"I know, I'll be careful what I say. Don't worry, I won't give him the opportunity I suspect he keeps looking to break me, flog me or maybe worse. I'll go now and get it over with."

"I'd get cleaned up a bit first if I were you."

"He can see me the way I am. Maybe some honest dirt will blow off me and on to him. Perhaps it will inspire him to get off his ass and get us some replacements."

"Don't antagonize the man any more than you normally do. If you'll calm down, I have information for you that does not please General Gallius. I recall you once shared a tent a long time ago with Vitellius Turbo back in Germania. Well, General Turbo arrived here in Judaea since you left."

"I'll be damned! I wonder why he's here."

"Turbo is now second in command in Judaea to General Severus. From what Gallius let slip, I understand Gallius and Turbo are not exactly on the best of terms for reasons he wouldn't say. Anyway, there's more. Rumor has it that the emperor himself is coming here. No real news to us, but there's a perception in Rome the war's not going well, and Hadrian is furious."

"I'm not surprised. From what I know and recall of Hadrian since he was a tribune, he was always ready to step in and look things over for himself. I doubt there's another individual in the empire that's walked or ridden over more of the empire than he has."

"I understand he intends to do more than just visit and listen to the generals tell him how great things are. According to Gallius, Hadrian's taking command himself. If that doesn't move things along, I don't know what will." He paused before continuing, "Evidently, your friendship with Turbo must not have been all boast. A courier arrived two days ago and brought an invitation for you to come and see him just as soon as you returned."

"Does Gallius know?"

"Yes, and he's not too happy about it. He doesn't understand why he asked to see you and not him. We can talk more about it when you dismiss the cohort, and I accept your invitation for a libation in your quarters. In return, I will give you the benefit of friendly counsel that will help you remain primus pilus after you see Gallius."

Arrius laughed and excused himself to join the cohort standing in front of the principia. After a few terse orders to the centurions, he dismissed the formation then rejoined Varro. The two men walked toward Arrius's tent where Philos stood by the entrance waiting for them.

"Look, Attius, my faithful Philos waits for me. Should at any time you fail to tell me when I'm about to piss on my boot, he will."

"You are fortunate to have such a man to call friend. How long have you been together?"

"You are more right than you can know. More than ten years. I would not be where I am today without him."

"I believe he was once your slave before he became your steward. Why you picked a one-armed slave is a wonder to me. Where did you find him?"

"In a Parthian slave market, soon after I left Britannia. I had just been appointed to the centurionate and needed a slave to take care of my kit. As a new centurion, I didn't have much more than my armor and a spare sword at the time; consequently, all I was able to afford was an aging slave with one hand. When he said he could read and write Latin as well as Greek, I took a chance and bought him. I didn't realize what a bargain I made until much later. Eventually we became friends, and our roles were reversed; I took over the menial tasks intended for him, and Philos gave me lessons in philosophy, logic and the art of debate while improving both my capability to speak and write Latin. More importantly, he taught me to be inquisitive and think beyond the reach of my sword. I don't know which one of us was more pleased the day I gave him his freedom; after I removed his slave collar, I crossed my fingers he wouldn't leave."

As the two men neared the tent, Arrius saw how frail Philos was beginning to look. Since their arrival in Judaea, the gray fringe of hair remaining on his head had turned white. He wondered just how old Philos was. Too old for the rigors of campaigning, he thought. Kindness would be to send him back to Greece or wherever else he wanted to go to finish out his remaining days in soft sunshine with enough denarii to maintain him in relative comfort. Yet, he hated to suggest it partly out of concern he would insult Philos, but mainly out of selfish concern he would miss his friendship and counsel.

"Philos, how are you, my friend?"

"Much better now that you've returned, Marcus. Was the patrol successful?"

"If successful means we killed more Jews than they did Romans, we were successful. If, on the other hand, it means we made a difference bringing the rebellion to an end, the answer is no, we did not."

Inside the tent, Arrius took a flagon of wine a slave offered and handed it to Attius while taking the other.

"Attius, I'm tired of razing villages and watching individuals kill themselves to avoid becoming a prisoner of Rome. A few days ago, I watched a father throw his wife and four children off a cliff before he jumped after them. I wonder when we are done here if there will be any Jews left."

Philos pointed to the dirt-stained bandage on Arrius's forearm. "I'll have Sartos attend to that, and you'll need to change into something more presentable before you see General Gallius."

"How did you know I'm going to see Gallius?" After seeing the guilty expression on Varro's face, Arrius said, "I think you and Praefectus Varro are conspiring against me. General Gallius will see me as I am."

"How did it get so bad between you and Gallius?" Varro asked.

"I'm not sure, but he listens to no one. All the legion commanders I ever served under or knew of sought counsel from their centurions, but it seems Gallius is the exception. I'm probably to blame. I criticized the outcome of our first engagement after he took command. My comments were not personal and intended only to be constructive to avoid making the same mistakes in the next battle. He didn't take it well. I suspect if it weren't for you he would have run me off or found a reason to run me through. It was the gods who sent you to the *Deiotariana*. It's a pity they didn't send you here sooner."

From the window, General Gallius watched Arrius coming toward the headquarters still wearing his dirt-encrusted field armor. He was no longer clear why he disliked the centurion. He refused to consider his feelings were a product of envy resulting from the centurion's confident bearing and his quiet but effective leadership, qualities which accentuated Gallius's own feelings of insecurity. There were frequent occasions when he woke up at night terror-stricken from a nightmare that almost never varied, a dream in which he had somehow survived to suffer the disgrace of defeat. He realized from his first battle years ago it wasn't death he feared; it was failure that occupied him whether awake or in his dreams. Perversely, Arrius represented the one man who could ensure he did not fail. It was that very dependency that he had come to resent, believing it somehow diminished him.

Tiberius Querinius, the senior tribune and second in command of the legion, regarded the general's taut expression. "I don't know why you've tolerated Arrius and his insolence. Look at his appearance. He hasn't even done you the courtesy of making himself presentable. He shows no respect for his superiors."

At first, Gallius did not intend to respond. He didn't like the man he had been required to take on as *tribunis laticlavius*. Handsome and physically impressive, Querinius was also young, spoiled and a dilettante in military affairs. Gallius resented the fact Querinius had the advantage of wealth and privilege he never had or would ever achieve. However, it would have been unwise to refuse the request to appoint a senator's son to the post. A debt had to be repaid since it was the senator who had been instrumental in getting Hadrian to appoint him to command the legion. Querinius was a self-serving bastard who served his and his father's interests more than his general, a fact that did not necessarily differentiate him from others of his class.

"I considered getting rid of him soon after I took command, but it would have been a mistake to have him demoted or transferred to another legion. Arrius is too well-regarded and highly-respected. Now I'm beginning to think I would be well-served if the Jews solved the problem for me."

"He seems to go out of his way to insult me," Queriniussaid. "Not that he ever says or does anything improper to give reason to take disciplinary measures. No, he's far too clever for that. He pays no attention to the other tribunes."

Gallius did not respond since he considered the young tribunes assigned to him by the Senate more nuisances than assets and generally beneath notice except as protocol dictated otherwise.

The senior orderly entered the room. "General Gallius, Primus Pilus Arrius is here. Will you see him now?"

"Give me a few more minutes with Tribune Querinius." He had no real desire to continue a conversation with Querinius about Arrius or any other subject for that matter, but the delay, petty as it was, would assert his authority.

For a few minutes longer, he tolerated the tribune's complaints about Arrius and the centurions before cutting Querinius off in mid-sentence, yelling through the doorway, "Send in the primus pilus."

Without so much as a glance at Tiberias Querinius, Arrius marched into the room cradling his battered field helmet under his left arm and came to a halt in front of Gallius. He struck his cuirass in a salute vigorous enough to raise a cloud of dust.

Each time he saw Gallius, Arrius was struck by the incongruity of Gallius's physical appearance and bearing with his erratic performance as a general. If looking the part of a legion commander was sufficient then Gallius would have been the model for all legion commanders in the Roman Army. Middle-aged, tall and physically impressive, Gallius initially had made a favorable impression on him and the other centurions. Time and circumstances had altered that impression. By now and for reasons no longer completely clear to either man, they harbored a deep, irrational dislike for each other.

Gallius said nothing for several moments while he silently took in Arrius's disheveled appearance. He noted the blood-caked bandage wrapped around the centurion's left forearm.

"Centurion, is it your habit to report to your general without taking the time to be presentable?"

"Praefectus Varro informed me you wanted to see me. He indicated I should do so without delay."

"It could have waited."

"In that case, I'll return later." Arrius turned to leave.

"Since you're here, you may as well give your report."

Arrius faced Gallius and recounted the highlights of the patrol. Gallius listened attentively, interrupting now and then to ask a question. Arrius ended his account by listing the casualties.

Despite his dislike of Arrius, Gallius was impressed with the succinct account. He knew the centurion had understated his own significant role in the conduct of the patrol. In a moment of objective clarity, he realized it was Arrius who was more prepared to command the legion than he was. If their positions were reversed, he doubted he had the ability to perform the centurion's duties. He realized his mind was drifting, and the centurion was looking at him strangely. He regained his focus.

"Do you have any suggestions how we might be better able to defeat the Jew?"

Arrius was surprised Gallius had given him the opportunity to reiterate previous recommendations that so far had yet to produce any positive change in the legion's tactics and organization.

"General, we need to adapt more to the nature of the terrain and enemy. We are essentially fighting an enemy that will not stand and fight a prolonged battle at close quarters, preferring instead to attack quickly and melt away into the hills. Without adequate intelligence, we will continue to search the hills and mountains to find the Jews while wearing down our legionaries in the process. We need cavalry and more ..." his voice trailed off as Gallius impatiently silenced him with a peremptory wave.

"Enough, I tire of listening to things I can do nothing about." He already regretted having opened the door on a subject that always placed him on the defensive with suggestions he knew should have been implemented long ago but that he had been unable to convince his superiors to follow. "You've said much the same on other occasions. The resources simply aren't there, and given the protracted nature of the war, it's unlikely to change. This war will probably get worse before Rome's prospects for victory improve. In short, we must make do with what we have." Then Gallius abruptly changed the subject. "Do you know General Turbo?"

"Yes, General, we served together as optiones in the VIII, *Augusta* in Germania,"

"Do you have any idea why Turbo would want to see you?"

"I do not."

Gallius regarded Arrius with narrowed eyes. "A courier arrived yesterday with orders you are to report to him without delay. Have you had any correspondence with him?"

"I've neither seen nor heard from General Turbo since we served in the *Augusta* nearly twenty years ago."

Apparently satisfied Arrius was telling the truth, Gallius said with obvious irritation, "General Turbo is now in Judaea. For the time being, he's established his headquarters with the *Fretensis* legion several miles northeast of Jerusalem near the village of Gazara. Turbo is now in command of the entire region. Julius Severus is expected to be the new governor of Judaea with authority extending from the northern boundary of Parthia to the southern border of Egypt. Apparently, Severus is also bringing additional reinforcements with him. Perhaps we may yet receive the replacements that so far have gone to the other legions in greater number. It is said the emperor himself may be coming here. In short, it appears the war here in Judaea is about to escalate along with the opportunity to distinguish the *Deiotariana.*"

With effort, Arrius refrained from saying anything, thinking the legion's capability to distinguish itself under Gallius's command was remote.

"Well, whatever the reason, Turbo wants to see you as soon as possible. You will leave tomorrow and report to him. You may take a cavalry troop as befits your rank. I expect you to return here immediately after meeting with General Turbo."

Arrius saluted and turned to leave. "Centurion, one more thing. Your cohort will report to Tribune Gabinus tomorrow to continue work on the west wall and gate. We're behind in completing the camp, and now the first cohort is back, I intend to make up for lost time."

"General, it's customary to grant a returning patrol time off to rest and recuperate. Perhaps a day to visit the taverns and whores would not cause a significant delay in the building program. The men are expecting more and will be greatly disappointed if they aren't granted at least some time off. Morale is low enough as is without offering additional reason for a legionary to desert."

"Centurion, do not think to question my authority or judgment. You have your orders."

For a moment, Arrius considered keeping his mouth shut rather than risk inflaming the general even more; however, he was unable to restrain himself.

"General, I would not think of questioning your orders, but wouldn't our time be better spent in the field chasing the Jews than continuing to build a camp we may abandon tomorrow?"

Gallius's face went white. "Arrius, you go too far. When I want your advice, I shall ask for it. Now get out!"

Arrius clamped his jaw shut. He'd already pushed the point farther than he should have. Since Gallius said nothing about today, he decided the usual post-patrol equipment cleaning and repair would be abbreviated in favor of giving the men at least a brief opportunity to visit the village. He was certain Tribune Gabinus, the legion's junior tribune, would not be altogether happy with the condition of the first cohort in the morning. The thought brought a smile to his face as he headed for his quarters.

Chapter 3

Ben Kosiba looked about the cramped confines of the tunnel with distaste. This tunnel and those connecting it were near what was left of the town of Beth Thera in the foothills southwest of Jerusalem. Over the past several years, the subterranean refuge had grown large enough to conceal a small army. A token village population remained above ground to give the Romans the idea there was nothing special about the location, least of all that it had become a focal point for the Jewish rebellion.

"We live like rats in a sewer," he said wrinkling his nose in disgust at the fetid smell of too many unwashed bodies living in close confines.

Sarah looked up from the small brazier she was using to roast scraps of lamb, the last vestiges of their weekly meat ration. They would have to exist exclusively on millet cakes for several more days. Noting his uncharacteristic burst of emotion, she wondered what was bothering him. He'd said little since returning early this morning after several weeks in the northern hills.

She recalled the early days of the current uprising when Rabbi Akiva became the voice that ultimately set the stage for rebellion. However, it was Shimeon ben Kosiba who had become the spark, igniting to open flame the smoldering coals of discontent and hatred. At first, she was captivated by his fiery speeches, but it wasn't long before she was physically attracted to him. Shamelessly she had thrown herself at him even though she was fully aware she wasn't the only one with whom he shared a bed. As time passed, she alone finally claimed his favors.

The Roman response to the growing rebellion was both predictable and swift as village after village was destroyed in retaliation. It was to be expected. After all, Romans had been doing that for as long as anyone remembered, prompting droll humor that sarcastically gave thanks to the Romans for the chance to build anew with an ample supply of building materials always available. Some saw the destruction as a tangible sign it was time to move or rebuild.

Ben Kosiba stood up and restlessly began pacing back and forth causing the small fire Sarah was tending to flare erratically. "Take care, this is the last of the meat." She carefully poked the meager rations. "Sit down or go outside until I call you."

Meekly, ben Kosiba did as she said and took a seat nearby. He was still considering the latest report from one of the spies earlier that day. It was information he had yet to share with the council or anyone except Eleazar.

Sarah gave him a searching look. "Shimeon, something is bothering you."

He looked at her for a long moment before replying, his expression grave. "I've asked Eleazar to assemble the council in one hour's time. What I tell them will not be received well. The Romans are bringing in reinforcements, possibly as many as three more legions. There are those in the council with faint hearts who will view this as reason to seek terms rather than continue to fight."

"Would the Romans even consider terms?"

"Not likely. Oh, perhaps a year ago it might have been an option, but now it's too late. The fact the Romans are sending in additional legions tells me they intend to lay waste to Judaea and destroy us both as a people and a country. We've shown the world the empire can be challenged and even defeated, but I now fear time is on their side. I've seen the signs among our own people. They grow tired of a struggle that seems unending and in which sacrifice after sacrifice is made with little to show for it except to live underground like animals. We grow weaker while the Romans grow stronger. Perhaps it's time I made overtures to the Romans."

She was taken aback by his discouraging words. She had never heard or seen the slightest hint of it until now. More than his pessimistic words, his body and face were already taking on the appearance of defeat. Rather than feeling sympathy for him, it had the opposite effect, and she felt only anger.

"How dare you talk that way? You of all people who wanted resistance and sacrifice from the beginning, encouraging even those unfit to fight to help defeat the Romans. You made resistance to Roman rule a testament to religious conviction and gave us hope for a new day when Jews would once again rule their homeland. Now you sound as if you are ready to give in." He was astonished at her anger and stared mutely at her.

"Sacrifices are still being made in the name of ben Kosiba. Did you look closely at your latest recruits when you spoke to them this morning? They are only children, but they are ready to die for you before they've even had a chance to live. They weren't afraid to show their commitment when they cut off a finger to show they are ready to fight for you and, if necessary, die for the rebellion. Some tried not to cry, but they couldn't help it, and I cried with them. Don't you dare turn away from the hopes and dreams of these people who have already suffered and done so much for you and Judaea."

Abruptly she turned away and began to weep. She felt his arms around her, his face buried in her hair and she said, "I'm sorry, I don't know what came over me. Your words frightened me. I'm not afraid of dying, truly I'm not. For the first time, you raise the specter of defeat. It's the thought we will lose this war with consequences far worse than death that frightens me."

"No, Sarah, it is I who must apologize. You're right. I'm ashamed that ever since I received the information concerning the Roman reinforcements, I've been thinking and acting like a coward. To tell the truth, I'm frightened, too. The war does not go well for us, and we cannot continue as we are much longer. We've lost nearly half our fighting strength, food is scarce and the nominal help we've been depending on from across our borders is disappearing as confidence in our ability to defeat the Romans lessens. Even the belief in Bar Kokhba among the Jews is beginning to erode. Have you heard some are starting to call me another name — Bar Kozeba, Son of Disappointment?"

She turned and put her arms around him, holding him tightly. "You've always spoken the truth. You are the voice and the strong arm of our people, and no one else would have been able to accomplish what you have. From the beginning, you've had detractors, people who watch and wait for the opportunity to take advantage of any misstep, hoping to gain power at your expense."

"Your words make me even more ashamed. I think it was a good thing you spoke up. It's exactly what I need to hear to remind me of why we must fight until there is no longer anyone left to carry on. You've changed what I will say to the council and how I will say it. I will make the additional legions sound like the Romans are desperate and proof our efforts are proving successful."

Suddenly, they became aware of the acrid odor of burning meat permeating the tunnel. "Oh, dear, look what I've done, and there's nothing left but lentil soup."

He gave her a comforting squeeze. "Just as Jews are used to doing when food is scarce, I'll simply tighten my belt another notch. Tonight, I'm certain my empty stomach will take comfort from the rumbling chorus of other hungry stomachs around me."

Ben Kosiba looked at the expressions on the faces of the war council members and knew he would have to summon the best of his oratorical skills to interject a positive note to the gloomy report he presented. Even Eleazar looked more dour than usual. The council, represented as it was by the predominant political-religious factions, was typically fractious, argumentative and continually on the brink of complete dysfunction. It was apparent that tonight would be no exception. The Sadducees continued to advocate a political solution as more advantageous to their higher economic class. The Pharisees by contrast, although tending to be more open-minded and tolerant by nature and custom, were the more resolute in continuing the conflict at whatever cost. Other factions with smaller representation within the council were just as ready to assert a contrary opinion on every issue broached or decision made. If it had been feasible, he would have disbanded the council long ago. But even with the considerable powers he'd accrued as the leader of the rebellion and accepted head of the Jewish State, his authority was still insufficient to take such a step. After all, it was deeply ingrained in all Jews they had a God-given right to be heard and to disagree with anyone they chose. Ben Kosiba sighed as he listened to the heated exchange and thought it was going to be an exceedingly long night.

Finally, ben Kosiba decided he had heard enough and stood up. "The news the Romans are bringing in additional legions changes nothing except to accelerate our plans. We still outnumber them," he said with more conviction than he felt. He straightened his shoulders. "We will defeat the Romans because it is our destiny to do so, but our tactics must change as the Romans are adapting too much to our methods."

"Are you suggesting we fight them in large numbers as we did in the beginning?" Sapphias asked with an incredulous expression.

Ben Kosiba was not surprised the first sign of opposition came from Sapphias, a political adversary who had been biding his time to replace him since the rebellion began.

"Not entirely. We need a bold stroke to convince the Romans, our foreign allies and most of all our own people that we still have the means to defeat the Romans on the battlefield. We need to be bold and destroy one or more legions before more legions arrive."

At first there was profound silence in the council chamber followed by shouts of derision and disbelief. He allowed the uproar to continue until gradually the noise began to abate. He noted Sapphias's resolute expression and knew his leadership was now hanging by a thread. He looked over at Eleazar who had remained silent during the uproar and saw that he, too, was doubtful. He realized as he looked about the chamber he would have to win them over with more than bold words and oratorical skills. He held up his hand for silence.

"By now, the Romans have concluded that we will continue to rely on isolated skirmishes in the belief we cannot stand up to them in a prolonged battle; they have ample justification to believe so. What we must do is to catch them off-guard and strike them decisively in such a way they will not expect."

Normally one of his staunchest supporters, Zachariah was the first to speak with an expression clearly indicating his skepticism. "How do you plan to bring about such a miracle? We proved several years ago we were no match for the Romans when it came to fighting the way they do." Murmurs of agreement broke out, and once again he held up a hand for silence.

"We will do this gradually. Our objective now is to convince the Romans we are on the run and unable to fight a large battle."

A sardonic voice spoke up from the far end of the chamber, "That will not require a lot of convincing. In fact, I'm already convinced." The deprecating comment drew hoots of laughter and even brought a smile to ben Kosiba's face.

After the laughter died down, he continued, "With winter approaching, the Romans will soon suspend field operations and retire to their camps to train and prepare themselves for the campaign next year. This gives us time and opportunity to use to our advantage. We will stockpile supplies here in the south to be used when we bring our warriors from the north to join the forces fighting here. Our best opportunity to face the Romans will be somewhere south of Jerusalem, perhaps in the Sorek Valley near Beth Thera where the terrain provides sufficient concealment and ample room for a large force to maneuver. We'll let the Romans believe we have enough strength in the region to attract the interest of a legion, perhaps two. We'll choose the time and location of the battle. When the Romans attack in the belief a few thousand Jews have been caught by surprise, they'll soon find out that instead of a small, unprepared force, they are facing a Jewish army of ten or more times their number. After destroying them, we will once again melt away into the mountains to resume our present tactics. A major victory will be the psychological impetus for our own forces to rededicate and intensify our efforts. In addition, success will regain the confidence of those who have been supporting our cause beyond our borders."

Ben Kosiba paused to search the faces of the council members for affirmation he was winning them over. He was gratified to see the majority were leaning forward in interest. His best indicator he'd at least captured their interest was the scowl on Sapphias's face, suggesting that even if he was opposed to the concept, he realized it was gaining favor. He alone might be the one individual who privately harbored the most doubt. *If I'm wrong, the rebellion will end near Jerusalem where it all began.*

Chapter 4

Although Arrius was looking forward to seeing Turbo again, he still wondered why the general wanted to see him. Even though they had been close friends more years ago than he cared to think about, it had been a long time since then. Their past friendship alone hardly seemed reason enough for the summons.

He noted the farther southeast they traveled the countryside that at one time had probably teemed with life seemed more barren. Once prosperous villages had been razed to further emphasize Hadrian's resolve to put down the rebellion no matter the cost. The closer they came to the coast, the more travelers they encountered. Most appeared to be refugees attempting to escape the inevitable consequences of a war where an entire population had either been enslaved or cast adrift to wander aimlessly looking for a safe place to live. Once, they passed a procession of Jews shackled together and guarded by a military detail conveying the walking spoils of war to a ready market. From the slovenly appearance of the guards, it was only too apparent they represented the dregs of the Roman Army willing to perform a task most legionaries considered unworthy. Arrius did not bother to acknowledge the casual salute of the unshaven centurion who led the detail.

They reached Gazara by mid-afternoon, a village no less nondescript than most others he'd seen in Judaea except that it was larger. Even this early in the day, the taverns appeared to be doing a brisk business as off-duty legionaries, most in various stages of intoxication, staggered from one canteen to another. He saw a small knot of men surrounding two legionaries squaring off, both too drunk to do more than swing ineffectually at each other to the raucous amusement of the onlookers. They passed a narrow side street where Arrius saw lines of legionaries waiting to obtain relief in one of the many brothels located there. Each smiling legionary that left was greeted by those still in line with cheers and ribald comments.

The encampment of the Tenth was situated a half mile from the village. Arrius was struck by the size of the guard and their polished accouterments as he rode up to the gate nearest the village. He noted a tribune standing to one side dressed in full armor and surmised the presence of General Turbo was responsible for the additional and polished guard detail. The *decurion* commanding his escort spoke to one of the guards who then hurried over to the tribune. After a brief exchange, Arrius saw the tribune nod. The guard signaled for the mounted detail to enter. The tribune looked incuriously at Arrius, acknowledging his crisp salute with a casual wave.

In front of the principia, Turbo's personal standard consisting of a large white flag embossed with a gold lightning bolt billowed lazily in the slight breeze. Arrius dismounted and entered the headquarters. After giving his name to a harried clerk who looked as if he had not slept in some time, he was directed to a wooden bench and told to wait until summoned. Arrius removed his helmet and sat down prepared for an indefinite wait or to be told to return at some later time.

He'd barely settled back when he heard his name shouted from somewhere beyond the orderly room. The various staff members who were in the room came to attention as General Vitellius Turbo entered the room. Dressed in a simple tunic and ignoring the other occupants of the room, Turbo came toward him, a warm smile reaching from ear to ear. Turbo grasped Arrius's forearm in a firm grip of genuine affection.

"Marcus, my old friend, it's good to see you." The men in the orderly room stared in astonishment at the senior commander's effusive welcome of the tall centurion.

"You do me honor, General." Arrius saw Turbo had aged considerably since they had last seen each other, but he suspected the general was probably thinking the same about him. Unlike him, in which continuous life in the legions had of necessity kept him lean and hard, Turbo's rounder features reflected the more leisurely garrison duty with the Praetorian Guard in Rome. Unchanged were the intelligent grey eyes that Arrius knew flashed as quickly with anger as amusement. Above all, there was still a magnetism Turbo possessed that had always set him apart from other men, a quiet belief in his own ambition and destiny that underscored his confidence he would one day achieve high office. Nearly forgotten memories surfaced again when both suffered the hardships of border patrols and winter camps, confiding to each other their dreams of the future. He realized then his own aspirations had never been as ambitious as Turbo's. Perhaps if he'd dreamed bigger, he might have progressed higher than a lifetime serving in one legion after another. He realized the difference between himself and Turbo was that he had merely dreamed, and Turbo had planned.

"Marcus, you haven't changed at all except for a few more scars and a few more lines on your face. You still look like every Roman soldier should and with a face mean enough to scare the shit out of any poor son of a bitch within the reach of your sword. By the gods, it's good to see your ugly face. Why haven't you been to Rome to see me? I would have given you any posting in Rome including the Praetorian if you'd only asked."

"General, with all due respect, the last place I ever wanted to serve was in Rome. I think I'm better suited for legion duty than risking the unfamiliar terrain of political battlefields."

"Spoken like a primus pilus and the field soldier that you are. I understand more than you realize, and you're better than the rest of us for the choice you've made." Then taking in the various phelorae adorning Arrius's cuirass, he said, "I've followed your career from afar and envied you for what you've done. Your name and reputation are widely known. I do not exaggerate when I say you could ask for much, and there would be no one to refuse you."

"You praise me more than I deserve, and any success I have had is nothing to what you've achieved. Congratulations for being appointed to command all legions and auxiliary units in Judaea. I cannot imagine command being vested in a more able man than you."

"I appreciate the sentiment. I hope Julius Severus, the new governor scheduled to arrive soon, will share your opinion. Perhaps as the general responsible for coordinating and commanding all field operations in Judaea, I may even come to appreciate the honor." Then looking around at the silent spectators in the room, he winked at Arrius and commented loudly, "Now, no one heard that last remark. I want it clearly understood I am deeply gratified for the trust the emperor has shown me." Turbo stepped back a pace and faced Arrius with a sober expression. "Marcus, dine with me tonight. I have people waiting now and matters requiring my immediate attention. Later, we'll have more time to talk of old and better times including why I sent for you." He beckoned for one of the orderlies to come forward.

"See to the centurion's needs and find him suitable quarters for the night. Bring him to me at nightfall."

Turbo disappeared through the doorway as quickly as he'd come leaving behind an entourage curious about the badly-scarred centurion.

Arrius, more presentable because of a bath and the assistance of an orderly, entered the vestibule of the spacious tent and saw Turbo bent over a table littered with scrolls and scraps of parchment intently studying a map of Judaea. He saluted and waited silently for Turbo to initiate the conversation. He noticed that unlike the buoyant demeanor shown earlier that afternoon, Turbo appeared tired and distracted, his age more pronounced, the lines on either side of his mouth made deeper by the dim flickering of the oil lamps. With no more than a brief welcome smile, Turbo dispensed with any preamble and got right to the point.

"Marcus, I'm happier to see you than you can imagine," a statement that both surprised and bewildered Arrius. "I've been in Judaea only a few days but long enough to get the impression I'm told only whatever someone thinks I want to hear. Some I've talked to believe there's no hope of subjugating Judaea except through a prolonged and costly war; others have blind faith in the supremacy of Rome that will be sufficient for a speedy end to the rebellion. I suspect the truth is somewhere in between. You're here because I need someone like you I can rely on to tell me what conditions are like, what we should be doing or what we should stop doing. From experience, I know you'll tell me what I need to know, not what I would like to hear." Turbo sprawled in a camp chair and motioned Arrius to another.

"General…"

"Here in private, I am Vitellius. I want you to talk to me as we were a long time ago, as friends and not as general and centurion." Turbo smiled briefly erasing the cares on his face. "That way I can shamelessly take advantage of a friend and drain him like a sponge before I let you go back to your legion."

"General…" Arrius started before correcting himself. "Vitellius, since I don't know what you've been told, I hardly know where to begin. No doubt you've already formed an opinion of your own."

"Oh, I didn't need to come all the way to Judaea to form an opinion. I had that before leaving Rome and reading the dispatches coming from Judaea not to mention listening to Hadrian. The emperor's angry, more so than I've ever seen him. The war has not played well in Rome. Our casualties continue to mount with little or no end in sight. The last time I saw Hadrian, he'd convinced himself he should come to Judaea and personally take the field as the senior general, and it now appears he intends to do exactly that. Can you imagine the emperor doing such a thing? Better a general to take the blame for a Judaean quagmire than the emperor to get the stink of it on his own hands. I'm merely the latest general whose career will likely end in this godforsaken place. Rome is tired of this war and wants it to end now. So far, I don't see that it will end soon or at least soon enough to satisfy Hadrian."

For a moment, Arrius said nothing. "All right then, but what I have to say may be at odds with what you've already heard. First, we are too few, and the Jewish tactics have changed. At first, we killed them on the battlefield by the thousands until they realized they couldn't defeat us that way. Now they attack in small numbers; consequently, our own advantages and opportunities to destroy them have been reduced."

"I understand they did well enough to destroy the Ninth Legion and control Jerusalem for over almost two years."

"True, but that was an early success the Jews have been unable to repeat. Jerusalem was retaken, and ever since, they've resorted to small unit actions relying on surprise and ambush. They choose the time and location for an attack after which they melt away into the hills and mountains honeycombed with caves and tunnels. Except for the southern region which is relatively open, the country is rugged in the far north. We spend our time in useless pursuit, wearing ourselves out and leveling villages they no longer depend upon and have mostly abandoned anyway. In short, we are accomplishing very little in our attempts to ferret out an elusive enemy who has nothing to lose by prolonging the war in the belief Rome will seek terms rather than proceed indefinitely with an unprofitable war. The soldiers see little gain in what we do, and frankly, neither do I."

"The Jews are wrong if they think Rome will seek terms. That opportunity has come and gone for any peace. Nothing will satisfy Hadrian except the destruction of Judaea."

"I'm no politician, nor do I have any interest in commerce, but is the destruction of Judaea a wise investment?"

"Hadrian no longer cares about commercial and financial interests. He's concentrating on the fact this is the second major rebellion in Judaea in the last sixty years, and if he has anything to say and can do about it, it will be the last. He means to subdue Judaea once and for all even if it takes killing or enslaving every Jew in the country. He's bitter by what he feels was a Jewish rejection of his well-intentioned attempt to understand their religion. He tried to reach an accommodation with their beliefs and his. The Jews focused on one god, and we have more than I can remember on a good day. The Jews believe in circumcision, a practice Hadrian abhors. The rabbis wouldn't compromise, and in the end, neither did Hadrian. Hadrian's plan to rebuild Jerusalem after we did our best to destroy it during the last rebellion was probably the last straw. The strange part was Hadrian thought he was doing the Jews a favor by rebuilding the city even if he had intended once it was completed to rename the city after himself and Jupiter."

Turbo reached into a small leather purse hanging from his belt and withdrew a small coin that he handed to Arrius.

"What is this for? Is this an advance on the pay we haven't received for months?" It was a pointed reminder of the usual delays in receiving pay routinely experienced in the Roman Army.

"Take a close look at it."

Arrius examined the small gold coin unlike any he'd seen. On one side was a palm tree with the inscription he knew was the Hebrew word for Jerusalem. The obverse depicted a cluster of grapes in abstract form with another inscription also in Hebrew which he was unable to understand.

"What does it say?"

"It says 'For the redemption of Jerusalem' or something like that. I doubt anything made Hadrian angrier than when he saw one of these for the first time. Although Jews have been allowed to mint coins in years past, this time it picked the scab off as far as Hadrian was concerned. Hadrian's objective is to kill as many Jews as possible. By the time we're through with Judaea, there won't be enough Jews left in Judaea to fill this tent. Now you know why I said what I did this afternoon about the honor of the appointment." Then with a note of bitterness, "I fear there will be no glory for anyone when this war is over, no triumphs for any general for a war the majority in Rome didn't want, and if the truth be known, didn't care about except that a bad outcome threatens the rest of the empire."

"Then what's the answer?"

Turbo leaned forward, eyes narrowed, and said in a soft voice, "Make no mistake, if we lose this war, or even if it appears to the rest of the world the Jews have somehow won terms, the future of the entire empire is in jeopardy. We cannot afford to lose; the stakes are too high. The Jews have already made too many people think the unthinkable, that Rome can be defeated, an attitude that is now being shared by some in Rome. Rome cannot long survive if the Jewish revolt continues much longer and manages to ignite the unrest always lying beneath the surface in other parts of the empire."

"Then you'll have to double or triple the number of legions now in Judaea, and even that may not be enough. I don't know how the other legions are faring, but the *Deiotariana* is no longer a legion, reduced in strength as we now are. We've lost over a thousand men, and we were hardly at full-strength when we left Egypt. My own cohort is fewer than seven hundred, and at least a hundred of those aren't fit for field duty."

"The increase in our forces is already underway. Julius Severus is bringing two legions and additional vexillations from other legions throughout the empire. More legions will follow later if there is still need for them. In six months, there could well be as many as ten legions in Judaea. Hadrian is leaving Britannia and the eastern borders in grave danger by reducing our strength on those frontiers. He's willing to risk the consequences to put an end to a rebellion that has gotten out of hand. We need to get this rebellion finished quickly, or we risk rebellion in other places in the empire."

Arrius tossed the coin back to Turbo and stood up motioning for Turbo to join him at the table where he pointed at the map of Judaea. "You're looking for a quick solution to a problem for which there may not be one."

"A quick solution is precisely what Hadrian demands, whatever the immediate cost."

"Then we are expendable just so long as Hadrian achieves his goal?"

"Make no mistake, even the senior general is expendable in Judaea."

Arrius pointed to the map. "During time the *Deiotariana* has been in Judaea, we've covered much of the province almost as far north as

Syria. Rome now owns the coastal plain from Syria to the southern deserts; I doubt there are enough Jews left in this area to make a difference. It's the far mountain country in the north and the central highlands where the greatest concentration of Jews remain. The central highlands region is important because of the abundant water available, and its fertile valleys are a principal food source. The problem with both regions is that it also presents the Jews with terrain where a Jewish army can very well remain hidden if they so choose. If reinforcements do arrive, these are the areas where it will require the greatest concentration for that is also where the Jewish strength lies. The farther south along the Dead Sea and beyond Jerusalem the country becomes increasingly arid and more desert-like. The comparatively more open and rolling hills south of Jerusalem would allow a couple of legions or possibly a single legion with an additional cavalry vexillation to maintain control. This would allow the bulk of our legionary force to be concentrated in the other and more rugged hill and mountain regions. Even then, it will take considerable time, effort and legionaries to comb this region searching every cave and valley to dig them out."

"Minerva's teats, I don't have that kind of time. It would take years to accomplish such an effort. There must be another way."

"Not necessarily. I grant you if we continue to fight the way we have been, it will take time. I think we may be able to accelerate the process by changing our own way of fighting."

"How?"

"I said earlier we are wearing ourselves out with patrols that find little and accomplish less. We need to better adapt to the kind of warfare with which we are now confronted. That means better focused and more coordinated operations instead of each legion approaching the war as if it's the only legion engaged."

"Yes, I agree, and the very reason the last governor was replaced. He never grasped the fact we were helping the Jews to defeat us by squandering our strength. What else?"

"We need to train our legionaries to fight effectively in small units in the hills and mountains instead of expecting the Jews to come down and fight us in conventional battle in open terrain."

Turbo looked doubtful. "To do so will reduce our own cohesiveness and the advantage we have in fighting a battle where tight discipline and organization have always been the Roman way to fight and win a battle."

"Hear me out, Vitellius. That is exactly what I'm talking about except we must apply those qualities in a different way. I'll explain. The first thing we must change is to do a better job at finding the Jews. In most cases when we do engage, it results from an attack the Jews have initiated and at a time and place they choose. We need to reverse this. We would do better by keeping our forces deployed in the field instead of marching around the hills for a few days or weeks before returning to let our soldiers spend too much time in garrison visiting taverns and brothels as I witnessed when I passed through Gazara."

"I've noticed since I've been here the reluctance on the part of the Tenth to take to the field."

Arrius noted the disgusted look on Turbo's face and was encouraged to continue. "Once a mountain or valley has been cleared, we should retain sufficient forces nearby ready to prevent the Jews from re-occupying the area. What I'm saying is that we first must find the Jew before we can engage him. The best way to do that is with continuous reconnaissance and pressure. Once we find a stronghold, we should strike without delay with a force that is located close by and prepared to move quickly as soon as a report of enemy activity is received." Arrius swept his hand across the map. "Mountain by mountain, hill and valley, we should push them out of Judaea north into Syria as far as Parthia if necessary and east across the river that flows from the fresh water lake in the north to the Dead Sea in the south. Let them try and exist in the trackless wastes of Arabia or the desert south of Jerusalem. They'll find the country and the Arabian tribes offering little if any hospitality or tolerance for their religion and their presence."

A worried frown darkening his face, Turbo reluctantly nodded in assent. "I fear such a strategy, even as practical as it may be, will require more time than Hadrian will allow. With winter approaching and the campaign season rapidly ending, I'll lose additional time to win a quick victory."

"The answer is not to sit out the winter months in garrison but to keep on pressing them."

Turbo shot Arrius a doubtful look. "The legions will not like taking the field in the winter; they'll expect to suspend field operations then as we traditionally do." He hesitated. "However, perhaps you're right."

Arrius saw the harried look on Turbo's face and realized he'd said little thus far to dispel the hopelessness in which the general seemed to view the situation. He supposed he might feel the same way when confronted with an angry emperor who wanted a quick solution for ending both an unpopular and unprofitable war. He decided there was nothing to lose by contributing some of the ideas he'd voiced to Gallius, but which thus far the legion commander had ignored.

"If you're interested, I have a few suggestions that may help to improve the effectiveness of our efforts to find the enemy and after we do, inflict more casualties."

"I'm interested."

"When we do engage the Jews, it's seldom in the close-in fighting that gives us the advantage of using our most formidable weapons, the spear and the gladius. The Jews' most effective weapon is the bow. Their arrows can engage us from a distance and much farther and more accurately than we can throw our heavy javelins. You may wish to augment our regular forces with archers. We should also reduce the length and weight of the spears with which our legionaries are now equipped. A lighter javelin would allow a legionary to carry three perhaps four instead of the standard two. A light javelin can also be thrown farther. Finally, employ the cavalry in small numbers for reconnaissance in the less mountainous regions and in larger numbers along the coastal plains. As I said earlier, I would also consider sending additional cavalry to the southern hills south of Jerusalem should you decide to limit legionary forces in that region. It is still a risk leaving the south less protected, but I believe concentrating more strength in the north and central highlands where the bulk of the enemy forces are located may help to shorten the war."

Turbo's interest was apparent by the attentiveness with which he listened, now more animated since the centurion had entered the tent.

"Excellent, Marcus, well said. These are the first positive and practical suggestions I've heard since I arrived. I'll ensure your ideas are taken into consideration as we develop our battle plans." Turbo looked curiously at Arrius. "Have you said anything to anyone about these ideas?"

"I may have mentioned them a couple of times."

"Well, they're good and practical ideas. You should have done more to elevate them."

"I did try." Arrius did not offer further elaboration.

"I have an idea whose deaf ears did not hear what you had to say. I think Gallius has not changed very much from when he exchanged his seat in the senate for a general's baton." Not expecting Arrius to comment further, Turbo continued, "Gallius is an ambitious man, and while that describes most of us either in the army or in politics, including me at times," he said with a self-deprecating grin, "it's a quality Gallius can and will carry to an extreme. I'll speak no more on the matter."

"Nor will I."

Turbo leaned forward, elbows on his knees. "Why don't you join my personal staff here? I'll make you one of my senior advisors and give you the rank and authority to implement your own ideas. I need someone I can trust with experience and fresh ideas. I must admit, I've been too long in Rome and away from the army. I need your considerable and more extensive field experience."

"I appreciate your offer, and I'm sorely tempted to accept, but I've no wish to leave the field to serve in a staff position, even if it's on your staff. I realize I'm getting old for field duty, yet I don't wish to end it any sooner than I must. I still have time to serve as primus pilus. I want to serve out the full year of my appointment after which I may be more than willing to consider your offer — that is if no other legion will have me."

"I had a feeling that would be your answer. I'm disappointed but not surprised. I think you're making a mistake by not taking advantage of my offer to win higher office when it can be handed to you as I'm trying to do now. Such an opportunity may not be there a few months from now, especially if Hadrian doesn't see this war coming to an end quickly enough. If it doesn't, I will certainly no longer be able to extend anything but my sword, and then it will be in my own belly. But, so be it, the offer stands should you change your mind. I respect and understand your decision even if I don't agree with it. Now it's time to eat, drink and talk of other things and better times."

As several orderlies cleared the table and brought in platters of food, the two men relaxed, and the talk switched to lighter subjects as they reminisced of years gone by. It was much later when Arrius lurched somewhat unsteadily back to his quarters already regretting the long ride back to the legion in the morning.

Chapter 5

Sitting astride his horse on the dock at Joppa, Tiberius Querinius watched the replacements disembark. Most wore eager, interested expressions at their first close look at Judaea. The older and more seasoned veterans looked straight ahead, giving not the slightest sign of interest in the dockside activities.

Curiosity and boredom had brought him down to the docks. It would be several days before the legionaries would be parceled out to the legions. Gallius had made it clear the senior tribune would be responsible for ensuring the *Deiotariana* received a fair allocation. So far, Querinius was not impressed with most of the men he saw. Many appeared to be past their prime with no other options left but to serve Rome no matter where the service would take them. The best of the lot appeared to be a contingent that by dress and speech were likely Tungrians brought in from Britannia. At least the Tungrians appeared healthier in comparison to the rest and looked as if they were ready for field duty. Despite his distaste for native legionaries, he resolved to have the Tungrians assigned to the *Deiotariana*.

He was about to turn his mount around and ride back to the holding area to make his case for claiming the Tungrians when he saw a man leaning over the rail of one of the ships watching the disembarkation with a look of bored resignation. Querinius thought there was something vaguely familiar about the broad-shouldered, swarthy-featured stranger. Querinius walked his horse closer to the small ship while the man observed his approach without any visible interest.

Querinius casually raised a hand. "You look familiar. What's your name?"

"I doubt we've met, and if we have, I don't remember you."

"See here, I asked a civil question. I expect a civil response, or I may well invite you to come down here and see the measure of my sword."

The stranger did not appear in the least discomfited by the threat. "Tribune, perhaps it's you who may wish to come aboard and inspect the point of my sword."

Querinius felt the blood rushing to his face as he angrily slid off his horse and strode toward the gangplank with every intention of teaching the stranger a lesson in manners. As he stepped onto the deck, Querinius began to feel some apprehension when the stranger continued to lean on the rail without any apparent concern.

"You're an insolent bastard. How dare you talk to me that way?" He began to draw his gladius. "Draw your sword or I'll spill your guts as you stand."

Leisurely, the stranger pushed himself away from the rail. "I am indeed a bastard as it so happens; therefore, I selected my own cognomen when I came of age and named myself Marcello Aculineous. Perhaps you've heard of me? Now, Tribune, you have my name at last." Noting Querinius's dawning recognition, he continued, "I take it you have heard of me."

Lowering his sword and stepping back a pace, Querinius said, "I've heard of you," recalling the last time he saw Aculineous was the day the centurion had defeated his third straight challenger at a legionary gladiatorial contest in Rome. The legion-sponsored events were supposed to be relatively bloodless, emphasizing as they did battle skill and spirited rivalry between legions; however, Aculineous had achieved notoriety for the merciless way in which he frequently left his opponents severely wounded and maimed for life. Querinius had seen his fighting skills exercised and knew enough of his reputation to realize he would have stood little chance besting a man with such expertise. Absent-mindedly sheathing the gladius, he asked," What are you doing here?"

"I am presently awaiting assignment to whatever legion may require my services."

"Yes, but why are you here?"

"I'll spare you the long story. I became too successful in the arena on the last occasion I fought. Afterward, I was made to understand it would prove to be in my best interests if I were to volunteer for service in Judaea. Now that I've seen Judaea, albeit a small part from the deck of this ship, I feel I may have made a poor bargain. I have but one desire left, and that is to return to Rome just as soon as I can do so."

The beginning of an idea began to take shape as Querinius listened to Aculineous's brief explanation. The centurion might well be the solution to General Gallius's problem while serving his own interests in the bargain. "Centurion, I believe I may be able to assist you in achieving what you want."

Aculineous listened with growing interest as Querinius outlined what he had in mind.

Arrius was pleased when the contingent of badly-needed replacements eventually arrived as part of the general increase in Roman strength throughout the province. Surprisingly, Gallius had taken a more aggressive interest in obtaining the legion's fair share of the reinforcements and sent Tiberius Querinius to Joppa where the arriving legions and replacements were marshalling. Ten days later, Querinius arrived at the head of a dust-caked column. The first cohort was increased in strength by an additional two hundred men and a centurion, much less than he hoped for; however, any increase in strength was an improvement.

Most of the replacements assigned to his cohort were Tungrians from Britannia who had been relocated from Belgica along the upper Rhine River following the tribe's subjugation by Julius Caesar over a century before. The relocation of conquered barbarians was in keeping with Rome's practical belief that far away from their native land they were less likely to rebel again. Despite the Tungrians' heavily accented Latin and clannish behavior, Arrius was relieved to see the cohort's ranks strengthened.

At first, the Tungrians were greeted with mixed enthusiasm by the cohort's veterans. The replacements were initially as much of a liability as an asset. As was the usual case with reinforcements hastily recruited to meet the needs of a sudden build-up, a levy never included the best legionaries. Arrius and his centurions quickly went to work to forge a disciplined and cohesive fighting unit. Some of his veterans resented the infusion of the replacements as disruptive to the already established fraternity of the centuries. The Tungrians had their own set of complaints at being split up and simply regrouped at every opportunity in sullen hostility, frustrating his attempts to achieve unit integrity. Within a few weeks, there were fewer and fewer disruptions caused by real or perceived slights as Romans and Tungrians began to concentrate on preparing to fight Jews more than each other. As always, the centurions and optiones were instrumental in facilitating the transition and gradually the smack of vine staffs on bare flesh occurred with less frequency. As time passed and patrols increased, Arrius began to see the results when he saw the cohort melding into a single entity, reacting to his orders with smooth precision. The *Deiotariana* veterans also began to accept the Tungrians accented speech, their habit of cutting off the heads of the Jews they killed and, if given the opportunity before battle, painting their faces blue as a lingering vestige of their heritage.

The one notable and serious problem facing Arrius was Marcello Aculineous, the centurion who had been arbitrarily assigned to the cohort by Tiberius Querinius. Arrius had reason to expect the elevation of a centurion from one of the other cohorts to fill the vacancy as tradition mandated. He had counted on one of several candidates he had recommended to Attius Varro; therefore, it came as an unwelcome surprise when Aculineous, a complete unknown, had been arbitrarily assigned to the first cohort. When he objected, Varro said it had been at the direction of Tribune Querinius.

Arrius concealed his irritation, determined not to blame Aculineous for the arbitrary assignment; however, despite his best efforts to accept the centurion, it did not take long for him to form a strong dislike of the new officer. It was evident from Aculineous's half-hearted attempts to fit in that he was indifferent to the honor of being assigned to the first cohort.

Although Aculineous appeared competent enough in the essential skills Arrius demanded of his centurions, the morale in Aculineous's century quickly plummeted, principally because of the excessively brutal measures taken to punish the smallest infraction. His aloof, abrasive manner quickly alienated him from the other centurions. Aculineous appeared to go out of his way to be argumentative and confrontational to such an extent he had effectively isolated himself from any social contact, a fact that seemed not to bother him at all.

Arrius determined it was time to intervene on the occasion when he watched Aculineous supervising sword practice. Using one of his legionaries for an opponent, Aculineous was demonstrating a maneuver the legionary seemed unable to replicate to the centurion's satisfaction. Showing increasing impatience over the legionary's clumsy attempts, Aculineous finally bore down in a vigorous assault that knocked the man to his knees. Then to Arrius's surprise,

Aculineous stepped forward and brutally thrust the point of his gladius into the legionary's shoulder.

"That may teach you to pay closer attention. Next time it might be your throat." The other legionaries and Arrius looked on in shocked silence.

After the training was over, Arrius drew Aculineous aside. "Aculineous, that's the second man you've sent to the infirmary in as many days. As short of men as we are, I can't afford to have you helping the Jews."

Aculineous smiled as if nothing had happened. "Whatever you say, Primus Pilus, but I was attempting to put a little emphasis on the lesson. I've always believed there's nothing like a little scratch to make a man remember the basics."

"You go too far. Heed what I say; I'll have no more of that. The next time you see fit to blood one of my legionaries, it will be my gladius you'll face."

Aculineous smiled. "Now there's an interesting proposition. Perhaps we should give a little demonstration to the men here and now — that is if you're game for it?"

"Another time. It's the men who require the sword practice, not us."

"A pity," the centurion looked disappointed. "It might prove to be interesting."

Later, Arrius described what he had witnessed to Strabo who said, "There's something strange about him. He's skillful and experienced well enough, but he's made no effort to fit in at all. As far as I know, he's made no friends since he arrived and seems to prefer keeping to himself, which by now no one objects to."

"I can't afford to have him continue to act the way he does. He'll have to change his ways and attitude, or I'll have him moved to another cohort."

In the days that followed, there were no further reports of Aculineous's training excesses. Soon Arrius thought no more about it, believing the centurion had wisely taken heed of the admonishment and ultimatum he'd given him.

Chapter 6

Varro reached for the pitcher and poured a generous measure of wine into Arrius's empty cup before refilling his own. The two men were sitting by themselves in a small village canteen favored by the legion's officers. Conversing quietly and enjoying the warm glow from one pitcher already consumed, Arrius was glad Varro talked him into going with him. He hadn't really wanted to with so much to do before leading the cohort into the hills for an extended patrol, but Varro was finally persuasive when he reminded him of the coming weeks when there would be no such opportunities. Arrius wasn't fooled. He knew wine wasn't the only thing Varro had on his mind. It wouldn't be long before the portly officer would announce it was time for other pleasures and lurch off to one of the brothels. He resolved to finish the cup before him and then head back to the fort.

Sitting with his back to the door, he was aware someone had just come in but paid little attention until Varro leaned forward and said in a low voice, "One of your centurions just walked in."

Arrius turned and saw Aculineous taking a seat at a distant table. For a moment their eyes met, and the centurion flashed a disarming smile. Expressionless, Arrius nodded and considered whether he should invite the centurion to join them. He quickly decided against it in the belief sharing a cup of wine wasn't going to improve their relations.

"How is Aculineous doing?" Varro asked.

"Well enough."

"I heard he sent a couple of legionaries to the infirmary."

"It's true. I put him on notice because of it. I'm pleased with my replacements except for Aculineous. I've no complaints with his skills, but his attitude needs improving. Attius, there's something about him that isn't quite right. Apart from not making any effort to socialize with anyone since he arrived from Joppa, I don't know what it is about him that gives me reason to be concerned. Once we take to the field, I expect he'll begin to fit in. If not, I'll request his reassignment to another cohort." Arrius drained his cup and stood up, already beginning to regret the amount of wine he'd consumed and the long walk back to camp now facing him. "It's time I was getting back," he said, throwing a few coins on the table. Arrius buckled on his *balteus*, the wide military belt that supported the gladius and dagger worn on the opposite side.

"I'll see you back in camp," Varro called after him.

After the comparative gloom of the tavern, the glare of the late-afternoon sun intensified the feeling he'd drunk more than he should have. Instead of taking the road and easier way back to the fort, he decided to travel the steeper but more direct route through a ravine that cut nearly in half the distance between the fort and the village. After reaching the bottom of the ravine and stumbling several times in the process, he continued to make his way along the well-worn path meandering through the brush and trees. He paused briefly to relieve a full bladder in the shade of a rocky outcropping. Behind him, he thought he heard someone approaching. He assumed Varro had changed his mind and decided to return to the fort. He sat down on a large rock off to the side of the path to wait for him.

A few moments later, it was Marcello Aculineous who came into sight and not Varro.

Aculineous's face broke into a smile that failed to reach his eyes. "Arrius, here you are. I was beginning to think I might have delayed too long and missed the pleasure of your company. I must say I was disappointed you and Praefectus Varro didn't invite me to your table for a cup and the opportunity to become better acquainted."

"Next time, I'll make a point of it."

"Primus Pilus, I do not believe there will be a next time. I'm on my way to Joppa so this is the last opportunity we shall have to get to know each other."

Perplexed, Arrius said, "You're leaving? No one spoke to me of it. I'm surprised General Gallius would approve a transfer when we're still short of replacements and about to go on patrol."

"In truth, General Gallius knows nothing of it. In fact, it's my own idea. I'm about to finish the business I came here to do; therefore, I see no reason to remain in this pesthole any longer than I have to."

"What business would that be?"

"Why to kill you, Arrius, and this place seems to be as good as any to take care of it." He drew both his dagger and sword.

Taken completely by surprise, Arrius stood up and stared, making no attempt to draw his own sword.

"Are you mad? What's the meaning of this?"

"It means I intend to gut you from neck to belly. Draw your sword, and you will at least have a chance to stay alive — although it will be a very small chance."

Arrius drew his sword. "Why are you doing this?"

"I'd be happy to tell you, but I'm in a bit of a hurry. I've already been here longer than I ever intended while waiting for an opportunity to do this; therefore, I'm not really in the mood for a long conversation. Frankly, I'd hoped the sword training the other day would be a convenient way to end the matter, but you're difficult to provoke. Even though I'm being well compensated, I've had to wait far too long for this opportunity."

Arrius was more bewildered than ever. "Who's paying you and why?"

"Tribune Querinius doesn't seem to like you. For what reason, I have no idea, but then it doesn't really matter to me. Enough of this, let's get on with it."

For the second time, Arrius regretted that last cup of wine and tried to shake off its lingering effects. He took stock of his opponent standing resolutely before him. Aculineous was smaller but had the advantage of being at least ten years younger; he had a longer reach and more experience in his favor.

Aculineous confidently assumed the loose, crouching stance of an experienced combatant. As the two men circled warily, each looked for the slightest weakness or hesitation that could be exploited. It was Aculineous who made the first move, advancing with an aggressiveness and agility that nearly ended the affair at the start. Almost too late, Arrius realized Aculineous's dagger was just as deadly as his sword when he felt it penetrate the loose folds of his tunic.

Both men backed away showing mutual respect for each other's skill. Aculineous smiled and said with an equal measure of respect and ridicule, "Not bad for an old man. This may take longer than I anticipated."

"Whatever the reason for this, you can't possibly leave Judaea alive if you succeed in killing me."

"Oh, that will not be a problem. Let me assure you, arrangements have been made, and by tonight, I'll be well on my way to Joppa and on the first boat back to Rome."

Aculineous had no sooner stopped talking when Arrius saw the muscles tense in the other man's right shoulder. Arrius was ready and countered Aculineous's aggressive attack. For the next few minutes, each man cautiously probed the other's defense, waiting for a careless move. As time wore on, Arrius was pleased to see Aculineous was no longer smiling. A grim look now replaced the cocky, confident smile, but he also realized he did not have the stamina of the much younger man. Aculineous appeared to stumble and seeing an opportunity, Arrius lunged forward only to discover too late it had been a ruse. The consequence was a cut to his shoulder that would have found his throat had he not reacted as quickly as he did. Although the wound itself wasn't very painful, the bleeding was making the sword hilt slippery to hold.

"You're slowing down, old man. Not much longer now before you sleep with the gods. I'll grant you there have been few I've faced who lasted this long. For that, I congratulate you."

A moment later, Aculineous lunged, and Arrius reacted automatically by dropping to one knee and raising his sword. Aculineous's sword slid harmlessly the length of his before stopping at the guard. Caught off balance, Aculineous staggered. It was the moment Arrius had been waiting for as he thrust the dagger up and into Aculineous's throat. Eyes wide in shocked surprise, Aculineous slumped to his knees and struggled with both hands to pull the blade out before falling lifeless to the ground, the dagger still protruding from his neck.

Arrius heard a noise behind him and turned, sword at the ready, and saw Varro standing nearby.

"Marcus, aren't you getting a little too old for this sort of thing? I was beginning to wonder how much longer you were going to last before you foundered."

"You've been watching the entire time?"

"Long enough to wonder how it was going to turn out."

"How did you happen to be here?"

"I saw Aculineous leave right after you did without touching the wine he'd ordered. I thought it was strange so I thought I'd follow him. It was apparent he was following you. The truth is I was having difficulty keeping up with both of you."

"Well, I'm grateful you did."

"I was beginning to think you might need a little help."

"Attius, I wouldn't have refused if you'd have offered to help. The bastard came close to sending me to a place I'm not yet ready to go. I may be getting too old to hold my own with the likes of him."

"So, Marcus, how did all this come about?"

Arrius quickly summarized the brief conversation with Aculineous. "It makes no sense to me, Attius. He said Querinius paid him a substantial amount to kill me."

"Querinius? Minerva's sweet ass, I wonder why."

"I know Gallius and I do not get along, but I have difficulty in believing he would resort to such a thing as this."

"I agree. Perhaps not Gallius but Querinius might think if he took care of you, he would gain additional favor. It isn't any secret you and Gallius are not exactly on the best of terms. I think Querinius is the one to explain this. Are you going to ask him?"

"I don't think so. What's to be gained? He'll only deny it. No, I intend to say nothing about this although it will be difficult to explain why I killed one of my centurions."

Varro stared thoughtfully at the body. "The answer is you don't. Let the Jews get the blame." Then without explaining further, he knelt and rolled the dead man over until the centurion lay facing the cloudless sky. Arrius watched Varro pull the dagger out of the dead man's neck and then thrust the metal tip of the arrow he'd been carrying into the wound.

"That should do. When the body's discovered, the logical assumption is Aculineous met an untimely death from a Jewish assassin while returning from the village."

Arrius gave a short laugh, reassured Varro's idea had every chance of being accepted without question. While Arrius bound up his wound from a strip ripped from Aculineous's tunic, Varro gathered up the dead man's weapons and deposited them in a narrow rocky crevice, kicking dirt on top to conceal them.

"The Jews would never leave a good sword and dagger behind," Varro commented when he was satisfied the weapons would not be found. "Let's go on back to the village and get you cleaned up. While you're doing that, I'll attend to other matters."

Chapter 7

Turbo was nervous. So far, the meeting had not gone as well as he'd hoped. He'd been a close confidant and friend of Hadrian for years, but that counted for nothing with the angry man he was now facing.

Sprawled in a chair, Hadrian was in a foul mood. Several months had passed since Turbo had last seen the emperor in Rome, and the mental and physical changes that had occurred in the intervening time were startling. Gone was the calm, almost stoic demeanor along with the physical stamina characteristic of the man. It wasn't that long ago when Hadrian would shoulder the pack of a common legionary and march for days with a legion in the field, sharing the same rations and sleeping rough, much to the admiration of the men. There was little resemblance to that man now. Hadrian had put on so much weight his cuirass had to be enlarged on the increasingly rare occasions he wore it. His legs were too swollen to wear greaves, and it was difficult for him to walk without assistance. Hadrian now traveled in a mule-cart on the infrequent occasions he chose to visit a legion instead of mounted on a horse. The visits to the legions, which at one time gave him the greatest pleasure, no longer appeared to have the same effect. He seemed content to remain in the headquarters where he spent almost as much time consulting with the court physicians as with the generals.

Turbo thought the most obvious example that Hadrian's thinking was not entirely rational was in assuming the title *Imperator* emphasizing his assumption of command of all legions in Judaea. Given the dismal outcome of the Judaean war thus far and the distinct possibility the war might drag on indefinitely, there was little for Hadrian to gain from the act and much to risk if the outcome was less than successful. Had he been emperor, he would have remained in Rome and let Severus take the blame for a war thoroughly unpopular in Rome. The result of a Roman victory was negligible, and the consequences of losing would be unthinkable.

Feeling a trickle of sweat run down his side, Turbo said, "Caesar, the disposition of the legions is forcing the Jews to fall back farther and farther in the mountainous regions to the north and east. As a result, most of the province is now under firm Roman control. In the last two months, we've killed over 25,000 Jews and shipped almost that many slaves through the ports of Judaea and Syria. Our reports indicate many of those still able to resist are already crossing into Arabia."

"How many Jews are still left in Judaea and able to put forth any significant resistance?"

"It's difficult to say although estimates range anywhere from 75,000 to twice that number."

Hadrian threw his wine cup across the room then stood up and waddled towards Turbo who instinctively stepped back a pace convinced the emperor was about to throttle him. Hadrian stopped in front of Turbo, towering over him, face only inches away from his.

"General Turbo, I sent you here along with ample reinforcements to end this rebellion once and for all. So far, all you've told me is that you are making progress. By the gods, a turtle makes progress, albeit slowly. Are you asking me to accept the pace of a turtle and results that at this rate will take years instead of the weeks and months I expect this campaign to take? Do I have the wrong man for this task?" Hadrian looked at Severus. "Or should I put you in command and send Turbo back to Rome to explain to the Senate why he failed to do as his emperor directed?"

Severus knew it was time to intervene and attempt to calm the emperor down — less for Turbo's sake than to preserve his own position that he believed was about to become as precarious as Turbo's.

"Caesar, I believe the situation is better than General Turbo may have indicated. There is ample justification to be confident a quicker solution is still achievable. If I may persuade you to allow General Turbo to continue, perhaps we may yet assure you that your purpose and objectives will be achieved as you desire."

For a moment, Hadrian continued to glare at the two men before returning to his chair. "Very well, General Turbo, continue, but I warn you my patience is ended. I want no more promises. Each day this rebellion continues, the empire becomes weaker. I want actions that will give me an end to this god-cursed rebellion, or I will have a new governor and a new field general who will do the job the way I want it done."

Strangely, Hadrian's angry outburst had a calming effect on Turbo who decided he had absolutely nothing left to lose. He might just as well proceed to define the strategy he believed was the only way to bring the rebellion to a fast end as Hadrian demanded.

"Caesar, it is clear to us, as it must be to the Jews, we are beating them at their own tactics of seeking battle in small engagements over a wide area. They have the memory of Masada to remind them the Romans will not rest until the Roman eagle is unchallenged in Judaea."

Hadrian banged his fist on the chair arm. "I don't want to hear the name *Judaea* again. This province will be called *Palastina*. Nor do I wish to hear the name Jerusalem; the city will be named *Aelia Capitolina.*"

Turbo and Severus exchanged looks of surprise. Both were aware the name Jerusalem had been proscribed, but this was the first either had heard the name of the province would be changed, still another indication of Hadrian's implacable hatred of the Jewish people and the province. Turbo acknowledged the emperor's interruption. "Yes, Caesar, I will inform the map-makers. Our reports indicate there is considerable dissension within their ranks with many who now wish to end the rebellion by seeking the best terms or any terms offered."

"General Turbo, I told you in Rome, I neither seek, nor will I accept, any Jewish terms. I want the Jews destroyed. I don't want any possibility the Jews will ever disrupt the empire again."

"That is fully understood, and we are making no provision to seek terms although I've let it be known terms would be possible only to sow dissent among the Jewish factions. We know there are many who no longer see ben Kosiba, who until recently was known as Bar Kokhba, as their leader and would welcome the opportunity to end hostilities. I believe the Jews may be preparing to intensify their efforts in the spring and are using the deteriorating weather conditions and the expectation we will withdraw to winter quarters to disguise the signs they are consolidating their efforts in the southern region. We're not certain if this indicates a desire to escape the harshness of the mountainous regions or suggests they may be getting ready to launch an attack or attacks on a larger scale. Regardless of their intentions, it seems clear from intelligence reports our recent efforts are the reason Jewish forces are moving south."

Turbo was relieved to see Hadrian leaning forward, his full attention now focused and reminiscent of the practical soldier he once was. He continued with growing optimism. "For my part, it's my intent to ignore, at least for now, the build-up in the south and continue to maintain pressure in the areas we are currently occupying during the winter months. I do not wish to let the Jews know we are aware of their movement south by shifting our own forces in that direction. I've instructed the legion commanders to rotate their cohorts through the base camps to allow the legionaries to rest up without losing ground we've so far gained. I remain hopeful the Jews will again try to attack in large numbers in the mistaken belief they can defeat us. If the Jews are encouraged to fight more conventionally, that will be their undoing."

"Assuming your information is accurate, when do you anticipate the Jews will launch an offensive."

"There are no signs it will be before late spring or early summer. They show every indication they will remain generally quiet during the winter months. I also suspect it will require time to position sufficient stores and men to begin a major offensive. In any event, we should have ample warning before they begin to move."

"You sound very confident, General. What makes you so sure the Jews are going to do as you've described?"

"We have a well-placed spy who so far has proven to be reliable. In fact, we even know the general area where we believe ben Kosiba has his headquarters near Beth Thera south of Aelia Capitolina."

"Then why not go after him now? Kill the bastard, and the rebellion will crumble."

"Caesar, it is said he moves about and does not stay in any one place for long, and I'm not certain that if we are fortunate in killing ben Kosiba, it would necessarily signal a final Jewish defeat."

"How large a force can the Jews muster?"

"It's difficult to say, Caesar. Our best guess is the Jews have left a total fighting force spread out over the country of between 50,000 and 75,000. It could be less but unlikely it is more than that. In any event, I do not expect the Jews to begin an offensive with more than 30-40,000."

"What strength do we now have close to Beth Thera?"

"The Tenth Legion, *Fretensis*, is located five miles due north and northwest of Aelia Capitolina with a near full strength of 4,235 legionaries. The Twenty-second Legion, *Deiotariana*, is operating 40 miles north of Beth Thera located west of the Dead Sea. I intend to lure the Jews in consolidating their forces to fight us on our terms. When that happens, I will order the *Deiotariana* south to the vicinity of Beth Thera."

"What is the current strength of *Deiotariana*?" Hadrian stroked his beard.

"Somewhat under 4000 legionaries."

An irritated look flashed across Hadrian's face, "Come, General, somewhat is a bit vague. I'll ask you again. What is the current strength of *Deiotariana*?"

Turbo looked uncomfortable, "The most recent strength report had the legion's strength at 3,753; however, 342 are unable to take to the field either because of injury or disease. These numbers include the replacements sent two months ago."

"Perhaps in view of your latest intelligence regarding Jewish dispositions, it's time to improve the strength of the *Deiotariana*," the emperor said in a surprisingly mild voice.

"That is precisely what we must not do, for to do so might indicate to the Jews we are aware of their build-up in that region."

"So, *Deiotariana* is the bait for the trap you hope to spring."

"That is exactly my intent. I will order five legions to move south to reinforce the *Deiotariana* when I think the Jews are about to launch their attack."

"What other legions do you intend to use?"

"The Third *Augusta*, five cohorts each from Third *Galicia* and Third *Cyrenaica*, the Sixth *Ferrata* and the Tenth *Fretensis*."

"Your plan is dangerous for the *Deiotariana*. If the reinforcing legions are delayed, the *Deiotariana* will become the sacrificial lamb instead of the bait," Severus said.

"Who commands *Deiotariana*?" Hadrian said.

"Metellus Caecilia Gallius." Turbo's reply was neutral. He was surprised Hadrian had to ask which seemed additional proof the emperor was not operating with his former mental acuity. He recalled it wasn't long ago Hadrian was still extensively involved in all senior legion appointments including junior tribunes and senior centurions.

"Ah, yes, Gallius. He's only been in command a short while, has he not?"

"He joined the legion a few months after *Deiotariana* arrived from Egypt."

"He's gained some experience then in fighting the Jews?"

"The legion has done well under Gallius considering its low strength when it arrived from Alexandria. Thus far, the legion has not been engaged in many large battles. By the time the legion arrived, the Jews were resorting almost exclusively to skirmish tactics."

"And what about Gallius himself? Can he be relied upon to hold out until the other legions are able to respond?"

"That is my expectation, Caesar."

"General, you had better back up that expectation with an extra offering to the gods, for if your plan succeeds or not, there will be little left of *Deiotariana* by the time the other legions arrive to assist Gallius."

"It's a calculated risk that we may lose one legion to end the war quickly and on our terms."

"I understand, General. I like the plan, and if it unfolds as you think, it offers an excellent opportunity to speed my return to Rome. Does Gallius understand his role in this endeavor?"

Turbo felt a momentary feeling of unease before answering, "No, he does not, Caesar. I do not intend to inform him. I don't want to risk that in knowing, Gallius will begin to prepare in ways that are out of the ordinary, and by so doing, warn the Jews we have a purpose in deploying the legion near where we believe they will concentrate their forces. I also believe the reduced strength of the *Deiotariana* will further convince the Jews we do not believe there's a real threat in the southern region."

Hadrian's face registered surprise, and Turbo prepared himself for the tirade about to follow; therefore, he was shocked when the emperor merely shook his head and said quietly, "By the gods, Turbo, your plan is diabolical but clever. Now I know I have the right man to get this rebellion stopped. Well, bad luck for Gallius even though I do dislike the prospect of losing so many legionaries. If that is what we must do, so be it. I only hope Gallius has some first-rate centurions, for they'll be the ones that will make the difference if any part of the *Deiotariana* is left."

"You need have no concern; they have some of the best in the Roman Army." Turbo had only a brief twinge of remorse after saying it as the image of Marcus Arrius flashed before him. *When it is all said and done, we're all expendable, including senior centurions and — generals.*

Chapter 8

Arrius leaned back and allowed Philos to carefully unwrap the bandage from his shoulder. The wound inflicted by Aculineous had begun to fester, and he finally relented to having the older man inspect the wound. Philos regarded the reddened flesh and pus oozing forth.

"How long were you going to wait before doing something about this? Until your arm fell off?" He began to swab the wound with a clean, wine-soaked rag.

"I didn't think it was all that bad until today when it started to throb a bit. Besides, you know I've had much worse wounds, and this wasn't much more than a scratch." Then he attempted to deflect further criticism. "What have you heard about Aculineous's death?"

"Only that there are those who are not sorry a Jewish arrow found his throat. He will not be missed. For someone who was here for such a short time, he managed to make more enemies than friends. Strangely, the only one who appeared to show any concern was Tribune Querinius. It was rumored he seemed unusually angry when the body was brought in yesterday. Still, there was talk. The patrol that found him thought it strange Aculineous was not mutilated as has been the usual case when the Jews had the time and circumstances to do so. Apart from that, no one seems to have connected you with his death. When will you take the field again?"

"In a few days, and then I expect we'll be gone for some time." Arrius looked at Philos with a rueful smile. "I shall have to make do on my own without your careful attention. In the meantime, do the best you can to get my shoulder back in service."

"Where will you go?"

"Does it matter? I believe the difference this time is that we will be gone longer than we have before. We'll establish and maintain field camps during the winter months to keep the Jews off-balance and from reoccupying the land they've lost."

"Can the Jews still win?"

"It's possible, but I don't think so. With the additional legions now here, and I understand more may come, the Jews are losing the means to resist. It really is more a question of time and not outcome. General Turbo said Hadrian intends to lay waste to the land to ensure the Jews will never rise again. I think the destruction in Judaea already achieved has met much of the emperor's goal."

Three days later, Arrius led the cohort east for what was expected to be a prolonged campaign and a bold departure from normal Roman practice of suspending military action during the winter months. He could hardly complain about the uncommon decision and discomfort of an extended fighting season since he had suggested the idea to Turbo. However, Arrius was disappointed to hear a rumor the legion was eventually going to be redeployed from the more mountainous region in the central highlands to the less active southern region. He didn't fault Turbo's logic in replacing the comparatively small *Deiotariana* Legion with two larger legions to deal with the more demanding northern terrain and the greater Jewish strength presumed to still be there.

As the weeks and months wore on, the pace of the campaign became a familiar, if not a welcome, way of life to the legionaries. The routine was characterized by brief periods of rest and recuperation and prolonged time spent in temporary camps and extended patrols under harsh, primitive conditions. The Jews fared no better and were kept on the move by the relentless Roman patrols.

The strain of intermittent clashes with an elusive but tenacious adversary began to erode the morale of the legionaries even more than the physical hardships of dealing with the cold, poor rations and fatigue. To counter the effects of sagging morale, Arrius won grudging approval from Gallius to rotate the centuries of the first cohort more frequently in and out of the main camp. The practice further cemented the centurion's popularity while inspiring the legionaries' willingness to accept an otherwise unpleasant and physically arduous ordeal. Because access to any brothels was non-existent except for the brief time a century was permitted to go to the fort, Arrius occasionally arranged for prostitutes to visit the field camps. The diversions were another key factor in keeping morale from plummeting while maintaining the momentum of the campaign.

At first, Jewish resistance had been fierce with each hillside and cave the scene of intense fighting during which the Jews gave as much as they got. Success was difficult to measure as hills taken one day were quickly reoccupied the next, frustrating the legionaries who grew tired of the seemingly monotonous and physically demanding pursuit of an enemy that refused to stand and fight. Roman casualties continued to mount as disease and Jewish arrows launched from ambush found their targets.

By contrast, it was difficult for Arrius to determine the extent of enemy losses as the Jews had become adept at carrying off their dead for secret burial. He guessed the enemy must be experiencing at least as many casualties as their own. Even after prolonged and painful interrogation, Jewish prisoners refused to reveal any useful information although recently he'd begun to see a trend. It wasn't the fact the resistance had become less but more a suspicion the number of Jewish fighters they were encountering seemed to be fewer. He thought it was just a matter of time before the Jews would have to make a stand rather than continue to endure the gradual constriction of what little was left of Judaea that remained under Jewish control.

Warfare in different provinces against different ethnic civilizations should have inured Arrius to the brutal way in which a Roman Army defeated an enemy. The war began to reveal a depth of cruelty and merciless intent beyond anything he had ever experienced. When the Romans realized it was a deeply-imbedded Jewish custom to bury the dead on the day death occurred, Jewish bodies were left to rot under guard without burial in a conscious attempt to further undermine Jewish morale. This practice along with the wholesale slaughter of women and children had exactly the opposite effect, stiffening resolve and encouraging the Jews to escalate their own forms of retribution. It didn't take long for a legionary to prefer death on the battlefield to Jewish captivity. Roman prisoners were treated without mercy, and when the bodies of those legionaries who had the misfortune of being captured alive were recovered, Jewish savagery proved every bit as brutal as that of the Romans. The stench of rotting corpses permeated the damp winter air. The countryside was dotted with cairns of bleaching bones in mute testimony of the aftermath of battle and Roman progress in the subjugation of what once had been one of the most cooperative and lucrative provinces in the empire.

As time passed, tempers in the Roman camps began to flare as the legionaries dwelled on the comforts of a traditional winter encampment. The centurions began to resort to more stringent forms of discipline than relying on the sting of a vitis. Insubordination was no longer a rare occurrence. Officers developed the habit of bedding down at night near each other to thwart any attempt for retaliation from a stealthy dagger.

Arrius was unaware of any specific day or event when he began to have profound doubts about the war and his role in it. He recalled Turbo's prophecy there would be no glory and laurels when the war ended, and he began to realize the truth of it. The day he became convinced of it began routinely enough. At the last minute, he'd decided to join Strabo's patrol in part to escape the boredom of camp routine. An early morning fog and a light rain allowed the patrol to surprise a Jewish enclave tucked away in a remote ravine. Caught unaware, the occupants had little chance to resist. While some managed to put up a stiff but short-lived resistance, they were either quickly killed or captured.

At the edge of a steep, rocky drop-off was a small, roofless enclosure that appeared to have been an animal pen from the abundance of animal dung present. Inside were three bedraggled men sitting with their shoulders hunched against the drizzle. One of the prisoners looked about nervously while in contrast the expressions of the other two indicated resignation as they waited either for execution or a lifetime of slavery.

Arrius approached the last stone enclosure where a legionary, older than most, stood peering through a large hole in the roof oblivious of his approach. Drawing closer, Arrius heard the familiar heavy breathing and grunts inside and realized a legionary was losing no time in taking advantage of the opportunity to satisfy a primal urge while the other legionary evidently waited his turn. He turned and started to walk away disgusted but tolerating a practice that was too ingrained to ever change when he heard a commotion behind him followed by loud, angry curses. Only partly turned, he was caught off-balance and nearly stumbled when a disheveled barefoot woman, hair wet and plastered to her face, ran full force into him. Instinctively, his arms went out to grasp her as much to steady himself as to prevent her escape. At first, she struggled and lashed out with a bare foot before surrendering to the inevitable as two legionaries ran up to assist him.

Her features distorted with hate, eyes blazing, she said defiantly, "Now, Roman pig, I suppose it's your turn. Go ahead and give me back to them," gesturing with a toss of her head in the direction of the two legionaries. "I would prefer to have their smelly bodies over me than to be soiled by a godless Roman officer."

He quickly spun her around twisting one of her arms up until she gasped with pain. The two legionaries stood mute and undecided nearby, suspicious they were about to be deprived of their prize.

For a moment, all remained as they were until Arrius said, "Off with you and finish looking around. I want to talk to her."

Arrius wondered briefly if they were about to disregard his order. He saw the surly looks turn more threatening. One of the legionaries nearly as big as he was and powerfully built with heavy eyebrows and prominent jaw started to take a step forward, hand resting on his sword hilt. The other legionary, showing more presence of mind, held him back with a restraining hand and said in an undertone, "Let it be, Rufus. When the centurion's through *talking*, I'm certain he'll give her back. Isn't that right, centurion?" His voice was neutral but nonetheless conveyed an unspoken threat.

"I'll do as I see fit. Now obey me or draw your sword. If you do, consider carefully whether this woman is worth dying for."

Sullenly, the two legionaries walked away. He heard the older legionary mutter to the other in a voice meant to be overheard, "Curse all officers! I'd like to take my sword and shove it up the backside of every one of those prick-sucking bastards."

Maintaining a tight grip on the woman, he half-dragged, half-shoved her to the closest shelter and pushed her inside. She stumbled and went sprawling on a straw pallet. Suddenly she reached down and pulled up the modest, ankle-length robe that covered her body.

"Go ahead, Roman, get it over with."

"Cover yourself. I'm not interested in your body."

He removed his helmet and placed it on a nearby table. Her eyes widened at the horrific scar on the side of his face.

"What's the matter, Roman, are you so old the only sword you can wield is the metal one?" She hoped he would come close enough to give her an opportunity to draw his dagger. She wanted a chance to kill the tall Roman, thinking the centurion's life would be some reward before her own ended.

When Arrius remained silent, she pulled her dress down. "What do you want?"

"I want you to tell me about this place, and depending on how well you cooperate, you may keep your life. If you don't tell me what I want to know, I'll turn you over to my legionaries to finish what they were doing, after which no one will care any longer if you live or die, especially you."

"Why should I? The choices are degradation, death or slavery, and in the end, you'll be the one to decide, not I."

"You are correct. I will be the one to decide, but you haven't considered what will happen to you if I give you back to my men who, I assure you, are most eager to enjoy your body while I am not. If I were in your place, I would consider choosing to live if only to preserve the possibility your situation might one day improve. Decide quickly, for I've no time to waste."

"What do you expect me to tell you? Where our camps are located? Where you can find Bar Kokhba? Where we intend to attack you next? If that is what you expect from me, you may as well call your men and have done with it. Do you think so little of Jewish honor that I would tell you anything?" She brushed a strand of damp hair back from her face. She was beginning to regret her recent insistence to do more for the rebellion than the mundane camp-related tasks that she'd been performing over the last year. Now, the desire to be back in the forefront of the fighting as she once had been during the early days of the rebellion seemed a foolish act. Reluctantly, ben Kosiba had finally agreed, and she was given the task of assessing the extent sufficient supplies had been stockpiled in the southern region to support a spring offensive. This had been her last stop, and if she'd left last night as originally planned instead of delaying until this morning, she would have been well on her way back to Beth Thera with the information ben Kosiba needed.

Arrius made no response to her impassioned outburst. Gradually, his silence had a calming effect. The look of desperation on her face slowly gave way to resignation. "All right, what do you want?"

"You can first tell me your name."

"Miriam." She feared if he learned her name was Sarah, he might somehow discover her relationship to ben Kosiba. She dreaded the possibility the Romans would use her as a trophy if they knew her real identity.

"That's a start. How long has this place been here?"

"A long time, why does it matter?"

"I was curious why my patrols did not find it until now."

"You don't know how many times we've laughed when your patrols passed by one of our camps without knowing it was there. We led you where we wanted you to go while we rested and continued to store our provisions against the day we will force you to leave Judaea or destroy you if you remain."

Arrius ignored the wishful sentiment. "There are other camps like this?"

"Yes, Roman, there are many more. We know these hills and the mountains in ways you will never learn. We have enough weapons and food to last for years, certainly longer than your emperor wishes to spend in a land so hostile to everything you Romans hold sacred."

"Assuming the camp is a storage point and you are truthful there are others like it, why would supplies be stored here rather than farther north where your capability to resist is much greater?"

"Perhaps it's better to be where we are least expected." He saw her hesitate, her face registering some confusion as she realized she may have said more than intended.

"While we flail around in the north, the Jewish army moves south presumably to attack where our numbers are fewer. Very enterprising; however, you may find the surprise to be more in our favor than yours. The movement of your warriors south has not gone unnoticed." He hoped the remark might draw a revealing response. He was not disappointed.

"You are mistaken. We avoid your patrols with ease, and we'll continue to do so until it's too late for you to do anything but die as surely you will. If a mere woman can travel under your very noses and not be discovered as I have done for the last month then you may be assured our warriors have no difficulty in doing the same."

Arrius thought he had learned as much from her as he would without resorting to the harsher forms of interrogation commonly employed. He didn't know why, but he regretted she might be subjected to such methods on her way to the slave market. He thought it might have something to do with reminding him of the woman in

Alexandria even though there was little physical resemblance between them. Perhaps it was her dark eyes that under different circumstances, he would have found alluring. Min-neferet also had spirit, and despite many amorous hours spent together, she made it clear she had no love for Rome. He supposed the best thing to do now was to turn the woman over to the men as they expected, but he found himself reluctant to do so. She presented him with a dilemma where any solution seemed equally unsatisfactory. He realized the problem was she had become someone other than a faceless enemy combatant. The revelation was disquieting. He had a fleeting thought of allowing her to leave unharmed, but it was an idea quickly discarded. The best thing to do was to have done with her as soon as possible before he succumbed to some irrational notion that sparing her life would serve any useful purpose. He regretted taking her away from the legionaries.

"Why do you continue to fight in such a hopeless war?"

"We have no other choice. You Romans have driven us to it. You've robbed us of our country, persecuted us because of what we believe and ignored the sanctity of our holy places. Then you wonder why we rebel? I cannot decide if you and your godless soldiers are merely naïve or stupid to wonder so. Your attitude is that of a misguided father to a child who has misbehaved. If you beat the child hard enough and long enough, he will eventually submit. The Judaean child was once the crown jewel of your empire, and Rome's most loyal and obedient of all its children. For many years, we accepted the reality of Rome's power and, yes, even occasionally welcomed the security it represented. Then the beatings became more frequent, the restrictions more pronounced. The final blow came when your emperor took away Jerusalem and began to build a new city foreign to our belief and hateful to our eyes. May God curse Hadrian for a thousand years to come for what he has done to our beloved land and, more importantly, our faith. There, Roman, is that sufficiently clear for you?"

He was moved less by her argument, much of which he'd heard before, than by her passion. Objectively, he wondered if he was committed to anything as deeply as she was. Other than a strong sense of duty to his men and less so to Rome the older he got, he decided he didn't really care how the war turned out.

Arrius picked up his helmet. "You'll not be further harmed while you remain my responsibility. I cannot promise the same once you leave my command. For what it's worth, I hope you fare well in the slave market. You are young and will fetch a good price that may help to place you in a better position."

"I have no intention of serving any Roman willingly or unwillingly. I will die before I do that, so you may as well draw your sword and have done with it now."

"Suit yourself. It's your life I'm giving you. It's up to you what you do with it." He no longer cared what became of her as his mind was already focusing on other matters at hand. "Get up and come with me." He stepped aside and followed her as she went out the doorway.

He pushed her toward the enclosure where the other prisoners still sat looking even more bedraggled than before. As they approached, the younger prisoner jumped up and said, "That woman is Sarah; she's Bar Kokhba's woman."

Arrius saw the woman stiffen in shock as the other two prisoners leaped up and started kicking and beating the younger man. The guards quickly intervened and beat the other two men senseless with the flat of their swords.

"So, your name isn't Miriam?"

Her body went limp as she looked at him. "Please, I beg you, kill me now."

"I will not do that. If you are who he claims, you know much more than you told me."

Seeing Arrius look his way, the prisoner said, "She can tell you everything. I've given you the chance to find Bar Kokhba. That should be worth the price of my freedom."

"I'll say nothing no matter what you do to me!" She drew herself up in defiance and pointed a shaking finger at the prisoner. "As for you, you're nothing but a gutless coward. When your family finds out what you've done, they will cast you out, and you will wander the rest of your worthless life as a slave and pariah hated as Josephus is today."

Arrius admired her bravado but knew before the interrogators were through, she would tell all she knew; however, his immediate concern was to get her back to the fort where the interrogators would do what was necessary to learn about Bar Kokhba.

Keeping a tight grip on her arm, he led her toward the enclosure intending to have her tied with the other prisoners. He stopped inside and forced her to the ground where she sat disconsolate, hair streaming down on either side of her face. He felt a vague and unexplainable uneasiness sweep over him as he watched her, wishing again the circumstances had been different. He focused his attention on the prisoner who had called out.

"What do you know about this woman?"

"Just what I said. Her name is Sarah, and she's Bar Kokhba's woman."

"Why is she here?"

"She was sent by Bar Kokhba to inspect our storage camps."

"How many other storage camps are there and where are they located?"

"I don't know, but she can tell you." The man was stammering, his eyes shifting nervously.

"In short, you've told me who she is and why she's here, but that is about all you can tell me."

The prisoner hung his head in silent assent. With a desperate look on his face, he gestured toward the two unconscious prisoners. "Please let me go. If you don't, they will never let me get to Joppa alive."

"My advice then is sleep with one eye open."

Arrius heard a curse from one of the guards behind him. He turned around and saw Sarah with the guard's dagger clutched in her hand running toward the edge of the stone enclosure, outdistancing the burly legionary chasing her. She jumped up on the low wall with the dagger pointed at her throat. Arrius and the guard stopped as she turned to face them.

Arrius took a step forward, hand outstretched. "Don't do this." He searched for the words to persuade her to get down, already knowing she would not.

Her face softened and assumed a resigned expression. With a sudden thrust, she plunged the dagger into her throat and fell backward. A moment later, Arrius heard a muted thud from the gorge below followed by silence broken only by the soft sound of rain on his helmet.

Chapter 9

Marius Strabo finished checking the guard and walked over to the small fire over which Arrius sat hunched, his damp cloak pulled around him against the chill as the shadows of dusk began to deepen. Earlier the rain mercifully began to abate providing a respite from the last several days of cold rain and occasional dense fog. Based on the success of the day's efforts and the break in the weather, the men should have been in fine humor, yet they were strangely quiet as they settled in for the night consuming their evening ration without the usual banter that was the normal pattern. Strabo knew the legionaries were more tired than usual because of the additional burden occasioned by the captured supplies they were taking back to the legion's main camp.

He was also concerned with the hostility that dominated the low conversations among the men that quickly broke off when he drew near. He'd heard enough to have a general idea what was causing it. The focus had mainly to do with the primus pilus and the perception Arrius had usurped the rights of legionaries to do what they always expected to exercise after a battle, expectations that entitled them to the spoils of war. Rufus wasted no time in making it known the primus pilus had crossed a line. Strabo did not like what he was hearing. It was time he had a talk with Arrius, but he was not looking forward to it.

He sat down on a rock opposite Arrius stretching his boots toward the fire, grateful for the opportunity to warm and rest his aching feet. Deep in thought, Arrius did not acknowledge the other's presence and continued to gaze vacantly into the fire. For several moments, the two centurions sat quietly. Strabo studied the somber face of his friend and mentor and searched for the words to say what he wanted to. It was obvious Arrius's behavior during the past several hours was uncharacteristic. Under normal circumstances, Arrius would have passed up and down the column joking with the men, exhorting the laggards to keep up with friendly ridicule and supervising the night encampment to ensure it was properly secured. Instead, he had been silent and apparently uninterested in the activities of the patrol since leaving the Jewish camp.

When it became obvious Arrius wasn't going to say anything, Strabo cleared his throat and said quietly to prevent being overheard, "Marcus, we've had a successful day, and yet you look as if you've lost your best friend, which you haven't since I'm sitting in front of you." His attempt at humor was intended to initiate a conversation.

Arrius looked up with a blank look and registered surprise when he saw Strabo sitting in front of him.

"I didn't hear you come."

"By all the gods in the universe, Marcus, the entire Jewish Army could have marched in here, and you wouldn't have known it until they were about to cut off your balls." Strabo was rewarded with a brief smile.

"I suppose I've been somewhat preoccupied. Are the guard and *tessera* posted?" He referred to the wooden tablet upon which the password was inscribed in wax and carried by each successive watch officer during the changing of the guard.

"Of course, if you hadn't been so preoccupied with other things, you'd know the defensive wall is in place, the men have eaten and the first relief is posted. The camp is secure, and it will soon be dark enough to put this fire out before we attract Jewish arrows."

Arrius smiled. "You've grown cautious, my friend."

"I was taught well by a centurion who now risks much to warm his old bones."

"Have a care, Marius, these old bones aren't much older than yours, and I can still out-march and out-fight any man in the cohort including you. But you're right," he reached over with a stick to disperse the fire in a shower of burning sparks until only a faint glow remained, "there's no point in making it easy for them."

Strabo coughed, uncertain how to put his concern into words without appearing to criticize. He decided the only way was to address the matter directly.

"Marcus, the men are talking about what you did back at the Jewish camp."

"And what do they say?"

"They say it wasn't right to take the woman from them."

"As their commander, I can do whatever I want, whenever I want. It isn't for them to question what I do. Besides, it wasn't like that at all. I never touched her."

"The men think you did. You were certainly in the hut long enough, and if you didn't, you might as well have because that is what they believe. They think they have a right to do as they please with female captives. It has always been that way, and they resent your interference."

"Am I supposed to fall on my sword just because they got their cocks up for nothing? Perhaps they'll take better care to spare more of the women the next time we engage the Jews."

"Why did you take her away from them?"

The long silence that greeted his question led Strabo to think there might not be an answer. He was about to change the subject to a less controversial topic when Arrius finally spoke.

"To tell the truth, I'm not sure. The deed was done before I really knew what I was doing. I guess it was an impulse once started I was unable to resist, but it had nothing to do with wanting her."

Strabo recalled the speculation caused by the centurion's frequent trips into Alexandria. Only speculation, as Arrius confided in no one except possibly Philos. "I thought she might be able to tell me something worthwhile about the camp or anything else about the people we're fighting. I never intended anything more than talk to her. After which, I was going to give her back to the men." There was another slight pause. "I'm not sure that's entirely true either. Who knows? Although it hardly matters what I might or might not have done with her, does it?"

"Do you think she was really Bar Kokhba's woman as the prisoner claimed?"

"Perhaps. If so, it was a loss. I imagine she could have told us much including where he could be found, that is if they were able to make her talk."

Strabo's laugh was humorless. "Oh, she would have talked all right. I've known few prisoners able to withstand a Roman interrogation. Our techniques are refined and impossible to resist."

"You may be right, but this woman might have been one of the exceptions. There was something about her, a quality I'm not sure I understand or can put into words. No, I'm certain of it." Without waiting for a response, Arrius continued. "She caught me by surprise when she stabbed herself." Then he seemed to speak to himself. "No, I did not expect that, and yet I should have anticipated it."

"Why should you have known?"

"Her commitment"

"By the dark cave of Mithras, what do you mean by that?"

"Have you ever thought about why you took the sacramentum?"

"I don't need to think about it at all; the answer to that is easy. I wanted to have a better future than farming a small plot of land like my father. I wanted booty and more than I would ever get raising chickens and hogs. And I wanted to get away from a small village in northern Italia that got even smaller when a young girl's belly started to swell. Mind you, I was not the only candidate, but unfortunately, for good reason I was the one most likely to be held accountable. I still think fondly of her and not just because I miss her delectable body. She gave me a reason to get off my ass and leave."

"All good, honest reasons and not all that much different from most of us when we took the oath, but did you ever think about why you joined other than escaping a restricted life with no prospects?"

"What other reasons are there? I don't know what you mean."

"I mean extending the limits of the empire for the glory of Rome or defending the right of Rome to rule the world."

"Marcus, you aren't going to tell me that's why you became a legionary, for if you do, by Minerva's lower beard, you'll never convince me."

"That's exactly my point. Practically all of us came into the army for precisely the same kind of reasons you gave. We were committed to objectives mainly to do with personal gain. I'm not saying our commitment to each other and to the legion and legions we've served is not real and important, because it is; however, I don't think it's the same thing with the Jews. Their commitment seems to have nothing to do with personal gain, or they would never have started this war."

"Marcus, I have no idea what you're talking about, and I strongly advise against speaking openly about such notions." Strabo again lowered his voice hoping they were safely out of earshot from anyone else.

Arrius sighed, reflecting a mixture of both resignation and frustration. "Possibly I don't either, but I can't help wondering why the

Jews started this war and why they keep fighting when everything Is against them. I think we're facing an idea that I wish I better understood."

"You think too much." Strabo was uneasy, distinctly uncomfortable in the direction the conversation was heading. "You would do better to concentrate on being a centurion and leave such ideas alone."

Arrius refused to let it go. "Have you noticed how willing so many Jews are to take their own lives?"

"What does that signify? Taking your life is not unknown in the Roman army, nor is it dishonorable."

"True enough, but for us it usually results from personal failure. With the Jews, it seems to me almost an act of defiance as if to say, 'You may have won a battle, but you haven't defeated me, and my death is my way of showing you that you are the one who lost.' I never realized that when I saw Jews kill themselves or Jewish fathers take the lives of their family before taking their own. Today, after talking to that woman and watching her choose death, I saw it in her eyes, and by the gods, I've been trying to understand it ever since. I wonder if I ever will."

"That's enough for me." Marius stood to stretch, anxious to terminate a conversation that was too abstract for him and wading in waters too deep for his comfort. "You make my head spin with such talk. I'm going to take another look around before I get some sleep. By the way, sleep light just in case one of the legionaries you frustrated today decides to tuck you in."

"The last thing they'll do is to try that, but I thank you for the warning all the same."

"Suit yourself, but keep in mind a dagger in the night does not reveal the owner of the hand that wields it."

Arrius spread his cloak on the ground next to the dying fire to catch what little heat was left and laid down to stare up at the night sky. He watched as the bright stars were slowly erased by gathering clouds signaling the strong possibility of more rain before morning. He thought he would be unable to sleep, not for worry what the two legionaries might do, rather because of the disquieting ideas he'd tried to talk to Strabo about. Despite his concern he would have difficulty sleeping, he quickly drifted off undisturbed by either concept of commitment or the light rain that fell just before dawn.

Chapter 10

The news of Sarah's death and the circumstances in which it happened was a shock. Ben Kosiba knew it was less for personal reasons than the remote possibility she might have told the Romans about the approaching offensive. He would miss her pliant body on the increasingly rare occasions now he required physical relief and the opportunity to talk to someone about his fears and doubts he couldn't share with anyone, not even Eleazar. Sarah alone had claimed a dimension of him no other woman came close to possessing. The thought made him feel abandoned.

Despite the risk of whatever Sarah may have said, he was reluctant to advance the timetable for a summer offensive. They were still a long way from consolidating sufficient men and supplies. To his surprise and frustration, the Romans had not abandoned the field for winter quarters, a departure from their usual practice. The Romans continued to press them, and if not preventing his mobilization plan from being executed, his timetable was nonetheless disrupted. He would have to accept slower progress in assembling a force to apply at a precise time and place of his choosing. A decisive blow was essential. There was no alternative except a slow death through starvation and attrition.

The loss of the supplies was a serious blow. It had taken months of preparation and sacrifice to obtain the stores for use when the forces now engaged in the north arrived to join his and those assembling south of Jerusalem. Despite the fact it was only one of many such sites, the loss of the supply depot meant that much less for an army that was already close to starving. Even if all sites remained undiscovered, the supplies left were barely adequate for a short campaign and not at all sufficient for a protracted one. He was gripped in a paralysis of indecision. His skin itched with a rash that had broken out over his body the day before. He was having difficulty sleeping, a condition he knew was caused by incessant worry he was leading the rebellion in the wrong direction. Sarah had once told him months ago that she did not fear death, only failure; he now realized that was precisely the way he now felt. He worried his own egotism and desire for greatness would be the downfall of Judaea. The name Bar Kokhba that still echoed across Judaea was a constant reminder of his selfish and blatantly opportunistic beginnings.

This was no time for vacillating over what he should do. With the day drawing closer for executing the plan, he needed resolve and confidence without which he would be unable to instill the same in those he led. To continue as they were, it was simply a matter of time until the last Jewish warrior died under a Roman boot or fled the country as so many were already doing. The stakes were too high to risk the consequences of failure. If the Romans prevailed, his leadership was probably finished even if a significant Jewish force remained large enough to carry on the fight. He was sensitive to the growing animosity present at council meetings, the eagerness by the opposition to seize on every bit of bad news as justification to challenge him. He began to see his staunchest supporters starting to falter, question his decisions. He knew the only reason he hadn't been deposed was because no one had come up with a better vision or concept for defeating the Romans. There was still a loud minority who continued to plead the case for reconciliation with Hadrian, apparently oblivious to the fact the Romans displayed absolutely no intention to accomplish anything less than total subjugation of Judaea, total annihilation. His sources had informed him there was now such a glut of Jewish slaves crowding the ports that Rome had Jewish captives slaughtered rather than being encumbered with the logistics of an unprofitable commercial enterprise.

Lost in his own thoughts, he did not hear Eleazar enter the cave and quietly take a seat opposite him. After a few moments, Eleazar cleared his throat. "Shimeon, what do you intend to do?" The question was pointed and devoid of any sympathy for the other man's worried expression, a departure from his usual attentive and supportive manner. Eleazar knew he alone was privy to ben Kosiba's confidence, a trust inspired by his unswerving loyalty formed early-on in the rebellion. As confidant and senior advisor, he was among a very few privileged to speak openly without sparking ben Kosiba's well-known volatile temper or undermining the messianic view ben Kosiba had of himself. "Can we be sure Sarah told them nothing?"

"We cannot; therefore, we will have to advance the timetable for implementing our plan. That will still give us time to build our strength to nearly 45,000, less than the 65,000 warriors I was hoping for. Nevertheless, it should prove more than sufficient to defeat the Roman forces here in the south. After defeating them, we will disperse again and make our way north to resume pressing our offensive there. We'll keep the Romans off-balance by forcing them to deploy their forces where we are not. That way we create the opportunity to isolate one legion at a time and at a place of our choosing."

"Easy enough to say, but will the Romans cooperate? I confess to certain misgivings the Romans will do as you believe they will."

With his own deeply-rooted doubts concealed in the recesses of his mind, it required effort on Ben Kosiba's part to hide his similar concerns from Eleazar.

"Benjamin, you worry too much. We shall play the Romans like a lyre and with a tune melodic to us and dissonant to Roman ears."

Unimpressed with the music-related analogy that he privately thought trivialized the reality of their situation, Eleazar tried once more to verbalize his profound doubts harbored since Shimeon presented his plan to the council. He was beginning to regret not voicing his concerns during the council meeting instead of remaining silent. He'd rationalized his failure to speak against the proposal in the belief his reluctance to support it would be detrimental to the larger issue of maintaining solidarity, a critical factor if there was to be any chance of defeating the Romans. The reality was he did not have a better alternative to offer. Eleazar was beginning to suspect the plan's appeal was based more on hope than realistic expectation and the council's equally desperate wish for a success.

"Shimeon, before I speak my mind, I would have you know I will do all that I can to ensure your plan is successful; however, you must know, I no longer believe it will succeed." Eleazar held up his hand as he saw the angry expression on the other's face. "No, let me say what I should have said when you first proposed it to the council. I believe the plan is severely flawed for several reasons. First, it depends too much on what the Romans may do, notably what their dispositions will be at the time you plan to execute the plan still months away. Second, the sad reality is the Romans can mobilize their forces much faster and more effectively than we can. It has taken us months to assemble the modest force we now have here in the south. Dispersing our forces quickly following the battle will prove to be equally challenging, assuming the Romans will react aggressively as they surely will. I am concerned about their cavalry and our distinct lack of it. Once we concentrate our forces in terrain suitable to the plan, it also follows we increase our vulnerability to Roman cavalry. Third, if we should lose the battle, we will no longer have the means to resist in any credible way. In sum, the risk associated with this plan is great. I've never pretended to have the military experience or foresight you have, but this time, I think you're wrong. I urge you to abandon this plan and let us fight the Romans as we have been doing with a jab here and a jab there. We can keep on weakening them until they become too weary and disillusioned to continue the fight."

Ben Kosiba's face softened as he listened, his anger slowly dissipating replaced with sympathetic understanding. "Your points are well taken, and I agree with each one."

"If so, why do you want to persist in such a risky endeavor?"

"Because I believe we no longer have a choice. Even before the Romans began to bring in additional forces, we had little time left. Our people are starving. We no longer have the benefit of annual harvests upon which to rely, and food supplies we once could obtain from neighboring countries have steadily declined until there is barely enough to sustain those whose responsibility it is to bring it across the border. Eleazar, we can either slowly starve to death, or we can fight with the slimmest of possibilities the plan may work. Our people are disillusioned, and many press for peace in a vain attempt to obtain it when the Romans have no intention of granting it except on their terms, terms that will mean the end of our homeland as we have known it since our ancestors came here from Egypt. If I thought for one minute my death would provide the means to obtain a peaceful settlement, I would ride to the nearest Roman outpost and give myself up. But that alone is not enough, and by living, I can provide the leadership our people will require to win our last chance, no matter how slim, to preserve Judaea as a Jewish homeland. In the meantime, I've given them the one thing that can make the difference between success and failure — I've given them hope and the belief we can overcome the impossible."

Eleazar stood up and walked toward the entrance without a word, pausing a moment before turning to say, "Shimeon, you have led us well. There is an old proverb my mother was fond of saying. 'It is never a good idea to change cooks when the meal is only half prepared.' You say we have no alternative other than to do as you have outlined, and I say we have no alternative to ben Kosiba. You may count on me to do

whatever I can to help you succeed despite my own reservations."
Without waiting for a response, Eleazar disappeared into the night.

Chapter 11

As the weeks passed, the morale of the first cohort slowly improved in part because of a temperate weather change. In the upper elevations, the nights had become pleasant where a relatively short time ago the legionaries had huddled in their cloaks at night cold and miserable, frequently getting up to stamp around to keep the blood flowing. They were even grateful for the additional warmth of the calf-length winter breeches issued for wintertime use that they thoroughly detested. Made of animal hide, they were a tight fit and caused chafing and more so after getting wet when they dried and became even tighter. Only the Tungrians, used to a colder, wetter climate, slept comfortably, a fact that created one more irritant for men already fed up with long, physically uncomfortable marches with little action and almost no tangible reward to show for it. The few Jewish hold-outs they did find did not put up any prolonged resistance. Arrius began to see a pattern emerging. At first, the Jewish forces fought resolutely and invariably stopped the Roman advance before melting away soon after the initial contact. Much to the disgust and disappointment of the legionaries, the Jews left nothing of material value behind to claim as booty.

One day as he walked along the edge of what remained of a small village, he heard a rustling noise in the dense undergrowth behind several large boulders. He approached the boulders and parted the bushes. A young boy had his arms wrapped tightly around two smaller children. As soon as they saw him, they began to whimper piteously. For several seconds, he remained there taking in the scene. Then raising a finger to his lips to signal silence, he stepped back and released the bush so that it once more concealed them. As he walked away, he tried to blot the faces of the children from his mind. He was conflicted with what he had done feeling both guilt and bewilderment for not revealing their hiding place. It would be a long time before he understood his actions.

It was becoming apparent the Jews were avoiding any large-scale engagement. Arrius wondered if there were simply fewer Jews left in the Central Highlands, or a widespread redeployment, possibly to the north, had taken place. He also noticed the poor physical condition of those they killed or captured. The few prisoners taken seldom provided any useful information, resisting even the cruelest methods of Roman interrogation. Increasingly, he felt disgusted with the post-battle blood lust when the legionaries took out their frustration in ever more brutal ways. Mercifully, there were fewer and fewer female prisoners taken, for regardless of age, they fared worse than the male captives. They lived longer and suffered more from savage use after which they were slaughtered and their bodies left to rot indiscriminately with the men.

A rumor quickly spread among the Romans that the Jews were swallowing their jewels and gold coins to prevent them from being taken. The rumor fostered a frenzy with legionaries hacking bodies apart and sifting through entrails with blood-soaked hands and daggers in a fruitless effort to satisfy an insatiable desire for plunder. When the Jews saw what was happening, they quickly abandoned the practice; however, it took a long time for the desecration to stop. In retaliation, Roman prisoners were treated just as brutally, and it was apparent when the bodies were found many had been disemboweled alive, emphasizing savage behavior was not an exclusive Roman practice.

Arrius grew sickened at what he saw and tried in a vain attempt to reduce if not stop the worst of the behavior that was undermining the cohort's effectiveness. It was prompted less in sympathy for the Jews and more to stop the erosion of discipline. There were too many incidents when legionaries, preoccupied as they were with their own quest for booty, were slow to respond to orders, some even staying behind after the cohort moved off, focused more on plunder than preparing for the next battle. Without consulting the other centurions, whom he reluctantly believed were part of the problem, he developed a plan to curb the breakdown of discipline.

As the cohort moved on following the destruction of a village, Arrius remained behind a walled enclosure to catch any stragglers. He didn't have long to wait. He heard the low murmur of conversation and the scrape of hob-nailed sandals on the rocky path becoming louder as the stragglers drew near. He was not surprised when two of the three turned out to be the same legionaries who had been entertaining themselves with the Jewish woman called Sarah. While two exchanged uneasy looks, the one called Rufus appeared not in the least discomfited by the sudden presence of the senior centurion. Without saying a word, Arrius motioned for them to follow him. He then proceeded to set a blistering pace to catch up to the cohort already some distance away. Soon he heard labored breathing as they exerted every effort to keep up with him, realizing from the stern expression on Arrius's face this was no time to lag.

A few minutes later, they reached the cohort. Angry but outwardly calm, Arrius ordered the centurions to post perimeter guards and then formed the cohort in a hollow square around him with the three legionaries standing in the center. Rufus alone did his best to maintain an air of bravado while the other two legionaries began to look around apprehensively. He called for the centurions who laid claim to the three men to step forward. A centurion recently transferred to the cohort stepped briskly into the center of the square and stood at attention silently waiting for whatever was about to happen next. Although impassive, the centurion understood he was about to be held accountable for allowing his century to move on without a headcount.

Arrius slowly walked around the square saying nothing but looking directly into the faces of the legionaries he passed; few met his penetrating stare without looking away. The only sound as he made an entire sweep of the square was the quiet noise of shuffling feet as anticipation intensified over what might happen next.

"These men are guilty of desertion," Arrius's voice carried to the farthest ranks. He knew the use of the word desertion would raise the prospect of branding or a *fustuarium*, death by clubbing routinely practiced by the Roman Army for desertion. "Why desertion? After all, many of you are thinking what is so serious about being late to formation when so many have been guilty of such a minor infraction in the past? Such a charge is doubly surprising when these three were most likely in the process of returning when I apprehended them. If I ask them, they will tell me that. They will say they had no real intent of being absent permanently just as those of you who have been guilty of straggling in the past thought similarly and received a token punishment from your centurion for the offense."

Arrius paused, holding up his hands to silence the swell of angry shouts that erupted, waiting until it subsided before continuing. "Well, no more will there be token punishments. For those of you too thick-headed to notice, we are at war. We are in a hostile land where the Jew here and there is still very much ready to take advantage of every opportunity to kill Romans. Every time I lose one of you, it reduces my capability to carry out the orders given to me by the legion commander who in turn is expected by the emperor to win battles. I cannot win battles if I do not have the means to fight them. For that, I need live legionaries and discipline to keep them alive. I and my centurions have been lenient far too long in deference to the unusually harsh conditions and the continuous patrols that you have endured over the long winter. Cold lodging, worse food and the rigors of chasing the enemy up and down these mountains have required much from you. My centurions and I have turned a blind eye to things I would normally not tolerate; the leniency of your leaders has reduced discipline by allowing you to believe you can do what you want without fear of any consequences. Discipline is the bedrock of the Roman Army, and without it we are no better than a rabble making us more vulnerable to Jewish sword and arrow. When individual legionaries begin to take it upon themselves to do what they want, when they want, the result is a gathering of individuals who are no longer part of an organized fighting unit capable of defeating any army anywhere. Have we become brigands seeking plunder without understanding why we are here?" After a momentary pause for dramatic effect, he continued. "I will not command brigands. I command Roman legionaries who think of their contubernium, their century and their legion before they think of themselves, risking not just their own lives but those of their comrades without pursuing selfish interests."

The formation was silent as he resumed a slow walk within the square looking at the faces of the legionaries until each one was convinced he was being singled out.

"Legionaries, you must understand from now on, if there are any further incidents such as the one that occurred here today, I will apply the full measure of my authority without mercy and without hesitation just as these men before you can expect nothing else."

He noticed the clenched jaws on the stoic face of the centurion who now expected the worst. One of the legionaries, his knees having given out, knelt on the ground; the defiance Rufus initially showed was gone replaced with a look of worried concern. Abruptly, Arrius turned and faced the centurion. "I depend on my centurions to be the sharp edge of my sword, charged with instilling and maintaining discipline. You have failed not just me, but the men you lead. You are no longer welcome in the first cohort. You are relieved of your duties immediately. You will return to the main camp with the first supply detail for reassignment to another cohort."

He turned to the three legionaries. "Now for these sorry excuses for Roman soldiers. I will not request General Gallius to sentence you to the fustuarium as is within my authority to do so and to serve as an object lesson to all." A collective sigh of relief seemed to rise from the ranks. "But there will be a price to pay for my leniency. I will give you a choice. You may receive twenty lashes now or risk death one at a time by drawing your sword against me. By allowing you to fight me, I provide the opportunity for my own punishment merited for my failure to bear down harder on my officers, that is, should one of you prove to be capable enough to administer it." An excited buzz broke out. The disciplined ranks began to waver as the men in the rear ranks began to maneuver for a better view of the unfolding drama. Hands on hips, Arrius asked, "What is it to be, the whip or the sword? If you choose the lash, strip now."

With only the slightest hesitation, two of the legionaries began removing their armor. They stripped off their tunics and stood at attention naked except for loin cloth and *caligae*, their white bodies from just above the knee to the neck in marked contrast to the dark weathered skin exposed to the elements. Rufus alone stood motionless, right hand on the hilt of his sword and a smile of satisfaction exposing the wide gaps between his teeth. It was apparent from the legionary's expression he was about to realize a dream come true.

Arrius motioned to the stone-faced centurion. "Carry out the sentence."

Quickly the centurion moved to the two legionaries and without hesitation began to flog them with his vine stick. Soon, their backs were wet with blood. The rhythmic sounds of the flogging interspersed by occasional, muted gasps of pain were the only sounds heard as the assembled legionaries watched silently. Other than wincing slightly in reflex at each blow, neither man cried out maintaining a stoic countenance throughout the ordeal. When the centurion finished the prescribed number of lashes, the two legionaries retrieved their armor and tunics and faced Arrius waiting to see if they were dismissed. He nodded slightly signaling both his approval for accepting their punishment and their dismissal. As the two legionaries made their way into the ranks of legionaries, Arrius removed his helmet beckoning to the nearest centurion to assist him in removing his armor. He turned and faced Rufus standing several paces away who by now had removed his armor.

"If by fortune, this legionary should prevail, let no man turn his hand against him, for this matter is now in the hands of the gods." He silently hoped he would have more influence on the outcome than the divinities.

As soon as the two men faced each other and assumed a crouching stance, the legionaries erupted, loudly placing bets, jostling each other for a better view of the two men slowly circling the open area. Arrius was pleased there seemed to be at least an equal number willing to bet on him. In terms of size, he was taller, but his opponent was powerfully built. Rufus also enjoyed a reputation for his skill with a gladius. The numerous scars on his right forearm gave ample testimony to the legionary's fighting experience.

Rufus was the first to initiate an attack with an agility that indicated a competent, if not imaginative, swordsman. In the ensuing clash of blade against blade with no apparent harm to either man, the two men appeared to be evenly matched in skill. It required only a few minutes for Arrius to confirm he was by far the better swordsman. All the same, he refused to underestimate his opponent's skill at the risk of overstating his own. There was always a chance an unguarded moment might be his undoing.

At first, Arrius allowed Rufus to be the aggressor as he quietly evaluated the extent of the legionary's skill. In a short time, he began to see a pattern in the way Rufus initiated an aggressive attack only to withdraw abruptly, momentarily pausing before once again resuming the assault. He was also quick to note that although Rufus was indeed agile and capable, he communicated the beginning of each new attack by unconsciously clenching his left fist as if he was still grasping a non-existent shield. And his style was somewhat mechanical, limited to the traditional thrust, hack and step back maneuver relentlessly drilled into every legionary from the time he was a fresh recruit.

Eventually, the predictability of Rufus's movements allowed Arrius to draw first blood. A lightning parry deftly warding off a downward slash gave him the chance he was looking for in the form of a quick thrust to the legionary's left shoulder. While the wound was neither deep nor serious, it began to bleed freely. Rufus stepped back in astonishment, automatically reaching up to feel the wound. He showed no sign of pain, only surprise. Arrius saw the man's expression change from confident assurance to caution. If he thought the slight wound would undermine the legionary's composure, he was mistaken. The legionary became more careful and deliberate, now waiting for his opponent to initiate the attack. Arrius obliged with a series of thrust and parries that soon had Rufus backing away from the unrelenting assault. The legionary's face mirrored his growing concern as he did his best to defend himself. It wasn't long after that Arrius caught his opponent slightly off balance leaving his torso exposed just enough for him to aim a backhand slash across the legionary's chest. Rufus stepped back several paces and looked down to see the front of his tunic gaping open, blood flowing from a shallow cut. Now confident of the outcome, Arrius saw the first glimmer of panic beginning to take hold as the legionary realized he was outmatched. The end came quickly as Rufus, by now thoroughly rattled, clumsily missed a parry and felt the tip of Arrius's sword pressing on his throat. Rufus froze as the noise from the excited legionaries around them died down until the only sound left was the heavy breathing of the two combatants standing motionless, frozen in place. Arrius looked Rufus in the eyes and no longer saw fear, only calm acceptance.

"Go ahead, Centurion," Rufus said in a flat voice without the least hint of bitterness or fear "Finish it as I would do if it was my sword at your throat."

For a moment longer, Arrius held the position before stepping back and lowering his sword until it pointed toward the ground. A quizzical expression came over the legionary's face.

"It's finished, Rufus. I can't afford to lose another legionary; I have few enough as it is. Consider your wounds punishment enough." Arrius turned away from Rufus and slowly moved in a circle addressing the entire cohort still standing quietly. "There better not be another incident by Rufus or anyone else, or by all the gods that watch over us, next time I will not hold my sword. From now on serve me better than you have this day. You fight well, but in the future, save your fighting skills for the Jews."

A slow smile spread across the legionary's face, a renewed look of respect in his eyes. "That I'll do, Centurion, you can depend on it."

"I expect no less. Centurions, form your centuries, deploy flankers and the advance guard!"

As the legionaries began to reassemble in a marching column, there was an undercurrent of muted conversation as they processed what had just transpired. Arrius was practical enough to understand a positive reaction would not be universally accepted within the ranks — that assessment probably included his centurions as well.

Chapter 12

The mid-summer heat descended on the land like a suffocating blanket remaining week after week with no relief in sight, oppressively sapping the strength and will of Jew and Roman alike. The rain that normally fell in early spring had been less than usual, and the heavier summer rains that should have been soaking the fields by now were late. A cloudless sky with a scorching sun made the roads an ordeal to travel. Any movement raised clouds of choking dust that seemed to hang in the air discouraging the casual traveler from venturing forth any farther than was necessary. Farms quickly dried out leaving cracks in the earth like dried veins snaking across fields usually verdant green with half-grown crops. The villages where enough of the non-Jewish population was still left to till the soil were surviving with small hand-watered gardens. The valleys could not provide enough food for a market both the Jewish resistance and Roman occupation depended upon. The Romans were substantially better off as they could rely on food supplies brought in through ports over which they had complete control. To supplement their food supply, ben Kosiba ordered additional raids on Roman caravans transporting supplies to the legion garrisons. For a time, the results provided a much-needed supplement to the meager food rations that barely met a subsistence level. The Romans quickly counteracted with more heavily guarded columns that reduced further Jewish successes.

Switching back to conventional warfare from the guerrilla-style tactics followed during the last two years required the Jewish forces to retrain using more conventional formations and employing tactics not unlike the Roman style of warfare. Moving by night with a small entourage, ben Kosiba traveled to the isolated training areas where small units were being drilled. The trainers consisted of a small cadre of ex-Roman legionaries who had deserted their legions attracted by the gold the Jews were willing to pay for their services. With each camp he visited, he found a renewal of his own sense of commitment and was heartened by their militant fervor. It was a welcome relief from listening to those who spent most of their time complaining incessantly over the slow progress of the rebellion while doing little to provide tangible support. He had no illusions that enthusiasm alone was enough. When it came down to fighting, the only possibility of Jewish success lay in surprise and overcoming the target legion quickly with overwhelming strength. He knew the result, even if successful, would demand a terrible price and prayed the results would be worth it.

After visiting the last training area, ben Kosiba returned to his headquarters in the subterranean caves and tunnels beneath the town of Beth Thera where the Sanhedrin was also located. The proximity of the Sanhedrin represented both a convenience and a curse with emphasis on the latter. He resented the Sanhedrin's interference in military affairs and did his best to circumvent their attempts to exert authority. Overtly, he tolerated the meddling and carping of a minority of raucous members because he had no choice, but privately, he followed his instincts.

Beth Thera was situated on top of a prominent ridgeline overlooking the Sorek Valley located a dozen miles southwest of Jerusalem. Possibly because of the Roman fixation for rooting out the resistance in the Central Highland and northern regions, the southern part of the province had been largely ignored. He thought it would only be a question of time before the Romans switched their attention and began looking south. The village of Beth Thera appeared harmless enough after having been partly destroyed early in the rebellion. What the Romans had not discovered during their brief occupation, lasting just long enough to lay waste to it, was the extensive number of caves that honeycombed the ridgeline above the ruined village. Over the past two years, the caves had been further extended and now consisted of a tunnel complex large enough to conceal a small army.

Shimeon ben Kosiba felt increasingly pressured to act before the effects of slow starvation caused his grand strategy to fall apart. Daily the provisions so carefully stockpiled were beginning to dwindle at an alarming rate while waiting for additional forces to arrive from the northern region. The active and constant patrolling the Romans maintained through the winter upset his timetable. The patrols forced the infiltrating units to break down into smaller-sized elements and to move at night to better escape detection. The net result was that only 35,000 warriors had been assembled in four staging areas in the hills south of Jerusalem, far less than double the figure he'd envisioned months ago. He also realized during his travels throughout the far recesses of Judaea that there were now far fewer men left to fight than he had originally thought. Starvation, disease and the Romans had taken a greater toll on Jewish strength than he planned, a fact he carefully concealed from all but his dedicated inner circle of advisors. He worried that if a general understanding of their true situation became known, the will to continue the rebellion would spiral down to certain defeat. Even though he would have preferred at least another month to finish training and increase the size of his army sufficiently to ensure success, he knew it was time to launch the attack. Eleazar was right. He was out of time.

Adding greatly to his worries was the spy that had been apprehended a few days ago. He vaguely recollected meeting the individual on one of his visits to a camp near Jerusalem but knew little of him except what others had reported. He was confident the informant would not have detailed knowledge of any plans underway, but he at least knew about the gradual shift of Jewish forces to the southern region. There was no longer any doubt in his mind that to delay longer risked losing the element of surprise should one or more of the staging areas be discovered. That very afternoon, he reluctantly issued the necessary orders to set the final part of the plan in motion.

Superficially, the legionaries of the *Deiotariana* first cohort no longer looked the part of Roman soldiers, resembling as they did a rough-looking band of mercenaries that only an impoverished prince of the poorest country with little to spend would consider hiring. For months, the cohort had subsisted off what they were able to capture from the enemy and the infrequent supplies Gallius was able to get to them. Most of the legionaries now sported ragged beards. Arrius tolerated the unkempt appearance out of necessity and as a concession to the arduous nature and privations of their extended patrol. Prolonged, he thought ruefully, at least in part by his own recommendations to Turbo. Their faces were lined with fatigue. To a man they had lost weight and had the fierce, hungry look of seasoned campaigners. The Tungrians looked especially lean in contrast to their customary heavier builds that resulted from a cultural predisposition to consume vast quantities of food and to imbibe excessively whenever circumstances allowed. The torn and dirty cloaks, badly-nicked sword scabbards and armor reflecting the wear and tear of battle and weather spoke eloquently of their physical hardships. As what remained of the cohort filed through the gate, the legionaries from the other cohorts watched silently as the gaunt legionaries passed by. By several weeks, the first cohort was the last to return to the main encampment from the extended field campaign.

Arrius was not disappointed when Gallius's cryptic message to return reached them in a remote mountain pass. He thought it was way overdue for his men to get some relief from the field and enjoy the relative comforts of the main camp. He credited the perseverance and skill of the optio who led the small detail for eventually locating him so far away from the main camp. Without slighting the detail's fortitude, Arrius thought it was strange it had not only survived unscathed but had done so without a single encounter or enemy sighting consistent with the dramatic decrease in enemy contact over the past few weeks. Occasionally, his patrols glimpsed groups of men moving generally in a southerly direction but too far away to intercept. There had to be some significance to the observations, but he was too tired to think much about it.

Arrius was not in the least embarrassed by the appearance of his legionaries. He realized the efforts of the centurions the night before to address the more egregious examples of disarray had concluded without any appreciable improvement. With little prodding, the men were willing to do what they had to with good humor, reflecting a morale that had every reason to be low and yet surprisingly remained high despite the prolonged hardship. As he stood at attention and watched his legionaries form up in perfect alignment, shoulders back, facing straight ahead and ignoring the occasional catcalls, he didn't see the frayed tunics, the rust stains and battered shields. He saw the finest legionaries he'd ever served with. If given the chance at that moment, he would have proudly marched them in review before Hadrian himself. What he knew of Hadrian, he was certain the emperor would appreciate what they had been through without any criticism of how they appeared. He privately doubted if Gallius would feel the same.

Gradually the ribald comments and jeers from the crowd of onlookers began to die down as they continued to watch the first cohort now fully assembled and standing motionless in the wide expanse of the via principalis. He was dimly aware of sounds behind him as the headquarters behind him emptied, its inhabitants curious to see the legionaries that in their prolonged absence had been the subject of so much controversy. No other unit in the legion had been in the field so long without periodic visits to the base camp for rest or had been posted so remotely as the first cohort. All who watched knew the stern senior centurion and the legionaries he commanded had endured prolonged and arduous conditions well beyond what the other cohorts experienced. For centurion and legionary alike, the cohort's reputation had achieved near legendary status as reports of their actions, considerably embellished each time they were related, continued to circulate until the line was blurred between truth and myth. A profound silence descended upon the camp.

Oblivious to all who watched silently, Arrius focused his entire attention on the ranks arrayed before him. After several moments and in a firm voice that carried to the far reaches of the camp, he said, "The first cohort has done all that I asked of you. It has been a long and difficult march, often with little to show for it except sore feet, a cold bed and rations a goat would refuse." The last raised a laugh that quickly subsided as they waited for him to continue. "The glory of what we have done is only in your own hearts and the knowledge you have done your duty for your legion and for your emperor. There can be no greater glory than that. I do not know how long we shall enjoy the comparative comforts of the camp including the willing ministrations of the whores who are only too willing to ease your distress," he then paused before adding, "for at least as long as you have a sesterce to pay them." Laughter greeted an acknowledgement of what was predominantly on their minds. When silence prevailed, he continued.

"These are my orders. You will immediately begin to refit. Centurions, coordinate with the quaestor for necessary repair or replacement of swords, armor, sandals and tunics. I want all repairs and replacements completed in two days at which time there will be a full kit inspection. If necessary, the cohort will be prepared to march in three days. Centurions, at your discretion you may release half your century at a time for recreational activities in the village." Arrius saw the smiles breaking out on the faces of the legionaries as he emphasized the word recreational. "I expect all those who have been released from duty and excused to be back within the camp confines by commencement of the second evening watch. Centurions, take charge."

As Arrius turned away, he heard the centurions adding their own obligatory emphasis to his orders accompanied by dire threats for any who contemplated the smallest departure from the orders. A loud cheer broke out signaling the legionaries had at last been released. In the brief ensuing lull, a single voice called out, "Arrius!" There was a slight pause followed by the same shout from another voice, "Arrius!" Arrius turned to see who it was that called his name and saw Rufus standing in a cluster of legionaries facing his direction. By then, the cry was being taken up by a few more legionaries until there was a spontaneous joining in by the rest of the cohort that continued to swell in volume reverberating within the walls of the camp in a rare display of admiration and respect. Arrius stood frozen at the unexpected honor, for once utterly at a loss for anything to say. He held up his hand in acknowledgement to the now wildly cheering legionaries before turning on his heel and walking briskly to his quarters.

Observing unobtrusively from a window in the principia, Gallius watched enviously the spontaneous display accorded the senior centurion. How he'd fantasized that he, too, would one day be the recipient of such an accolade, the legion lined up, crying his name in recognition of his brilliant leadership. Bitterly, he turned away from the window resentful over the unlikely prospect he would ever have that privilege. In a rising tide of self-pity, he wondered why it was a man like Arrius seemed to lead naturally while he had to work so hard even to convince himself he was capable. It was becoming more and more difficult to maintain a confident façade when self-doubt dominated his every waking moment clouding his thinking and judgment. He wanted to be able to invite the centurion's counsel, yet it was his own insecurity that made him do just the opposite.

He felt more isolated and lonely than he'd ever been in his life. Not so long ago, Tiberius Querinius had been the only one that had come close to offering a degree of companionship, someone that he could occasionally share some of his inner thoughts. In time, he'd come to understand Querinius was not worthy of his trust. He said and did things designed to ingratiate himself including the despicable act of contriving to have Arrius killed by Aculineous in a trumped-up duel. He had been blind concerning Querinius. How was it that he'd so misjudged him that he would unwittingly encourage the man to conceive such a thing? The last thing he wanted was to lose the one individual who was likely the most critical to his success as a legion commander. He sat down and massaged his temple in a vain attempt to relieve the ache that never seemed to go away. He knew the chronic headaches were a major contributor to his irritability and a principal reason his staff did their best to avoid him except when duties obliged. He picked up the cryptic order from Turbo and read again the instruction to consolidate and prepare the legion for a campaign hoping that at long last he would be given the opportunity to prove himself worthy, less now for the glory of Rome than for himself.

For once, Hadrian seemed close to being his normal self. Severus thought of late the emperor appeared less quarrelsome and more tolerant of a war that while generally progressing favorably from the Roman point of view still had the potential for grinding on for some time. Hadrian had somehow managed to lose weight, no longer showing the bloated, jaundiced appearance when he first arrived in Judaea nearly six months ago. He thought perhaps the more Spartan and healthful field environment in comparison to court life in either Rome or Athens may have had a beneficial influence. Hadrian was once more beginning to look and sound like an emperor rather than the caricature of the commanding presence he had once been.

Severus waited for Hadrian to signal for the meeting to begin even as he stifled his rising anger at Turbo's absence. If Turbo failed to appear, it would be up to him to conduct the meeting; it was an irritant, but it did not concern him. He was as knowledgeable as Turbo concerning perceived enemy dispositions and the evolving plans for the forthcoming campaign.

The council had been convened to provide recommendations for what he hoped was the beginning of the final phase of the war. Following the emperor's approval, orders would be issued to the legion commanders. Severus was seated to the right and just below the dais upon which Hadrian now sat. Hadrian listened attentively to several members of his personal staff standing in close attendance and speaking in voices too low for him to hear. Whatever was being said, he was supremely confident he would hear about it later in detail. He and others were now quietly looking beyond Hadrian and the reality of the emperor's deteriorating health. Thus far Hadrian had not uttered a word concerning whom he would declare to succeed him. Trajan had adopted Hadrian and made him his heir, and there was no reason to believe he wouldn't be similarly considered by the emperor particularly if the current war in Judaea ended quickly. Until Hadrian declared his intentions, the field was open. He saw every reason to advance his own candidacy by whatever means possible including making sure those closest to Hadrian were well-disposed to him and sufficiently ambitious to consider their own futures.

His reflections were interrupted by the sudden arrival of Turbo, an expression of harried concentration on his face. Turbo nodded perfunctorily in the direction of Hadrian and waited until the emperor cut short whatever one of the young tribunes was whispering in his ear and looked at Turbo.

"Good of you to join us, General Turbo," an unmistakable edge to his voice. "As I seem to recall, it was at your request this council was convened."

"Yes, Caesar, it was, and my apologies for being late. I was delayed by the arrival of a dispatch having a direct bearing on the purpose of this council." Half turning to include Severus, he continued. "Over the last several months, we've received reports of enemy movements that seemed to have a pattern. Specifically, they confirm Jewish forces are moving south. Recent interrogations of prisoners confirm this. It appears ben Kosiba is concentrating a significant number of his forces three to four miles southwest of Aelia Capitolina. Indications of this were suggested some weeks ago by one of our informants. Regrettably, we've lost contact with him; it's possible he may have been discovered. Based on our information to date, I estimate ben Kosiba may have a fighting strength of at least 30-40,000 warriors, perhaps more. Caesar, this is the opportunity we've been waiting for. We have the Jewish forces flanked by the Mare Mediterraneum to the west and the Dead Sea to the east. With the desert to the south, he has no place to go."

"And what do you plan to do?"

"We must continue to encourage him to concentrate his forces. It does us no good if he sees our legions on the march and decides to disperse back into the mountains where we may have to spend the next year or two hunting the Jews down one by one. We must give him an incentive to attack."

"I seem to recall you had a way to make this happen using the *Deiotariana* as bait. Is this still how you intend to accomplish this?"

"Yes, Caesar, it is. I've already taken the liberty of alerting General Gallius to prepare his legion for a fresh campaign. With your permission, I will issue the necessary orders directing him to proceed south. Except for enough legionaries to maintain our positions in the west and north, all legions will begin marching as soon as they receive their orders. By the time the other legions are within one day's march of Aelia Capitolina, the *Deiotariana* will already be in position in the south ready to conduct operations in the region. Even as I speak, the legion has terminated further patrols in the Central Highlands and is in the process of preparing to march."

"General Turbo, does Gallius understand his role?"

"Not entirely. As we have discussed before, I did not wish to give the plan away by having Gallius appear too aggressive. General Gallius has only been told to conduct patrol activities in the south against the possibility the Jews may be preparing to launch an attack from there. I want the legion to look as if it is undertaking a routine march."

"So, Gallius still knows nothing of the build-up in the south?"

Severus interceded. "Caesar, it is a calculated risk. If we can execute the campaign as envisioned, the outcome will have justified the risk and the uncertain fate of the *Deiotariana*. I'm certain General Turbo will agree the *Deiotariana* is not a legion that will simply blow away at the first sound of a ram's horn. They've fought well and accumulated an impressive record in the time they've been in Judaea."

"My dear Severus, if Mars himself stood next to Gallius, he couldn't save that legion. We should not presume otherwise. I will leave it up to you whether you tell Gallius what fate undoubtedly awaits him. For me, if I was in his position, I would wish to know. I would thank you for telling me and giving me time to make my peace with the gods. I believe Romans fight best when they know what is expected of them." Hadrian stood up signifying his participation in the council had ended. "General Turbo, issue the orders and may the gods be with the legions and especially with the *Deiotariana*." He beckoned to an aide hovering close by. "I want four bullocks sacrificed in the name of the Twenty-second to whatever deity they claim as theirs."

That afternoon couriers under heavy cavalry escort spread out across Judaea to each legion headquarters. The pouches contained similar orders and a detailed assessment of enemy strength except for the Twenty-second which conveniently omitted any detailed information concerning the growing Jewish strength south of Aelia Capitolina. Turbo decided it was not in the interests of a successful campaign to tell Gallius more than he needed to know.

Within hours of receiving General Turbo's orders, Gallius convened a *consilium* of his own attended by the tribunes, Attius Varro, the praefectus castrorum, and the centurions from the first cohort and the senior centurion from the other nine cohorts. The fact Gallius had called for a meeting that included the centurions was itself unusual. Until now, he evidently preferred relying almost exclusively on the council of his tribunes especially his senior tribune, Tiberius Querinius. Arrius decided months ago that excluding the primi ordines from war councils as exception to normal practice was simply another way to avoid his own outspoken participation.

While waiting inside the spacious vestibule of the principia for Gallius to call the council together, Arrius stood off to one side with Attius Varro. Both paid only half attention to Marius Strabo excitedly describing his activities in the brothel the night before in lurid and graphic detail while an orderly circulated offering cups of watered wine.

Arrius noted Tiberius Querinius was wearing a broad purple-striped toga instead of armor in an ostentatious display of his status as a future legate. Querinius detached himself from a circle of centurions and junior tribunes and made his way toward him. Arrius had nothing personal against the senior tribune who on the surface had always been pleasant enough treating those subordinate to him with outward cordiality. On the surface, the tribune was affable if somewhat ingratiating, but there was something about Tiberius Querinius Arrius instinctively disliked without knowing why. He was certain Querinius was somehow responsible for the fight with Marcello Aculineous, but if so, the reason was beyond understanding.

He was surprised when Querinius stopped in front of him. "That was quite a speech you made to your cohort the day you returned from the field."

Arrius was trying to recall what remarks he'd made that had been noteworthy when Querinius obligingly reminded him. "I'm referring to when you said something about 'there can be no greater glory than serving your legion and your emperor.' That was well-spoken, and you said it as if you really meant it." He gave a short laugh.

"I did."

Querinius's smile became fixed as he darted a quick look at Varro and Strabo who remained silent, expressionless. Aware he'd said something that might have given offense but unsure what it might be, he attempted to make light of it. "Well, the words had a catch to them, even memorable. Perhaps one day I may even have occasion to say the same."

"Tribune, I would be honored if you did, but only if you truly mean what you say as I did."

This time there was no mistaking the message. Querinius flushed and said. "Centurion, of course, I would mean it. Why would I say such a thing if I did not believe it?"

"That is something only you can answer and for others to wonder."

Querinius eyed Arrius coldly and looked as if he was ready to reply. Apparently thinking better of it, the tribune stalked off without another word.

Watching Querinius walk away, Varro said, "Marcus, your words are often as sharp as your sword. In his own clumsy way, the tribune was trying to compliment you, and in return, you might have treated him better by ramming your sword up his ass." Arrius heard Strabo stifling a laugh.

Arrius looked at Varro and said part in disgust, part in anger, "What does that bastard know about being a soldier and serving the eagle? He spends a year or two in a legion and then goes back to Rome as a legate, possibly one day to return to field duty for a couple of years in command of a legion. The likes of Tiberius Querinius will never understand those of us who spend our lives defending Rome, calling home the legion we currently serve. He will never believe what we believe, nor will he bother to understand why. I have nothing but contempt for those who pretend to be more than what they really are which describes most of those like Querinius. Such men dip their hands in legionary blood and claim it as a testament of their sacrifice and justification for advancement."

Strabo coughed nervously and darted a covert look around to see if anyone else had overhead. Varro laid a restraining hand on Arrius's arm. "Marcus, lower your voice. Think what you will, but say less of it. Your sentiments may be all too accurate, but it accomplishes nothing and others who hear you may make more of it than you ever intended, which will serve you ill. Not only that, it's dangerous. It does no good to undermine the legion's senior leadership at a time when you, the other centurions and the legionaries most depend upon it. You attack a system that for centuries has served Rome well." Then continuing in a more conciliatory tone, he gestured toward the small cluster of tribunes. "Besides, I happen to believe young Gabinus, and, yes, Quintus Flavius as well have the makings of fine officers and undeserving of your criticism."

At first, Arrius remained silent considering what Varro said. Then with genuine contrition, he said, "Attius, you're right, but by the gods, I feel better for having said it, and I have no intention of amending a thing I said to or about Querinius."

Varro laughed. "I wouldn't think of asking."

Further conversation was curtailed when an orderly appeared and announced the general was ready to proceed with the council.

The next three days saw a frenzy of activity as the legion prepared to depart on its first major deployment in almost a year. The hammers of the armorers rang across the camp making equipment repairs, mending wagon wheels and ensuring the six small scorpiones were functioning properly before being dismounted from the camp walls and stowed in ox-drawn wagons. Additional food supplies and casks of water were being loaded as the poor growing season made it unlikely the legion would be able to forage sufficiently to sustain the nearly four thousand men for the fourteen days or so Gallius expected to be in the field.

Arrius noted there were few extra rations being loaded to supplement the monotony of *bucellata*, the hard-baked biscuits each contubernium made from the ration of wheat grains ground to flour each night. Biscuits and cheese washed down with diluted wine-vinegar was the staple diet while on the march. There was a considerable amount of grumbling when Gallius ordered the usual assortment of personal slaves, camp-followers and contractors that normally supplied extra foodstuffs to satisfy hungry legionaries would not be permitted to follow. Despite Gallius's directive to travel light, Arrius knew from experience that behind the marching column, there would be a second column consisting of those whose livelihood depended on the legion.

119

The centurions inspected and re-inspected equipment to ensure each legionary was properly accoutered and carrying the prescribed amount of equipment and supplies that would weigh almost seventy pounds per man. On four-foot poles with a short cross bar at one end hung the cooking utensils, ration bag with three days of rations, water skin and *dolabra*, the small pick-ax essential for digging entrenchments, a basket for carrying dirt and additional articles of clothing. Slung over the left shoulder by a leather strap and buffered by the hooded *sagum* serving both as cloak and blanket was the shield with each legionary's name written on the inside. The helmet without plume hung across the chest and was fastened to the cuirass by a small metal hook. In the right hand, they would carry a pilum; the smaller javelins remained lashed in bundles and carried on a wagon pulled by two mules along with personal baggage and the leather tent housing an eight-man contubernium.

Cohorts took turns drilling on the large open space in front of the headquarters, practicing the various maneuvers that made the Roman military machine a formidable adversary on the battlefield. Such maneuvers had seldom been followed by the legion during the decentralized operations characteristic of the guerrilla warfare conducted over the past year. Arrius was concerned the mountain operations had degraded the cohort's capability to maneuver effectively in open terrain. He was worried about his Tungrians who remained an unknown insofar as their capability to fight in more conventional ways.

Arrius took extra pains to integrate his detachment of archers into the cohort's drills in the belief their long-range capability would do much to break the momentum of an attack before the enemy reached the considerably closer range for launching the heavy spears. As the other centurions from the other cohorts observed his emphasis on the unorthodox manner of placing the archers just behind the first rank, they also began to practice the technique.

He drilled unmercifully and was secretly pleased by the cohort's progress and willingness to suffer the grueling pace with no more than the usual grumbling without which he would have been worried. By the time the legion departed, he was confident the cohort would be as effective as time and circumstances would allow. He wished there was time to work the Tungrians a bit longer. In the heat of the moment, they seemed to have an inbred tendency to break away from the formation resorting to individual action instead of maintaining their place and function as part of an integrated unit. He was certain in his own mind that even if he had more time, the Tungrians would probably not change significantly. Still, they had more than proved on countless occasions their capability to be tenacious fighters once the battle was joined.

On the day before the legion was scheduled to depart, Attius Varro approached Arrius during a break in the training.

Marcus noted the older man's taut expression. "Attius, what's bothering you?"

"Gallius and Querinius had a falling out. Apparently, it was quite a row. Gabinus happened to be outside the doorway and heard what happened. He then came and told me."

"What was it about?"

"It was about you."

Marcus laughed. "By the gods, tell me more."

"It started out pleasant enough with the two of them discussing the details of making the legion ready. You may not be aware, Querinius spends a lot of time with Gallius and seems to be the only one he is comfortable with — just one more shortcoming our commander apparently has. At some point, Querinius made mention of replacing you since your time as primus pilus is nearly up. At first Gallius waived off the comment saying something to the effect he needed you, 'insubordinate as he is' — yes, he used the word insubordinate. Querinius kept pushing the matter, and finally Gallius got angry. Maybe for Gallius it was like pulling off a scab before the wound is healed. Gallius told Querinius to get out of his sight and not to come back unless he had something important to say."

Marcus was troubled. "I care even less for Querinius than I do for Gallius, and yet this is not welcome news. To have the two senior members of the legion not on speaking terms does not serve the legion well, most particularly on the eve of a campaign. It also means that if we do engage the enemy, I'll have to work extra hard to ensure nothing happens to Gallius, or Querinius will assume command. Now that's irony for you. It's strange that Gallius would take my part under any circumstances."

Varro looked thoughtful. "I'm hardly his confident although I can venture an opinion. It may be Gallius is both afraid and envious of you. You have great experience and influence, neither of which he has."

Arrius was skeptical. "Gallius afraid of me? Attius, the man dislikes me because I've a bad habit of not keeping my mouth shut when I should. Gallius is right. I have been insubordinate. I admit one of my faults is an unwillingness to sit back and think more carefully about what I say and when I say it. I suppose I should be more diplomatic, but it isn't in my nature to be that way. My mistake was after Gallius's first battle when I spoke up in council what was on my mind in the mistaken belief that it was expected of me. Jupiter's balls, Attius, I wasn't criticizing the man on a personal level; I even thought I was being tactful. Looking back, I suppose I should have gone to him and talked it over privately. I suspect it's too late for anything like that now, and besides, in a few more weeks, he'll be well rid of me as will I of him."

"Have you decided yet what you will do? Where you'll go?"

"It's strange, the closer the time comes, the less I think about it, probably because despite the problems I have with Gallius, I don't relish the idea of leaving. I have a place with Turbo if I want it. I never told you, but he urged me to be part of his staff when I went to see him."

"Maybe you should have taken him up on his offer."

"Perhaps I should have. I wasn't ready to leave the legion then — in truth, I'm still not. Next to commanding the legion, there isn't a better job in the army. I can't say I'm looking forward to being just another underling even if it happens to be on the staff of a man like Turbo." Arrius laughed. "I also have to keep in mind, given my less than successful attempts to give counsel to Gallius, I may not be entirely suited to the role."

It was still dark in the early morning hours as Philos helped Arrius with his last-minute preparations for departure. Outside the two men heard the myriad sounds of a camp coming to life, mules braying in protest at being harnessed, the rattle of the carts being maneuvered in the darkened streets and the murmur of low voices interspersed with occasional curses as the contubernia struck their tents. On the far side of the camp, they heard the neighing of the cavalry horses excited at the prospect of being released from the confines of the stables. It would not be long before the horns would blast giving notice to the optiones to form the centuries in preparation for the arrival of the centurions. The optiones would descend on the silent ranks of legionaries prepared to deal harshly with the smallest infraction in a time-honored rite common enough to any military formation.

Arrius knew the priests were busy preparing for the obligatory sacrifices that would commence just as soon as the sun lifted above the horizon. He hoped the auguries would be favorable even though he no longer placed much stock in such matters. He concluded long ago the priests saw in the steaming, bloody mass of entrails precisely what they wanted to see. Still, it was the superstitions of the legionaries that mattered. If the signs were favorable then the men would willingly march off, confident the divinities were with them. If, on the other hand, the priests declared the opposite, he'd known cohorts that refused to budge regardless of the threats made until the signs were once again in their favor.

He wondered if Gallius would take the opportunity to address the assembled legion before they marched off. He'd known many commanders who would never miss an opportunity to keep the legionaries standing in formation for an interminable amount of time in an excessive display of self-importance while others said little, confident it was action that motivated more than words. He hoped Gallius, if he spoke at all, would keep it short.

He looked closely at Philos in the dim light of the lamp wondering what was bothering him as he watched him carefully finish packing the small trunk containing the few personal items he was taking with him. Finally, he grasped the older man by the shoulders.

"Old friend, what troubles you? You who are usually so cheerful, why do you wear a long face now? This campaign promises to be no different than the rest."

"I do not like the idea servants and slaves are not permitted to go."

"Ah, Philos, for that I'm glad. I would spare you the dust and thirst of a long march. I prefer you remain here to look after the household and make ready to leave here for whatever destination may follow. By the time this campaign is finished, so will be my time as primus pilus. I certainly have no expectation General Gallius wants me to remain in the position one day longer than it takes to satisfy tradition."

Philos regarded Marcus with a grave expression. "Marcus, the signs are not good."

"What signs? It will be much later before the priests slay the bullock and make their pronouncements."

"I had a goat sacrificed last night, and the signs were not auspicious." Despite his own personal reservations sacrifices made any difference, he knew Philos thought the opposite, and for that reason he was always careful to refrain from making any comments critical of the practice. "The entrails were all twisted and black with disease. What is it about this campaign that is different from the rest?"

"Why nothing at all. We will look for the enemy, and he will be elusive as usual. After marching fruitlessly for several weeks, we will declare victory and return here. I shall no longer be primus pilus, and we will then seek a new life in another legion."

"Do not mock my concerns. I know you place little stock in sacrifices and omens, but I know what I saw. I do not like the signs."

Arrius saw his attempt at humor had further upset Philos and was immediately contrite. "Philos, I do not belittle your beliefs. I was merely trying to ease your mind. I do not know what the gods have in store for me, but I do not believe they have in mind for me to die here in Judaea."

Except for the jingling harnesses and snorting cavalry horses, silence settled on the closed ranks of the cohorts standing six deep filling the streets and open spaces where the tents of the contubernia had recently been pitched. Expectation hung in the air as the legion waited in the predawn for the ceremonies to begin. The rose-colored sky became brighter and brighter as the sun edged over the horizon. A raucous blast of trumpets from the cornicines marked the traditional commencement of the departure ceremonies. It was the signal for the standard bearers to file into the shrine located in its own guarded room beneath the principia. The first standards to emerge were those bearing the image of the emperor, recognizable by the Hellenic beard Hadrian habitually wore and the clean-shaven image of King Deiotarus. As each cohort signifier came forth, he took position to the left of the senior centurion. Common to each cohort standard was an open-palmed hand with thumb and fingers joined that occupied the top position and signifying the *manus*, a tangible reminder of the sacramentum each legionary took as a raw recruit. Below the manus were various circles and crescents and a bar from which appended tassels indicating past honors bestowed on the legion.

There was a dramatic pause as General Gallius stepped forward and met the aquilfer dressed in his leopard skin headdress. The bearer slowly with great solemnity raised the standard upright in full view of the legionary ranks. Marcus heard a collective sigh from the ranks as all eyes fixated on the ultimate symbol of their service, blending as it did both secular and religious aspects that gave special meaning to their lives as legionaries.

Accompanied by a fanfare of trumpets and horns, Gallius led the aquilfer to the raised dais upon which stood the altar dedicated to Jupiter *Optimus Maximus*. Off to one side of the dais stood the priests, one holding the halter of a bull made docile with drugs to ensure it met its fate without risking the solemnity of the occasion.

The sun was now fully above the horizon, and at the appointed time considered most auspicious to begin the sacrifice, one of the priests skillfully drew a sharp knife across the bull's throat severing the main artery. Moments later, the bull swayed and collapsed without a sound. Marcus was close enough to hear the final whoosh of air from its lungs. After filling a cup with blood, one of the priests mounted the dais and placed it on the altar, stepping back with hands outstretched beseeching Jupiter to accept the offering. Two other priests deftly slit the belly and gathered the steaming entrails onto a large tray for an examination that seemed to go on longer than usual. He heard the restless moving of the legionaries as they craned their necks for a better view, superstitiously waiting for the results. Finally, one of the priests beckoned for Gallius to join them beside the carcass of the dead bull. Marcus watched as a whispered conversation took place but was too far away to hear; however, he noticed Gallius' expression was grim, and the priests seemed agitated. Gallius abruptly turned on his heel signifying the ceremony was over.

The legion commander, with the aquilfer following close behind, strode to the raised tribunal centered on the formation and with one bound leaped on top to stand with one hand resting on his sword hilt, the other upraised to still the murmuring in the ranks. The legion's eagle provided an impressive backdrop silhouetted against the sunrise. In armored cuirass and helmet that glinted in the early morning light,

Gallius fulfilled the image of what a Roman general should look like. Arrius was relieved to see Gallius radiate a confidence that quickly communicated to the upraised faces of the legionaries. Despite his dislike and misgivings of Gallius, he had to admit the general presented a commanding presence that quickly overcame whatever concerns which may have been raised by the prolonged results of the sacrifice.

"Legionaries of the *Deiotariana* Legion," Gallius began in a voice that carried to the rear ranks, "we are about to embark on what may be the last campaign of the war, marking the final defeat of the Jews and the end of Judaea. I say the end of Judaea for the emperor has decreed the province will no longer be referred to by that name, but henceforward, it will be known as Palastina. I expect that in the days and weeks to come, we shall know difficult days not unlike what you have already experienced and suffered. This is nothing more than the common fare of a Roman legionary. Before this campaign is over, I have no doubt some of us will sleep forever with the gods. The glory you want and deserve will be yours to seize. We will now march forward under the eagle we proudly serve and win this land for our emperor and for Rome. Centurions, legionaries, we march!" A loud, sustained cheer followed Gallius as he jumped down and walked directly to his horse while the aquilfer proceeded to his post behind the first century of the first cohort.

Arrius thought it was an impressive performance, and one he hoped marked a renaissance in the general's behavior, including his own relationship with the man. He resolved to do better in his dealings with Gallius for the remaining days left to him in the legion. There was no time to linger on such thoughts as the first cavalry troop assigned the lead and followed close behind by a mounted contingent of archers exited the south gate at a jingling trot. He vaulted onto his horse and gave the signal to march.

Chapter 13

Arrius envied the cavalry advance in front and flank guards to the side, each a bowshot distance away from the main column. Even this far forward in the marching column, the dust was almost unbearable and fine enough to find its way into every pore. He imagined how bad it must be for those in the rear. He rotated the centuries in the cohort to give those in the rear some respite from the relentless, nose-clogging dust; however, the relief was more psychological than real, for unless you were among the very few in front, there was no relief. A cloudless sky and unrelenting heat made it worse. The conditions were some of the worst he'd ever experienced, possibly even worse than the bone-chilling cold along the borders of Germania or Dacia when touching bare metal risked losing the skin off your fingers. Now that he thought about it, perhaps the present conditions weren't quite so bad after all.

As he rode the length of the cohort, he was pleased to note the men seemed to be taking the hot, dusty conditions in stride. Most of the time, he preferred leading his horse and walking beside the centuries, exchanging a few words with the men to better assess their morale. The few complaints he'd heard were less a reflection of a fatalistic acceptance of unpleasant conditions and more to do with the practical necessity of keeping your mouth shut to avoid a mouth full of gritty dust. He noted the position of the sun and estimated another three hours before Varro selected the site for the night encampment.

Occasionally, albeit more frequently than he liked because of the extra clouds of dust created, General Gallius, accompanied by members of his personal staff, would canter the length of the column exhorting the legionaries to step lively. To his credit, the legion commander did his share of walking, remaining in the center of the column and suffering the consequences of the dusty march along with everyone else. Absent in the legion commander's entourage was the senior tribune. Arrius wondered how much of what Attius Varro had relayed to him accurately represented the relationship between Gallius and Querinius, or was it merely an embellishment of a minor dispute by a young and inexperienced Gabinus? In any event, Querinius's absence from Gallius's side was silent testimony the senior tribune was in disfavor.

As the column crested a hill, Marcus saw a knot of horsemen flanking a four-wheeled cart on a nearby hill. At the foot of the hill was a large contingent of cavalry. The standards were too far away to identify, but the size of the cavalry escort seemed to indicate someone of importance. When a slight breeze lifted one of the flags, he saw the gold lightning bolt on a field of white, the personal flag of General Vitellius Turbo. As the column drew closer, he realized the person in the cart was none other than Hadrian himself. He immediately turned and ordered the centurions of the first cohort to straighten ranks before bellowing to the trumpeters to signal honors as they passed by the hillside; he heard the command being echoed the length of the column. Marcus saw Gallius accompanied by Attius Varro and two of the tribunes riding toward the hill. The presence of the emperor and Turbo here was puzzling. He saw a cavalryman detach himself from the group on the hill and ride toward him. He was mystified when a moment later, the rider reined to a halt beside him. "General Turbo's compliments and would the primus pilus attend him?"

Without a word, Arrius followed his escort up the hill at a gallop. As he drew closer, he saw Gallius astride his horse a few paces from Turbo and looking at him inscrutably. Not looking the less regal for sitting in a cart instead of on a horse, Hadrian watched impassively as he rode up. There was no resemblance to the robust and impressive figure he recalled in Britannia years ago with the corpulent man sitting on the wagon with the cares of an empire etched deeply on his face.

"Caesar, may I present the primus pilus of the *Deiotariana* Legion, Marcus Junius Arrius," Turbo announced as Arrius came abreast of the cart.

A flicker of interest crossed Hadrian's face as he acknowledged the introduction. After a slight pause, he nodded slowly and said in a gravelly voice, "I know you, Centurion. You were an aquilfer in the Sixth Legion, *Victrix* when I visited Britannia. What I do recall even more clearly was the wet weather. That was one of the wettest, most unpleasant times I ever spent. My crotch didn't dry out for three months after I left there. You've come a long way since then, Arrius."

"I think you've traveled and achieved far more than I, Caesar."

Hadrian smiled at the glib understatement. Arrius heard the chuckles of those nearby. "General Turbo has mentioned your name to me a time or two. It appears Turbo and I both claim prior service with you. He tells me you provided valuable counsel when he first arrived to assume his command." Arrius dared not risk looking in Gallius's direction, who by now he thought must be mortified he was being largely ignored at the expense of his senior centurion. Hadrian leaned forward. "Arrius, I have no doubt you are a good primus pilus, and I see by the decorations on your cuirass you've seen and done much. We are depending on you to do your duty to the fullest in the days to come for General Gallius and for me. Will you do that for me?"

"It will be my honor, Caesar." He wondered what was in store for the legion. He glanced in Turbo's direction, receiving a nod confirming the audience was over.

Arrius saluted the emperor and was about to ride back to the column when Turbo kneed his horse alongside his and reaching out with his right hand, grasped Arrius's forearm and said quietly, "May the Gods be with you, Marcus!" For a moment longer, Arrius felt the tight pressure of Turbo's grip, tighter and longer than convention usually required.

Taken aback at the intensity of Turbo's gaze, Arrius said, "And with you, General," before urging his horse into a gallop to rejoin the column.

Attius Varro had selected the site well for the legion's third marching camp since its departure from the main camp. It was in the center of a large valley defined by low hills on either side. Dominating the hills on the south side of the valley, Arrius noted a long ridgeline running generally northeast to southwest.

The quartering party had barely completed their survey before the main body arrived and began marking off the prescribed distances and positioning the markers where the tents, corrals and latrines would be located. The markers also defined precisely the dimensions of the outer walls, a configuration designed to achieve a fortified night camp quickly and efficiently.

Constructed in the shape of a rectangle, the camp was bisected by two wide perpendicular avenues meeting in the center with two narrow streets located on either side of the longest avenue. The latrines were located at one end where the cavalry horses and mules were tethered to iron rods driven into the ground. The infirmary was situated at the opposite end of the camp from the corrals. In between in a series of parallel straight lines were the cohorts located in specific pre-designated places that maintained the integrity of each cohort, century and contubernium.

Arrius stood to one side with the other primi ordines and watched the optiones directing the centuries to their appointed places. There was little chatter as the legionaries grounded their equipment and stood with wicker baskets for carrying dirt and the two six-foot long palisade stakes sharpened at each end that each legionary carried.

As the other cohorts continued to move to their assigned positions and grounded equipment, the optiones of the first cohort were ushering the centuries to the row of marking stakes defining the outer wall that when completed would soon enclose the fortified camp. Varro gave the order to prepare the walls, and the legionaries immediately moved to the section they were assigned and began to dig a V-shaped ditch approximately four feet deep and five feet wide at the top. Varro had ordered a deeper than normal ditch suggesting the legion would occupy the location longer than the usual overnight camp. There was little idle chatter as the men dug energetically knowing they would not be allowed to prepare any food until the last stake had been positioned. The legionaries in each contubernium took turns digging and hauling dirt to erect a wall four feet high. After the objective height was achieved, the parapet would be topped by the palisade stakes lashed together at the center handgrip. Each of the six *carro-ballista* would then be positioned on a slightly raised platform behind the stakes and high enough for the bolts to clear the palisade when the weapons were fired. One catapult was emplaced on each corner of the encampment with the remaining two located to protect the east and west entrances.

There was still at least two hours before the sun would disappear, and Arrius decided to invest some of that time to investigate the hills nearby. After informing and receiving permission from Gallius and leaving Marius Strabo to supervise the cohort, he rode out accompanied by a small escort. His intention was to travel first west then swing toward the east in a long arc extending several miles from the camp. As he rode, he surveyed the countryside searching for anything out of the ordinary. He saw only isolated and deserted farms. As was the case everywhere else, fields were lying fallow either because of the drought or the war. Only the well-cared-for gardens close to the dwellings showed any indication of recent habitation. Although he had little appreciation of farming, he thought the valley looked to be a fertile land when normal conditions prevailed. Numerous rock fences enclosed fields where now only dried stubble remained amid unrelenting drought. Small groves of olive trees and an occasional stand of palms displayed splashes of green in an otherwise sepia-colored landscape.

Arrius indicated a small knoll ahead that he thought was as far west as they needed to venture before angling south. As they drew to a halt on the crest, he shielded his eyes from the sun and scanned the horizon, seeing only a still and empty landscape. His attention was diverted by one of the cavalrymen who had been looking toward the north in the direction from which the legion had come.

"Centurion, there's a haze in the distance too large to be caused by the wind."

Arrius looked in the direction the cavalryman indicated and saw a faint dust cloud but nothing to indicate it was caused by anything more than the wind. Realizing they still had miles to go before completing the sweep, he kicked his mount into a canter and led the troop in the direction of the night camp.

Ben Kosiba watched the progress of the scouting party from behind a rocky outcrop and began praying fervently it would soon turn east or west. If by chance the Romans continued south another four miles, they would inevitably find the valley was nowhere as empty as it seemed but instead filled as it was with 30,000 Jewish warriors. The considerable dust raised by a marching legion had given ample notice and signaled the time to move into the designated assembly positions. Tonight, he would order the army into attack position surrounding the Roman night camp. When the Romans prepared to leave in the morning, they would see more than the approaching dawn. He wished he could see the legion commander's face when he saw the overwhelming force arrayed against him. Nothing short of total annihilation would be satisfactory. He had already given the order no

Roman would be allowed to escape or leave the field as a prisoner. The time for reinvigorating the rebellion was at hand.

As if answer to his prayers, he saw the scouting party begin to turn north away from the ridge above Beth Thera. He signaled to the two men accompanying him, and they quickly made their way to the horses tethered among the rocks below.

It was nearly dark when Arrius returned to the night camp. The parapets were completed, and the palisade stakes were emplaced. Marius Strabo was organizing the first of four guard watches while the remaining legionaries erected their tents and began preparing their evening ration. The joking and horseplay indicated morale was good despite the hot dusty march. He saw Attius Varro conferring with General Gallius and Tiberius Querinius and walked over to report the results of his reconnaissance. In contrast to Gallius's impassive face, Querinius shot Arrius a dark look, a clear indication he had neither forgotten nor forgiven the centurion's comments prior to Gallius's last council meeting.

Arrius spoke first. "General, I saw no sign of the enemy. I traveled a wide arc from west to east. The ground is generally open with low hills in abundance and posing no obstacles except they restrict visibility out to any distance; therefore, I recommend the cavalry extend their reconnaissance to that distant ridgeline to the south. Although I was too far away to see clearly, it appears there's a settlement, possibly a stronghold on the crest."

"I will so instruct the cavalry commander." Turning to Varro, Gallius asked, "Does this valley have a name?"

"The Jews call it the Valley of Sorek. The road that runs through the center leads to Jerusalem. The settlement the primus pilus just pointed out is called Beth Thera."

Arrius recalled the dust he sighted in the north and described the flash the cavalryman thought he'd seen. Gallius seemed uninterested, and he decided there was no point in saying more about it.

Arrius excused himself to accompany Varro in an inspection of the walls before it was too dark to see. Varro always made a point of walking every inch of the defenses after they were completed. The night before, they'd found a section of the wall and ditch unsatisfactory. The entire fifth cohort was turned out to make repairs in the dark. Tonight, the camp defenses passed muster.

After completing the inspection, Arrius remained at the wall near the west gate that was the first cohort's responsibility. He leaned against the carro-ballista lost in thought. The heat was still oppressive, and he would have given much for fifteen minutes in a bathhouse to rid himself of the dust that seemed to fill every pore of his body. For reasons he didn't understand, he felt uneasy. Tomorrow would likely be the same as today — a dusty march and after that, a repeat of the same. He was doubtful the Jews would ever challenge a legion in the field, even an undersized legion such as the *Deiotariana*. Still, he couldn't shake the feeling something wasn't quite right. He recalled Philos's agitation over the augers and hoped it was unfounded. Even Turbo's farewell now seemed in the growing darkness to take on a significance that in daylight would be dismissed as no more than curious. It finally occurred to him what had been bothering him during the reconnaissance. He'd been looking for anything out of the ordinary; the vestiges of an enemy camp, grass trodden down indicating the possibility a body of men may have passed that way or sightings of movement in the distance. Apart from the dust sighting far to the north, he'd seen nothing. In spite of the effects of the drought, the small farms they'd passed over the past several days continued to show life as the owners struggled to exist until the rains came to turn the fields green. In contrast, the homesteads they passed by that afternoon showed no sign of habitation although the gardens dotting the area continued to show signs of care. It was his sixth sense coming into play once again. At the risk of being viewed as an alarmist, he headed for the general's tent to share his concerns.

General Gallius was surprisingly receptive to his assessment and immediately ordered an increase in the number of sentries above the twenty-percent strength usually comprising the night guard. Arrius remained awake well into the second guard relief, occasionally mounting the parapet wall much to the anxiety of the optiones and guards who wondered why the legion's primus pilus was not asleep as the other officers were.

The sliver of moon low in the sky provided little illumination to pierce the blackness of the night. When his eyes began to feel heavy and there was nothing to suggest other than a quiet night, Arrius thought it was time to put aside his unconfirmed feelings something was amiss and get some sleep. After instructing the officer of the guard to awaken him before dawn of if anything unusual occurred, he made his way to his tent.

Chapter 14

Arrius had the ingrained habit of soldiers in the field to fall asleep quickly and come awake just as fast as circumstances dictated. Therefore, when the officer of the guard came into his tent two hours before dawn and said in a low voice, "Centurion, there are sounds beyond the walls." He immediately came awake and followed the officer past the rows of tents to the west wall. After climbing the parapet, the officer leaned toward him and whispered, "Listen."

At first, Arrius heard nothing but the usual noises of the sleeping camp behind him and the sound of a restless breeze rustling the dried grass beyond the walls. It took a moment longer to realize there was not a breath of wind stirring. He knew then what was making the low rustling sound, indistinct and undefined beyond the palisade stakes.

"Do you hear it?" the guard officer asked in an anxious whisper.

"Aye, I hear it."

"What is it, Centurion?"

"It's the sound an army makes when it's on the move. When the sun comes up, we are going to see more Jews than we ever wanted to see. I'm going to check the other walls."

"Should we sound the alarm?"

"Not yet. For now, we'll let the Jews believe they've surprised us, which I suppose is true enough."

He left the guard officer and made his way across the camp to the east wall and stood motionless trying to filter out the camp noises behind him. Once again, he heard the sound. Now there was no mistaking what was causing it when he heard a muffled cough followed by a low, urgent voice admonishing whoever it was that had broken the silence. After checking the other walls and verifying the camp was surrounded, he left the parapet and went to the principia aware the camp was stirring as the guards began to report what they heard. He stopped first at the tents of Attius Varro and Tiberius Querinius and reported what he suspected then recommended they join him at General Gallius's tent.

Arrius waited in the outer vestibule as the orderly went to awaken Gallius. The legion commander emerged so quickly and wide awake Arrius suspected he had not been asleep. Moments later, Varro and Querinius entered the tent.

Arrius wasted no time in preliminaries as he addressed the legion commander. "General, there is movement beyond the walls. I believe the Jews have us surrounded."

"Do you think an attack is imminent?" Gallius's voice betrayed no hint of nervousness or fear.

"I don't think they will attack before first light."

"What makes you so certain?"

"The darkness will make it more difficult for them than for us. If I was planning to attack, I would do so when there's enough light to control the formations and for archers to acquire a target. I estimate at least another hour before first light."

"What do you advise we do, Primus Pilus?" Gallius asked as he searched the faces of the other officers, still not showing any sign of anxiety. Arrius noted Querinius's fixed expression resembling a frozen mask in contrast to Varro's calm demeanor that reflected only reassuring confidence.

"We should rouse the men quietly without sounding the trumpets to prevent giving notice we think anything is amiss. In the event the enemy attacks sooner than I believe they will, we should take up positions on the walls and prepare for an assault at dawn."

"I don't like the idea of skulking behind walls waiting for an attack. We should take the initiative and carry the attack to them," Querinius sounded bombastic and quarrelsome at the same time. "After all, the Roman Army is at its best fighting offensively."

Attius Varro said, "Tribune, there may be ample time to do as you say after we know better what we're facing. In the meantime, I agree with Arrius. We need to make ready for an imminent attack. Let the Jews be surprised when they see us ready to receive them."

Gallius nodded. "That makes sense. I must know what we're facing. Arrius, I believe your assessment is correct. We are probably quite outnumbered, or they would never attempt an assault." Cutting off Querinius abruptly with a wave of his hand as the tribune started to speak, Gallius turned back to Arrius. "What else?"

"As a precaution, I suggest we move the baggage carts and supply wagons and position them to bisect the camp in a defensive line from the east to the west gate in case we have to reduce our perimeter. We should prepare to defend the southern half of the camp; therefore, all water casks should be moved in proximity to the infirmary"

"Excellent suggestions," Varro said.

"I agree," Gallius said. "What of the cavalry? How can we use it effectively?"

"There is little it can do. When there's enough light to see, I can better determine the extent and depth of the enemy formation. If, as I fear, we are significantly outnumbered, the cavalry will be of little use. On the other hand, should the enemy numbers be smaller than I believe, the cavalry can make the initial attack which will then give us time to assemble the legion in an attack formation outside the camp as Tribune Querinius suggested." Arrius paused. "If the Jews are in great numbers, we will have little choice but to remain in a defensive position, and if that is the case, it may be necessary to slay the horses and mules and have the cavalrymen take positions at the walls with the other legionaries. This will prevent the animals from getting loose and threatening our own defense."

Gallius's expression was dubious. "We'll wait and see if we have to resort to that. If the situation requires it, I will so order. All your other suggestions, Centurion, will be implemented." He turned to Varro. "Supervise the defense of the camp. Use the tenth cohort to assist you in repositioning the carts, supplies and water. Inform the Medical Officer he may also use my tent and those of the tribunes to expand the infirmary should it be necessary to do so. Tribune, you're in charge of the wall defense. Inform the other tribunes and assign each to one of the walls to assist you. Primus Pilus, alert the other cohort commanders to implement the measures you've outlined and attend to any orders Praefectus Varro and Tribune Querinius may issue. When the legionaries and archers are in position, all tribunes and senior centurions will report here to coordinate and implement the details of the defense. I want absolutely no noise. Let the surprise be for the Jews when they see us ready to fight."

At first, the shadows appeared to be nothing more than an extension of the small hills nearby. Then as the sky began to take on a golden hue, the Jewish army was revealed in rank after rank an arrowshot away extending into the less visible distance. Arrius turned around and beheld the same sight on all sides. The Jewish numbers were staggering and far surpassing anything he imagined a few hours earlier. The enemy ranks were even more ominous for their total silence, and he felt a hard knot in the pit of his stomach. He noted absently an archer a few paces away stumble to the edge of the parapet where he kneeled and vomited, overtly giving in to the fear that by now all were feeling to varying degrees.

"By the gods," he heard Gallius exclaim quietly, unconscious he was even speaking. "I had no idea. They didn't tell me there would be this many."

Arrius looked at Gallius sharply and asked, "General, did you know anything about this before we came here?"

"Turbo told me the day we last saw him to expect some resistance as we approached Beth Thera, but I did not expect the entire Jewish Army. We will need Jupiter's help this day for certain. What do you estimate their strength to be?"

"Possibly 20-25 thousand, perhaps more behind those hills." As he continued to view the silent ranks now becoming more visible as the sun rose higher above the mountains, Arrius now understood the intense expression on Turbo's face when he said farewell three days ago.

"General, I believe it was not intended for you to know more than you were told. But then, the Jews haven't been told either. We are the sacrificial goat staked out as Turbo's bait. Unless I am mistaken, the dust cloud I saw yesterday is Turbo's advance cavalry. Unfortunately, from the size of the force now facing us, Turbo may encounter more than he expected. I certainly hope there are at least three legions following the cavalry."

"It may be the *Deiotariana* will be a tougher goat than the Jews bargained for. I intend to make them pay dearly if they succeed in taking this camp," Gallius said. "Arrius, what can we expect them to do next?"

"They've already accomplished their first objective by surrounding us in a manner designed to shock us into surrendering. We may receive a delegation seeking to convince us we should give up without a fight on the promise our lives will be spared if we accept their terms. Since that is an unlikely event, we can then look forward to a fusillade of arrows before they initiate the main assault. It is even possible they will remain where they are and wait until we run out of water. Personally, I hope they do, for that will give Turbo time to reach us."

"What if he doesn't?"

"Then before this day is over, the buzzards will have their fill while we kneel before the gods."

Ben Kosiba was irritated as he surveyed the Roman camp from a hilltop. It was apparent from the deliberate preparations and the calm demeanor of the legionaries lining the walls they had not achieved either the surprise or the reaction he expected. He decided to dispense with the offer to surrender believing it was a waste of time. He would proceed with the next phase designed to loosen Roman bowels. He beckoned to Eleazar standing a short distance away. When the younger man approached, he said, "Sound the signal to begin the serenade."

"What about asking for their surrender?"

"It's a waste of time. Besides, a decisive battle well and truly won will serve my purpose much better. Now they will hear our voices before they feel the bite of our arrows."

Eleazar shrugged and motioned to a warrior with a ram's horn attached to a thong around his neck. "Sound the signal!" The warrior blew several long blasts followed by a short one. A single, clear voice sang out in Hebrew the first part of a chant that was quickly taken up by the ranks of warriors until the valley echoed with the swelling rhythm that went relentlessly on and on.

Gallius turned to an orderly and said something Arrius couldn't hear because of the loud chanting. The orderly jumped off the parapet and ran to Attius Varro who was supervising the last of the baggage carts being maneuvered into position to form a line dividing the camp. Moments later, the horn and trumpet players began to blow a series of parade medleys and calls in response to the Jewish chanting. The legionaries erupted in spontaneous loud cheers at the Roman response. Arrius turned to Gallius and smiled his approval. Thus far, the legion commander had conducted himself surprisingly well; the legion's survival in the next few hours depended upon Gallius continuing to do so. He was beginning to wonder if he'd misjudged the man.

Arrius surveyed the Jewish army standing in neat ranks, and even though they were dressed in widely-differing garb, they gave every appearance of a disciplined fighting force. The front ranks carried long shields not unlike the large Roman scuta in contrast to the smaller, rounder shields normally favored and still carried by the warriors standing in the rear ranks. Archers and slingers stood in the third rank similar to a tactical Roman formation. There was no question the Jews had been busy for a long time preparing for this battle. It remained to be seen if they would be equal to Roman discipline. But then what did it matter? With the overwhelming superior Jewish force arrayed before them, the question was not whether they would survive; rather, it was a question of how long.

"Arrius, what say we begin by inflicting the first casualties? You there," Gallius called to the legionary standing next to the bolt-shooting carro-ballista, "a denarius if you can hit any one of those warriors."

"General, for a denarius, I'll put one through any of those bastards you want, and for another one," as he bent to sight along the bolt already in its cradle, "I'll go out and bring his head back." Those within earshot laughed.

Seconds later, a heavy three-foot arrow-shaped missile went streaking toward the Jewish ranks. The target was too far away to hear the bolt striking the shield of one of the warriors in the front rank, but the effect was clearly visible. Arrius watched as the shaft penetrated the shield striking the bearer in the chest with such force that the man was thrown backwards into the rank behind knocking two other warriors off their feet. A cheer rose from the Roman ranks inspiring the other carro-ballista operators. Soon, the distinctive twang of bolts being launched filled the air. Insignificant as the number of Jewish casualties may have been, the results were enough to give a welcome albeit brief psychological lift to Roman morale.

Arrius saw Flavius Verres, the decurion in command of the cavalry detachment, mount and leave the nearly 100 cavalrymen standing next to their mounts since early dawn waiting for orders. Verres had been told to be ready to slay the horses and presumably had passed the order on to his men. The decurion reined in next to Gallius, saluted and said with an urgent note in his voice, "General Gallius, give me the order to attack."

Gallius glanced at Arrius who shrugged and remained silent. Both knew the cavalryman preferred certain death in a doomed assault to the alternative of slaying the horses and waiting for a no less certain fate inside the camp. Gallius looked at the eager face of the cavalryman and nodded without trusting himself to speak. Verres flashed a triumphant smile and galloped off to join his troop. Before the troop rode through the gate, the cavalrymen donned their bronze face masks normally worn only on parade that gave the riders a surreal appearance. The horses pranced and lifted their heads in excitement while the troop formed up in an extended attack formation in front of the wall. Arrius saw the Jewish ranks to their front preparing for the charge as spear butts were planted in the ground, points angled in the direction of the attack. He saw archers moving between the warriors holding the long shields in the front rank.

A hush descended and both sides heard the decurion's commands clearly. The line began to move forward at a walk then a trot before quickly accelerating the gait to a canter. Halfway to the Jewish lines, lances were leveled as the troop broke into a full gallop with Verres centered and leading by several lengths. In a desperate effort to postpone the inevitable, Arrius cupped his hand and ordered the archers to begin firing at the Jewish ranks over the heads of the advancing cavalry. The Roman arrows had little effect in comparison to the devastating impact of the Jewish arrows that dropped half the troop in a single volley. Moments later, the only thing moving between the two armies were several horses bristling with arrows, limping away only to be mercifully dropped by a final volley of Jewish arrows. This time it was the Jewish ranks that erupted in wild enthusiasm, cheering loudly while the Romans looked silently at the lifeless bodies of men and horses strewn about haphazardly. Not one cavalryman had reached the Jewish front ranks.

Sensing the time had come when the first assault would commence, Arrius gave the signal to position their shields in anticipation the impending ground assault would be preceded by a fusillade of arrows. As the archers kneeled behind the first rank, the legionaries in the second rank lifted their scuta above their heads while the third rank faced to the rear. The result was a wall of shields from sides to top that provided protection from arrows coming from any direction. He motioned for Gallius, who had been standing unprotected by the carro-ballista, to take cover even as the first Jewish arrows and sling missiles arced over the camp. Although most of the arrows landed harmlessly within the compound, many struck legionary shields producing a rapid staccato sound; here and there, a few archers and legionaries were struck.

Looking over the shoulders of the two legionaries to his immediate front, Arrius saw the first three ranks of the enemy force beginning to move slowly forward as the archers and slingers continued to launch volley after volley. He noted the calm, orderly ranks marching toward them and contrasted the disciplined maneuver with the generally disorganized manner that had characterized past Jewish attacks. Had the Jews been wearing helmets and cuirass, they would have looked like Roman legionaries. The sight lent credence to the reports Roman deserters had indeed joined the Jewish cause.

"Arrius, when do you suggest we give the signal for our archers to begin shooting?" Gallius asked.

"When the enemy ranks are much closer and the archers are able to engage specific targets. As soon as the Jewish infantry begins to break into a run, the archers will fall back to join the next wave, and that's when the infantry will be the most unprotected. We'll inflict the most casualties at that point and hopefully break the momentum of their attack."

The two men watched intently as the Jewish ranks marched toward them. Jewish arrows continued to rain down finding unprotected limbs attested by sharp cries and gasps of pain. Marcus heard thudding hooves off to his left in time to see a mule maddened by arrows protruding from its back and flank break through the rear legionary line standing thirty feet behind the walls. While legionaries and archers on the wall tried to get out of the way, the animal reached the top of the palisade and attempted to jump over the sharpened stakes; it was not successful and ended up impaled, thrashing about with flying hooves. From the number of legionaries and archers lying on the ground in the immediate vicinity, Arrius realized the animal had caused more casualties than Jewish arrows had so far. The incident supported his earlier suggestion to slay the animals to avoid that very occurrence. Verres's doomed cavalry charge had solved the problem of the horses but not the mules that remained a lethal problem in their midst.

"General, you must give the order to slay the baggage animals. Alive they will do us at least as much damage as the Jews." Gallius summoned an orderly to relay the order to Attius Varro standing next to an overturned baggage cart.

Arrius determined the advancing enemy ranks were now within effective range. "It's time for the archers."

Gallius nodded and gave the order for the archers to engage. At the last note of the trumpet blast, the second and third ranks stepped back far enough to give the archers room to commence firing between the legionaries standing in the front rank. Although many of the arrows imbedded harmlessly in the attacker's shields, others found an unprotected shoulder or leg. Arrius saw one warrior drop his shield to claw at the shaft protruding from his jaw; divested of his shield, two more arrows struck the man simultaneously in the chest. At such close range, the ballistae operators couldn't miss, and because the velocity of each bolt was great enough to penetrate the enemy shields, the target area was correspondingly greater in comparison to the archers. At first, the growing number of Jewish warriors falling seemed to have no effect as the ranks were quickly filled by those following behind. Gradually the front ranks of the attackers began to thin noticeably. By the time the attacking force had covered half the distance to the fort, most of the Jewish warriors in the first three ranks had either been wounded or killed. Arrius looked down the length of the parapet and was pleased to see that Roman casualties so far appeared to be comparatively light. He hoped it was the same elsewhere along the perimeter.

When the first wave drew close enough, Gallius gave the signal for the first rank on the parapets to hurl their spears. The weight of the spear when it struck a shield made it difficult for the bearer to hold it upright, which then made him more vulnerable. By the time the second volley of spears was thrown, only a handful of attackers had managed to reach the outer ditch. The next volley of spears was enough for the survivors to turn back, leaving them exposed to the archers who with deadly accuracy took their time selecting their targets.

A ragged cheer broke within the camp that rapidly escalated to a roar at the clearly one-sided results. The initial outcome did much to erase the stunning defeat of the Roman cavalry and at least for the moment, lifted the morale of the defenders. Arrius surveyed the battlefield and knew that for every Jewish warrior lying on the ground, there were probably fifteen to twenty more waiting for the order to attack. Optimistically, he tried to think of some way to look at their situation and believe there was at least a chance of avoiding annihilation. Realistically it was not about survival but how much longer they had to live.

Arrius surveyed the fort and estimated more than fifty legionaries were either dead or incapacitated to the point of being ineffective. Some of the archers were making their way to one of the carts and returning with bundles of arrows to supply the forward lines. Legionaries in the rear ranks sprawled on the ground or kneeled in place talking quietly among themselves while optiones were already seeing to the distribution of water and additional javelins to replace those already thrown. Noting the mule carcasses and the dead legionaries piled next to a baggage cart, he knew what it was going to be like by tomorrow when the hot sun began to take effect on the dead legionaries and animals. On the other hand, he doubted any Roman would be left alive by then to be concerned about it.

"We've done well so far," Gallius said. "Even though our casualties are light, next time we must kill more of them, or we'll not last the day assuming they mean to continue the attack."

"I believe they mean to do exactly that, and I agree we can't afford the loss of a single legionary."

"Have you noticed the Jews attacked in much the same way we might have done?"

"I did, General. No doubt we have some deserters to thank for that. I've not seen them fight like that before today. But the Jews made a mistake in not pressing the attack; it's one I hope they repeat."

The two men separated as Gallius went one way to inspect the walls and Arrius went the other, each man stopping briefly here and there to pass on words of encouragement. He found Marius Strabo sitting on the ground, his back against a baggage cart, stoically clutching his right upper thigh from which protruded the shaft of an arrow. Attempting to make light of it, Strabo said, "It could have been worse, a little higher up and more centered, and I wouldn't care how this fight is going to turn out."

Arrius beckoned for two of the legionaries to join him. "Take Centurion Strabo to the infirmary. The sooner that arrow is out, the faster he can get back into line. And Marius, when you do, see you do a better job of getting behind a shield." He gave the centurion a playful slap on the shoulder. "The time is fast coming when we will need every sword."

He saw Querinius talking with Gallius on the far side of the fort and recalled Attius Varro's story relayed by Gabinus concerning the conversation he'd heard between the two men. He hoped that whatever had transpired between them did not affect their actions now that would further diminish their chances of surviving long enough for Turbo to reach them. He'd had no opportunity to see how Querinius was acquitting himself, but so far, his observations of Gallius had been favorable. The general now seemed willing enough to seek other opinions and rein in his impulsive nature. Further thought on the matter was interrupted by the sound of a ram's horn. Marcus hurried back to the center of his section of the wall to prepare for the next attack.

Chapter 15

Eleazar watched the survivors stumbling back and in keeping with his habitually cautious outlook on life, began to doubt the chance for an easy victory as ben Kosiba had predicted the night before. He walked the short distance to where a scowling ben Kosiba was conferring with his field commanders. From the heated comments coming from some of the men, he realized he wasn't the only one with criticism for the unimpressive results thus far. He was in time to hear ben Kosiba admonishing them with icy calm.

"I will review the signals and actions one more time. Remember, when the horn signals the first ranks to switch from a walk to a run in the final charge to the walls, the next wave should be walking forward until they too are in position to make a final charge. In this manner, we can continue to press the attack and overwhelm them with our superior numbers. I do not want a repeat of the last attack. Do you hear me? I would rather Jews die on the walls than limp back alive and defeated. Now let's get this battle over and done with. I want the legion commander's head hanging from the eagle standard within the hour." Chastened, the field commanders returned to their horses without another word.

The next attack took on the pattern of the first, and the Roman response was the same. Arrius noted one major difference. The Jewish commander instructed successive ranks to move behind the first line of attack, making it clear the Jews had learned from the mistake of the first attack. Once again, the archers took a toll on the approaching ranks as warrior after warrior fell. He heard the distinctive twang of the nearest ballista maintaining a steady barrage and wished now they had not left the other ballistae behind. Another volley of javelins blunted the advance of the first wave with few survivors able to reach the ditch below. Those that did were quickly dispatched by either arrow or javelin. By then the second wave was nearly upon them. Arrius realized the battle was about to enter a new phase with arrows and spears that so far had held the enemy at bay replaced by the close-in thrust and

146

slash of swords. This time there was no preventing the inevitable as Jewish warriors vaulted over their fallen comrades into the ditch below and attempted to clamber up the opposite side. Most were quickly cut down disadvantaged by the depth of the ditch that made the low palisade wall difficult to climb.

As the legionaries in the first rank grew tired, they were replaced by those in the ranks behind. Under the circumstances, Arrius thought they were more than holding their own when he heard a loud commotion at the east end of the camp. He stepped back to see what was happening and was alarmed to see Jewish warriors swarming over the northeast corner of the parapet wall. He saw Attius Varro leading the reserve century already moving in that direction. Given the number of Jews coming over the wall, Arrius realized Varro would have difficulty pushing them back. He yelled to the optio in charge of the small force positioned behind the south gate barricade and told him to take his legionaries and join Varro.

As the reinforcements ran to assist Varro, he began to pull legionaries from the third rank on either side of the gate to reconstitute the gate defense. His action proved timely as Jewish warriors began streaming through the entrance. He stepped forward to engage the lead warrior whose skill was no match for his. He made short work of the encounter with a quick, lethal thrust and turned to meet another man who was just as aggressive but no more skillful; after a few quick parries, Arrius buried his sword so deep into the other man's stomach he had difficulty withdrawing the blade. He was dimly conscious of the legionaries fighting on either side of him were acquitting themselves equally as well. Moments later, the gate was once again secure.

He rushed back to the center of his line where the legionaries manning the parapet were grimly holding on; however, in the short time he'd been gone, their situation had become increasingly precarious. He assumed it was no better elsewhere along the walls. Too many legionaries were lying behind the rear rank either wounded where they were no longer able to fight or so winded they labored to catch their breath. One positive note was the presence of Marius Strabo, now divested of the arrow in his thigh and wearing a blood-stained bandage.

Arrius made his way to the front rank where the legionaries on either side were happy to make room. He saw one of them was Rufus whose sword arm was red from the numerous cuts he had sustained so far. The legionary glanced his way and gave him a gap-toothed smile.

"Hail, Centurion, it must be worse than I thought if the officers are joining the front rank. I'm glad you're here."

Arrius noted the legionary's bleeding arm. "I seem to recall cautioning you about maintaining your guard, but then before this day is gone, you will have many opportunities to practice."

Both men then gave full attention to the attack that continued unabated. It seemed as one Jewish warrior was dispatched, there were two more to take his place.

Although the Romans were holding their own, it was apparent to Arrius the dead and dying Jews and Romans were rapidly filling up the ditch making it easier for the attackers to reach the top of the walls. There was no longer a third rank of standing legionaries waiting their turn to move forward and replace the rank in front. Many legionaries left in the second rank were wounded so severely they were barely able to stand. Under normal circumstances, most would have left or been carried off the battlefield. Those that were no longer wielding a sword had armed themselves with a spear that they were using to thrust between the legionaries in the front rank to discourage any Jewish warrior from coming over the palisade. He felt a burning thirst as his lungs heaved, and the weight of the shield he had taken from a dead legionary seemed to increase by the minute.

Arrius sensed rather than saw the momentum of the attack beginning to waiver. He looked beyond the immediate line of engagement and saw Jewish ranks withdrawing. Within minutes, the attack was over. Legionaries collapsed where they were. This time there were no cheers, only labored breathing as they stumbled, sweat-soaked, toward the water buckets to cool down parched and burning throats.

Arrius and Rufus were among the few who remained at the wall watching the fleeing Jews. Even the archers who took delight following the first attack in sending arrow after arrow into the backs of the attackers did not rise this time to reprise their efforts. The archers closest to him sank to their knees using their bows to prop themselves up. He looked closer and saw the quiver of one of the archers contained Jewish arrows indicating the supply of Roman shafts was quickly becoming exhausted. Well, no matter, he thought, there seemed to be an inexhaustible enemy supply from which to draw. His eyes took in the nearest carro-ballista and saw the crew on their raised and more vulnerable earthen platform lying motionless looking like human pincushions. It was obvious that section of the wall had been singled out by the Jewish archers. Gallius would not have to part with a denarius after all.

On his way to the nearest water bucket, Arrius gripped Rufus's shoulder. "Rufus, you serve the legion well."

Rufus called after him, "No more than you, Centurion."

He saw Gallius, Querinius, Varro and the two other tribunes talking together a few paces away and walked over to join them. Varro was kneeling, and it was obvious he had suffered wounds in repelling the breach. Gallius was facing his direction and so was the first to acknowledge his arrival. Without wasting time in idle remarks, Gallius asked, "Arrius, what is your assessment?"

"We must give thanks to faulty leadership on the part of the Jews, or they would have owned this camp an hour ago; however, we can't rely on enemy mistakes to hold out much longer. I believe we've lost half our fighting strength, and that assumes some of the wounded are still able to contribute in some way to the defense, no matter how limited."

"Varro says it's time to consolidate the camp and abandon the east side. Do you agree?"

"I do, but we should arrange a reception to make them pay dearly to reach the center barricade." Arrius quickly outlined what he had in mind, and the other men nodded in approval. He looked at Gallius and said, "I claim the privilege of using my century to do what I just described."

Varro began to protest, but Gallius waved him to silence and said not unkindly, "Praefectus, your wounds preclude you from the honor rightfully yours." Then he looked questioningly at Querinius who looked apprehensive. "Very well, Arrius. What else do we need to do to prepare?"

"There is one more thing. We need to slow down the next assault by placing the dead on the far side of the ditch."

"Won't that give that much more cover for Jewish archers?" Querinius asked.

Marcus shrugged. "With the number of attackers pressing in on the walls, the Jewish archers will have difficulty finding a Roman target; however, you have a point, but it's a risk we'll have to take."

"I like the idea. See to it, Querinius. Varro, report to the infirmary and have your wounds looked after. I need you to organize and supervise the defense of the internal barricade." Varro nodded and limped off to the infirmary. "The next assault will likely be the last one we can resist. Thank you for what you have done here today. May the gods strengthen our hand and grant us the courage to face our last hour."

Arrius nodded and without comment hurried back to that section of the wall the first cohort was responsible for and turned over further defense to Strabo. With the assistance of another centurion and two optiones, he began pulling every tenth man from the wall east of the barricade until he had almost a hundred legionaries and 30 archers assembled. He ordered the carro-ballistae located at the southeast and northeast, too heavy to be moved quickly, disabled by severing the catapult strings. He then formed the century-sized contingent into three curved ranks with the archers spread out and positioned just behind the first rank.

"Pay attention to the signals. The first trumpet call is the signal for the remaining legionaries left at this end of the camp to withdraw behind the east barricade. As soon as the enemy starts coming over the walls, the first rank will kneel allowing the archers to shoot arrows over the heads of the first rank. I want the archers to launch as many arrows as they can. Two trumpet calls will signal the archers to withdraw to the center of the formation and continue to engage targets as opportunity presents. After the archers pull back, the first rank will rise and throw their spears; you will have time to launch only one, after which you will draw swords and kneel to allow the second rank to step forward and throw their spears. After the second rank launches their spears, the front ranks will stand and prepare to meet the enemy with sword and shield. A final and extended trumpet call will be the signal to withdraw behind the barricade."

Minutes later, the Jewish assault began.

Chapter 16

Ben Kosiba felt a knot of desperation in his stomach. He never expected the Romans to resist this long. And while the ultimate outcome for the Roman camp remained certain, the cost already had gone far beyond anything he'd thought possible. In truth, he'd half-expected the Romans to capitulate when the rising sun revealed the overwhelmingly superior strength of the Jewish army. He had badly underestimated the Roman commander, and now the number of Jewish casualties alone, regardless of final victory, would likely be his undoing. Maybe Eleazar was right that another victory such as this would finish the rebellion. He thought about his rise to power and wondered what he would do different if given the chance. He was yet unwilling to admit it may have been a mistake to try and fight the Romans using Roman-style methods. He reluctantly realized Eleazar and the others might have been right after all. Perhaps all he had accomplished with the latest strategy was to ensure a bloody and faster Jewish defeat.

He noted the legion's eagle was still standing and prominently displayed on its long pole with other various symbols below. He didn't understand the Roman's reverence for the eagle attaching a religious meaning that was both unfathomable and an abomination to Jewish belief. Perhaps when the legion's eagle was paraded through the streets of Beth Thera and all the other remaining strongholds and enclaves, it would serve to re-energize flagging spirits. Buoyed by his own thoughts of the captured eagle, he redirected his attention to the scene below. He watched in grudging admiration as the Romans appeared to be consolidating the camp on the west side thereby reducing their defensive perimeter to adjust for their losses. He was not so blind of his hatred of the Romans that he was unable to marvel at their discipline and tenacity in prolonging the inevitable. He felt a chill of excitement at the signal to begin the next and, he hoped, final assault.

Arrius signaled for one trumpet call as Jewish warriors began to swarm over the east wall. On cue, the archers released arrow after arrow in rapid succession over the heads of the kneeling first rank and the last of the legionaries withdrawing from the walls. At first it looked as if the archers alone had swept the area clear; however, the appearance was illusory as another wave poured over the wall.

The fresh attacking force advanced at a run but suffered heavy casualties from arrows launched at such close range easily found a target. Arrius signaled for the spears to be launched. No sooner had the first rank hurled their spears than he called for the second rank to do the same. Although the effects of the arrow and spear onslaught had been lethal leaving dead and dying Jews strewn about the ground, there were many more times that number still advancing. With a clash, the outer ranks of defender and attacker met with grim determination. Arrius moved about within the hollow of the formation shouting encouragement. One side of the formation began to buckle, and he leaped forward to take his place in the first rank. His movements were automatic as the familiar routine of blocking, parrying and thrusting left an adversary bleeding on the ground or limping away. Unfortunately, for every Jewish warrior killed or wounded enough to leave the fight, there were still too many to resist for long.

Arrius ordered the few archers left to fall back behind the barricade. What was left of the defensive line now consisted of a shallow semicircle manned by no more than a fraction of the original force. He guessed from the number of Jewish bodies covering the ground that his legionaries had acquitted themselves well, but so had the Jews. Individually, the Jews lacked the physical stature and the experience of the Romans; yet they continued to press the attack fearlessly and seemingly uncaring of the considerable losses they were sustaining. He felt a sharp pain in his right side as a Jewish sword slipped past his guard. Ignoring the wetness spreading down his side, he continued backing up as the enemy pressed them toward the barricade until he felt the hard resistance of a baggage cart at his back. He waited only long enough for the few survivors left to reach the comparative safety behind the barricade before he, too, abandoned the bloody field.

Arrius leaned against a baggage cart long enough to catch his breath. He surveyed the walls and saw that while they still held the western portion, the legionaries still defending them were alarmingly few. Rufus remained where he last saw him, thrusting and hacking with machine-like precision and showing little sign of the fatigue he himself was feeling. The smaller form of Marius Strabo stood with the aid of a pilum and looked even smaller next to the hulking forms of the Tungrians who seemed to represent the majority of those left to fight on the south wall. His attention was drawn to Gallius standing near the eagle standard and being supported by an orderly. The general's gilded cuirass was red from the blood flowing across the front of his chest; he appeared to be moving with difficulty and required the support of one of his orderlies to remain standing.

Arrius made his way toward the general feeling the effects of his own wound with every step. He saw Querinius emerge from the infirmary tent and wondered what he was doing there when it was apparent he had suffered no wounds. Just as quickly, the tribune ducked back inside, and he knew the answer to his question. The leather tent was virtually impervious to the Jewish arrows still raining down.

He reached Gallius's side just as the general slumped to his knees. Arrius saw a feathered shaft protruding from the base of Gallius's neck in the narrow space unprotected by cuirass and helmet. From the angle of the shaft, the arrow had penetrated in a nearly vertical trajectory deep into Gallius's chest. He knelt beside the wounded man.

"Can we hold out?" Gallius asked with difficulty as blood spilled from his mouth.

"No, it will be over soon, General. We've done well, but we are too few left to resist much longer."

Gallius mustered a faint smile. "To tell the truth, I didn't think we would last this long."

"Frankly, I didn't either."

"Better to die this way than hand over the eagle without a fight." Gallius started to say something else, but a spasm accompanied by a fountain of blood cut off his last words as he fell forward.

Arrius looked down at the dead legion commander and felt vaguely disconcerted. Perhaps Gallius would fare better with the gods when he knelt before them than he would. Possibly they would ask if he had truly fulfilled the sacramentum he had made to Gallius. If he thought as much, there may also be doubt in the minds of the immortals as well.

He stood up and walked toward the leather tent of the infirmary where he found an ashen-faced Querinius standing inside the sweltering inferno. He looked at the tribune with undisguised loathing and wondered why it was so many good men were dead and Querinius was not only still alive but possibly among the very few who remained unscathed. He was almost tempted to save the Jews the trouble of finishing Querinius and reached for his sword with the intent of doing so. At the last moment, he restrained himself.

"Why are you in here, Tribune?" He knew full well why the Tribune was cowering there but wanted to hear him say it.

Querinius attempted to bluster his way through an explanation. "I'm here to see how the wounded are doing and to give them comfort."

For a long moment, Marcus stared contemptuously at Querinius before opening the tent flap.

"Tribune, look out there. If you wish to attend the wounded, there are enough outside to occupy your remaining time in this life. What's left of the legion out there needs leadership not comfort. General Gallius is dead, and you now command the legion. I suggest you focus attention on the ones who are still on their feet and doing what they can to preserve the remains of the legion. For the sake of what little is left of your honor, perform your duty as the gods have seen fit to assign it. If you remain here, I'll save the Jews the effort to kill you."

Without further response, Querinius left the tent with Marcus following behind, his sword ready to cut the tribune down at the least hesitation.

Outside the battle continued to rage. The defense was rapidly crumbling on all sides. There were no longer any legionaries left on the walls. The Roman perimeter had been reduced to a mere hundred paces across. In several places, there were gaps and Jewish warriors and archers were pouring through. Arrius felt a shock and sudden pain to his left shoulder followed quickly by numbness in his arm and fingers. He lost the grip on his sword. He looked over and saw the arrow shaft sticking straight out just as another struck him high on the left thigh. A wave of dizziness swept over him, and his knees started to buckle. Gradually, the sounds of battle became fainter until they faded altogether as he surrendered to the onrushing blackness that enveloped him.

The horseman rode with great concentration, holding on grimly, willing himself and his lathered horse to go just a little farther. The initial, needle-like agony of the Roman arrow in his back had by now subsided to a throbbing ache. The Roman cavalry patrol had surprised him. His concentration had been so focused on rushing back to report the dust clouds, three in the north and a closer one to the northeast, that he'd failed to notice the dismounted Roman patrol resting their horses in a small stand of trees until he was nearly upon them. A hail of arrows had come toward him with most passing him except for two; one arrow struck the horse's hindquarters leaving a bloody but relatively harmless wound, while the other arrow lodged in his back. He was conscious of a burning pain, but even more alarming was the taste of blood in his mouth. He was certain he had probably observed his last Sabbath. He pulled up the horse just long enough to lean over and retch resisting the temptation to simply get off and lie down and relieve himself of the painful jarring of the horse. He summoned his last reservoir of strength to remain astride the horse. He had to warn ben Kosiba the Romans were on the march.

He heard the din of battle before he saw it, the clash of metal on metal and the muffled roar of thousands of voices. He thought he heard Roman trumpets and worried his pursuers were closing in on him until he recalled they had turned back miles ago. Coming over the top of the hill, he saw the dust of the battle still in progress. He felt the horse under him stumble, and he prayed it would last just a little longer. He knew if the horse went down, his painful ride would have been in vain, for he had little strength left to go much farther.

Fighting off the lassitude slowly taking over his body, he guided the horse toward a cluster of men on horseback hoping they would quickly direct him to where he could find ben Kosiba. He reigned in clumsily in their midst unconscious of the irritated comments his actions provoked until they saw the arrow protruding from his back. He managed to mumble ben Kosiba's name and was relieved to see the Jewish leader's face.

"The Romans are coming behind me." He gestured in the direction from which he had come.

"What Romans?" ben Kosiba asked in surprise.

Trying not to lose consciousness, the scout relayed what he'd seen. Ben Kosiba leaned closer as the man's voice began to fade, his words becoming more slurred until he tumbled lifeless to the ground. Ben Kosiba lashed his horse up the hill with Eleazar following close behind. Let it be the wind kicking up the dust from parched fields, he silently prayed. At the top, he reigned in and looked toward the northeast, north then northwest, horrified to confirm what the scout had just reported.

He heard Eleazar gasp, "My God, there's more coming from the south. Where did they come from? There must be at least three legions coming this way."

"We are fortunate if there are only three, but I fear there are more. We have three hours, perhaps less before they get here."

"What should we do?"

Ben Kosiba did not reply at first but turned instead to look at the Roman camp below. He estimated another hour would be required, possibly less, to finish off the remaining defenders who resisted with unexplainable tenacity. He pounded his leg in angry frustration at the thought he would be deprived of victory. His anger quickly passed, and he began to assess the situation with calculated logic.

"If we continue to press the attack, we will destroy the legion and achieve our objective. Unfortunately, we have no choice but to stop the assault. Sound the signal to withdraw and inform the commanders we march to the ridgeline above Beth Thera. There we will wait for the Romans."

"Why not disperse the army as we planned?"

"It's too late for that. We have a better chance of surviving if we remain together and fight as an army."

"Shimeon, I fear all is lost."

"Perhaps, but if so, we will sell our lives dearly."

After Eleazar left, ben Kosiba remained where he was observing the ominous dust clouds. He began to focus on the practical details that needed to be considered for repositioning the army in the ridge above Beth Thera. Gradually, the full consequences of the Roman Army now marching relentlessly toward them began to sink in forcing him to come to terms with the unthinkable. Reluctantly, he accepted the rebellion was over. There were undoubtedly a thousand reasons providing rational thought why mounting a rebellion against Rome was doomed from the start. He recalled there were many who had counseled passionately against it. He had taken savage delight then in relegating their fears to the inconsequential maunderings of the fainthearted who were convinced Rome's war machine was omnipotent. He slowly rode down the hill resolved to make Rome's success just as bitter as the Jewish defeat.

Chapter 17

Followed by only a few members of his staff, General Vitellius Turbo slowly threaded his way through the battlefield in the late afternoon sun. He did so with difficulty as the Jewish dead lay thick upon the ground. His horse shied away at the grotesquely contorted bodies. He walked the horse toward the nearest entrance of the camp and was struck by the silence. He thought there was nothing quite as silent as a battlefield when the fighting was over. This was in marked contrast to what it must have been like a few hours before, filled as it was with the loud and raucous din as the opposing forces tried to annihilate each other.

The dust of the retreating Jewish Army had long since dissipated over the nearest hills, and the Sorek Valley was now a Roman valley, achieved without the launch of a single arrow or gladius thrust from the relief force. He agreed with Severus that the Jewish Army was making its way south toward the distant ridgeline range overlooking the valley. It had been too much to expect to engage them in the open valley as they'd hoped. No matter, it would take a little longer rooting them out of the hills, but the result would be the same. Hadrian would have his victory although the emperor had already made it clear there would be no triumph in Rome, preferring instead a quiet return with the less said and recalled of the rebellion the better. So be it. He would settle for the latter so long as Hadrian's plans continued to include him.

He guided the horse past the defensive ditch that was now filled with dead Jews and legionaries locked together in a macabre embrace. He entered the camp and saw at a glance how the final defense had been organized with the baggage carts bisecting the camp. The progress of the battle was visible by the successive lines of Roman and Jewish dead.

He saw an officer's helmet on the ground. Dismounting, he nudged it with his foot rolling it over and saw it was not just an empty helmet as the half opened, sightless eyes of Praefectus Attius Varro stared back, his mouth already formed in a rictus. Handing the reins of his horse to an orderly trailing behind, he walked on toward the eagle standard surprisingly still present although leaning precariously to one side. He saw a legionary stand up next to the standard. Startled at first, he realized what he had assumed were all dead bodies lying about included a few survivors who began to stir lethargically. Several more stood up swaying unsteadily; one grabbed the shaft of the standard to keep it from falling. Looking closer, he saw the final stand had evidently taken place there, whether in a conscious or unconscious effort to protect the eagle to the very end. Others began to move although most appeared too badly wounded to expend more effort than raising their head to stare blankly at his approach. Turbo estimated less than four hundred legionaries were still alive with most of those severely wounded. He saw the still form of Metellus Gallius recognizable by his ornate cuirass. It was apparent, as his eyes swept over the enclosure, that despite his hopes, Marcus Arrius did not seem to be among the survivors. He saw the tribune, Tiberius Querinius struggling to gain his feet and walked quickly toward him to help. Normally not an emotional man, Turbo was overcome by the dreadful scene and the desperate actions taken to resist certain defeat. His jaw tightened as he worked hard to maintain his composure.

With effort, Querinius drew himself up and attempted a salute that only resulted in a feeble wave.

"General Turbo, with the death of General Gallius, I, Tribune Tiberius Querinius, command the *Deiotariana* legion." Returning the salute with deliberate precision, Turbo waited to see if Querinius had more to say; however, it appeared after his continued silence the officer was unable to summon the strength to say more.

"What of the centurion Marcus Arrius?"

The tribune pointed vaguely in the direction of Gallius's body. "He's dead." Turbo motioned to the nearest officer to attend to Querinius until the arrival of the medical staff.

Turbo turned to leave and was confronted by a burly legionary who from the gray showing in his close-cropped red hair had seen many years of service. Although his arms bore the bloody marks of numerous cuts, he appeared among the very few survivors in reasonably good condition. "General," the legionary said with a slight lisp, not bothering to salute and revealing widely-spaced yellow teeth, "he still lives."

"Who still lives?"

"Centurion Marcus Arrius."

Turbo gripped Rufus's shoulder. "Where? Show me!"

Rufus turned without another word and led him toward Gallius's body near which a shield had been propped up with spears to shade the still form of Marcus Arrius lying motionless underneath.

Turbo knelt and quickly examined the wounded centurion. He immediately discounted the numerous and typical sword cuts on the centurion's right arm focusing instead on the broken arrow shafts, one protruding from the centurion's left shoulder and another shaft buried in his upper left thigh. Both wounds, serious as they might be, were not life threatening, but the caked blood below the cuirass on his left side looked bad. He said a silent prayer to Jupiter to save him whatever the cost.

Turbo turned back to Rufus who had remained hovering nearby. "Did you do this?" gesturing to the shields shading the centurion.

The legionary nodded. "I gave him water, but I didn't do anything about the arrows. I was afraid to cut on him."

"I see. What's your name?"

"My name is Rufus, and Arrius is my centurion."

Turbo was struck by the simple declaration that spoke eloquently of a bond he continued to miss and hadn't experienced for many years.

"Well, Rufus, he's a special friend of mine, and I thank you for watching over him. Your duty now is to continue to look after him. Will you do that for me?"

The legionary's face wreathed in a wide smile. "I will, General, with pleasure. Why, if it hadn't been for Marcus Arrius, there wouldn't be any of us still left alive."

"I'm certain of it. Continue to serve him well, Rufus, for there are few left of his kind."

Sprawled on the ornately carved ivory chair that served as a field throne and shaded by a gold-colored canopy, Hadrian stared at the bearded head impaled on a spear held upright by a legionary from the sixth legion. "How do you know it's him?" he asked General Julius Severus. Then before Severus had a chance to respond, "It could be anybody."

"It's the man they called Bar Kokhba or Shimeon ben Kosiba right enough. One of our spies confirmed it. Strange as it might be, he wasn't killed by a Roman sword or by his own hand; rather, it was the Jews who ended his life. Apparently, he was killed in retribution for the failure of the rebellion. From the procession that handed over his body, there was some expectation that in so doing the act would provide amnesty for those left alive."

"I'll grant no amnesty. I thought I made that clear."

"It was perfectly clear, Caesar, and none was given. There is not even so much as a dog left alive in Beth Thera. For all practical purposes, the rebellion is over. The few that are left do not have the numbers or the will to continue resisting much longer. I can assure you there will not be another Jewish rebellion in our lifetime or for that matter, many lifetimes to come."

"I've no doubt that will be the case for the time left for me," Hadrian muttered, appearing to be somewhat mollified by the general's response. "I'd like to believe you're right, Severus. I want no successor of mine ever to be bothered by these people again, and if that is my only legacy, by Jupiter, it is enough. I leave for Joppa and Rome immediately. I want no more of this accursed land and its misbegotten people. I leave it to you to finish up here. I do not wish to hear of this place ever again. Do you understand that? Never, or so help me, they will never speak of anything again."

When Turbo entered the tent carrying a small leather bag, Arrius was propped up on a camp bed with Philos in the process of changing the bandage on his leg. Turbo saw the same legionary he had commissioned to look after the centurion standing on the other side of the bed watching carefully. Rufus noticed the general's presence first, acknowledging it with a cheerful smile and saying with embarrassing informality, "Welcome, General, I'm still doing my duty."

"Vitellius, I mean, General," Arrius said attempting to sit up, "it's good to see you."

"Stay as you are, Marcus," motioning with an outstretched hand to prevent Arrius from rising, "and Vitellius will do. I must say you're looking better than you were a few days ago." Turbo smiled at Philos and Rufus. "It must have a lot to do with the excellent care you're getting."

"Apparently some general told Rufus to look out for me, and I've been saddled with his company ever since. It seems I'm in your debt. I doubt I would have survived the trip back here to Philos without Rufus. I promoted him to optio against my better judgment. I should tell you Rufus once tried his best to put his gladius in my belly." Arrius smiled noting the uncomfortable expression on the legionary's face. "But that's a story for another time. Tell me, Vitellius, is the war over?"

"Severus says it is, and Hadrian evidently believes it to be; therefore, it must be so. The emperor is already on his way back to Rome and vows never to return even to see Aelia Capitolina when it's completed. Strange when you think about it, if it hadn't been for his grand design for rebuilding Jerusalem, the war might never have taken place." Turbo looked thoughtful. "That's probably untrue. Sooner or later the Jews would have rebelled again, and another Bar Kokhba would have been there to lead them."

Arrius turned to Philos and Rufus and said quietly, "Leave us. I would speak with General Turbo in private." When they were alone, Turbo knew what the centurion was going to say before he spoke. "You knew from the beginning what was going to happen to the legion. Was it your plan, or did Severus conceive it?"

"I won't try and deny it or pass the responsibility elsewhere. It was my plan from the start. And no, I didn't know or expect how bad the *Deiotariana* would fare although Hadrian did. Hadrian was surprised anyone survived. To tell the truth, I thought we would get to the valley sooner, but the sixth and tenth legions were slow to move. I wanted to press on sooner with three legions. Severus wanted to wait until all the legions were in place before we did, and Hadrian agreed. They were right to overrule me."

"So, the legion was the sacrificial bait?"

"In a manner of speaking. We had indications the Jews were consolidating in the south, but we didn't know where. A few weeks ago, we learned Beth Thera was being extensively fortified. I had hoped to engage the Jewish Army in the Sorek Valley where we would defeat them in the open before they escaped to the mountains. My expectation was the *Deiotariana* would occupy them long enough for the army to catch them in the open. We were too late and the legion, while surpassing all expectations, ultimately suffered the consequences. We did manage to catch up with the Jewish Army but not soon enough to prevent the remnants from gaining the Beth Thera stronghold. It required several more days to finish up."

"Gallius said he didn't know. Was he telling the truth?"

"For the most part. I told him to establish the camp in the valley and send out patrols for a few days believing that would bring the Jewish Army out. The truth is ben Kosiba moved faster than I thought he would. I expected to move at night into the valley to the north of you and wait for the Jewish Army to consolidate. Gallius was smart enough to know something was up and sufficiently ambitious not to press the point. Did Gallius perform well?"

"He did. In fact, I believe I may have misjudged him from the beginning. We did not get along, and it may have been as much my fault as it was his. He was ambitious, but then if that is a fault, it is one we all share. I have regrets although in the end I doubt it mattered or would have changed anything."

"I confess I didn't much care for Gallius either. I thought he was just another political general ready to stab anybody in the back to get where and what he wanted. Perhaps I owed him a full explanation of what we were trying to do. Hadrian thought Gallius deserved to know. I argued against it believing if he knew, he might somehow alert the Jews. Do you think I was wrong not to tell him or the other senior officers?"

"Yes, but I understand why you didn't. You did Gallius and the legion a disservice. Would it have made any difference to know we were being sacrificed? Would we have fought less or harder? The answer to both questions is probably no, and yet most men, including me, would prefer to know why they are going to die. If you're looking for forgiveness and to ease your conscious, you won't get it from me, but I won't hold it against you."

"So be it. I understand, but I'm not sure I would do it any different, and I'm not altogether sure you would have either assuming our positions had been reversed."

"Perhaps so, I'll concede that much." He lapsed into brief silence before resuming. "Vitellius, I don't fault your plan, only the fact you didn't see fit to trust us enough to include us. What's to become of the legion, or at least what's left of it? Will it go back to Egypt or remain here for a time?"

Turbo regarded Arrius with narrowed eyes. "You haven't heard," he said more as a statement than a question.

"Heard what? I haven't been anywhere for days, and most of the time, all I recall is Philos trying to put some ungodly tasting concoction either on my wounds or in my stomach."

"The legion's being disbanded. I'm here to preside over the ceremony tomorrow. Severus declined to attend."

"But why? We acquitted ourselves well enough."

"More than enough, but Hadrian wanted it done. He's aware of the sacrifice made by the *Deiotariana*. What you don't understand is how much Hadrian has come to hate the Jews and this province. No matter how well the legion did, he believes it was destroyed by the Jews. If you look at it from Hadrian's view, there's logic in the decision, or at least to him there is. If you're the emperor, that's reason enough."

Arrius slumped back and closed his eyes, trying to absorb what he'd just heard. Still with his eyes closed, he asked, "How many survived?"

"Not counting the hundred or so left behind to guard the camp here, less than three hundred were still alive when we reached you. Many of those died of their wounds over the past several days. If it's any consolation, the emperor has approved generous donatives for all the survivors including gold torques for the centurions." Turbo opened the leather case he had been holding and withdrew the heavy decoration. Designed to be worn at the neck, it was made of thick, twisted wires of pure gold in the shape of a three-quarter circle and hinged at the back. Each open end at the front was crafted in the shape of an eagle's head. Turbo laid the decoration on the table adjacent to the cot. "Regrettably, with the death of Strabo Marius this morning, you are the only surviving centurion."

"Strabo is dead? I was told he would live."

"He would have lived except the loss of his leg was more than he could accept. Marcus, he took his life. Can't say as I blame him much, might've done the same thing."

After a brief silence, Arrius asked, "What's to become of those who are left?"

"That's part of the reason I wanted to see you. I want to persuade you to join me in Rome. If you don't want to be on my staff, I'll see that you command the Praetorian Guards. I guarantee it."

He realized Turbo was making him both an attractive offer and a singular honor coveted by any Roman officer. He was sorely tempted. The thought of easy duty without the rigors of field duty was seductive, particularly as he felt the throbbing pain of his wounds. "What will you do with the rest of the survivors?"

"Some will remain here to replace losses experienced at Beth Thera. Severus wants to send the rest to Britannia where things there are a bit precarious. Poor bastards, as if they haven't suffered enough fighting the Jews. I was there years ago. Fortunately, the gods saw to it I wasn't there for long. I rarely saw the sun it rained so much. Worse even than Germania where at least we saw the sun a few times even when our balls froze and disappeared not to appear again until the spring thaw."

Arrius, barely listening to Turbo, stared off into space. When he looked up at last, Turbo was regarding him with a quizzical expression on his face.

"Maybe Britannia is where I need to be. It was there I became a centurion. I was only there a short time. They asked for volunteers to go to Parthia, and I was the first to do so." Ruefully he reached up and felt the scar on his face. "Perhaps I should have stayed in Britannia after all. For different reasons than Hadrian, I'm ready to leave Judaea or Palastina, if that is what we're calling it these days. I appreciate your offer, Vitellius, but Rome isn't the place for me. No offense, but I'll take my chances on finding a position in one of the legions, maybe even work myself back into being a primus pilus."

Turbo's expression was a mix of incredulity and disappointment. "If that's what you want, I'll talk to Severus and see what can be arranged. But we can do better than just assigning you to one of the legions. How would you like to be a commander of an auxiliary force along the frontier? That will give you more authority and autonomy even then being a primus pilus."

Marcus nodded slowly, "That would suit me well enough."

"Good, then that's settled. I'll arrange it with Severus, and I'll assign you to command the detachment returning to Britannia."

The two men continued to talk for a few minutes longer until it was apparent there was nothing left to be said. Awkwardly, Turbo made a few more banal comments and departed. Arrius had a feeling he would not see him again. Events in Rome would eventually prove him right.

Bareheaded, still wearing the armor Rufus had convinced him to wear to board the ship, Arrius stood at the rail absent-mindedly fingering the gold torque around his neck and watched as the Judaean shoreline slowly receded. Gradually, the noisy sounds of the busy port of Joppa became fainter and fainter until they were lost to the shouts of the busy crew and the loud crack of the sails as they began to fill in a fitful offshore breeze accompanied by the slapping of the waves against the hull. The wind finally filled the sails, and the small ship heeled over. Instinctively, he grasped a nearby rope to steady himself momentarily forgetting his wounds. The movement caused him to wince in pain, giving a sharp reminder he still had a long way to go to full recovery. He was mending well enough, although his leg was giving him the most trouble. The arrow had driven deep, and Philos had cut extensively to free the iron point. It would require a lot more time before he would be able to walk any distance without the assistance of Rufus, a man he was still trying to get used to having around.

Rufus had attached himself to his household and clearly showed no sign of departing. If it weren't for the physical frailties becoming more apparent with Philos, he would have sent the burly legionnaire back to one of the legions. As it was, he was a help to Philos, and despite their profound mental and physical differences, they seemed to get along well enough.

It had been several weeks since the final ceremony that punctuated the end of the *Deiotariana* legion. Rufus described what happened. Arrius hadn't really wanted to hear about it, enduring the account only because he didn't have the heart to silence the legionary.

The legion's few survivors had been assembled with the Legion VI, *Ferrata* dressed in full regalia and paraded to witness the decommissioning of the twenty-second legion. Mainly because he was one of the few who did not have any serious wounds, Rufus was given the honor of aquilfer carrying the eagle for the last time. Accompanied by a fanfare of trumpets and the solemn beat of drums, the eagle was removed from its staff and cast into a brazier that eventually reduced the soul of the *Deiotariana* to nothing more than a puddle of molten metal. He could forgive Hadrian and Severus for approving the plan Turbo crafted that caused the destruction of the legion and even the delay in reaching the legion in time to save it. Such plans and occurrences were acceptable if unfortunate consequence of war. What he was unable to forgive was their absence when the eagle was destroyed. It was as if the death of so many and the eagle they served were of no importance.

The fact Querinius was the senior officer present after Turbo made him doubly thankful he was bedridden. Turbo would have expected him to be there, and he would have had to go or else explain why he refused. Querinius would doubtless return to Rome where he would take up the business of being a senator immersed in the political intrigues he suspected Querinius was more suited to deal with than the perils of a battlefield. If there really was a Jupiter, he thought bitterly, it would have been Gallius, Varro, Strabo or nearly four thousand other legionaries of the Deiotariana spared their fate instead of the craven tribune. Not for the first time, he silently questioned the existence of the gods that had caused him to be the legion's sole-surviving centurion. Perhaps it would have been better had he not lived to wonder so.

His mind drifted to Min-nefret, the Egyptian woman he had known in Alexandria. He tried to picture her face and was disturbed when he no longer recalled her features as clearly as he once did. Strangely, it was the face of the woman called Sarah that came more to mind, a woman he had never lain with and had known for only a brief time before she killed herself. In some ill-defined way, he suspected he would never fully understand why she had, but she'd become a face to an enemy that until then had been impersonal, nothing more than a military abstraction Rome expected him to defeat by whatever means and methods required. Vaguely, he resented the intrusion of the woman's face in his thoughts. It raised disturbing questions threatening to provide answers he neither sought nor wanted to know.

He tried to shake off the malaise enveloping him. The trouble with wounds, he thought, is they oblige you to sit around too long and think about things best not considered at all. He was glad he hadn't volunteered to remain with one of the legions remaining in Judaea — or Palestina as it was called now. Perhaps he should have accepted Turbo's offer, but then he decided he had been right in not going to Rome. For now, he wanted to forget everything about Judaea with its persistent images in his mind; cairns of bleaching bones; endless lines of slaves destined for the auction block; and legionaries pawing through the bodies of dead Jews looking for gold and jewels.

The shoreline was now merely a ribbon on the horizon rapidly fading into the distance as the ship quickened under a fresh sea wind. For a time, he stared absently into the white-capped waves letting the soothing rolling of the ship clear his mind. Impulsively, he reached up and undid the hinged clasp that kept the gold neck decoration secure. For the first time, he minutely inspected the costly decoration. From its weight, he knew it was valuable beyond the honor it represented. He wondered why some survived a battle and others did not. Was it the gods who decided such things long before a battle took place, or did they simply watch from above then arbitrarily point to the ones who would live and those who would die? Or those unfortunate to be horribly maimed, a fate most legionaries feared more than death. He was certain it had little to do with worth, or certainly men such as Attius Varro and Marius Strabo would be standing on this deck instead of him. Even Gallius had proven to be worthy in the end. But then had he been worthy? Perhaps he had been so during the battle, but what about before Sorek? Had he been as loyal to Gallius as the sacramentum demanded? He wasn't sure he had, and he feared doubt would be with him until the gods claimed him.

Gradually, he became aware he was still holding the heavy torque. Without any conscious thought of what he was about to do, he tossed the medallion into the foam-capped water below where it flashed briefly as it twirled away into the depths. With its disappearance, he felt strangely better. The decoration had become a tangible reminder of things he no longer wished to dwell upon. So much for Judaea and the *Deiotariana* Legion, he thought. It was time he occupied his mind with other things. Perhaps Britannia would prove to be a turning point in his life. In time, he would come to realize that it had already occurred in Judaea.

Chapter 18

The fifty days to travel from Joppa to the port of Puteoli on the west coast of Italia included intermediate stops at Alexandria and Carthagae on the coast of Africa. During the two-day stop-over at Alexandria, Arrius was tempted to find Min-nefret. The more he thought about it, the more he delayed until finally he realized there was no purpose. He ended up drowning his memories of the Egyptian woman and Judaea in too much wine and the loveless embraces of dockside whores which did more to aggravate his wounds than to ease his mental or physical well-being.

Days after leaving Alexandria, they reached Carthagae where they stopped for a week to replenish the water and food supplies before the final and longer 10-15-day voyage to *Puteoli*. The sea air and comparative storm-free crossing had done much to improve Arrius's physical well-being even if it had not completely dispelled a lingering discontent. He spent long hours standing silently on the afterdeck staring vacantly at the empty horizon. Philos assumed Arrius's despondent behavior was based on the loss of so many friends in the Sorek Valley. In that, Arrius would have said Philos was partly right. Mainly, he was still trying to understand the point of the Judaean war. It had nothing to do with the carnage and brutality of the battlefield, which as a Roman soldier he had long since accepted as a natural consequence of war. Rather, it focused on why the Jews had challenged Rome when it should have been more than obvious they had no hope of succeeding against Hadrian's legions. He tried to comprehend the religious fervor of the Jews that motivated them to give up their lives so readily for a cause that was doomed from the start. His growing ambivalence in his own belief in the gods made it difficult for him to understand the apparent and deeply-rooted faith of the Jewish people. In time, he resolved the conundrum by concluding their religion must not have been any different from his sense of duty and loyalty to the legions and to Rome.

As time passed and his wounds continued to heal, Arrius spent less and less time pondering issues for which there were no clear answers.

He took the enforced captivity of the ship to study the Tungrians more closely. He had a practical interest for doing so since his new command in Britannia would more than likely include the Tungrian *auxilia* stationed on the frontier. Apart from similarities in terms of their large physical stature, fair complexions and heavily accented speech, he also discerned subtle differences among them. Although nearly all wore shoulder-length hair in contrast to the close-cropped style of the typical Roman legionary, some had partially braided hair in identical patterns. Others had similarities in the tattoos they wore and the various copper or gold amulets encircling their upper arms. One day to satisfy his curiosity, Arrius approached Decrius, the senior Tungrian optio, to learn more about them. If anything, Decrius was even more exotic than the others. He was one of the largest men Arrius had ever seen with arms the size of a large man's thighs. Except for braided side locks, Decrius's shoulder-length black hair was gathered at the back of the neck. His left cheek was partly covered in a blue tattoo consisting of a spiral design that continued downward winding around the neck until it disappeared beneath his neck scarf.

Decrius was only too happy to answer his questions. He explained the small differences in hair and body decoration reflected tribal differences among the Tungrians and remained a carry-over from their ancestral origins in Belgica. What surprised Arrius the most was that Decrius was not even a Tungrian but a Britannian by birth and a member of the Briganti Tribe.

Arrius occupied part of his time learning some of the Tungrian and Briganti languages. Not a natural linguist, he worked hard to acquire a basic ability to understand with an even more limited capability to converse in the guttural-sounding languages. The Brigantian proved to be a patient tutor, and soon he could master simple phrases. His efforts with the Tungrian language proved to be easier based upon his previous duty in Germania where the language there was not so dissimilar. At first, the Tungrians found his clumsy attempts amusing, but they soon realized he was making a concerted effort. Once they realized this, it was a communal undertaking to help him improve.

The only tangible reminder of his wounds apart from the red, puckered scars on his shoulder and left thigh was a slight limp; he had resigned himself to the probability it would likely be with him for the rest of his life as a lasting reminder of the Sorek Valley.

Philos and Rufus were relentless in their efforts to get Arrius back into shape. Philos continued to provide herbal concoctions he insisted would help restore Arrius to his former vigor while Rufus concentrated on a physical regimen that included increasing practice with gladius and shield. Eventually, Rufus's efforts inspired Decrius to prod the Tungrians into similar activity until the sight and sound of sparring legionaries on the narrow deck became a common occurrence. To relieve the monotony of the drills and the idle days, Arrius organized competitions until even the crew began to enter the spirit by wagering among each other and with the legionaries. Surprisingly, it was Rufus who emerged time and time again as one of the consistent favorites to the chagrin of Decrius. His enormous bulk compensated for swordsmanship that was at best average and was sufficient to maintain dominance over all but Rufus. Arrius wondered as he watched Rufus continue to improve his swordsmanship if he would prevail now as he had done when they'd fought in the Judaean highlands.

By the time the ship found a berth in Puteoli, crew and passengers alike were more than ready to leave the cramped confines of the ship for the opportunity to feel the ground instead of a pitching deck beneath their feet. Arrius was anxious to continue the voyage to the port of *Massilia* in southern Gaul. He was concerned any delay along with approaching winter would make the land march across Gaul an even more challenging endeavor. If fortune smiled and the winter was relatively mild, he thought they might reach the channel port of *Portus Itius* on the west coast of Gaul in two months. At Portus Itius, the detachment would once again board ship for the short voyage across the narrow channel to Britannia; however, should the winter weather prove more difficult than expected, they would have little choice but to go into winter quarters in one of the army garrisons along the way until spring made travel possible again.

Several days were required for the ship's captain to arrange for a new cargo of wool, wine and olive oil to replace the consignment of copper and spices off-loaded at Puteoli. Arrius chafed at the delay but realized there was little he could do about it. He therefore decided to make the best of it and allow the legionaries sufficient time and money to enjoy the taverns and brothels of one of the busiest port cities in Italia.

He also enjoyed the brief interlude. In the company of Philos, and with the assistance of a stout walking stick for each of them, the two men toured the streets of the city, taking in the sights and stopping at the various market stalls. The exotic merchandise for sale reflected the diverse mercantile commerce of the Mediterranean. The walking proved to have the additional benefit of loosening the stiffness in his leg. When the ship's captain determined it was time to cast off several days later, he no longer depended as much on the walking stick, although the leg remained tender around the wound.

Only one of the legionaries failed to return before the scheduled departure. Arrius sent out search parties to canvass the now familiar waterfront establishments, all of which had a common purpose of relieving the sailor and traveler from whatever coins they might have. Had it been any other legionary than Rufus, he would have left him without giving the matter a second thought. But what Rufus had done to save him and assist in his recuperation, he wouldn't forget; consequently, he sent out search parties to comb the whorehouses and taverns. More by luck than design, the wayward optio was found in a narrow alley in a drunken stupor just in time for the impatient captain to catch the outgoing tide. Once on board, he looked at the battered optio and was convinced Rufus had been punished enough.

A few days later under a cloudless sky and unseasonably warm temperatures, the ship arrived in Massilia in southern Gaul. Arrius regarded the temperate climate as a favorable omen and an unexpected bonus against the rapidly approaching time when they would have to endure winter temperatures as they made their way across the length of Gaul. Told there was a small Roman garrison on the city's outskirts, Arrius obtained directions from one of the port officials. For the first time since leaving the port of Joppa, he donned cuirass and helmet and led a small detail similarly accoutered to requisition enough supplies, wagons and mules to support their journey north. He left Decrius to keep a watchful eye on the legionaries left behind in full realization that without a vigilant supervision, he would be lucky to find a single man left on the ship when he returned. He had no wish to comb the waterfront bars and brothels looking for the legionaries. Based on experience, Arrius selected Rufus to command his escort, concluding it would be Rufus who would likely be the first to seek the comfort of wine and whores.

After a short walk from the waterfront, he found a small fort that from its size appeared to house no more than a century. As he passed through the gate, his initial impression was that it had been abandoned as indicated by the absence of any sentries and the generally rundown condition of the buildings. He halted the detail inside the gate and entered the guardhouse in search of a sentry. He found the guard lying on his back fast asleep on a bench, his head propped on his helmet, mouth gaping open and his spear leaning against the wall. Arrius placed the tip of his vitis in the sleeping man's open mouth and shook the stick, rattling it against his teeth. When the sentry's eyes opened wide in sudden alarm, he saw the towering figure of a scarred, forbidding centurion looming over him.

"On your feet!" After the guard sprang to his feet, Arrius leaned forward until he was only inches from the legionary's face. "What unit is assigned to this fort and who commands it?"

"Auxilia Century II, *Galicia* commanded by Centurion Santorius Lucius Caecilius, sir!"

Arrius had already surmised from the fort's rundown appearance and the lax behavior of the guard that it was probably garrisoned by an auxiliary unit. He winced thinking about what he might find when he assumed command of his own auxilia in Britannia.

"Tell me where I can find Centurion Caecilius."

The guard's face took on a worried look. "Sir, I believe he is at the baths in town."

"This time of day?"

"Why, yes, every day he goes there." The guard clearly found nothing amiss in the practice. Arrius wondered about a commander who indulged himself so regularly in the middle of the day.

Further conjecture was interrupted by the sound of a commotion outside in the gateway. Arrius heard an angry, imperious voice demanding to know the purpose of the armed detachment blocking the passageway. Evidently, one of the legionaries must have gestured inside the guardhouse for a moment later a short, slightly-built man with a receding hairline dressed in an expensive linen tunic entered the guardroom. Silent and expressionless, Arrius saw a look of surprise replace the irritated look that had pulled down the corners of the other man's mouth. For a moment, the two men studied each other in silence. He saw the younger man's eyes sweep over the military decorations fastened to his battle-worn cuirass before asking in a tone undoubtedly intended to be assertive but managing only to sound querulous, "Centurion, who are you and what are you doing in my guardhouse?"

"I am Primus Pilatus Arrius. I command a detachment of Tungrians being redeployed from Judaea to Britannia. I presume you are Centurion Caecilius and the commanding officer of this garrison?" When he received a mute nod, Arrius continued briskly, "Good, I shall need your assistance in preparing my detachment for an overland march across Gaul to Portus Itius. Specifically, I need supplies and transport. As it is already late in the year, and winter is fast approaching, I should like to be on my way within a few days."

"By whose authority do you make such demands?"

"By order of General Vitellius Turbo." Arrius noted a flicker of uncertainty in the other man's eyes. "I trust you've heard of him?"

"I suppose you've some proof of who you are?"

"It so happens I do." He retrieved a parchment scroll from a leather pouch appended to his belt. "This document signed by General Turbo gives me the authority to command the Tungrian detachment and to seek any assistance required from any Roman garrison while traveling to Britannia."

Plainly irritated, Caecilius unrolled the document and quickly scanned it. After noting the elaborate seal and signature of Vitellius Turbo, he handed it back. "Well, I suppose I can spare rations for a few days for a dozen or so men."

"Oh, I believe my requirements will amount to a great deal more than that, Centurion." Arrius handed the centurion a list of needed supplies and equipment.

After only a glance at the long list, the centurion said, "Wagons, mules, rations for 55 men for 60 days! You must be joking! I've no intention of complying with such an outrageous request. Why, that would deprive my own command and create an inconvenient shortage."

Arrius turned to the legionary still standing at attention and doing his best to remain inconspicuous. "Leave us," he said in a quiet, firm voice that left no question in the legionary's mind he should obey. "Close the door behind you." When the two centurions were alone,

Arrius said, "Now that we're alone, Centurion Caecilius, perhaps I can clarify the situation a little better." He grasped the hilt of his sword.

Alarmed over Arrius's threatening manner, Caecilius began backing away, his eyes wide with alarm. "I'm afraid in the end I will have to 'inconvenient' you. I'll give you three days to acquire the items on that list, at which time I will depart. If you're able to meet my demands sooner, that will be even better. You will then be rewarded by my earlier departure. Now, Centurion, I suggest you find your quaestor and begin to make the necessary arrangements before I begin to lose patience."

Caecilius made one final attempt to assert his position. "Now, see here, I can't possibly comply with your unreasonable demands —"

He got no farther as Arrius leaned closer. "Listen carefully, you little prick, I've no intention of repeating myself. You must understand you have absolutely no choice in the matter unless you wish to accommodate me and my legionaries for the winter. I can assure you as miserable as this place appears to be, it is far better than what I and my men have been used to for the past year or more in Judaea. If we must remain here for the winter, we will. The inconvenience of remaining here for the winter will be less for me and my legionaries than it will be for you. I'm not certain why, but I've a feeling you and I would not get along well over the course of the winter months. In fact, it might very well 'inconvenient' you in more ways than you can possibly imagine. Now are you going to waste my time and yours with further debate?"

Realizing further protest was useless, Caecilius managed to nod in grudging assent. "Very well, but I want a signed document for all you receive."

"Of course, I wouldn't have considered otherwise." Arrius's smile did not reach his eyes. "By the way, I should mention that I want the wagons and mules now. I need them to transport the equipment here from the ship we arrived on this morning."

"What do you mean here?"

"Very simply because I intend to quarter my detachment in one of your barracks until the supplies and wagons have been assembled. You can't expect us to remain on the ship while we prepare for our journey across Gaul. Of course, I shall require suitable quarters as well."

"But I have no room available."

"I'm certain you'll find a way to cope. Perhaps this may be an excellent opportunity to send some of your legionaries to the field for training, assuming they know how and where to find the field."

"Very well, I'll see what I can do."

"Good, then that's settled. I'll return to the ship with my escort to supervise the off-loading of our equipment. Since you've much to do, I wouldn't want to get in the way. I'll leave one of my men behind to guide the wagons to the ship."

Later that day, Arrius saw what looked to be a column of legionaries filing over a nearby hill. He felt reasonably confident their quarters that night promised to be considerably better than if they had remained on the cramped ship.

Despite the unpropitious beginning, Centurion Caecilius proved to be more cooperative than Arrius expected. He suspected the threat of having to put up with his uninvited guests for a prolonged stay was the principal incentive for quickly producing the required supplies and the five wagons requested along with the mules to pull them. Fearing the worst and expecting additional confrontations with the local commander, Arrius was pleased to find the wagons and stock in surprisingly good condition.

Philos took charge of accounting for all rations and forage requisitioned and supervised the legionaries as they loaded the wagons. The Tungrians quickly acquiesced to the older man's uncompromising demands during the loading. It did not take long for them to realize the former slave had a sharp eye for any attempt on the part of the local quaestor to pass off inferior supplies on them or to use short measures when weighing the bags of grain.

Possibly to make amends for his initial lack of cooperation, or more likely as an additional inducement for a speedy departure, Caecilius went out of his way to assist in the preparations. He proved helpful in locating two horses from one of the local stables. Although one of the horses was unremarkable, the other was one of the largest stallions Arrius had ever seen, standing more than fifteen hands high. It didn't take long to realize the bargain price for the horse resulted from its intractable temperament and persistent habit of trying to bite any who ventured too close. He named the aggressive black stallion *Ferox* after the animal's bold, arrogant nature. To his chagrin, the one individual

Ferox seemed to show any affection at all was Philos whose quiet and gentle nature seemed to have a calming effect on the horse.

During the few days required for the Tungrian detachment to prepare for their departure, there was little social contact between the members of the Auxilia Century II *Galicia* and the remnants of the *Deiotariana* Legion. Decrius kept a short leash on his Tungrians fearing it would take little for his legionaries to express their contempt for the local legionaries in stronger ways than mere condescending looks. The two groups were separated by more than ethnic background. Accustomed to frontier duty, the battle-hardened Tungrians presented a marked contrast to the legionaries stationed in the tranquil port garrison.

Arrius breathed a quiet sigh of relief when it was time to leave and no serious incident had thus far occurred. As a final gesture of respect to the veterans of the Judean conflict, Centurion Caecilius formed up his century, and while they did not present the most polished military formation, it was at least credible, and Arrius appreciated the effort the garrison commander had undertaken on their behalf. As the small contingent filed through the gate, Arrius thought as dismal as the prospect of the long march to Portus Itius and assignment in Britannia was, he preferred that to the Masillia garrison or one like it in a place where tedium was the only enemy.

Part II

Britannia

135-136 CE

"Of the islanders most do not sow corn* but live on milk and flesh and clothe themselves in skins. All the Britons, indeed, dye themselves with woad, which produces a blue color, and makes their appearance in battle more terrible. They wear long hair, and shave every part of the body save the head and upper lip."—Julius Caesar, 55 BC, *Commentaries, Book V, The Gallic War.*

* wheat

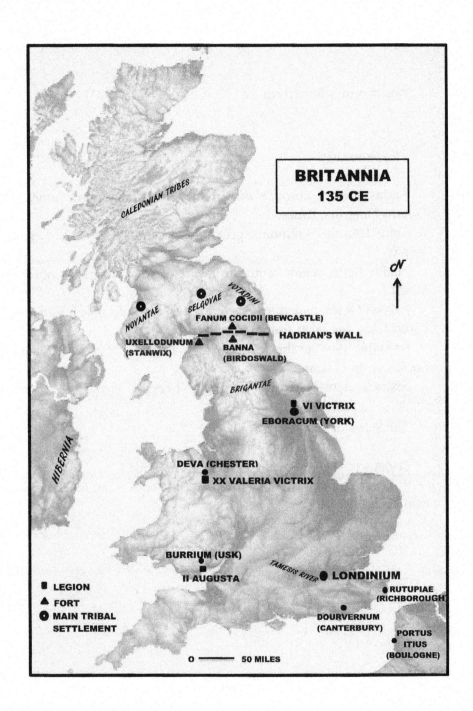

BRITANNIA
135 CE

CALEDONIAN TRIBES

NOVANTAE

SELGOVAE

VOTADINI

FANUM COCIDII (BEWCASTLE)

HADRIAN'S WALL

UXELLODUNUM
(STANWIX)

BANNA
(BIRDOSWALD)

BRIGANTAE

VI VICTRIX
EBORACUM (YORK)

DEVA (CHESTER)
XX VALERIA VICTRIX

HIBERNIA

BURRIUM (USK)
II AUGUSTA

TAMESIS RIVER

LONDINIUM

RUTUPIAE
(RICHBOROUGH)

DOURVERNUM
(CANTERBURY)

PORTUS
ITIUS
(BOULOGNE)

◼ LEGION
▲ FORT
◉ MAIN TRIBAL
  SETTLEMENT

O ——— 50 MILES

Additional Characters

The Romans

Antius Durio, *cornucularius* (chief of staff/administrator), II Cohort, *Tungrian*, Banna

Gaius Labinius Arvinnius, general and commander of VI Legion, *Victrix*

Matius Betto, senior centurion in the Second Tungrian Cohort at Banna

Publius Gheta, *quaestor* (quartermaster) Second Cohort, *Tungrian*, Banna I Ala, *Dacian* at Fanum Cocidii

Seugethis (Soo ge this), Commander First Ala, *Dacian* at Fanum Cocidii north of Banna

Sextus Trebius, Senior tribune of the VI Legion, *Victrix*

The Selgovi

Beldorach, High Chieftain of the Selgovae Tribe

Ilya, widow and owner of a local roadside tavern and inn; cousin of Beldorach

Joric, Ilya's young son

Chapter 1

Outside, the wind was cold and blustery on a clear, moonless night. Ilya sat facing her cousin across the table while an errant draft disturbed the flame of the oil lamp sitting on the table, causing the shadows on the wall to dance in flickering shapes. She listened attentively as Beldorach told her of the latest events among the Selgovae, one of three prominent tribes living north of the extensive stone wall Hadrian had commissioned some thirteen years before.

Her nostrils flared slightly as she breathed in the faint and unforgotten scents coming from him, a combination of forest, wood smoke and heather that brought forth a momentary longing for a homeland she still missed. She wondered if she would ever become fully used to living on this side of the Roman wall. Tall and willowy, Ilya had inherited her mother's legendary beauty, or so Beldorach claimed. She had to take his word for that. Her mother died in the process of giving her life nearly thirty years ago. She guessed she was comely if only because of the unwelcome attention she had to put up with from both the local Briganti men and the legionaries populating the nearby Roman garrisons. Only the faint lines at the corner of her eyes and mouth betrayed the fact she was perhaps older than first appearance might suggest. Had she been so inclined, she would have applied the usual oils and powders women had always used to appear younger than they were; however, her physical appearance was something she gave little thought to and assigned even less importance. She wore her long blonde hair with its coppery highlights loose and flowing down her back. The latter was a distinct departure from the traditional single braid favored by female members of the Selgovae after experiencing their first bleeding. The hair style was a tangible sign of her rebellion against tradition and a tribe that had cast her out.

"Why do you risk coming here?" she asked. "You know what will happen if the Romans catch you."

"I have to take the risk. I'm going south near the city the Romans called *Eboracum* to convince the Briganti to join in an uprising against the Romans. Getting the northern tribes to set aside our differences

183

was difficult, but I've managed to persuade the Votadini and Novantae, at least for now, to stop fighting among ourselves. If I can persuade the Briganti to join us, we have a better chance of defeating the Romans."

She nodded acknowledging what had been obvious ever since the Roman occupation that the perpetual state of armed conflict existing among the tribes had only benefited the Romans. But she was skeptical. She had seen such attempts in the past, all of which had failed. She thought the chance of keeping the various tribes on either side of the Roman wall in a lasting alliance was slim and temporary at best.

Ilya noted her cousin's gaunt, chiseled features bronzed from weather and sun and thought in the months she had last seen him he had aged considerably; however, his penetrating eyes, thin lips and square-jaw still projected the resolute confidence and authority that had made the Selgovae dominant among the northern tribes. She studied her cousin's strong hands propping up his chin as he stared vacantly into the swirling flame of the clay lamp. They were the hands of a warrior bearing the scars of many battles. To disguise his tribal affiliation for his travels in the south, he'd gathered his long hair at the neck instead of loose as was the custom among the Selgovi. The streaks of gray in his copper hair were more prominent, and the long moustache drooping down on either side of his mouth was grayer instead of the deep red it once was. He was not wearing the customary gold neck torque signifying his rank and status. Beldorach had become High Chieftain instead of her, a fact that had nearly split the tribe when many believed her closer relationship to Bhatar gave her rather than her unpopular cousin the right. However, there had been another and more compelling reason than tradition for his selection as tribal leader and that required her to take shelter behind the Roman barrier. Beldorach had helped her escape with enough gold to allow her to live modestly in her new haven as befitting her royal blood. Over the years, he'd continued to see she was provided for in ways hardly lavish yet sufficient to sustain her. She had come to live among the Romans out of practical necessity, but in the intervening years, her life among the Romans and Briganti still amounted to an existence only marginally acceptable. She had nothing but contempt for the Briganti she lived among for their growing complacency to the Roman presence. Unfortunately, she had no other place to go. She was grateful for

Beldorach's interest in her welfare even though she believed her cousin's attention had more to it than mere kinship and regard for her. Her proximity to the Romans made her a reliable source of information. As the proprietor of a tavern and roadside inn just outside the wall fort the Romans called Banna, she was well-situated to monitor the activities of the Roman garrison. She also suspected his efforts to help her live in the south were motivated by a concern she might one day choose to return to the tribe and assert her rights, a decision that would challenge the legitimacy of his claim to tribal leadership.

"It will take more than an agreement with the Novanti and Votadini to convince them," referring to the long-time rivalry with the neighboring tribes claiming the territory to the west and east of the Selgovan lands. "All know any treaty among the three tribes is at best temporary and usually lasts only until warm weather when the raiding season begins."

Beldorach took another long drink then wiped his hand across his drooping mustache. "I must try again. In the past, they've never said no, and I believe with the reduced Roman presence along the border, they may be more willing to join us. I suspect they're also waiting for the northern tribes to strike the first blow and achieve success before they commit to a joint alliance. Together, we can drive the Romans out. Sometimes I think we hate each other more than we do the Romans." He threw up his hands in disgust.

She thought it was Beldorach himself and his aggressive raiding that was as much to blame as anything for the tense relations with the other two tribes. She stared silently into space. She was ambivalent about a general uprising. Except for Joric, she no longer felt bound to anyone. Her son was her sole reason for enduring the Romans. In fact, the best she hoped for was a status quo. Peace would allow a better chance for Joric to reach manhood when he decided for himself who and what he wanted to be, Roman, Briganti or Selgovae. It was a decision she had no wish to make for him.

She turned to face Beldorach and saw he was studying her, eyes narrowed in speculation. When he had her attention, he asked quietly, "How has it been with you?"

She shrugged tiredly. "We survive. What more can I say? I suppose by Roman standards, I've prospered." With single-minded purpose and hard work, she'd turned the rundown estate she bought into a popular inn and tavern frequented primarily by a Roman clientele dominated by off-duty and thirsty auxiliary legionaries assigned to the nearby wall forts.

Beldorach tried to conceal the disgust he felt for the life she led but knew she'd had little choice. He had only contempt for a lifestyle so different from his own. He couldn't understand why anyone would tolerate an existence so divorced from the land. Her decision to leave the Selgovae to save her son was the reason he was now the High Chieftain of the Selgovae instead of her. He had returned from a raid to find Bhatar, his uncle and High Chieftain, dead and the village burning. The Roman patrol was quickly defeated; he beheaded each Roman prisoner himself. When he found Ilya naked, she was still stabbing with grim determination the lifeless body of the last of the undoubtedly many legionaries who had used her that day. Later, when Ilya gave birth to a son because of what she endured, he and the tribe were mystified by Ilya's last-minute refusal to allow the child to be killed, choosing exile instead.

"What of the boy?"

She bristled. "The *boy* has a name."

"Ah, so he has. How is Joric?"

Her face relaxed, and a slight smile softened her features erasing the angry look she'd flashed at him. "Joric prospers. He's very bright, and he grows tall and is fair like Bhatar. He stands apart from other boys his age for he has a keen interest in everything he sees or encounters. He can describe things to me he's seen or experienced during the day that reveal a degree of inquisitiveness and analytical capability far beyond his years. He speaks Latin better than I do and several dialects of the Briganti. I've also taught him our tongue as well."

"Why? It serves no useful purpose to teach him Selgovan."

"I want him to have choices; the kind of choices I didn't have and still do not. He also bears the royal mark," referring to the intricate blue-green spiral design she had tattooed on his chest.

"Why would you do that? You know he can't venture north without risking death."

"That may be, but only if you approve it."

"You know the custom. Once the priests have decided, the sacrifice must be carried out."

"And you know the High Chieftain has the power to overrule the judgment if he so chooses."

What she said was true even though it had seldom been done. The thought made him uneasy, and he wondered if it was genuine reluctance to rule against the priests, or if it was because she and the boy still posed a threat. His position was precarious. With three wives and innumerable concubines over the years, he had yet to father offspring of his own. His failure to sire a child was beginning to cause talk. He also continued to be conflicted over his feelings and motivations concerning Ilya. What she'd said was true. Had he wished, he could have intervened on her and the infant's behalf, but the prospect of assuming leadership of the tribe had overcome any guilt for his inaction.

"To go against the priests is unwise and jeopardizes the welfare of the people."

"What you really mean, cousin, is that it might not be in your best *welfare* since my son and I represent a more direct line to the royal dais than your own. I think it is for that reason you prefer Joric and I remain here."

"The boy is a bastard and part Roman; he would not be accepted, and your defiance of the priests has not been entirely forgotten or forgiven. It would be better for you, your son and the tribe if you stayed here."

"The fact he is a bastard has no bearing. You forget he has half my blood flowing in his veins, and according to tribal law or tradition, succession through the maternal line takes precedence. Do I need to remind you when my father was killed I had the right to succeed him? There is nothing in custom or law that forbids him to rule because of any question of his birth."

"What you say is true." He conceded the point without rancor. "But you've made a life here now, so why would you wish to leave?"

"I have an existence here, not a life. One day I may decide to leave and go back to the hills and forests."

"That may be as you wish, but I do not advise it. I can make no promise concerning your safety, or Joric's, if you come back."

"Perhaps it's only you and you alone who is against our return."

Their attention was diverted by the whisper of footsteps as a young boy on the cusp of manhood entered the room rubbing the sleep from his eyes. Fine-featured, tall and strongly-built for his age, he bore an unmistakable resemblance to his mother. Beldorach was reminded of Bhatar, not physically, but in the way the boy looked at him boldly. Bhatar had that look. He felt a pang of anguish wondering why the gods had not seen fit to give him a son like Joric.

When Joric saw who it was talking to his mother, the last vestige of sleep left him, and he stopped, hesitating as Beldorach stood and waited for the boy to come closer. Silently, man and boy regarded each other, neither one speaking until finally Beldorach broke the silence.

"Your mother is right; you've grown since I last saw you." Joric nodded silently and continued to stare intently at Beldorach. "She also tells me you are gifted in languages." Again, there was no response apart from a slight nod.

Just as Beldorach was beginning to doubt Ilya's earlier assessment of the boy's mental abilities, Joric said abruptly before sliding onto the bench next to his mother, "You've changed your hair. Mother told me the Selgovi do not have braided side locks." Caught off guard, Beldorach realized the boy's silence until now was occasioned by Joric's appraisal and not because of timidity or lack of intelligence.

"Aye, I have indeed. Do you know why?"

"You don't want anyone to recognize who you are," Joric said matter-of-factly. "Because no one likes the Selgovi here, or so mother says. We only speak in the Selgovan tongue when no one else is around."

"Right you are, and it would be better if you didn't tell anyone I've been here or who I am. Will you promise that?"

"I'll not tell anyone, even my best friend Rialus."

Beldorach looked inquiringly at Ilya who smiled indulgently. "Rialus is a Briganti boy about the same age as Joric who lives in the village. His father is one of the auxiliaries stationed in the fort, or at least he used to be until he and a number of the other auxiliaries were sent to Judaea over a year ago."

Beldorach looked at her with interest. "How many legionaries are left here?"

"A few hundred in the fort here, perhaps more. I heard some were withdrawn from the other forts as well." Ilya saw the calculating look in her cousin's eyes and knew what he was thinking. "I've also heard the war in Judaea is over, and the Romans will soon increase their strength to what it was before."

"It would seem the Briganti have allowed opportunity to pass them by. Who won in this place called Judaea?"

"The Romans, of course. Don't they always?"

For the next hour, the three talked quietly with Joric listening and asking occasional but penetrating questions. It didn't take long for Beldorach to form a new opinion of the young boy even as he resolved to ensure Ilya, at least for the time being, continued to remain south of the wall. Out of a deep respect for Bhatar, he would do his best to see that no harm came to her and the boy; however, he saw too much steel in Ilya and too much promise in the boy to risk having them return north.

Chapter 2

Although there was no shortage of ships in the harbor of *Portus Itius* to take them across the narrow stretch of water separating the mainland from Britannia, finding captains and crews who were willing to chance a winter crossing was another matter. The ships' captains were adamant against risking their vessels further with the added burden of the animals. Arrius finally gave in and accepted the fact if they were to reach Britannia, the mules would have to remain in Gaul. He sold the mules at a reasonable price and hoped he would be able to procure replacements once they reached Britannia. The one exception to the edict for no animals was Ferox. Arrius had no intention of leaving him behind. He had no pangs in parting with the one horse, but it was unthinkable to consider giving up the black stallion. Arrius had to dig deep into his own funds to overcome the reluctance of one of the captains to include the horse.

After dismantling the wagons and loading them aboard the ships along with their other equipment and supplies, they waited for the weather to abate enough to set sail. Days later when Arrius expected to be underway, he was still being given one excuse after another why they were not able to leave the harbor — the tides weren't favorable, the offshore winds prevented them from leaving, the omens were not auspicious. Finally, he had enough, and with one hand on the hilt of his sword and the other holding a bag full of denarii, he was able to convince the senior captain, who then persuaded the other captains, to depart the next day.

Arrius delayed putting Ferox on the ship until just before departure anticipating the stallion might be a challenge to get on board. It was quickly apparent he had completely underestimated the difficulty in getting the spirited animal loaded. The horse proceeded to show his displeasure in every conceivable way and became increasingly contentious the closer he got to the ship. After considerable effort and risk, it took the combined efforts of Arrius and the crew to get a sling under the horse and lower him down into the hold. Even after he tied a cloth around the animal's eyes to keep it from kicking out the ship's side planks or doing any more damage than the horse had already caused, it was a nerve-wracking passage with Ferox creating as much risk to the safety of the ship as the heavy, buffeting seas. Arrius remained in the hold during the passage in case the captain tried to carry out his threat to kill the stallion. Before he heard the cry above they were nearing land, he was beginning to consider allowing the captain to have his way.

Arrius's first sighting of Britannia in nearly fifteen years was far from auspicious. The leaden sky with a light rain falling presented a dismal picture as the flotilla of four ships rounded *Tanatus Insulae*, the low island sheltering the port of *Rutupiae*. He vaguely recalled passing through here when he first came to Britannia; however, except for the stark white cliffs dominating the shoreline farther south, he remembered little else. In sharp contrast, the mainland directly ahead was flat, rising no more than fifty feet or so above a predominantly gravel beach. Here and there, low dips indicated where freshwater streams met the channel's tidal flows resulting in marshes where tall grass waved in the slight breeze. Because of the low scudding clouds that seemed to press down on the land, he saw nothing beyond the shoreline.

One by one, the ships entered a narrow strait formed by the island and the mainland. Arrius steadied himself as the ship turned on a new tack. The sail, briefly gone slack as the ship came about, filled again with a loud snap from a brisk offshore breeze. The captain told him the port wasn't much more than a mile away, but with the variable winds typical here, he warned it might take an hour to reach it. If the wind held favorably, they would be in Rutupiae in a fraction of that time.

"At least it seems warmer than Gaul," Arrius said to Rufus standing beside him on the foredeck as they watched the details of the shoreline becoming more distinct the closer they came. Promoting Rufus to optio despite initial misgivings had proven to be more successful than he'd hoped. The responsibility had done wonders for the once incorrigible legionary. He now took on responsibility and demonstrated a sense of purpose quite different from his former behavior.

"Aye, and I'll give thanks for that. I'll thank the gods even more when I get off this tub and feel land under my feet instead of a rolling deck."

Near the halfway point across the strait, Arrius pointed to a huge ceremonial arch standing near the edge of the bluff they were heading toward. The gleaming white marble stood out in a prominent display of Roman grandeur under a gray sky.

"When I came here the first time to join the Sixth Legion, the arch was under construction and no higher than a man's knee. Now look at it, it's magnificent."

"I hope the gods spare me from wasting my time building such things. I'd rather break sweat with a woman under me or a sword in my hand and the promise of booty at the end of a good fight than hauling dirt and rocks to build useless monuments."

"There was sweat and booty in Judaea."

"Aye, sweat for certain but little booty, thanks to a centurion who went out of his way to find battles without giving his legionaries the time and opportunity to profit from them. I expect it will be no different in this pigsty of a country."

"Rufus, all you think about is your cock and your purse. I wonder why you volunteered to come here when you apparently have so little expectation for what lies ahead."

"I didn't volunteer. General Turbo told me to look after you, and I said I would."

"Then I order you to take the first ship back to Gaul and join one of the legions there. I'm certain General Turbo meant for you to look after me only until I healed. I'm now healed; therefore, you are no longer under any obligation to serve me."

"Now is a fine time to tell me when we've reached the ass-end of the empire. You could have told me that back in Puteoli instead of putting me back on the ship. Besides, General Turbo didn't say when to stop looking after you. I'm just following orders."

"Jupiter's balls, when did you begin to believe you needed to follow orders so faithfully?"

"I learned the hard way from a centurion who was better with a sword than I was."

"I countermand General Turbo's order."

"You can't do that; he's a general and you're only a god-rotted centurion."

Both exasperated and touched, Arrius did not press the matter.

An hour later, the ship reached the port where a series of long docks extended out from the beach like outstretched wooden fingers. Even now in winter, the port was busy with several ships in the process of being unloaded. Several small fishing boats were pulled up on the beach between the piers. Arrius watched as the helmsman, responding to the terse orders of the captain, skillfully maneuvered the ship into a berth alongside one of the piers. Dominating the tiled roofs of the village on the bluff above, the triumphal arch appeared even more colossal. Standing over eighty feet high, it was covered with elaborately carved murals, each corner featuring a statue of a Roman deity. Additional and smaller statues were positioned in recessed niches along the facing side. Arrius thought if the purpose of the arch was to create an impressive gateway to Britannia underscoring the might of Rome, it had been well and truly achieved.

Standing next to the ship's captain, Arrius's thoughts now focused on the tasks required to offload men and cargo including getting Ferox unloaded with a minimum of destruction to the ship or injuries to either crew or animal. He decided any attempt to take the stallion off on the pier was out of the question. He motioned to Decrius and Rufus to join him.

"I want the stallion taken off first—"

"Centurion, if that beast does any more damage to my ship —"

"Hold your tongue. You've been well paid, and I do not wish to be reminded just how much. You would do well not to stick your hand out for more, or I may decide to remove it. This is what we will do and how we will do it. Captain, have the crew remove the side rail opposite the dock. We'll lift the stallion up out of the hold and over the side. Keep his eyes covered until just before the animal is lowered in the water. I'll be on the beach shore waiting for him to swim across. Optiones, go aboard the other ships and tell the men to unload the wagons first then assemble them on the docks. After the wagons are ready, load the supplies and equipment. While this is being done, I'll ride up to the fort and make arrangements for oxen and drovers to get the wagons."

Satisfied the arrangements were understood and underway, Arrius picked up the saddle and went ashore offering a silent prayer to *Epona,* the "Great Mare," for help in getting the stallion safely ashore.

The appearance of the stallion above deck was preceded by the shrill whinnies of the angry horse and the sound of splintering wood. Somehow, Ferox had managed to shed the cloth around his eyes, and the result was enough for all except the dozen crew members pulling on the hoist to scramble as far from the flailing hooves as the ship's deck would allow. Ears laid back, teeth bared, the stallion's frantic efforts to get loose were made more energetic by the sailors' cursing and loud cheering of the dockside onlookers who had stopped to watch the unfolding drama. Once the crew swung the jib over the water and began to slowly pay out the rope, Ferox seemed to sense freedom was near and began to cease his struggles. By the time he was lowered into the belly high water, Ferox gave a last disdainful look at the ship, loosened his bowels and calmly waded ashore where Arrius accompanied by a loud cheer from the spectators quickly saddled him. Leaving Decrius and Rufus to see to the unloading, he used the wheel hub of a wagon to mount Ferox. Predictably, the unruly stallion showed his displeasure by bucking in circles causing those nearby to scramble to safety to avoid injury. Arrius finally gained control and tight-lipped, guided the stallion up the steep bank.

The few villagers he passed gave him little notice. After nearly a century of seeing Roman legionaries coming and going, the sight no longer inspired more than a casual, disinterested glance. The huge arch was in the center of a small, unremarkable fort that was further reduced in size by the presence of the monument that dominated it. It was apparent Rome's influence in southern Britannia was no longer in question and in even less jeopardy. Most of the buildings inside the fort were constructed of stone as were some of those in the village surrounding the supply depot; however, most of the buildings in the village were timber and wattle.

Arrius dismounted in front of a large building he assumed to be the headquarters. Proven correct, he was pleasantly surprised to find an efficient and willing staff inside in marked contrast to the reception at the port of Massilia. The necessary arrangements for temporary quarters and ox teams to haul the wagons up from the docks below were quickly made. He was shown to a large building at the northeastern corner of the fort to quarter the legionaries for the few days necessary to prepare for the march to Eboracum. The inn with its dry quarters, clean latrine and small bathhouse would be a welcome relief to the legionaries after the wet and cold channel crossing and the miserable quarters they had to endure for several days before leaving Portus Itius.

A few days were required for the necessary number of mules to be procured during which time the Tungrian legionaries basked in relative comfort. Arrius was generous in granting time off, recognizing they still had a long way to go under less than ideal marching conditions. When it was time to depart, he was ready to leave Rutupiae in contrast to the legionaries who would have been quite content to remain there a few days longer.

As they left the village behind, the road stretched straight ahead just as Roman engineers had been constructing roads for centuries, curving or turning only when the terrain made it necessary to do so. Arrius listened to the familiar, rhythmic crunching sound of Ferox's hooves on the cambered roadbed and resisted the temptation to nod off. The farther inland they traveled, the landscape became more rolling and forested. There were ample signs of prosperity, and the number of small villages had increased considerably since he had come this way bearing the eagle standard of the Sixth Legion. Arrius thought the countryside was probably pleasant enough although he thought it would improve considerably if the rain would only stop. He'd forgotten how long it had taken to get used to being wet in Britannia.

They reached *Londinium* late on the third day. Arrius allowed the legionaries a leisurely two days to enjoy the comparative comforts of the large town with its sizable Roman garrison quartered there. He was both surprised and pleased at the warm reception the detachment received when it was learned the legionaries represented the survivors of the Twenty-second Legion; he hadn't expected the legion's fate to be known so far from Judaea. He didn't realize until they were ready to depart the main reason for the local commander's generous hospitality was based more on sympathy concerning the detachment's ultimate destination than for what had happened in Judaea. The latter gave Arrius additional reason to doubt the wisdom of refusing Turbo's offer for a position in Rome.

From Londinium, Arrius led the detachment north toward their initial destination of Eboracum over two hundred miles away. At some point early every day, it rained even if only briefly. On the rare days when it did not rain, the mood of the legionaries noticeably improved, and they marched with a lighter step, breaking into rhythmic songs and chants in a blend of the Roman and Tungrian language. On such days, even Ferox appeared less intractable than usual leaving Arrius to think of other things than giving full attention to the quirks of the unpredictable stallion. His thigh had healed sufficiently that he was now able on some mornings to vault into the saddle without assistance — that is if he first took the precaution of working out the stiffness before making the attempt.

The countryside they passed through was initially flat north of Londinium but gradually became more rolling the farther north they traveled. The terrain was not unlike Gaul with large tracts of forested land broken here and there by small villages and farms. The peasant dwellings with their thatch roofs and round walls constructed of wattle were not unlike those on the continent. From time to time, they passed handsome villas with tile roofs attesting to the influence of the Roman occupation. The villagers and farmers they encountered seemed friendlier since he was last here. Dressed in woolen clothing, they were virtually indistinguishable from what would have been worn in the colder climate of northern Italia this time of year. Occasionally, Arrius saw men garbed in animal skins, their faces liberally daubed with blue paint in various designs according to individual preference. Decrius told him the blue was obtained by boiling the leaves of a plant common to Britannia. Decrius also said the use of blue dye was even more common among the tribes populating the northern regions including his own tribe, the Brigantes.

Nine days after leaving Londinnium and with a wintry sun about to disappear over the distant snow-capped hills, the detachment topped a rise and saw the spiraling smoke of Eboracum in the distance with the gray crenellated walls of the fort occupied by the VI Legion, *Victrix*. The Sixth Legion was responsible for overseeing and as necessary reinforcing the auxilia forces stationed on the northern frontier. Given the lateness of the day, Arrius decided to wait until the next morning before making their arrival at the fort to allow time for the legionaries to make themselves more presentable after so many days on the road.

He had no intention of exposing them to the jeers and catcalls that would surely greet any contingent arriving at a legion headquarters looking as travel-worn as they did now.

Later that night as Philos kept a vigilant eye on the slaves cleaning and polishing the best cuirass in preparation for tomorrow's arrival, Arrius sat staring vacantly into the flames of the campfire while massaging his upper thigh.

"Marcus, does the wound still trouble you?"

"No more than usual since we came to Britannia. In truth, it may have been colder in Gaul, but the damp in this country seems to penetrate bone-deep. I fear I'd best get used to it, for it seems all I remember about the climate has not changed at all. It's easy now to miss the comparative warmth of Judaea although that's all I miss."

"Then it isn't the leg that troubles you?"

"No, it's nothing, I'm just preoccupied in thinking about tomorrow and what to expect."

"I know you better than that. You've not been the same since we left Judaea. What bothers you?"

"I'm not really sure. I should be relishing the idea of my own command even if it's only with the auxilia, yet for some reason, I can't shake the feeling it may not turn out to be what I expected." He leaned back and closed his eyes giving Philos the impression the conversation was over, but after a few moments, his eyes still closed, he continued. "It seems that ever since I can remember all I ever wanted to do was to serve under the eagle. Now that I've spent almost a lifetime doing that, I'm beginning to wonder if it's enough."

"Marcus, by any standards, you've been successful. You now have the privileges of equestrian rank and appointment to an independent command. You have the support and friendship of one of the most important generals in the empire, and you're financially secure if you left the army."

"You're right in everything you say, but it doesn't answer the question of why I feel there's something missing."

"Is it because you regret the decision to go to Judaea, and by so doing, you left Min-nefret?"

Arrius remained silent a moment. "No, it isn't that. Given who and what I am, I would not have decided otherwise, and I would probably do the same again today. My regret is that I had to make a choice. Yes,

I suppose in a way I still miss her, but what I miss more is what she represented, a life I've never experienced nor am I likely to ever know. Philos, have you ever had a wife and family?"

When there was no immediate answer forthcoming, Arrius turned and looked closely at Philos who sat staring silently into the fire as if he hadn't heard the question. Just as Arrius decided to let the matter lie, Philos said in a low voice. "Yes, I had a family a long time ago when I lived in Macedonia. My wife and three children were killed by the Thracians. That is why I became a warrior and how I came to lose this," holding up the stump of his right hand. "I guess I was better suited to be a scholar than a warrior." He lapsed into silence without further explanation.

"Did you never consider marrying again? Even slaves are permitted to marry if the owner agrees."

"No, I was never so inclined. Besides it's way too late for me. After all, who would want a one-armed man, especially an old, one-armed man?" His laugh was humorless.

"I did."

"You were looking for a bargain that you could afford at the time."

"That, too, and I got one with friendship as the better part of the bargain."

"Marcus, I owe you more than I can ever repay. You gave me more than my freedom. You gave me a reason to keep on living."

"You already have repaid me a thousand times over, old friend. Let me hear no more talk of repayment."

"It's not too late for you."

"What's not too late?"

"A wife, a family."

"I think perhaps it is. I came close with Min-nefret, but I turned away. After all, who would want a legionary, especially one who I fear is well past thinking of and less able to accept a life without a sword at my side?" Yawning, Arrius stood up and stretched. "Well, the hour grows late, and it's time we slept on such weighty matters. Tomorrow the sun will come up, and we'll both have done with gloomy thoughts." The next day he found out he was half right; the sun did shine.

Chapter 3

The fort was situated on a slight rise above an otherwise flat plain overlooking a large village sprawling haphazardly on both sides of a bridge crossing a wide river gently curving through the countryside. The crenellated walls with the rounded corners were massive and constructed of grey stone that added further to an intimidating presence made no less under a sun-lit sky.

Leaving Decrius in charge of the detachment standing at ease a short distance away, Arrius cantered Ferox toward the eastern gate, slowing the stallion to a walk as he approached the double-gated entrance. He heard one of the two guards positioned just inside the entryway announce his arrival, and an optio quickly appeared in the doorway of the guard room. As soon as the optio saw Arrius's crested helmet, he came forward and saluted briskly.

"Centurion, state your name and business."

Returning the salute, Arrius dismounted. "Primi Pilatus Marcus Junius Arrius. My orders are to report to the Sixth Legion prior to assuming command of an auxilia on the northern frontier. I'm presently in command of a Tungrian vexillation newly returned from duty in Judaea."

At the mention of Judaea, the optio's eyes widened slightly; however, he made no comment other than to nod and say, "Sextus Trebius, the senior tribune, is presently in command in the absence of General Arvinnius. You will find the tribune in the principia," pointing toward the colonnaded façade of a large building directly opposite the gate.

Arrius walked the short distance to the headquarters and entered a spacious anteroom in which a dozen clerks toiled away at tables arranged around the sides of the room. At the far end was a doorway leading to an inner office from which he heard muffled voices.

A clerk approached and Arrius identified himself and why he was there. "Centurion, Tribune Trebius is occupied, but if you would have a seat," motioning to a wooden bench, "I feel certain your wait will not be long."

Arrius sat down and heard an angry voice rise in volume. "If you ever do anything so stupid, by the gods above, I'll have your hide on the wall and your balls decorating the legion's standard. Now I suggest you go to your quarters and reflect upon what I've said, for if by some miracle you ever command a legion, praise the gods it will not be the Sixth. I do not want it said any of your shortcomings are attributed to a failure of Sextus Trebius to impart at least a basic understanding of what is required of a legionary officer."

He heard a muted response too low to understand and a red-faced, disconsolate-looking man walked past him. He was surprised to note the individual was wearing the thin, purple stripe of a junior tribune on his linen tunic. Nothing in his experience had quite prepared him for a tribune speaking to another tribune in such a manner.

The same clerk that greeted him disappeared into the inner office and quickly reappeared a moment later followed by a grizzled, one-eyed man that reminded him of a massive block of granite. Waiting for Arrius to come forward, Tribune Trebius stood in the doorway, hands on his hips with a glowering expression on his face that Arrius was soon to realize was habitual. Trebius was much older than a tribune normally assigned to a legion. Solidly built and muscular, he had a seamed, weather-beaten face with a thrusting square jaw. What little hair he had left had been shaven, leaving only a shadow in a narrow band above the ears. A deep scar extended from the top of his left ear across the cheek and under a leather eye-patch and continued to the flattened bridge of his nose. Arrius had never been intimidated by any man before, but if there ever was to be an exception, Sextus Trebius would be a prime candidate.

Arrius saluted and handed over the document signed by Turbo appointing him to the auxilia.

"I've heard of you, Arrius, and most of it seemed positive enough, but we'll see about that in time. I find reputations seldom stand up to close observation. Have you heard of me?"

"No, Sir." The response did not seem to discomfit the other man in the least, acknowledging it only with a non-committal grunt. Inside the office, the older man unrolled the document and glanced at the contents then tossed it aside as if it were no more important than a piece of routine correspondence.

Noting the cavalier treatment Turbo's order had just received, Arrius felt obliged to say, "I trust my orders will receive the attention of the legion commander?"

"It just did. For the time being, I command here by order of General Gaius Labinius Arvinnius, the commander of the *Victrix*, who as I speak is on the border. You're late, Centurion, we've been expecting you for the past several weeks. You certainly took your own sweet time getting here. I've no doubt you've been taking time out to dip your prick along the way, and if you haven't, you'll be sorry you didn't when you get to where you're going."

"The weather was poor in Gaul and there was a delay in finding ships to bring us over from the mainland."

"Be that as it may, you're here now, and we'll have to make the best of the short time you'll spend here before you leave for the frontier. How many legionaries did you bring back with you? The orders say only you're commanding a detachment from the returning Britannian vexillation."

"I have fifty-two Tungrians in addition to my two optiones."

"By Minerva's cracked chamber pot," the older man said irreverently. "Is that all you brought back?"

Arrius bridled. "That number, small as it may be, represents much of what is left of the Twenty-second Legion. Nearly all bear the scars of the wounds they received."

For a moment Trebius cast a baleful eye on his visitor, and Arrius prepared for another verbal onslaught thinking that if it were to come, he would no longer be able to curb his rising anger at the tribune's abrasive manner.

Trebius nodded in understanding and said quietly, "Aye, I'd heard there were heavy losses, but I didn't realize the extent. To think, an entire legion gone. Was the outcome worth it?" Arrius merely shrugged without comment. "Well, thanks to Hadrian's little war, we're holding on here by the skin of our teeth. The Sixth has half the legion posted to the wall pending replacements to the auxilia that are long overdue. If the local tribes ever figure out how things really are, we'd have trouble withstanding another major revolt in Britannia."

"Another revolt?" Arrius had not heard of any recent problems in Britannia.

"Aye, two years ago the Briganti managed to give us some trouble. It was a close thing at first. Fortunately, most of the tribes hate each other almost as much as they dislike us. But more about that later. No doubt you're more interested in where you're going and the nature of the command you've been assigned."

"It has been on my mind."

"General Turbo sent a dispatch to General Arvinnius with his expectations regarding you. He made it clear you're to be given an independent command. It must be nice to have influence in high places." When he saw Arrius beginning to bristle, he forestalled any comment by saying, "Easy, I meant no criticism. Evidently, General Turbo thinks highly of your abilities. He even said you refused promotion to come here. Now there's confirmation of your lack of brains and good sense even if it is a possible endorsement of your worth." His one eye held a glint of approval. "Well, time will tell if you're as good as he says you are. Turbo was one of the better men I've suffered the misfortune of having to turn into a half-decent officer."

At the mention of Turbo, Arrius recalled where he had heard of Sextus Trebius. Turbo had mentioned him during the one evening they had spent together in Judaea. Trebius was responsible for the early training of no less a personage than Hadrian himself when the emperor had been an obscure junior tribune in the Second Legion stationed in Pannonia. Evidently at the time, Hadrian was not grateful for the rough treatment at the hands of a young centurion whose aggressiveness and no-nonsense manner intimidated officers many times his senior. In later years, Hadrian softened his feelings to the extent of bestowing a special donative to his former mentor and an invitation to join the Praetorian Guard, an honor that Sextus Trebius quickly refused renewing Hadrian's displeasure. The fact Trebius was now in Britannia seemed proof of the emperor's hot temper and unforgiving nature.

"Arrius, General Arvinnius has accorded you the rank and authority of a junior tribune with the title *Praefectus*. You are now entitled to an officer's crest on your helmet. You have my congratulations and my sympathies. You've been appointed to command the II Cohort Tungrian Equitatae located at Banna and the I Ala Dacorum, at *Fanum Cocidii* located north of Banna."

The name Banna seemed somehow familiar, but he didn't recall where he'd heard of it.

"Banna is the cesspit of the empire, but then that doesn't make it any better or worse than the other forts out there. It's on the northwest border about four or five days march from here, give or take, depending on the weather this time of year." Trebius paused before continuing. "Do you have mules or oxen?"

"We have the mules we obtained at Rutipiae."

"Well, mules won't do at all. You'll need to exchange them for oxen. You'll find the snows up north and the steep hills are unsuitable for mules. See my quaestor to exchange them for oxen. They'll be slower, but at least you'll get there." Trebius frowned. "Where was I? Oh, yes, Fanum Cocidii. It's even worse than Banna. Have you ever served with the auxilia before?" When Trebius saw Arrius shake his head, he continued. "Well, you'll soon find the auxilia is not the same as you've been used to. At least by posting foreign legionaries on the Wall, it spares the Sixth from having to be there. The auxilia will fight if necessary, I'll give them that. But it takes a Roman boot up their ass to guarantee they'll stick long enough for the Sixth and Twentieth to get up there if the northern tribes ever decide they want to start any trouble again. The Tungrian cohort is *miliaria*, meaning that at full strength it should have a thousand men consisting of 750 infantry and 250 cavalry. Because of the drawdown for Judaea, you'll find the Tungrian infantry strength at Banna considerably less than that. The cavalry is also under strength but not to the extent the infantry is."

"The Dacian Cohort at Fanum Cocidii is *quingenaria* and consists of 500 cavalry, or it would be if it were at full strength, which as with all other units on the frontier, it is not. Without getting out the latest strength reports, I'd guess the combined strength of both cohorts is somewhere between 1,200 and 1,300. If you haven't found out already, the Tungrians are a prickly bunch of bastards and clannish, too. The Dacians are more disciplined than the Tungrians, but that doesn't mean you won't have your hands full. Frankly, none of them get along except with their own people."

"There's some truth in what you say. But as I can attest first hand by their service in Judaea, the Tungrians fight well. If the rest of them fight when and where I need them, I'll have no complaints. As for the Dacians, I'll wait and see before I judge them."

"It's not their fighting skills I'm referring to. I concede that on the occasions when there have been incursions, they've acquitted themselves well enough. The problem is when they aren't fighting the native tribes. They're an ill-disciplined lot as you'll find out for yourself. They'll need a firm hand." Then abruptly changing the subject, Trebius said, "You might ask why General Arvinnius agreed with my recommendation to assign you the command."

"You recommended me?"

"I did for three reasons. Turbo recommended you, you're a seasoned campaigner and you're not apt to put up with the shit you're going to get from those auxiliary bastards. Not like the whoreson who quit after six months and went running back to Rome." Trebius thumped the table angrily. "The gutless bastard thought he was too good for real field duty. After that, I told Arvinnius we don't need another tribune just putting in his military service time at Banna. We need a seasoned veteran who understands how and when it's time to kick a legionary in the backsides. Unless I'm sadly mistaken, I believe that once again with a little help from Turbo, Sextus Trebius has found just the right man for the job." Trebius spoke without a trace of humility.

"A word or two about General Arvinnius might serve you well. He's an experienced general and commander, but he's a cold one. He's survived the intrigues in Rome, Hadrian and the perils of the battlefield with distinction. His main interest is General Arvinnius and his own political ambition, but unlike most of the other legion commanders I've served under who had a similar outlook, Arvinnius is at least competent enough even if his first instinct is political survival. I'm here because of Hadrian, although Arvinnius would have preferred a senior tribune who has more influence than I do. Since I don't have any political importance, nor do I wish it, Arvinnius would have had me out of Britannia long ago. But that would mean confronting Hadrian, and that he will not do. If Arvinnius thinks you're an asset, you'll get along fine; otherwise, he will see you as an obstacle to his own interests. Mind what you say and do around him. He has a bad temper, and he never forgives a slight. He prefers men around him who thinks as he does. He hopes to be named governor of Britannia when he leaves the Sixth, that is if he gets on better with the next emperor than he has with Hadrian."

Trebius stood up and walked over to a table upon which a large map of Britannia was displayed. "Come here and I'll show you where you're going and how your command fits in to our northern defense. The Sixth is responsible for the entire northern frontier. The *XX Legion, Valeria Victrix* at *Deva* about 175 miles to the southwest provides the primary defense in the west and secondarily to the Sixth if we require additional strength in the north. Ordinarily, the auxilia provides for the Wall defense that includes forts located from 20-50 miles forward of the Wall. The Judaean levies have made it necessary to place some of the cohorts from the Sixth on duty at the border until we receive more levies from the native tribes in Gaul and Belgica. Headquartered at Banna, your command is assigned the defense of that location and is one of sixteen major forts comprising the border defense. It's a critical location as it protects a river crossing as you will soon see. Fanum Cocidii is a forward position north of Banna." He pointed to each of the locations on the map. "The western half of the wall is considered the most critical section. The Novanti in the far west and the Selgovi east of the Novanti are the most hostile of the other tribes in the region with the Selgovi the worst of the lot. Banna is centered on the lands claimed by the Selgovi. You'll be the senior officer at Banna and will be under the command of the senior tribune at *Uxellodunum* here," pointing again to the map, "located about twenty miles west of you."

"Who commands at Uxellodunum?"

"No one at present, but I'm told a battle-tested tribune from Rome is on the way. As soon as he arrives, General Arvinnius's intent is to position him at Uxellodunum and put him in command of the entire Wall. In the meantime, General Arvinnius is temporarily making his headquarters there. Do you have any questions?"

"What's the name of the tribune?"

"You should know him as he was also with the Twenty-second Legion. His name's Tiberius Querinius. I'm told he was highly-decorated. Sounds just like the kind of man we need out here."

Arrius stared at the tribune in stunned disbelief. Something about the look on the centurion's face caused Trebius to ask, "You know of him?"

Arrius nodded, not trusting himself to speak. He realized he had no way of proving Querinius's suspected involvement in the attempt on his life. Nor could he speak of his cowardice in the Sorek Valley without a witness. He had no choice but to refrain from saying anything negative for fear any such unsubstantiated claims would be passed off as a personal grudge.

"By your face, you look as if you know the man or at least know of him."

"I do." He did not elaborate.

Trebius waited a moment longer for Arrius to comment further, and when it was apparent nothing else would follow, he said, "It's obvious there's more to this than you care to say, but we'll leave it for now. How soon can you leave?"

It had been Arrius's intent to remain in Eboracum for a few days, but given the last piece of information, he had a compelling reason to leave as soon as possible for fear he would be tempted to say something about Querinius. "I'll leave tomorrow."

"Good. I'll have an orderly conduct you to the quaestor to arrange for provisions and barracks to quarter your men for the night. With half the legion on detached duty in the north, there's ample room. Later, I'll give you the details concerning how the frontier defense is organized including information about the indigenous tribes you'll encounter on both sides of the wall. By the way, did I mention you're going to escort one of the northern tribal chiefs back to Banna? His name is Beldorach, and he's the clan chief of the Selgovae Tribe. I've no doubt he's been down here trying to get the Brigantes to revolt along with the northern tribes. It isn't the first time, and it won't be the last. If it were up to me, I'd run a sword through him, but Arvinnius thinks that would only give the Selgovi another reason to start trouble. We can't afford to risk that now. Take him to the border and release him. Don't trust him; he's a tricky bastard."

"Before you leave, go to the *Sacellum* and give your oath to General Arvinnius. The standard bearer will be notified to await your call and accompany you to witness your oath."

Arrius left Trebius too numb to think of anything but how *Fortuna* had turned her back on him. He regretted not killing the bastard in the medical tent when he had provocation and opportunity.

Early the next morning, Arrius looked on with interest as Beldorach was brought forward in chains and under heavy guard walking behind Trebius toward the Tungrian formation lined up and ready to march. One of the guards carried a bundle presumably containing the prisoner's possessions, a bow with a quiver of arrows and a long spear. He was curious about the tribal chief who despite the cold temperature was dressed in a leather shirt over which he wore a sleeveless vest of sheepskin. A saffron-colored woolen cloak was draped across his right shoulder. He wore leather breeches not unlike the Roman-style brecae. From knee to ankle-length boots, his legs were wrapped with wide strips of animal fur. His long copper hair was shot with grey and partly-braided along the sides and gathered at the back of the neck from where it hung down loose nearly halfway to his waist. His only facial hair consisted of long moustaches that drooped down on either side of his mouth.

The manacles, a split lip and bruises on his face did nothing to diminish the Selgovan's haughty composure who seemed indifferent to what was happening around him. Arrius thought Beldorach was like a caged lion about to be released into the arena, high-strung, menacing and waiting for a chance to strike.

Stopping in front of Arrius, Trebius gestured in the direction of the Selgovan. "This is Beldorach. Keep a close eye on him until you reach the border then release him. I don't much care what kind of shape he's in when you part company if he's still alive. I don't want him dying on this side of the border. Now if the bastard freezes to death north of the Wall, I'd not consider that a terrible thing." If the Selgovan understood Trebius's blunt words, he gave no indication.

Deciding it was past time to be on the way, Arrius signaled to the guards to put the prisoner on one of the supply wagons. The guards picked him up and unceremoniously threw him and his bundles on top of the nearest wagon.

It was only when one of the Tungrians led Ferox over to Arrius that Beldorach showed any sign of interest, his eyes widening as he stared intently at the large stallion stamping impatiently nearby, its nostrils flaring. Taking note of the stallion for the first time, Trebius stepped back a pace.

"Arrius, where did you get such a beast? I'll wager there's none larger in all Britannia or meaner from the look of him."

"I bought Ferox in southern Gaul from an owner who seemed very anxious to part with him. I soon found out why. He doesn't take to gentle words or handling." Arrius vaulted onto the saddle and with a tight rein turned the prancing horse to face Trebius who remained a safe distance away.

"Well, he looks arrogant and ferocious enough to justify the name. Arrius, I've no doubt you'll have your work cut out to make up for the shortcomings of your predecessor. Keep a close watch on the barbarians in the north and an even sharper eye on the locals on this side of the border. Don't trust any of them." Without waiting for a response or a word of farewell, the tribune turned on his heel and walked back to the principia.

Arrius nodded to Decrius who bellowed the order for the detachment to march toward the north gate of the fortress. As he moved to the head of the column, he passed the wagon in which Beldorach rode. Expressionless, the Selgovan ignored him and stared intently at the stallion.

Chapter 4

Although Hadrian looked for every way possible to distance himself from the Jewish war, Querinius did just the opposite. At every opportunity, he wore the torque Turbo had placed around his neck. In Rome where self-aggrandizement was a well-established and accepted way of life, Tiberius Querinius had no difficulty blending in to the social and political fabric of the city's elite. He played the role of hero simply because he believed it from the time Turbo had finished tying the decoration around his neck. He was quite happy to ensure those who had not heard of the battle in the Sorek Valley were made aware of his exploits, modestly understating his own contribution in a calculated effort to underscore his heroic part in saving the legion's eagle. In time, he'd almost come to believe the mythical proportions of his steadfast courage in the face of such overwhelming odds, odds that continued to grow in the retelling. His military service most honorably completed for the time being, he looked forward to taking a seat in the senate and enjoying the perquisites associated with that distinguished, if not necessarily influential, body. As both a hero of the empire and a rising political star with influence growing by the day, he had every reason to expect his future was bright and unlimited.

When he received his summons to visit the palace, he was certain he was about to receive the personal, if somewhat belated, attention of the emperor himself. A private audience with the emperor was a still a highly coveted and envied symbol that you had *dignitas,* even if the prestige associated with seeing the emperor was perhaps no longer the honor it once was. The rumors of the emperor's failing health and worsening temper were the subject of much speculation and inspired growing interest in who Hadrian would choose as his successor. In any event, his perceived celebrity status made Querinius even more unprepared for the calamity that befell him.

After climbing out of the sedan chair at Hadrian's sumptuous palace on the outskirts of Rome, he was ushered unceremoniously into a small, unpretentious antechamber where he found the familiar figure of General Lucius Turbo in animated discussion with several men he did not know. He assumed correctly the other individuals were members of the emperor's or Turbo's personal staff. The small group was clustered around a table, attention focused entirely on a map spread out before them. Eventually, Turbo glanced up and saw the tribune waiting impatiently to be noticed.

"Querinius, there you are." Turbo turned to the other men and announced, "Gentlemen, this is Tiberius Querinius, senior tribune formerly with the Twenty-second legion recently disbanded in Judaea. I believe Querinius is exactly the man General Arvinnius had in mind when he requested an immediate replacement for one of his auxilia commands." Then turning back to Querinius, he said with a smile, "Querinius, you have a new appointment approved by the emperor that I'm sure will please you immensely. It may also present you with opportunities to add more luster to your already distinguished name."

With a sinking feeling, Querinius stammered, "General, I'm not certain I understand what you mean."

"Why, Querinius, you've been reappointed to the tribunate and posted to Britannia where you will report to General Arvinnius now commanding the VI Legion, *Victrix* at Eboracum. General Arvinnius will specify the command you will assume. May I congratulate you on your good fortune?" Then noticing the shocked look on Querinius's face, Turbo said, "I realize such an unsuspected honor has caught you completely by surprise, but your remarkable record in Judaea convinced me you're the right man for General Arvinnius. I'm happy to say, the emperor agrees. I can think of no one better qualified than you are for this important assignment."

Querinius's mind was spinning as he tried to think of some way to reverse the impending disaster without making it appear the last thing in the world he wanted to do was to reprise his military service until it was time to command a legion, which hopefully would then be in the most peaceful province in the Roman Empire.

"But, General Turbo, I'm to take my senate seat in a few days. I'm afraid I'm not free to accept another military assignment at present." He was doing his best to adopt a convincing tone of regret.

"Nonsense, Querinius. The senate can wait. You'll have time and opportunity to do your duty with the senate later. Besides, what real value is there in the senate these days when it's the emperor who dictates what laws they will propose." Turbo's humorless chuckle left no doubt as to his opinion of that body. "No, Querinius, one cannot compare the obligatory, not to mention unexciting, requirement to be a senator with the honor and responsibility of military service and the chance as a tribune to have a command of your own."

Becoming more desperate by the moment, Querinius tried another tact. "General Turbo, I appreciate the honor; however, since I've so recently returned to Rome, I have not settled many of my personal affairs badly neglected while I served in Judaea."

"Querinius, what is more important than going to Britannia and serving your emperor? You almost sound as if you're reluctant to accept the appointment." Turbo's eyes narrowed and his voice took on an edge. "You would not presume to refuse the emperor's bidding? Such a decision would, shall I say, be exceedingly unwise, perhaps even dangerous."

Querinius realized it was useless to pursue the matter further without risking more than if he simply went to Britannia and made the best of it. He forced a smile and an expression he hoped showed relief. "You reassure me, General. My conscience is now clear. I most humbly and gratefully accept the appointment."

"Good, good. That's settled. Now step over here to the map, and I'll give you an idea of General Arvinnius's needs."

As Querinius walked over to the table, he risked a question he was almost afraid to ask. "How soon must I leave?"

"Why, right away, of course. General Arvinnius reports the Britannian tribes are once again showing signs of unrest and hostilities. It's a long way there so I expect you should be on the way within a few days. Haste, Querinius, haste, there's no time to lose." Turbo handed him two scrolls bearing Hadrian's seal, one presumably his reappointment to the tribunate, the other his orders to proceed to Britannia. Querinius fancied there was a glint of amusement in Turbo's eyes as he reached to take the documents.

Without catching so much as a glimpse of Hadrian, he left the palace in shock rapidly descending into the depths of despair. As the bearers began the return trip to Rome, the usual comfort of the swaying sedan chair became annoying rather than relaxing. He began to feel the familiar icy fingers of fear. Was it his imagination, or was there something about Turbo's manner that in retrospect suggested another motive for his new assignment? Perhaps Turbo knew the truth of what really happened during the last hours of the *Deiotariana* and his less than glorious behavior. Britannia then was merely Turbo's solution to a potential problem, a problem that would prove extremely embarrassing to Turbo and the emperor as well if the truth of his questionable behavior were revealed. If that was the case, it would explain why Turbo had selected him to go to Britannia. The decision had to be a clever and diabolical way to avoid a public and most unwelcome revelation concerning Rome's most recent and celebrated hero.

A sudden thought struck him. If he was right, the only way Turbo could have learned the truth was from Arrius. He didn't have the slightest doubt Arrius would go out of his way to discredit him. He remembered the centurion's cold eyes in the medical tent. For a moment, he thought Arrius was going to kill him. He vaguely recalled there was a past friendship between Arrius and Turbo, or so Gallius once mentioned. Had there been any discussion between the two men, it would seem likely Arrius reported the incident to Turbo. On the other hand, he'd been told the centurion's injuries had been serious. He began to rationalize a scenario in which Arrius had been too badly wounded to have seen Turbo, and if they had, perhaps the matter never came up. The thought filled him with euphoric hope, and he took heart in the thought. He had another revelation. Perhaps Arrius was dead from his wounds. His elation was quickly tempered by the sober realization that if the centurion had succumbed, he would have heard about it. Again, a wave of depression washed over him. He couldn't believe how badly the high tide of fortune had not only ebbed but had left his ship of high expectation derelict on the rocks of despair. Somehow, it must be the fault of the centurion, may the gods punish him through eternity.

He wondered where Arrius was. Until now, he had not fully comprehended the extent to which Arrius represented a continuing threat to his reputation. His blood ran cold at the consequences of a public disclosure. He would be subjected to unspeakable humiliation if that happened. The emperor would repudiate him, and he would become an object of ridicule without any choice but exile and a life of obscurity somewhere in the far reaches of the empire — somewhere such as Britannia.

Querinius began to spiral downward into a well of self-pity. Why should he be made to suffer such a fate for a momentary lapse? After all, fear was common enough. He'd heard stories from those seasoned in battle laughing uproariously after relating how they'd lost control and pissed themselves or even worse. In the telling, it served to further emphasize the perilous circumstances of the battle experience, overcoming a paralyzing fear stark enough to loosen bladder and bowel. It was the extent of the carnage around him that triggered his numbing paralysis. The medical tent did not shut out the sounds of the raging battle, but it did conceal the horrific sight threatening to drive him mad. The limited battle experience he'd been exposed to before had not come close to preparing him for the scope and brutality of that awful battle. He had yet to shake the image burned into his memory of legionaries dying all around him, the sound of agonized screams as Jew and Roman fought without quarter and the earth awash with blood. In some perverse way, he almost envied the dead legionaries who no longer had to be concerned with the fear of dying or even the worse fate of exposure and public condemnation for being unable to deal with it.

He felt a sudden need to urinate, and the motion of the chair rapidly accentuated the feeling. He yelled to the bearers to stop and headed for the nearest shrubbery. Nearly doubled over with urgency and unmindful of the amused pedestrians passing by, he fumbled under his tunic freeing himself just in time as the stream cascaded onto the ground. He regained control of his emotions and motioned for the bearers to move on. Calmer now, he began to think more clearly.

Clinically, he recalled the meeting with Turbo, recounting in his mind every word and gesture to determine if Turbo really did know the truth. In a flash, he knew Turbo did not. If Arrius had said anything to Turbo before the ceremony, the torque would never have been awarded in the first place, and if Arrius told Turbo afterward, the matter would have been settled before Turbo and he left Judaea. Therefore, the posting to Britannia was just as Turbo said, recognition of his abilities and not a means to rectify an embarrassing mistake. That left Arrius the only one who knew what happened. If Arrius had not said anything to Turbo, it was likely he did not intend to. The only other person Arrius might have told was Attius Varro, the camp praefectus, and that hardly mattered as Varro had perished in the battle. But still, the

213

centurion represented a continuing threat to his peace of mind and to his future. He cursed Aculineous again for his failure to do the job he'd been paid to do.

By the time he reached Rome, Tiberius Querinius was resigned to the fact there was no way out of his dilemma. In self-pity, he wondered why the gods should lift him up to the pinnacle of fame and fortune only to cast him down. He indulged himself in the fantasy of running a sword through the centurion's belly and watching him die a slow lingering death. Perhaps the day would come when there would be another opportunity to finish what Aculineous was unable to do.

Chapter 5

Several miles north of Eboracum and with the city no longer visible in the distance, Arrius called the first halt. While the legionaries sprawled along the road taking their ease and talking among themselves, he dismounted and led Ferox to the wagon carrying Beldorach. As he approached, he saw the Selgovan's attention seemed to be focused only on the horse.

"Do you speak my language?" Arrius asked.

Beldorach's eyes shifted from the horse to Arrius and fixed him with an unblinking stare. Just as Arrius decided the captive did not, Beldorach nodded.

"I've always made a point to be able to understand and talk to my enemies," Beldorach said in accented but understandable Latin.

"Good, then you may get down from the wagon and relieve yourself if you wish."

"Aren't you afraid I'll try to escape if I do?"

"I doubt you'll get very far in those," Arrius gestured to the chains.

"Perhaps I'll take your horse."

"You may find that more challenging than you think. Ferox does not take to being ridden, particularly by strangers with ankle chains."

"Somehow, Roman, I don't believe either reason is very compelling. We barbarians have a way with horses you Romans do not. As for the chains, well, I don't believe that's a problem either."

Beldorach nimbly vaulted from the wagon, and Arrius saw the Selgovan was no longer wearing the leg chains. Then as if to prove the other point, Beldorach approached Ferox and laid a reassuring hand on the horse's neck while gently stroking its nose with the other. To Arrius's chagrin, the horse responded by leaning submissively into the Selgovan.

"I can see I'll have to keep you under closer guard."

"There's no need. If I had wanted to leave, I would have already been gone by now. There are two good reasons why I will remain with you. The first is you happen to be going where I wish to go; the second is that I prefer a Roman escort as a safer way to travel through the tribal lands of the Briganti who would be happy to separate my head from my shoulders."

"Do I have your word that you won't attempt to escape?"

For a moment Beldorach searched Arrius's face to see if he was serious. After a brief pause, he said, "You would take the word of a barbarian?"

"I would take any man's word if I had reason to trust him although Tribune Trebius said not to."

Beldorach threw his head back and laughed. "The old one-eyed bastard was right not to trust me anymore than I would trust him. He and I have crossed paths before, and one day one of us will probably kill the other. The only reason he didn't kill me days ago is that he knows it would risk another uprising. But to answer your question, Roman, when it comes to my friends, I can be trusted as well as the next. My enemies would surely say different."

"Since we're not friends, are we enemies?"

"Romans have been my enemy since before I was born, but I can make an exception in your case for the time it takes us to reach Banna. After that, should we meet in my tribal lands, I would not expect a friendly reception."

"Very well, I'll trust you. Do I need to remove the chains from your wrists, or can you manage that yourself?"

"I confess I was having a bit more difficulty with them than I did with the leg shackles." Beldorach moved away from Ferox and extended his hands.

Arrius motioned for his orderly to unlock the chains. "I warn you, if you abuse my trust in any way, you'll wish you were back with Trebius. Now, you may either walk or ride," indicating the wagon as he mounted Ferox.

"I would prefer to ride him." He pointed to the horse.

"That's not an option."

"Perhaps one day it will be. Have a care, Roman, if you go north, you may find it difficult to keep such a fine horse."

"You may find it more difficult to have him than you believe."

Later that day, the camp's defenses completed to his satisfaction, Arrius allowed the legionaries to begin preparing their evening rations. He watched Philos and the slaves making similar preparations for his own meal, and it occurred to him that he'd given no further thought to Beldorach since his conversation with him that morning. Now that he thought about it, he hadn't seen him since the legionaries began digging the camp entrenchment. After walking the length of the camp and not finding him, he was reluctantly concluding he had been fooled into believing Beldorach understood the concept of honor. Trebius had been right, and he cursed his folly in trusting the Selgovan. It was far too late to mount a credible search. He turned to walk back to his tent only to come face to face with the tribal chief calmly chewing on a root.

"Looking for me?"

"I was. I was beginning to think you may have decided to go on without your escort."

"I admit it was a thought, but I quickly realized there was nothing to be gained, and after all, I'd given my word."

"It was my intention to offer you something to eat, but I see you've already seen to that." He indicated the root-like tuber Beldorach was holding.

"Well, it didn't appear anyone was overly concerned whether I had anything to eat so I thought it best to see to it myself; however, if you have something better to offer than this, I'll be happy to accept."

"I believe we can manage. Come with me."

Arrius led the way back to his tent and told Philos to fill another bowl. After the two men seated themselves, Philos returned with another camp stool and seated himself across from Beldorach.

"Beldorach, this is Philos."

Beldorach looked curiously at Philos. "Is he your steward and slave master?"

"Philos is more than my steward. He is also my closest friend. But to answer your question, he does supervise the slaves."

Beldorach nodded at the introduction and for a moment made no response before commenting harshly. "Unlike you Romans, the Selgovi do not hold with slavery. We believe men should not be made to live in such a way. I'm told there are more slaves in Rome than free men. I do not understand if there are so many slaves, why they are willing to submit to it."

"It's true there are many slaves in Rome, and occasionally there have been uprisings. But there have always been slaves and no doubt always will. Some, such as Philos, do not always remain as slaves. They earn their freedom by purchasing it or earning it. Occasionally, a slave owner will grant his slaves their freedom when he dies."

"I find your customs curious. Your practice of making slaves of those you conquer is the worst possible fate for a man or woman."

"Possibly. I've never given much thought to the matter. What do the Selgovi do with those they capture in battle?"

"We kill them or ransom them. Some join the tribe if they request it. Captives are often sacrificed to the gods."

"Is it then better to kill those you capture than to let them live as slaves?" Philos said.

"It is better for a man to die than live under the boot of another. I would never choose to live that way, and for that reason, I will never give in to you Romans."

"Giving in to Rome by treaty is not the same as becoming a slave to Rome. Throughout the empire, countries are treated well and allowed to practice their own religions, govern themselves and trade with whom they wish."

"That may be true according to the way you see it. I see it differently. If it's the way you describe, it's only because Rome dictates the rules. The Briganti have become your slaves even though they may not wear the shackles. They live the way Rome wants them to live and not because they are free to do what they want and go where they wish."

Arrius wasn't in the mood to debate the matter further finding the tribal leader's comments somewhat tiresome and not very original; however, he couldn't resist a final comment. "If it were not Rome, it would be another country that would conquer the others. It has always been that way, and I think it always will be. Perhaps one day it will be the Selgovi who will defeat Rome. Would the world be better for it?"

"It would at least be different, and there would be no Romans left on this island — they would either all be dead or Selgovan."

"And what about the Briganti and all the other tribes, would they also be willing to become Selgovan?" Philos asked.

"If they chose to be."

"What if another tribe than the Selgovi prevailed? What would you choose to do?"

"An interesting question, Roman, but since that will never happen, there is no need for an answer."

For a time, there was silence as the three men devoted their attention to eating. Philos was the first to speak when he asked curiously, "Do the markings on your arms have significance, or are they decorative?"

For a moment, Arrius thought Beldorach was about to ignore the question then he said, "They are decorative; however, they are also distinctive designs associated with the Selgovi. Each tribe has their own way to set them apart from the others. The Briganti, for example, favor facial tattoos as do the Votadini, while the Novanti do not favor tattoos but merely paint their faces. We, too, paint our faces blue for ceremonial occasions and when we go to war." Beldorach looked at Arrius before continuing in a contemptuous voice. "I noticed by the markings on his face one of your soldiers is a Briganti."

"It's true, and Decrius happens to be a fine optio, possibly one of the best I've ever known."

"He's a Roman lapdog," Beldorach said. "You Romans are what you are, and I can respect that. You think you've conquered this land, but you merely occupy it for the time being. The Briganti have forgotten who they are. For that reason, such men will be among the first to die when you Romans leave."

"What makes you think Rome will leave?"

"One day you Romans will either go of your own free will, or you'll be made to leave. I favor driving you out with arrow and spear; it would be a quicker way to see the last of you."

"If we're defeated, then you will go back to fighting among yourselves."

"True, we do have our differences which I admit have proven to be advantageous to you Romans. One day we may overcome our mutual grievances long enough to end your detestable occupation."

"Are we so much worse than the tribes you make war upon?"

"Since the Romans have come, we can no longer move about the land as we were accustomed to do. You've built a great wall, and now we must seek permission to go when and where we once traveled as we pleased. You look down upon us because we live and depend on the land, while you Romans depend on those you conquer. You expect us to change our way of life and become more like you, and when we resist and tell you we do not wish this, you are angry and make war upon us. The tribes have been here for as long as anyone can remember. Yes, we make war on each other; however, that is the way it has always been long before you Romans came, and that is the way it will be after you've gone."

Arrius was impressed with the other man's passion. He considered Beldorach's words and found himself thinking of Sarah, the Jewish woman, who had expressed similar ideas.

Philos, who had remained silent, spoke. "Is it so terrible to change your ways and adapt to a new and better way of life? It appears the towns and farms we passed over the past two weeks are prosperous and the people seem content enough."

Again, Arrius wasn't certain the tribal leader would bother to answer. Slowly, Beldorach shifted his gaze to Philos, his lip curling in disdain before answering.

"We were more prosperous before Roman tax collectors arrived to make us pay for our own subjugation. We were more content before the Roman boot bore down on our necks. You insult me when you speak of changing our way of life, presuming to think as you say such a thing that our lives will be better for it. Because you have constructed large buildings, temples and great fortifications when we have not, is this reason enough to believe we should be grateful for your presence and choose to do similar things? If we did, does this make us less barbaric in the eyes of Rome? I think not, for we will always be the barbarian in your eyes and less than Roman in our own land. Perhaps if you took away the soldiers that man your forts and dismantled the wall that divides our country, we would be more willing to change our ways. But when change is forced upon us, do not expect us to thank you for it."

"It would seem if Decrius is an example, the Brigantes Tribe may not think entirely as you do."

Beldorach's expression and voice seemed less intense. "Unfortunately, I cannot dispute that as strongly as I would like. The day may come sooner than you think when the Briganti will wake up and discover they are no better than slaves. Then beware, Roman, for you will have difficulty holding on to what you now claim."

Beldorach abruptly drained his cup and then banged it down on the table. After carefully brushing the ends of his moustache with his fingers to remove any residue of the meal, he stood up. "I give thanks for the food and your fair treatment. I do not wish you to think me ungrateful; your hospitality is an improvement over that shown by Trebius these past several days. I've no doubt that old man would have kept me shackled if he were taking me back instead of you." His voice hardened. "But do not presume to think our truce of the moment is anything more than a temporary accommodation and an agreement that will not exist if you venture north. We are adversaries, you and I, and you should do well not to forget that. I assure you, Roman, I will not." With that, Beldorach turned and disappeared into the night.

"Marcus, I believe you have an enemy," Philos said with a wry smile.

"It's too bad, for under other circumstances, I would much prefer it if we were friends. There is something about this barbarian I find interesting. I have the feeling after we part at Banna, our paths will cross again."

Gradually as the procession traveled farther northwest, the land became more rugged. The rolling hills became steeper with treeless crests and heavily forested valleys in between. The narrow road often twisted around rocky and precipitous outcroppings. Frozen streams meandered in the lower elevations threading in between the hills creating now and then small icy ponds or marshes that even in the depth of winter provided a habitat for animals and birds. Under the snow-blanketed hills and forests, Arrius saw much of the land was under cultivation, and from the stubble poking up through the snow, the dominant crop looked to be grain. He recalled Trebius saying the auxilia forces, in addition to maintaining a forward defense, were also expected to assist the local farmers in the annual wheat harvest. Helping to plant and harvest the crop was considered an activity nearly as critical to Rome as repelling any attempted invasions. Of course, Rome extracted that much more in tax from the farmers who received legionary assistance.

Although there were occasional settlements, the population throughout the area they traveled was sparse and consisted mainly of isolated homesteads that appeared prosperous indicated by the number of sheep and cattle foraging on the hillsides. The Roman presence was noticeable. Tall stone towers manned by a handful of legionaries were spaced along the road a half day's march apart. Arrius was aware the towers were the primary means for relaying signals from the border to Deva and Eboracum should any trouble break out that would require reinforcements from the Sixth or Twentieth legion or possibly both. Reinforcement by the legions was the cornerstone of the frontier defense with the auxilia forces intended only as a delaying force in the event the northern tribes attacked the Wall.

Trebius had been right about the oxen. They encountered deep snow drifts in the valleys formed by the harsh winds that blew almost continuously baring the hill tops and slopes above at the expense of the valleys and draws below. On many occasions, the snow was too deep even for the oxen, and the legionaries had to clear the road.

Late on the fifth day, they reached *Bravoniacum*, a century-size fort of turf and timber construction with the now ubiquitous stone signal tower rising above it. The small fort was near a crossroads marking the way to Uxellodonum farther to the northwest or leading due north to Banna a shorter distance away. Decrius tactfully suggested to Arrius that since they were now less than a two day's march from their destination, it might be advisable to send word ahead of their impending arrival to allow time for an appropriate welcome for the new commander. Arrius agreed and decided to call an early halt to the day's march. Noticing a half-dozen horses standing in a corral next to the fort, he sent Decrius to find the commander of the tiny garrison with a request for a mounted courier to precede them to Banna.

Arrius had exchanged only a few words with Beldorach since the first night after leaving Eboracum. He had intended to talk further with the Selgovan to learn more about the northern tribe; however, the tribesman's taciturn demeanor and obvious effort to avoid any interaction discouraged it. Since they would be parting company as soon as they reached the Wall, he decided to make a final effort. He found the tribal chieftain leaning against one of the wagons silently observing the activities of the Tungrians preparing for the evening camp. Arrius noticed Beldorach no longer wore braided side-locks and instead wore his long hair loose and parted in the middle; a leather headband kept his face clear. Having always worn his own hair close-cropped, he wondered what it must be like to have hair that long.

"How much longer before you reach your home?"

"Three more days, probably four if I traveled as slowly as you Romans."

Arrius ignored the implied criticism. "Will you stay in Banna for a time, or will you travel on?"

"There's no reason for me to stay there any longer than it takes to piss. I've no interest in Banna except perhaps to destroy it one day."

Arrius pointed toward the small settlement a short distance from the fort. "Are your homes and villages like those?"

Beldorach looked contemptuously at the cluster of small, square-shaped dwellings with thatch roofs resembling stone islands in a sea of mud. "The Briganti are soft and do not live with the threat of raids as we do. Our houses are circular for better defense against the harsh winds and attacks from the other tribes," Beldorach paused slightly before adding, "and the Romans."

"I was led to believe there is peace between Rome and the Selgovi."

Beldorach laughed without humor. "You Romans think because you haven't been attacked for a few months, there's peace between us. Peace is more a wish on your part than a reality for us. There will never be a lasting peace so long as our lands are occupied by a foreign invader."

Arrius was becoming irritated at the Selgovan's belligerent and increasingly caustic responses. He suppressed his growing resentment and dislike of Beldorach in the interest of trying to learn more about the man and the people he might one day have to meet in battle.

"I believe if we Romans were not here, this land would not be peaceful. Your way is to provoke warfare, not to promote peace."

"That is a strange comment coming from a Roman, and one who has undoubtedly seen much of warfare. I'm told your empire is vast, and you won it at the point of a sword, not by words. When Romans speak of peace, it is only after you've taken what you want and to better secure what you occupy before you go somewhere else to take more."

Arrius thought Beldorach had a point. It was strange how the barbarian summarized a reality he'd never consciously considered. He preferred to think Rome had extended civilization throughout the world leaving behind a better condition than before the arrival of Roman legionaries. The wasteland of Judaea came to mind, and he wasn't so certain.

"I can see my words have given you something to think about," Beldorach said quietly, noting the other man's thoughtful silence. When Arrius continued to make no response, Beldorach continued, his previous antagonistic manner replaced with a speculative look. "You seem different from other Romans I've encountered. Why is that?"

Somewhat taken aback by the direct question, Arrius said, "I didn't realize that I was."

"Perhaps because you were too busy carrying out your orders to take what Rome wanted."

He was unwilling to leave the debate decided in the tribesman's favor. "What of the Selgovi and the other tribes? Do they not take what they can, when they can?"

"It's true, but most of the time we take only a few cattle and horses. Such pursuits merely allow our young men opportunities to prove their mettle and win individual honor."

"Have you never attempted to defeat another tribe and seize their lands?"

"It has happened from time to time," he admitted.

"Then what makes the Selgovi different from the Romans?"

"The difference, Roman, is that you come from somewhere else and then try to change those who you conquer into Romans, and that is the worst of what you do."

"You're wrong, Beldorach, we make no attempt to change the way people think or the gods they worship. The empire is comprised of many different civilizations, and the diversity has created a better life for most of those who have seen fit to take advantage of what Rome has to offer."

"But for those who choose to reject Rome's offerings, there is a bitter cost and a life of slavery."

"Would it then be a better world if the Selgovi were to replace Rome? Would you seek to let the world remain as you know it, or would you follow the destiny Rome has been given to rule the world and make it better than it was?"

"Possibly not, but then we will never know. The Selgovi are too few to do anything but try and keep what we have left — at least for now. Our strength lies in our willingness to wait until Rome is no longer able or has the will to hold on to what it has conquered. There are many tribes like the Selgovi that are waiting for the opportunity to destroy your empire."

"We see things differently, Beldorach. I accept things as they are, for I don't have the responsibility or the charge to lead a people as you have been given. My allegiance to Rome has nothing to do with conquering the Selgovi or even trying to change what you believe or how you live. My responsibility is to lead my legionaries as they deserve to be led. If I must lead them to do things I may not like, so be it, and I will not hesitate to take them where I must and do what I am ordered."

"Spoken like a true Roman soldier. I feel sorry for you," Beldorach said quietly without any sign of his former belligerence. "You think you have everything, yet you have nothing but the responsibility to defend what others own. You have no home but a stone fortress in a foreign land while I at least have fields and forests that I can lay claim to. You call us barbarian for you do not bother to learn our tongue; therefore, we seem uncultured. You say we are uncivilized and warlike because we resist. But then, Roman, who are the real barbarians?"

Arrius was more impressed with Beldorach's logic and eloquence than he showed. The Selgovan had come close to echoing some of his own thoughts.

"Beldorach, we'll leave the debate as it is for now. Perhaps there will be another time and place for one of us to change the other's mind."

Arrius walked away to meet a young centurion dressed in full armor hurrying from the fort in his direction.

Beldorach watched Arrius talking to the centurion and thought with surprising regret, if circumstances were different, there was a man you would want to stand beside you on a battlefield instead of opposite.

Chapter 6

Under a bright, mid-morning sun, Arrius reined in Ferox at the top of a hill to allow the detachment to catch up. He was arrayed in his best cuirass, helmet and greaves polished to a dazzling shine. Philos had kept the slaves busy the night before to ensure he would make a favorable first impression on the Banna garrison. The last time he had donned his parade armor was to board the ship at Joppa the day they left Judaea. If what Trebius had more than intimated was true about the previous commander's shortcomings, the garrison's initial impression of their new commander was critical and justified the discomfort of the heavier cuirass.

Arrius looked more closely at the valley below. *By the gods, I've been here before.* He suddenly recalled Hadrian standing on top of the escarpment ahead while conferring with the governor and the legion's officers. Now he realized it was the construction of the impressive monument stretching before him they had probably been discussing. The memories of the place began to slowly crystallize in his mind. It had been a rainy evening as the legionaries prepared camp, and as the legion's standard bearer, he had been doubly concerned about the sodden ground lest the eagle standard fall in the night. When he wasn't checking the standard to ensure it remained solidly positioned, he had stayed awake worrying that it might come loose and fall, a catastrophe that would have cost him his life.

He looked at the valley below and the long ridgeline that stretched east to west and saw why Hadrian had directed the monolithic barrier to be constructed where it was. The fort directly across the valley a mile away that he was about to command had been named Banna for the rocky spur upon which it was positioned and the small river that made an abrupt loop to the south before passing under the Wall. A half-mile from the fort's east gate was a stone bridge that gave additional reason for locating the fort on the high ground above. Built from sandstone, Banna was a natural defensive position with its north face forming part of the Wall.

The village sprawled outside the east and west gates with the greater number of buildings located on the east side. The settlement appeared to be a thriving community, undoubtedly owing much of its evident prosperity to the proximity of the fort. But it was the Wall itself extending on either side of the fort's north face that continued to hold his attention. The crenellated stone barrier stretched generally east and west, undulating across the rolling countryside until it disappeared in the far distance. Rising above the height of the wall at mile intervals, smaller forts were incorporated into the wall defense. Between each mile fort were two smaller square towers. Even this far away, the helmets of legionaries patrolling the wall glinted in the pale sunlight.

Arrius remained in the lead as they descended into the valley toward the bridge. He heard the blast of a trumpet from the fort, undoubtedly announcing their arrival. Alerted by the sound, villagers emerged from their predominantly stone dwellings to stare silently at the legionaries passing by, their expressionless faces giving no hint of either welcome or hostility. Most wore Roman-style clothing consisting of heavy woolen tunics and lighter weight leggings as a concession to the winter weather; however, here and there he saw the more traditional native attire made from various animal skins. Many of the villagers had intricate designs tattooed or painted in blue on their faces.

"Roman, it seems we are about to part company, and our truce, such as it was, will soon be over."

Arrius looked down and saw Beldorach keeping pace with Ferox and saw he had painted his face blue.

"Are you so anxious to leave Rome's hospitality?"

"I find Roman hospitality somewhat lacking, and I think your food is not fit for a dog."

Arrius privately agreed with him. "I see you've painted your face. Are you so eager to go to war with Rome?"

"I will always be at war with Rome as long as you continue to occupy our land and desecrate it with your great stone wall and forts."

"One day you may come to realize peace with Rome has advantages."

"Peace with Rome has advantages only for Romans, and what do you know of peace? You've been the sword of Rome for most of your life. I pity you for you will eventually die for Rome without ever knowing what it is to be free."

Arrius remained silent. This was the second time Beldorach had said these things during the past several days. The first time he countered the arguments. Since then he gave more thought to what the tribesman said. Reluctantly he had to admit there was some truth to it. He wondered if he would have thought about it at all if he hadn't gone to Judaea. He was about to respond when he saw a woman burst through the door of a Roman-style villa with two men in pursuit.

Ilya had a premonition the two off-duty legionaries at a corner table were going to be trouble. Their surly, belligerent behavior had already driven away the other early morning customers. After they began taking more notice of her than the wine, she became concerned and wished Attorix was here; however, he wasn't due to arrive for several more hours. When one of them asked for more wine, she decided it was time to close the tavern.

"There will be no more wine served this morning; the tavern is closing. Your bill is twelve sestercii. Pay what you owe and leave."

"We'll leave when we want to," the larger of the two said. "Now bring another pitcher, or I'll get it myself."

She put her hands on her hips and tried to look assertive. "Don't force me to report you —"

Before she finished, the legionary stood up and started toward her. She backed toward the door thinking once she got outside she would be able to outrun them. At that moment, Joric entered the room unaware of what was happening. Before she could warn him, the other man leaped up and grabbed Joric. Although Joric was almost full grown, he was no match for the burly legionary who drew his dagger and held the point to the boy's throat.

"If you don't want to see the boy carved up, you'll bring more wine."

Realizing she had no other choice, she nodded in assent and wordlessly left the room. While out of sight, she took the opportunity to slip a kitchen knife under her robes. She hoped the bulge would not be noticeable. When she re-entered the room with the wine, she saw the two men were once again seated. Joric sat between the larger of the two men and the wall. She tried to disguise her alarm thinking a calm presence might well be met by similar behavior. In the meantime, if they drank enough, the effects of the wine might itself be a solution to their dilemma. At the very least, it might delay any further unpleasantness until other customers arrived to intervene in their behalf.

As she poured the wine, she realized she was trembling. She accidentally spilled some of the wine on the arm of the legionary sitting across from Joric. Before she realized what had happened, she was sent sprawling against a nearby table from a backhanded blow to her cheek. Stunned more than hurt, she was dimly aware of Joric launching himself at her attacker. The legionary merely laughed and fended him off without effort sending the boy tumbling helplessly to the floor. She realized she had to do something now before matters escalated further. She didn't want to risk Joric's safety no matter what they might do to her.

While she was still trying to think of something, her assailant leaned over and roughly pulled her to her feet. She made a frantic grab for the kitchen knife but wasn't fast enough. Holding her by the waist with one hand and groping her with the other, she tried desperately to push him away. Her left hand brushed the hilt of his dagger, and she quickly seized the opportunity. She drew the blade and plunged it into the man's side. She knew the wound wasn't serious, but it was painful enough for him to release her. She yelled to Joric to run even as she herself made for the nearest door thinking the distraction might be enough for Joric to make his escape and get help. She burst through the door and ran.

Arrius saw from their distinctive and wide military belts the two men pursuing the woman were legionaries. A young boy ran after the trio. The woman was starting to outdistance her pursuers when she tripped and fell. The legionaries gave a triumphant shout as they caught up with her. Oblivious of the marching column approaching, one of the men grabbed the woman by the arm and pulled her roughly back to her feet. When she resisted, he struck her across the face knocking her to the ground. By then, the boy had caught up to the woman's assailants and grabbed one of them from behind. Moments later, the boy was also sent tumbling to the ground. Undaunted, Arrius saw the boy pick up and throw a rock striking one of the men on the side of the face.

Furious, the injured man drew his dagger and started toward the defiant boy prompting angry muttering from the legionary ranks.

Initially, Arrius intended to ignore what appeared to be a domestic quarrel, but the weapon and the threat to the boy quickly changed his mind. Reacting automatically, he kicked Ferox into a canter and guided the horse toward the man wielding the dagger. Preoccupied as they were, the two men still not perceive the gathering audience observing the spectacle, nor did they hear the horse bearing down on them. Carefully maneuvering the stallion to avoid running over the woman still on her hands and knees, Arrius drew his sword and with the flat of the blade hit the first legionary on the top of the head. He felt a spasm of pain in his injured leg as he gripped the sides of the horse harder to keep from losing his balance. He turned the stallion toward the second man who stood frozen in stupefied surprise. Belatedly seeing he was about to suffer a similar fate, the now alarmed legionary began to run in a futile effort to escape. The horse brought an end to the drama by shouldering the legionary roughly to the ground where he remained, fearing if he did not, he would suffer more.

Arrius ordered Decrius to come forward and take the two men into custody. As Decrius quickly took charge of the thoroughly subdued and battered legionaries, Arrius walked Ferox over to the woman and boy standing with their arms around each other. From the uncertain expressions on their faces, he thought they must be worried their ordeal might not yet be over.

Ilya watched the mounted man approaching on the largest horse she'd ever seen. As he drew closer, she saw a terrible scar on his right cheek that the side plates of his helmet did not entirely conceal. She had never seen a more forbidding-looking man. When he spoke, his voice was surprisingly gentle as he asked with some concern if she and the boy were all right. The residual effects of the last few minutes had left her shaken, but now relief the incident was over was replaced with anger fueled by the image of Joric being threatened.

"No thanks to you and your mercenary brutes." Her voice shook in anger. "If you can't control your men better than this, I would prefer you keep them locked up in your fort. Better yet, why don't you Romans go back where you came from and leave us in peace?"

Taken aback by the ungrateful reaction, he said nothing while he quietly studied the angry, bareheaded woman. He saw a red mark on her cheek where she had been struck that showed prominently against her pale skin. Had her face not been twisted in a scowl, he thought she might be comely. She had long, copper-burnished hair that swirled around her in disarray; it had been a long time since he had seen hair on a woman that beautiful, if ever. He was both surprised and angered by her unwarranted hostility and was beginning to regret he had interceded. Then the image of the legionary with the dagger moving toward the boy flashed before him, and he knew why. In spite of the woman's ingratitude, he was glad he intervened.

Deciding that answering the woman was pointless, Arrius turned Ferox toward the road and said over his shoulder, "I'm glad I could have been of service."

As the detachment passed by, Beldorach kept a wagon between him and the villa. Although he was certain Ilya would not call attention to him, he didn't want to risk how Joric might react. He was of two minds over what he had witnessed. Had the two legionaries not been interrupted, perhaps his position as High Chieftain would no longer be in jeopardy. He wished the gods would make up their minds and decide the issue one way or the other.

Chapter 7

Arrius thought the Wall was even more impressive the closer he got. Based on a legionary slowly patrolling the parapet, he estimated the height of the wall to be 14-16 feet to the parapet walkway and another six feet to the top of the crenellated merlons. At close range, the fortress appeared little different from other forts he had helped to erect or garrison during his lengthy service. Tile-roofed towers were located at each corner of the fort with interval towers positioned between the corner towers and each of the four gates. The one-hundred-foot-wide *vallum*, an earthwork nearly as impressive and monolithic as the wall itself, had been excavated on the south side of the wall. The trench was ten feet deep and centered between two parallel berms with sloping sides. A graveled causeway crossed the vallum leading directly into the fort's south gate.

As they passed through the village toward the east gate, he heard Decrius and Rufus behind him dressing the ranks and vowing dire consequences for any legionary unfortunate enough to be out of step. A detail of cavalry and legionaries was formed up to the left of the double-arched gate waiting for their arrival. Under the supervision of a stocky centurion, the honor guard consisted of four ranks of legionaries and a small cavalry formation in the rear.

Arrius guided Ferox to a position opposite the centurion while Decrius formed the Tungrian detachment behind him.

The centurion saluted. "I am Centurion Matius Betto. Welcome to Banna, Praefectus Arrius." The centurion's grim face was anything but welcoming.

Arrius was not pleased with what he saw including the man commanding the guard. If any extra attention had been given to his arrival, it wasn't evident in the slovenly appearance of the men standing before him. As his eyes slowly swept the ranks, he saw men whose appearance was not much better than the Tungrians behind him and with considerably less justification for it. He saw shields with badly-faded insignias, frayed tunics and helmets that had not seen a polishing cloth for some time. With more than a day's warning of his arrival, there had been ample time for the garrison to prepare for its new commander. Even the centurion who was either in the process of growing a beard or had not shaven that morning did not seem to have gone out of his way to make himself presentable for the occasion. He recollected Trebius's disparaging description of his predecessor and now saw indications the tribune's description of conditions at Banna appeared accurate.

Without dismounting, he raised his right hand and returned the salute. "By the authority granted by General Gaius Labinius Arvinnius, I assume command of Banna, the Second Tungrian Cohort and the First Dacian regiment at Fanum Cocidii. I want all officers and senior optiones present at the fort to report to the headquarters in one hour. Centurion, dismiss the honor guard and see to the quartering of my detail." He wheeled Ferox around and saw the tight expression on Decrius's face. He was certain the optio was embarrassed over the poor appearance of the honor guard. He had little doubt Decrius would have much to say to the other optiones before nightfall.

"See the men are assigned to barracks and the wagons unloaded. You and Rufus will also report to the headquarters with the others." He addressed Beldorach standing to one side. "I'll escort you to the north gate."

"I would prefer to leave through the fort farther to the west. It would save me most of a day to reach my village."

"Very well, but it will be a few more hours before we leave."

"I'm certain I can find my way there on my own if you consent to provide me with a pass. You no doubt have other more important things in mind besides me."

"My orders were to deliver you alive to the north of the wall. I intend to do exactly that."

Leaving Beldorach under guard at the gate, Arrius walked Ferox through the gloom of the high-ceilinged arch. The horse's hooves gave off a hollow echo from the cobblestones in the interior of the gate tower causing the horse to sidestep nervously. Emerging into the sunlight, he continued along the *via principalis*, the road leading from the east gate to the west gate and took in the interior of the fort with dismay. It was the small things that showed indifference. Dried horse dung still lying undisturbed, weeds growing between some of the cobblestones and a pile of debris someone had swept up and neglected to take away. While the shortcomings were quickly remedied, what concerned him was the underlying cause for them to exist at all. He hoped General Arvinnius would not visit Banna or Fanum Cocidii before he had a chance to ensure the garrisons were up to Roman standards.

He passed the spacious, tile-roofed praetorium on his left and was impressed with his new quarters that promised more luxury than he had ever enjoyed before. Opposite was a long building similar in size to the barracks but contained storerooms and workshops. Usually, the headquarters was the largest building in any fort; yet in the case of Banna, the praetorium was larger. Both buildings were dwarfed by a rectangular-shaped, two-story structure on the other side of the street Decrius had said was used for drill and indoor training because of the frequent inclement weather common to the region. Farther down the street were two long buildings with narrow ventilation slits instead of windows he guessed were granaries. Trebius had emphasized maintaining the supply and storage of grain was not only critical to the Banna garrison but to the Sixth Legion as well.

Arrius dismounted in front of the principia and handed the reins to an orderly before stepping inside the inner courtyard where he saw more signs of neglect. The latter was further indication of indifference on the part of the garrison officers and the long absence of an effective senior commander. When he entered the colonnaded hallway at the opposite end of the courtyard, his bleak expression was sufficient to cause the clerks clustered about the doorway observing his approach to scurry hastily back to their offices. Only two individuals remained where they were silently watching as he approached. They did not appear intimidated by his grim face.

"And who might you be?"

"I am Publius Gheta, your quaestor, and this is your administrator, Antius Durio."

Publius Gheta was a tall, saturnine individual with deep-set eyes that showed a lively intelligence. Arrius guessed his age at close to his. His forearms and hands bore the white puckered scars of severe burns. Seeing the focus of the centurion's attention, the quaestor said with a brief smile as he held up his hands, "The Parthians were fond of using incendiaries," referring to the phosphorous-based mixture called Greek fire that was virtually impossible to put out.

Given the severity of the burns, he was surprised Gheta had managed to remain in the army and attain the rank and position of quaestor; that alone said something positive concerning his abilities.

In contrast to Publius Gheta, Arrius was surprised by the other man's comparative youth. Where Publius Gheta was tall, lean and dark, Antius Durio was the physical opposite. Although young, he had the impression the administrator was both bright and capable.

With Arrius maintaining a grim silence, the two men conducted a brief, impromptu tour of the headquarters building stopping briefly at the Sacellum where all three men paused dutifully to give a quick prayer to the cohort's standard within. He was assured the *aerarium*, the cohort's pay chest, was present under the floor below; he was curious as to how many denarii might be in the pay chest and resolved to get an accounting before the day was out. By the time he was shown his office, Decrius arrived to inform him the centurions and optiones were waiting in the outer courtyard.

Arrius left his helmet on the table and with the quartermaster and chief administrator following behind, made his way back to the courtyard. Nine centurions, almost as many decurions, thirty-odd optiones and other junior officers associated with garrison supply and administration were talking quietly among themselves while waiting for his arrival. The doorways and windows on either side of the courtyard were crowded with the clerks assigned to the headquarters. The centurion in charge of the honor guard called attention. Arrius nodded and gave permission to stand easy. After hearing Trebius's doleful predictions of what he would find, he had given much thought concerning his first comments and orders. It would do no good, nor would it enhance his own position, if he simply rounded on them for any shortcomings, real or perceived. He was certain in the brief time he had been at Banna he had seen only indicators that likely did not reflect either the best or the worst he would find later.

"It is my honor to assume command. My recent experience with what remains of the Tungrian vexillation that returned with me from Judaea suggests how fortunate I am to have such brave men to command. I have no doubt I will be similarly impressed with the Dacian regiment at Fanum Cocidii when I go there. In case you are wondering, I asked to come here even though some would speculate, and others would suspect, I somehow displeased both the emperor and the gods." A ripple of laughter echoed in the courtyard. "It's true, there are perhaps more desirable places to serve the empire, perhaps even drier I'm told," he waited for the laughter to subside at the understated remark. "That may be so, but I see this place and our presence here as an essential link in the chain of Rome's defense. It is no punishment to be here; rather it is an honor to be entrusted with such an important mission as we have been tasked to perform." He paused a moment before continuing in a voice that rang with steel, "And any man, whether legionary or centurion, who does not believe so will wish himself far away from this place, for such a man has the profound misfortune to be under my command. Now, I wish to meet each one of you so that I can begin to know you."

The first individual he greeted was the centurion in command of the honor guard whom he correctly surmised was the senior centurion, Matius Betto. It was not a good sign the centurion avoided meeting his eyes while they exchanged a few words. Arrius's first impression of the centurion was not favorable, and the second did not improve it; however, he intended to give his nominal second in command the benefit of the doubt. Nevertheless, he had the feeling Matius Betto would bear watching.

A few hours later escorted by a cavalry troop, Arrius and Beldorach galloped out of the west gate. His destination was the third and most distant mile-fort that Matius Betto informed him marked the western limit of his command. His intent was to make a brief inspection of each fort and the smaller towers midway between the forts before returning to Banna. He intended to visit the eastern section of his command tomorrow and the most forward defense, the Dacian cavalry cohort at Fanum Cocidii, the day following. The visit to the forward post would require an overnight absence.

As they rode through the west village, Arrius observed the buildings seemed to be primarily commercial enterprises. Shops with open stalls displayed a variety of goods consisting of clothing, animal skins, shoes and food items. A blacksmith paused in his labors to watch them pass by. A long timber building separated from the rest he guessed must be the local brothel from several off-duty legionaries he saw lounging about. Just outside the settlement, they passed a large field that contained the training devices and targets for cavalry and archery practice. The patches of untracked snow on the field was indication enough it had seen little recent use.

Each turret and mile-fort they passed was similar in construction and appearance. The turrets were 20-foot square towers each housing an eight-man contubernium assigned to patrol a section of the Wall. The larger mile-forts were manned by 60 legionaries and functioned as turreted gatehouses with a wide, single-arched portal monitoring north-south wagon and pedestrian traffic through the Wall. Identical to the gates at Banna, the portal doors were constructed of thick wood faced on the outside with iron panels. A small guardroom flanked one side of the arch providing an opportunity for guards below to monitor the traffic passing through. Opposite the guard rooms was a small room where the despised wagon and pedestrian tax was assessed.

The legionaries occupying the forts were lodged in rooms above the gate accessible by an internal stairway. Within the small towers, the legionaries were billeted on the ground floor in a small bay that would accommodate six men, the assumption being there would always be at least two men on guard. The centuries occupying the forts and towers remained on duty for a week. Matius Betto had said the replacement shifts were staggered to prevent an erosion of vigilance along the wall that might be caused if the shift change occurred all at the same time. Arrius thought the routine was a good practice and planned to continue it. From long experience gained along the Rhine frontier, the soporific effects of monotonous duty reduced vigilance and created additional tension among the men.

Word of their impending arrival had preceded them; consequently, the centurion in command of the most distant mile fort was standing by the south entrance waiting for their arrival. Arrius saw nothing outwardly amiss as he dismounted and received the officer's report. His initial impression was favorable, suggesting the guard detail had taken advantage of the time it took him to get there to prepare for his visit.

Before inspecting the fort, he turned to Beldorach. "This is where we part company."

Beldorach, who had remained mounted, guided the borrowed horse toward the gate.

"Beldorach, the horse was not part of my commitment to Sextus Trebius." Beldorach reined in the horse and looked through the open gate as if weighing the odds of making a run for it. Seeing the tribesman hesitate, Arrius said, "After having come all the way from Eboracum, I should hate to order your execution for having taken one of Caesar's horses."

Beldorach slid gracefully from the horse. "I don't suppose you would consider parting from that stallion? For a good price, of course." Arrius's expressionless face was his answer. "Too bad, for I've a feeling one day I'll have him without having to pay."

"Don't count on it."

"We will see, Roman, what the gods have to say about that. Now that our truce is about to end, I trust you'll grant me at least a bowshot from the top of your great wall."

"Aye, I'll give my word on that even though Sextus Trebius would likely not oblige you."

"I believe you're right. I've a feeling you and I will meet again. Perhaps when we do, it may be under different circumstances that favor me more than you."

"I'll be ready, but I'd prefer if we do, that it will be on peaceful terms."

"Wishful thinking, Roman. Your gods and mine have decreed otherwise, and we must do as they bid. You and I will only know peace when your army leaves our land for the last time. Then, who knows, friendship is possible, and we could talk of other things than war." With that, Beldorach turned and walked through the gateway.

Arrius watched as the tribal leader broke into a loping run until he disappeared over a distant hill. He heard a discreet cough behind him and realized the centurion was waiting for him to proceed with the inspection.

The brief time Arrius spent at the mile-fort left him with an uneasy feeling. The barracks seemed presentable enough and the guard detail diligent in their checks of the pedestrian and wheeled traffic passing through. His doubts had been aroused by the legionaries he stopped to talk to. He was struck by their sullen expressions and guarded answers to his questions. His interest was oriented to the usual things that materially affected legionary morale such as pay, the quality and quantity of food and wine rations, length of guard duty tours, fatigue details, patrols and time off to go to the village for wine and whores.

The responses seemed less than spontaneous leaving him with the disquieting impression all was not what it appeared to be. He was concerned over the reply he received from one of the guards pacing the parapet after he asked how many days he had served on the current shift. The legionary said he was on his tenth day, an answer at odds with the seven-day shifts Matius Betto cited. Out of the corner of his eye, he saw the centurion's stern expression. Ten days was entirely too long to serve in one shift. When he started to query the legionary further, the guard, seeing the centurion's dark look, quickly amended his original answer and said six days. The guard's less than fluent Latin may have been the reason to misunderstood the question. His limited ability to speak Tungrian very well prevented him from probing further.

Not surprising, the bulk of the complaints he did hear predictably focused on pay, the extent of the fatigue duty endured and the quality of the food ration. Such complaints were familiar and would have been common enough for legionaries serving on other frontiers or throughout the empire for that matter.

Several hours later, Arrius passed through the west gate as the first shadows of the setting sun began to steadily lengthen. Even though his inspection had been cursory and conducted mainly to obtain a general assessment, he was disappointed to find many of the same deficiencies at the western gates and towers he had noted at the main fort. At every turn, he confirmed his initial impression there was a significant and widespread morale problem at Banna. He suspected what might be the underlying cause but decided for the time being to keep his thoughts to himself. He needed proof, and he wanted to wait until he visited the eastern forts and towers before taking any constructive action.

His immediate and overriding concern was to determine just how effective his legionaries were in the event the northern tribes chose to launch an attack. Beldorach had more than intimated the Selgovi were simply biding their time while waiting for the opportunity to strike. Then there was Trebius's suspicion Beldorach's motivation for traveling in the south before he was apprehended was to encourage an alliance with the Briganti. He wondered just how well the Banna auxiliaries would do if put to the test in the event of an uprising.

In the meantime, he didn't intend to rely exclusively on a static defense behind crenellated walls. His perception was there had been few patrols forward of the Wall. Then again, his auxilia legionaries weren't as effective as their Roman counterparts. As soon as the thought entered his mind, he felt guilty, reflecting as it did the common prejudice within the Roman Army for the auxilia. He would have to guard against thinking in such manner in fairness to the legionaries he now commanded. In any event, he resolved to commence frequent patrols north if only to offer a change to the monotony of static guard duty.

After turning Ferox over to an orderly for grooming and stabling, Arrius walked the short distance to his quarters. He passed through the entry room into the inner courtyard of the villa-style quarters and found Philos standing next to the wagon that had yet to be unloaded. He saw the slaves appeared to be in the final stages of a major house-cleaning effort. The usually cheerful and animated slaves were uncharacteristically silent and visibly tired as they passed by with buckets of water and scrub brushes.

"I've never seen a place in a more disgraceful condition. We've only now finished making this place fit to live in," Philos said with distaste.

Deciding it might be better to leave, he took time only to strip off his armor before leaving Philos to see to the unpacking. Arrius thought his time might be better spent in the headquarters studying the comprehensive reports both Antius Durio and Publius Gheta had prepared for him. In reflecting over the events and observations he had made so far since his arrival barely six hours ago, he already concluded the chief administrator and the quartermaster were the only two individuals who had made any visible attempt to prepare for the new commander's arrival. The thought caused him to wonder even more about Matius Betto, raising questions in his mind over the role the centurion may have played in his predecessor's hasty departure.

Chapter 8

A day had passed since the two legionaries assaulted her, and Ilya was conflicted on what she should do to make up for the way she treated her rescuer. She felt her face flame when she recalled what she said to him. At first, she rationalized her behavior by excusing it as a delayed reaction to what she and Joric had just been through. Later as she calmed down and recalled the officer's intervention more clearly, she began to realize how irrational and unfair she had been. She assumed he was an officer because of the ornate armor and crested helmet he was wearing. It was Joric's friend, Rialus, who later confirmed he was not only an officer but none other than Banna's new commander. Even if she did dislike Romans in general, that fact was not an excuse for ingratitude. The only way to make amends was to go to him and extend belated thanks along with an apology for her intemperate words.

At first the howling wind, the hail rattling on the tile roof and bitter temperature combined to provide an excuse for not going to the fort. She considered sending Joric with a note of apology to avoid the distasteful even embarrassing task, but the more she thought about it, she realized that would not be enough to relieve her conscience. When the weather began to abate a few hours later, she accepted what she had known all along — the weather was a poor excuse to avoid an unpleasant duty. Ilya told Attorix to hitch the pony cart while she reluctantly made ready to go to the fort.

Just as Attorix pulled the cart to a halt at the entrance of the arched gateway where two guards stood attired in armor and holding long spears, she heard the distant thundering of hooves behind her. She turned and recognized the same Roman officer whom she came to see from the helmet crest and the size and color of the horse he was riding. As the procession drew closer, she saw him turn his head in her direction, but if he recognized her, he gave no indication as the column cantered past and through the archway.

Ilya took a deep breath and tried to overcome her nervousness as she climbed down from the cart. In the process of turning and stepping off the cart, her cloak pulled tightly around her, providing an eye-catching view of feminine curves fully appreciated by the two guards observing her. Ignoring the crude comments muttered by the guards, she approached the one closest to her and identified who she was and the purpose of her visit. The guard looked at her admiringly subjecting her to a critical inspection focused principally on the visible swell of her breasts that even the heavy woolen cloak did not entirely conceal.

"I wish to see the Praefectus," she said.

The guard laughed as he turned to the other guard and said rudely, "Our commander works fast. Here only two days and he's already found himself a bed warmer." Then noticing the bruise on her cheek, he said, "From the look of her face, it may be the Praefectus likes it a bit rough, or perhaps that's your preference," he finished with a leer while the other guard snickered. "Go away, the commander has no time for the likes of you." A speculative look came over the guard's face. "Maybe you'd like to come to the guard room where we can get to know each other better."

"I suggest you do as I've asked and keep your disgusting remarks to yourself. Your commander may very well take as much offense at your vulgar behavior as I do."

The guard's expression changed to uncertainty over the possibility she was right. Caution evidently weighing the balance, the guard turned to the other and said with irritation, "Take her to the principia." Silently, the guard motioned for her to follow him.

She was intimidated by the stark functionality of the fort. A shiver ran down her back, and she had the urge to turn around and run away from this alien environment so completely different from what she was used to. The soldiers she passed looked at her curiously as she passed by but otherwise made no comment.

When she entered the headquarters, she saw it was arranged in many ways not unlike the villa she owned except that it was on a much grander scale. The courtyard appeared to be a noisy beehive of activity. Clerks ran back and forth across the open courtyard from one office to another, some carrying stacks of wooden tablets. In one corner, several men stood talking quietly; she thought they might be officers by the quality of their cloaks and armor. The guard led her to a small office and said something to a youthful man sitting at a table. The man looked so young she assumed he was just a minor functionary. He regarded her with interest as the guard, without glancing at her, left to return to his post.

"I'm Antius Durio, the cornicularius, what can I do for you?" he asked politely but clearly curious to see a well-dressed, attractive woman asking for Arrius.

She had no idea what a cornicularius was, but at least he wasn't subjecting her to the boorish treatment she received from the guards. She introduced herself and told the seated man why she was there.

He looked doubtful. "The commander is busy. Perhaps you would consider returning by appointment at a less busy time." He saw the disappointed look on her face and relented. "Wait here, I'll see if he has time to see you."

Resigned to the prospect of having to return some other time and suffer additional abuse at the gate, she was surprised when after a few moments, Antius Durio returned and beckoned her to follow him. He led her down to the far end of the colonnaded hallway and through an outer office where an orderly glanced silently at her with appreciative eyes as she passed by.

She saw the new commander of Banna sitting behind a wide table, head bent to the tablet he was reading. He was older than she initially thought. For a moment as he continued to read, she studied his face. Without his helmet, the scar she had only glimpsed the day before was now clearly visible. The vicious-looking scar dominated the right side of his face and extended from his hairline all the way to his chin. She wondered in what circumstances he had gotten such a terrible wound. His dark, close-cropped hair showed the first traces of silver. He was not handsome so much as he was impressive to look at. She thought he had the rugged features and resolute jaw suggestive of a man used to exercising authority. His weathered face and the lines radiating from the corner of his eyes were proof he had spent more time in the open and squinting into the sun than sitting behind a table reading documents. When he finally looked up, she saw his eyes were gray. He stood up and regarded her skeptically before saying, "Have you come to continue your criticism of me and the Roman Army in general, or is there another purpose to your visit?"

"My name is Ilya." She was doing her best to keep her voice steady and impersonal. "I own the tavern and inn where you saw me yesterday. My purpose in coming here is to apologize for my behavior.

I was upset and frightened; therefore, I did not fully appreciate what you did for me and my son. For that I am truly sorry for what I said to you."

Ilya saw his lips twitch slightly that may have been the beginning of a smile. "Your use of the word *fully* is curious as I am unaware you *appreciated* any part of my intervention."

Arrius saw her eyes narrow and a red spot appear on each cheek as she began to bristle at his sarcastic response.

"See here, I..." She stopped as Arrius held up a restraining hand.

"Peace," he said with a smile. "I accept your apology. Now would you like to sit down and tell me what happened so that I may decide what to do about the two legionaries I have in custody."

Ilya let out her breath and began to calm down, thawing somewhat in the warmth of his smile. She thought once you overlooked the terrible scar, he seemed not as brutish as she had first thought. His eyes were his most compelling feature, transfixing her with an unwavering gaze that was disconcerting in its directness. She had the feeling he might be slow to anger, but once provoked, he would be quick to take decisive action. His assistance the day before was proof of that.

As she seated herself on one of the stools he indicated, Arrius eyed his guest while trying not to stare. She was far more beautiful than she had appeared the previous day. Then again, the circumstances were hardly conducive to presenting a flattering image. Her hair and clothing were no longer in disarray, and her calm expression was in stark contrast to the fright and anger he saw before. Even with the noticeable bruise on her cheek, she was a remarkably beautiful woman. Finely featured with a heart-shaped face, she was taller than most of the native women he had seen and with a more slender frame. She wore a simple shift of dark linen edged at sleeves and neck with a pattern of finely stitched designs that was neither Roman nor native Britannian but a stylish blend of the two. The garment was gathered at the waist with a belt consisting of linked circles in gold that accentuated the curves of her breasts and hips. The reference to her son indicated she was probably older than she appeared.

Briefly and unemotionally, she related the events leading up to the assault, her hands folded together on top of the cloak draped across her lap. He admired the way she avoided embellishments providing sufficient detail without unnecessary and irrelevant comments. He also liked the way she omitted any strident demands for punishment of the two legionaries.

When she finished, she looked at him expectantly as if waiting to hear what he had to say about the matter. He wondered why her husband had not been there to assist her, a thought that began to lead to additional speculation concerning who she was and how she came to own a tavern way out on the frontier. Belatedly, he realized she was staring at him while his thoughts wandered.

He coughed self-consciously. "I'm sorry you were harmed, and I'm glad I was able to be of assistance. I also apologize for the behavior of the legionaries involved. I can assure you they will receive appropriate punishment for their behavior." She inclined her head in acknowledgement. He was curious she had yet to inquire as to the details of the punishment.

"It was unfortunate your husband was not there to provide some protection. I should think it inadvisable for an attractive woman and the owner of a tavern to be left unprotected."

He saw the bright spots appear on her cheeks again as she flared, "I have no husband, and I do not need to hear any lectures about what I should or should not have, particularly from a Roman at that. Perhaps if there were no Romans, I would not have to worry about protection."

Now irritated, his response was sharp. "Perhaps if we Romans were not here, you would not have a tavern and a clientele with which to make your livelihood."

"We were doing just fine before you Romans came here and built your great forts and stone walls. I would gladly burn down my tavern if it would cause you to go back where you came from. You Romans are so arrogant and feel so superior you think by your very presence you do honor to those you subjugate."

He was beginning to suspect now why she had no husband. *By the gods, she may be beautiful, but she has a temper and a tongue.* He stood up to end the conversation

"I can see we have differences of opinion on this subject that might be better to leave for discussion on another day." Arrius firmly resolved there would be no further occasion for a discussion with her on this or any other subject.

Ilya also stood up, lips compressed, eyes flashing. "I sincerely doubt you and I will have any reason to have another conversation about anything, for I believe we would find nothing upon which to agree."

Angered by her sweeping characterization of Romans, he found her words tiresome and a distraction he neither had the inclination nor the patience to deal with.

"If that is all, I'll have my orderly escort you to the gate. The sooner you leave the fort, the sooner we Romans will not trouble you further." Arrius called for the legionary. "Escort this lady to the gate and see that nothing happens to her while she is in the fort."

Without another word, Ilya donned her cloak uncaring of the melted snow that sprinkled the open tablets on his table. The wide-eyed orderly hurried to catch up with her as she stormed out. What a mistake it was to come here she thought as she walked quickly toward the gate oblivious of the stares from those she passed. Never would she come here again and be insulted, patronized. She would take their sestercii for the sake of Joric, but she would never be able to do more than tolerate these people. To think she had almost formed a favorable opinion of the officer.

She passed by the same two guards at the gate without acknowledging them proceeding directly to the cart where Attorix was standing ready to assist her. She vowed it would snow in summer before she would willingly have anything more to do with the insufferable commander of Banna.

After Ilya left, Arrius stared at the wall and reviewed the events of that morning hoping the rest of the day would go better but no longer optimistic it would. It was a shame such an attractive woman had the poisonous tongue of an adder. With a temper like hers, it was no wonder she had no husband he told himself for the second time. Possibly he left rather than put up with her, or perhaps he was killed by Romans which would clearly explain why she disliked Romans. In any event, he wanted no more to do with her. Before the day was out, he intended to instruct the staff that under no circumstances would she be admitted to the fort again. With some effort, his thoughts gradually turned to other and more pressing matters than his contentious visitor.

His visit to the eastern forts revealed they were in slightly better shape than those he had looked at the day before, a fact he attributed mainly to more time to prepare than the western forts had been given. While there were still visible signs of neglect, he was becoming less concerned over the physical appearance of the men and the forts and more so with his growing perception the legionaries were indifferent. The men he spoke to at least did not seem either hostile or disrespectful, typical signs of a serious morale problem. Rather, they seemed apathetic. He also believed the sloppy appearance of the legionaries and cavalrymen he had seen so far might result more from standards that had never been established or maintained instead of signifying passive rebellion.

There were also the now familiar complaints about the wine. It wouldn't be the first time the wine was being overly watered to allow an enterprising optio or centurion to make a profit by selling a portion of the ration to the local taverns. He asked similar questions concerning pay and received answers generally approximating what he had already heard. He was convinced Antius Durio would simply confirm his suspicions after completing his inquiries. At least the inventory of the pay chest completed earlier that morning revealed an accurate accounting down to the last sestercii, thanks to the careful record keeping of the cornicularius.

The two legionaries apprehended outside the tavern had surfaced another problem. Both men were properly chastened when they were brought before him. Normally, public brawling would not have been considered a serious matter with punishment for such an offense usually limited to a few days of extra fatigue duty. But after learning the incident was merely the latest of common occurrences, he knew he had to do something about it. He recalled the grim faces of the villagers as the detail rode past the village and began to understand better their less than enthusiastic reaction to the arrival of more legionaries. He was also influenced by the memory of the legionary threatening the boy with his dagger. Whether the legionary's belligerence would have resulted in injuring the boy would never be known; the legionary in question had been quick to deny he intended anything more than scaring him. He gave the two men ten days of fatigue duty with reduced rations and restriction for an additional ten days. He thought maintenance work on the vallum might very well cause them to modify their future behavior while sending a signal to the rest of the garrison.

Before leaving that afternoon for Fanum Cocidii, he wanted to inspect the granaries and the basilica. The barracks would wait until he returned, and by then they might be more presentable than he suspected they were now. Earlier that morning he had seen a detail busy pulling up weeds growing between the cobble stones and cleaning up horse dung throughout the fort.

Antius Durio entered the room and reported Matius Betto and the quaestor were ready for his inspection of the granaries and the basilica. A few moments later through a light drizzle more mist than rain, the three officers with Publius Gheta carrying an oil lamp made their way to the two granary buildings.

Two stories high, the granaries were each 70 feet long and 25 feet wide with a pitched and overhanging roof of stone tiles. The roof extension insured rain would not flow down the sides of the buildings thereby precluding any risk of moisture getting inside. The heavy weight of the roof was supported by a series of buttresses. Narrow louvered slits between each buttress allowed circulation within while keeping animals and weather out. After the three men mounted the several steps to the door, Publius Gheta produced a key that unlocked the stout wooden door. Gheta barely had time to step aside before Betto brushed rudely past him and entered the building. Arrius saw an angry look flash across the quartermaster's face.

It took a few moments for Arrius to get used to the gloom inside made even more so by the gray skies outside. Even a bright sunny sky would have provided only a dim light coming through the narrow ventilation slits. Betto held the oil lamp up, and the flickering light revealed stacks of large casks with wooden lids placed in bins on either side of a central aisle. The floor consisted of stone slabs placed on top of wooden channels that allowed a flow of air from above and below to help maintain a cool, dry temperature even during the hottest days of summer.

The walls of the bins were ten feet high and provided the support for the wood ceiling above. In the bins, the casks were stacked almost to the ceiling. Hanging beside each bin was a tablet marking the current tally for each numbered cask. Arrius slowly moved down the aisle, stopped at one of the bins and lifted the lid of the nearest cask. He was surprised to find it contained barley. When nothing else was available to eat, Roman legionaries would reluctantly consume barley, a food source more associated with punishment when a commander was displeased with a unit's performance on or off the battlefield. He plunged his hand in, grabbing a handful of the contents. The grains sifting through his fingers felt cool and dry to the touch.

Publius Gheta coughed and said, "Not all the barley is consumed as food. A portion of it is used to make beer, or at least it used to be. While the brew is not pleasant to a Roman palette, it seems to have an appeal to the Tungrians and Dacians. Evidently, the brewing of a similar beverage was common practice where they came from. Indeed, they do not much care for wine although they will drink it."

"Nasty stuff, I must say," Betto said in disgust. "It's a waste for the grain to be so used. There's nothing wrong with watered wine, and it's more than good enough for the likes of these worthless swine."

Arrius's estimation of the centurion dropped further. He let the disparaging comment pass for the moment and focused on Gheta's last remark.

"What do you mean used to be?"

Without pause, Gheta said, "Since Centurion Betto curtailed the practice weeks ago."

Arrius turned to Betto. "Why?"

"It required too much barley to make and would leave the supply short until the next harvest." Having no idea how much grain was used to make the beverage, he thought the reason seemed plausible enough until he noticed Gheta's expression.

"How much barley does it require to make this drink?" Arrius looked at Gheta.

"Very little in comparison to the supply we have on hand. There is more than enough available to make beer without risking a shortage here or the levy imposed by legion headquarters."

Betto shifted his feet uncomfortably but made no rebuttal. Arrius reflected on the comments he received from the legionaries when he asked about the wine. He was beginning to suspect he may have misinterpreted their responses. Now that he thought about it, their complaints may have been focused not so much on the quality and quantity of the wine ration as he had first thought, but rather they had been denied their preferred drink.

The inspection of the second granary was brief. Arrius found the same clean and dry conditions present in the other building. While the first granary was used exclusively to store grain, some of the bins in the second granary were used to store other consumables. Joints of meat suspended on chains hung from the floor above. Baskets of cheese, casks of olive oil and clay amphorae containing wine were also present.

By the time the three men made their way to the training hall, it was obvious Betto and Gheta had a deep mutual dislike of each other. He thought it unusual for a more junior officer such as the quaestor to deliberately antagonize a senior centurion such as Betto.

The interior of the hall was cavernous and large enough to accommodate the entire Tungrian cohort. The hobnails on their boots rang hollow on the flagstones as the three men walked across the large expanse of floor to the center of the building. The center and highest part of the two-story, three-tiered roof was supported by a row of tall square columns. Clerestory windows at the top of the ceiling provided additional light from the ground-floor windows.

Arrius turned to Betto. "I want all men in the cohort not on guard assembled here when I return from Fanum Cocidii tomorrow afternoon. At that time, I'll define my expectations and my requirements." He saw Betto nod slightly in assent. "During the following days, I'll inspect each century with their officers in full field kit as if they were prepared to go on patrol. You may schedule them in any order you wish. Quaestor, I want you present at the inspections to record the list of equipment that needs to be replaced."

"Centurion, I warrant the accouterments and arms are adequate," Betto said in a tone that bordered on defiant.

"I don't agree if your honor guard and those legionaries I've seen at their posts since my arrival are any indication. I've seen enough to know Publius Gheta and his assistants will be very busy seeing to a general refitting. I hope the local tradesmen represent a willing and able source for the items we will require and cannot make ourselves."

"I resent your implication the cohort is not presentable and not up to your standards. You'll find soon enough duty on this accursed wall is enough to drive men crazy. The men drink too much, fight with each other and sneak off to the village at every opportunity to bed the whores. I warn you, Praefectus, if you begin to treat these misbegotten bastards with a light hand, you'll find soon enough you've made a big mistake."

Arrius did not interrupt Betto's tirade or change his expression. When Betto was finished, he said to the quaestor, "I believe for the time being I will no longer require your presence here. Make yourself ready to accompany me to Fanum Cocidii within the hour."

Betto began to look uneasy as the quaestor's footsteps receded, and Arrius remained silent. A moment later, the heavy wooden closed with a booming echo in the stillness of the large room. When Arrius finally spoke, his voice was mild, almost conversational.

"Centurion, it appears you and I have much with which to disagree. We are alone; therefore, I will speak freely and candidly. I do not wish to risk leaving unsaid anything I, or you, might regret later." His voice took on an edge as he continued. "In the granary, you referred to the men as worthless swine. In my experience, if men are regarded as no better than swine, they will behave accordingly. In the brief time I've been here, my impression is the morale is poor, and I suspect the main reason is how the men have been treated. Another reason for low morale is boredom brought about by the monotony of constant guard duty. In that I agree with you. The very first legionary I spoke with yesterday let slip he had been on guard duty for ten days. I suspect I know why. He was paid to pull another legionary's duty. The reality of tolerating something like that is to risk the effectiveness of the watch. I'll wager after five or six days, it's time to rotate the guard before indifference erodes the main reason for us to be here. I'm told it has been sometime since active patrolling took place north or south of the Wall. This will change, but first there will be training to ensure the legionaries can do more than walk passively on the parapets while waiting for an attack that may never come."

Arrius paused momentarily to see if he had the centurion's full attention. "Let me say a word about appearance. If the appearance of the legionaries is allowed to deteriorate, they will take no pride in what they do and how they do it. A legionary acts the way he looks. If his tunic and armor are in a poor state, he will not regard himself and the duty he performs with pride. These are merely the first of many things I intend to change. You have a choice, Betto, you can change with the cohort, or you will leave it, possibly as something less than a centurion. Do I make myself clear?"

Betto's face was flushed with anger as he struggled to maintain his composure. "Aye, you've made your point plain enough. It remains to be seen if your way is better than mine. I believe corporal punishment gets a legionary's attention faster than kind words and soft treatment." He slashed the air with his twisted vine stick. "For now, you're the commander and I'm obliged to do things your way, although mark what I have to say. Be careful when you check the guard some night that appreciation for kind treatment is a dagger in the back — then I may well be in command again."

"Perhaps I have less to worry from the legionaries than my officers. I think you and I are not done yet, but enough has been said for now. Think carefully what I've said while I'm gone. If you decide you are unable to fulfill your duties in the manner I require, I'll see you're posted elsewhere just as soon as I can make the arrangements." Arrius abruptly turned on his heel and strode purposefully to the door.

After the door banged shut behind Arrius, the centurion said quietly, "Praefectus, you may well be right about one thing. You may have just cause to fear your officers."

Chapter 9

The harsh weather of that morning had dissipated as the cavalry troop approached the outpost of Fanum Cocidii under a cold, cloud-studded day. Named after *Cocidius*, a local Britannian deity worshipped by both hunters and warriors, the Shrine of Cocidius was located seven miles north of Banna and accessible by a well-cleared and raised road that snaked between the steep hills. Because of the icy conditions, it had taken the troop an hour to traverse the short distance to the fort.

When they arrived at the fort, Arrius saw at a glance the village opposite the fort of Fanum Cocidii had been accurately described by Sextus Trebius. Smaller than the one at Banna, the settlement was built haphazardly on the near slope of a hill. Pigs and chickens scratched and rooted about. The turf and timber fort was situated on top of a low hill nearby.

The fort was large to accommodate the 500-man cavalry regiment and their mounts. Unlike every other fort Arrius had ever seen or served which was either rectangular or square-shaped, Fanum Cocidii was hexagonal. The spoil from a wide and deep ditch surrounding the fort had been used as fill in the construction of the lower walls to a height of ten feet. Log palisades extended the height of the walls by another eight feet to the top of the merlons. There were two gates each dominated by a watch tower; smaller interval towers were located midway on each wall. The main gate was the only double-arched entryway, and the only one that was open. Above the gate, the regiment's *draco* hung limply from a slender pole. Signifying a cavalry unit, the four-foot long standard consisted of a cloth sleeve fashioned serpent-like and attached to a bronze dragon head with gaping jaws. When carried by a mounted standard bearer or inflated by the wind, the sleeve would fill with air and move sinuously. A device in the jaws created a loud whistling noise as the air passed through it. Apart from terrorizing the enemy, the standard also served a practical use for mounted archers to adjust their aim according to the direction of the wind.

As they approached the main gate, he saw a solitary figure mounted and waiting for him in front of the main gate. He recognized Seugethis, the Dacian commander, from Publius Gheta's earlier description. Arrius was very much aware that with the rank of praefectus, Seugethis was his equal in rank even though his appointment made Seugethis his nominal subordinate. What little he knew of the proud Dacian led him to believe tact and diplomacy would go farther than attempting to assert the fine points of his senior command.

Astride a white horse and wearing an elaborate plumed helmet with narrow cheek guards and a leather cuirass, the Dacian cut a dashing figure. Arrius thought the luxuriant blonde beard Seugethis sported would have been the envy of Hadrian himself. As he reined in, the troop commander brought the Tungrian cavalry escort to a halt. The Dacian's eyes surveyed the Tungrian cavalrymen with a sour expression. Arrius thought his escort was presentable enough and wondered how to interpret the Dacian's appraisal.

Thumping his chest with a closed fist, Seugethis said, "Hail, Arrius," while paying more attention to Ferox than his new commander. Belatedly, he said, "and welcome to Fanum Cocidii and the gateway to nowhere."

Arrius saw the glint of humor in the Dacian's eyes. "Hail, Seugethis, I've served for many years in nowhere and that is why this place looks familiar."

"Then you and I have much in common. And hail to you, Publius Gheta, for I've much to say to you as well as our new commander. If you please, Praefectus, I would bid you dismiss your escort for a time while I show you around. They'll find water for their mounts over by the stables."

The Dacian turned his horse about and waited until Arrius drew abreast before entering the fort. With Ferox at least 15 hands high and a hand larger than the mount Seugethis was riding, Arrius found he was looking slightly down on the Dacian as they walked the horses through the gate.

"That's a fine stallion you're riding," Seugethis commented with undisguised envy. "What name did you give the beast?"

"Ferox"

"I've no doubt he would make a fine cavalry mount for a Dacian cavalry commander." Just then the standard above let forth a whistling shriek caused by a gust of wind. Ferox snorted and Arrius had to rein the horse in tightly to keep the animal from bolting. Seugethis amended his comment by saying, "That is with better training."

Slowly, the Dacian Commander led Arrius and Publius Gheta around the inside of the fort pointing out each building and the wall defenses. From time to time, Seugethis did not hesitate to acknowledge shortcomings when Arrius probed a point. But he was equally unabashed in proudly extolling the virtues of his Dacians when it came to describing battle readiness and success in the infrequent clashes with the native tribes populating the area. Arrius noted the stark difference between the cavalrymen he saw from the legionaries at Banna in both manner and dress. Although conditions at Fanum Cocidii were more austere than Banna, the men were well turned out and seemed in better spirits.

Seugethis reined in before a squat building that apparently served as a headquarters and dismounted. Motioning to Arrius to follow suit, he tied his mount to a ringed post near the doorway and walked inside.

"Tell me of your routine." The three men removed their helmets and took a seat at a large table.

"As you may have noticed, I keep only the main gate open and a small contingent in the towers during daylight. The reason is that cavalrymen do their best on the back of a horse and not behind a wall. The reason I can reduce the guard on the walls is because I have patrols ranging out in assigned sectors for three days at a time out to 15-20 miles. I have smaller patrols operating closer in. In this manner, it would be very difficult for the Selgovi or Novanti to surprise us."

"What about the forest? I understand it's vast."

"It is certainly that and dense as well, and that's why I say it would be difficult but not impossible for a surprise attack. Arrius, my men are very good, but then so are the Novanti and Selgovi, particularly the Selgovi. If they were better disciplined, better mounted, more organized and had larger numbers, we'd be hard pressed to hold them back for long. They can ride as well as my Dacians, and their arrows seldom miss." Arrius had already decided the Dacian commander's praise was not freely given, and for that reason, his description of the native tribes carried additional weight.

"What do you know of Beldorach?"

"I've seen him from a distance a couple of times. The blue-faced devil is foxy. If they had a few more like him, I'd be asking for more men and horses than what I have now. You know of him?"

"Aye, we've met. In fact, I escorted him from Eboracum to Banna. He undoubtedly passed by you the night before on his way back to his village."

Seugethis pounded the table. "You should have gutted the slippery bastard."

"I couldn't by order of Tribune Sextus Trebius. Nor would I have done so even if I hadn't been under orders to escort him back."

"Why in the name of *Zalmoxis* didn't you?" He invoked the Dacian god of battle.

"Would you if you had been in my place?"

"Under those circumstances, I suppose not, but if I should ever get close enough for sword or lance, one of us will never need to piss again."

"Fair enough, and I'll likely do the same if the circumstances are presented. Still, I found him interesting. Too bad he wants only war — he would serve his people better if he would make peace with us."

The Dacian was skeptical. "When you've been here longer, you'll see that's a vain hope. It isn't just Beldorach although he's apparently the most powerful and the most influential. It's all the tribes, including the Brigantes Tribe at our rear. I worry more about the Briganti than I do the ones out there." He gestured north with a sweep of his arm. "At least the northern tribes make no pretense about hating us, but the Briganti, well, they act peaceful enough, but underneath the surface, they're like the rest of the tribes, waiting for the time to show what they really think of Rome. Hear me well, Arrius, you've as much or more to be concerned with those who live at your back as Beldorach who makes no pretense he wants a fight. They're all uncivilized savages. If they weren't busy fighting us, they'd be fighting each other which they often do anyway."

Arrius decided diplomatically to refrain from reminding Seugethis it had not been but a short time past when Rome had said similar things about Dacia.

"I look to the day when I have the opportunity to cross swords with Beldorach, and when we do, one of us will no longer be around to mark the outcome." Seugethis threw back his head and laughed, then seeing the look on Arrius's face, he said, "It's not the way of a Dacian warrior to grow old and useless. What better way to stand before the gods than to die gloriously in battle by the hand of a worthy opponent. Of course, I shall make certain Beldorach has every opportunity to see the gods before I do."

For the next two hours, their conversation ranged over a myriad of topics, all dealing with the usual problems, solutions and concerns common to any frontier command. At one point, Seugethis looked sharply at Publius Gheta and asked, "And what of the barley I requested weeks ago? Much longer and we'll have nothing to drink but water."

Arrius looked puzzled wondering what a shortage of barley had to do with having to drink water. Publius Gheta's reply quickly reminded him of the conversation in the granary. "I believe I can assure you a supply of barley will be ready for pick-up as soon as I return to Banna now that our new commander has allowed some of it to make beer again."

"So, it was Betto I have to thank for stopping the supply? I might have known it was that son of a dog that was behind it."

"I take it you have differences of opinion with Centurion Betto." Arrius wondered what the centurion had done to inspire the Dacian's ire.

"He tried to charge my cavalrymen for more rations and equipment than we ever received, and I called him on it as Gheta here knows full well."

Arrius looked at Gheta.

"It's true. Betto unwisely tried to do as Praefectus Seugethis suggested."

Seugethis was quick to point out. "If it hadn't been for Publius Gheta here, the bastard might have gotten away with it. He gave me fair warning by suggesting in front of Betto that I might wish to verify the amounts charged before we started paying the men. It was a good suggestion and gave me an opportunity to prevent my men from being cheated. As a result, I'll bet Gheta here is not on the best of terms with Betto. Your quaestor has earned my gratitude for certain. I'll not forget it, and there's my oath on it."

As the discussion continued, it was apparent to Arrius that he and Seugethis had much in common. He liked the cavalryman's no-

nonsense even irreverent attitude that did nothing to diminish his belief Seugethis was competent and dependable to a degree he doubted Betto would ever be. Finally, Seugethis stood up and invited Arrius to accompany him to inspect the barracks and stables while Publius Gheta sought out his counterpart to assess in more detail the Dacian supply requirements.

The two men continued their conversation as they walked toward the long, rectangular-shaped buildings constructed of logs accommodating both horses and men. Each building was built to house a 32-man troop with the horses stabled on the outside half and the inside half partitioned into small rooms occupied by the cavalrymen. The buildings were grouped in pairs separated by only a few feet. Facing verandas ran the length of each building on the side where the men were billeted. Although the fort in comparison to Banna was austere, there was an appearance of disciplined maintenance presently lacking at the Banna fort. Arrius was certain if he were to return unannounced, the condition of the barracks would be little changed.

It required only a few steps into the first stable-barracks they came to for Arrius to see the profound contrast to the stables at Banna. Beyond the pungent ammonia smell of dung and urine, there was little else in common. Here the stalls were clean and filled with fresh straw; the passageways were raked and free of droppings. Tack hung neatly next to each stall along with a rack for lance, arrow quiver, shield and *spatha*, the long, straight sword carried by the cavalry. The familiar smell of horse and human sweat permeated the buildings. Each building was exactly like the others. A small entryway served as an orderly room and office for each decurion. Past the entryway were small rooms each just large enough to billet three men. The wooden cots were built sturdy and strung with thick cord. A folded pallet and blankets were stacked neatly at the head of each cot. Personal clothing items hung from pegs next to each cot. The rooms for the three officers assigned to the troop were located at the far end of the building in and accessible by an outside entrance. The *calones*, the servants who mucked out the stalls and maintained the barracks, lived in the attic above the stalls and barracks rooms. There was nothing to criticize with the living conditions for either man or horse at Fanum Cocidii.

As the two men completed the inspection, Seugethis said, "You may have wondered why there was no honor guard to mark your arrival."

Arrius had noted the absence of the traditional formalities, but since he gave little importance to such displays, he had taken no offense and therefore said nothing about it. "I think such things are a waste of time. Instead, I invite you to observe one of my troops as they demonstrate their battle skills. In case you think the cavalrymen you will see have practiced for the occasion, I want to assure you they have not. The maneuvers they will perform are standard training drills, and the troop involved is neither my best nor my worst; it simply happens to be here in garrison for rest before going back on patrol."

The two men returned to their horses, mounted and walked them through the gate. Arrius followed Seugethis to a raised tribunal at the side of an open field. In contrast to the untracked snow on the Banna training field, this muddy field showed it was heavily used. It consisted of a variety of steep ditches and variously placed targets of wood and straw positioned in such a way to thoroughly test a cavalryman's riding and weapons skills. The cavalrymen were already lined up ready to commence the demonstration. Arrius noted half the men held small oval shields and were armed with several short lances; the remainder carried recurved bows with quivers of arrows worn across the back. The archers carried no shields and wore a spatha on the left side suspended by a baldric.

The first exercise consisted of each troop demonstrating the different patrol and attack formations. At first, the drills were routine and conducted at a slow pace. Just as he was beginning to wonder if Seugethis had exaggerated the capabilities of his men, the tempo of the drill dramatically increased. Soon the same formations were being conducted at full gallop accompanied by exuberant yells and war cries. The cavalrymen approached the first steep ditches with hardly a break in stride, and Arrius was certain he was about to see horses falling and cavalrymen tumbling in broken heaps, casualties of the slippery terrain. But to his amazement, not a single horse faltered or refused the difficult obstacles attesting to the skills of both riders and horses. Next was a weapons demonstration. If he had been impressed with the horsemanship he had seen so far, he was even more amazed at the proficiency the cavalrymen showed in the use of their weapons. He thought the Dacian cavalry skills surpassed even the superb Parthian Cavalry he had faced in battle.

Following the conclusion of the demonstration, the troop paraded past the tribunal before returning to the fort. Arrius turned to Seugethis. "That was a fine display of cavalry skills."

"I'll wager you've never seen better or as good."

"I believe you are right."

Later, Arrius had an opportunity to meet the other officers in the garrison while also being introduced to the locally brewed drink both the Tungrians and Dacians seemed to prefer over the watered wine favored by the Roman legionary. He found the frothy drink not unpleasant and similar to the drink he had sampled along the Rhine in Germania. After a few more cups, he was thankful he was not returning to Banna until the next morning.

The return to Banna seemed to take forever. The fog gradually became a drizzle mixed with snow that chilled him to the bone. Uncomfortable rapidly descended to miserable. The bitter cold aggravated his leg, and each time Ferox changed his gait to adjust for the slick road surface, his thigh throbbed. He heard the muttered cursing of the escort behind him and knew they were just as anxious to seek the comparative comfort of the fort as he was.

To take his mind off his discomfort, Arrius began to review the events since his arrival a mere two days ago. So far, he was well-satisfied with what he had seen at Fanum Cocidii. He was certain there was nothing so wrong with the Banna garrison that could not be improved quickly and faster if he got get rid of Betto. The centurion appeared to be a fundamental problem that required a solution sooner than later. He also had to consider there were some of the centurions who would remain loyal to Betto no matter what changes he made. It would be better if Betto requested a transfer instead of Arrius making a formal request to General Arvinnius to transfer the troublesome officer.

Without consciously realizing it, his thoughts began to drift to other things, and before he knew it, he was thinking back to his visitor the previous morning. At first, he was irritated as the face of the woman intruded. It was an unwelcome distraction. Her unwarranted and unfair characterization of him and Romans in general succeeded only in making him angry. He tried to redirect his thoughts, but her image persisted. Gradually, his anger subsided as he recalled her lithe figure, beautiful face and rich color of her long hair. Under different circumstances, he wondered if they might have gotten along better. He vaguely regretted there would be little chance for the opportunity to find out. She was a reminder it had been a long time since Alexandria and time spent with a woman he cared about. What was it about this native woman that made him wish their first meeting had gone differently? He surprised himself with the thought. Looking back on what he had said, he realized he let his temper get the better of him.

When they reached the fort, Arrius dismissed the escort and started walking the stallion toward the stables; however, before he reached them, he reined Ferox in and looked around. The fort's configuration, nearly identical to other forts he had known, was a familiar sight and a place he should have felt comfortable. Now it seemed only a collection of grim, stone buildings made more so under a winter sky. He recalled Beldorach's accusation that he only had a stone fortress to call a home and wondered if there was more truth to it than he wanted to accept. He had a sudden urge to get away from the fort, and without any thought of where he was going, he turned Ferox around and cantered toward the east gate.

Chapter 10

Joric watched the horse and rider coming toward him and knew it was the same officer who had come to their assistance a few days before. He was still puzzled at his mother's behavior toward their rescuer. He also didn't understand why his mother hated the Romans so much. Decrius, the father of his closest friend, Rialus, was not exactly a Roman, but he was in their army; he was also friendly and kind to him and his mother. Joric thought most of the legionaries who came to the inn were nice enough. He admired the way the Roman officer sat astride the spirited horse, his cloak swirling behind him. He had never seen anyone who looked so magnificent and so terrible at the same time. He resolved one day he, too, would ride a large horse and wear armor to compare with this Roman officer even if he must become a Roman to do so.

He would never be able to confide his adolescent dreams to his mother. She wouldn't understand much less approve of them. She would try to tell him again about the destiny he may one day fulfill. He pretended to understand, but he didn't really. He had endured the pain of the spiral tattoo on his chest years before to humor her. The reasons she gave were all too vague with her talk of royal marks. He loved his mother, but he suspected she was caught up in her own dreams that he did not share. She spoke of her tribe, but all he knew was his life at Banna. He humored her in the Selgovan language she insisted they speak when no one else was around. Apart from infrequent visits by his uncle when they spoke the Selgovan tongue, he didn't see any practical reason for learning the language any better than he did now.

Unaware of the impression he was making with the boy, Arrius reined in Ferox and asked, "Are you the son of the woman called Ilya?" When the boy slowly nodded and said nothing but continued to stare at him, Arrius wondered if the youth was either simple or unable to speak. Upon closer observation, there was no mistaking the boy for any but Ilya's son. Although more masculine, his features closely resembled her, and the color of his eyes were the same.

Just as he was about to repeat the question, the boy said, "I'm glad you came. I want to thank you for your assistance. Without your help, I would have had more difficulty defending my mother."

Arrius suppressed a smile at the boy's response. "I'm certain you would have been able to manage, but I'm glad I was passing by at the time. I trust you both have not been bothered since?"

"No, but Attorix now spends more time here than before, and he's even bigger than you." Arrius wondered who Attorix was.

The boy took a step forward and stuck out his hand to stroke the animal's muzzle. Arrius started to pull back on the reins to give some distance certain the horse would react predictably by laying his ears back and baring his teeth. To his surprise, Ferox resisted the reins and moved to meet Joric's outstretched hand.

Cautiously, Arrius relaxed his grip on the reins and watched in astonishment as the young man spoke softly to the horse while Ferox patiently allowed his nose and ears to be scratched. Only on rare occasions had Ferox shown him similar attention and it was usually when the horse thought he would be rewarded with a handful of grain.

"He's the most beautiful horse I've ever seen and gentle, too."

"Aye, beautiful he may be, but gentle he's not. Have a care, he can be unpredictable." Arrius realized he didn't know the boy's name. "What are you called?"

"My name is Joric."

"And what's your name?"

"My name is Marcus Junius Arrius."

"Why do Romans have so many names?"

"Well, Marcus is the *nomen* my family gave me in a naming ceremony when I was very young. Before that I was just called Quintus as I was the fifth child. Junius is my *praenomen*, or family name, from the tribe Junius and Arrius is my *cognomen*, derived from a clan of the Junius tribe. It's customary for my family and closest friends to call me Marcus. Those who are not address me formally as Arrius."

"Since I do not know you, is it proper for me to call you Arrius?"

"I suppose, but perhaps when we get to know each better then you can call me Marcus."

"Why does Decrius have only one name?"

"Decrius is not yet a Roman citizen. One day when he completes his military service, he will be granted citizenship after which he can add another name."

"Would you like to see my mother?" Joric hoped the invitation would keep the Roman officer from leaving right away.

"Perhaps another time. I wouldn't wish to bother her." He began to turn Ferox back toward the road.

"I assure you, it's no bother," a soft voice came from the doorway of the tavern. He turned and looked in her direction and saw she was even more beautiful than he remembered. She must have been brushing her hair as it was loose and falling to her waist. She wore a shawl over a sleeved shift of linen reaching to her ankles and cinched at the waist with a wide leather belt. She stood with her arms at her sides, fingers interlaced, expression neutral.

"Won't you come inside for a cup of wine?" This time he imagined there was a suggestion of sincerity in the invitation.

Arrius hesitated to give himself time to collect his thoughts, worried the unsettling effect she had on him would rob him of a coherent response.

"Surely a Roman officer requires little time to decide whether to accept a cup of wine. Or do you think by doing so you risk another argument? I promise, if you accept, you'll not be ill-treated."

The proverbial olive branch had been tossed, and he decided he could do no less than pick it up. Arrius smiled, and Ilya noticed how quickly it softened his severe features.

"I confess I was cautious given our past meetings. I thought to make friends with your son to gain an ally in the event we should meet again."

Staring at each other as they were, Ilya and Arrius missed seeing the delight on Joric's face. Had Ilya noticed the admiration in her son's eyes as he looked at the tall Roman, she might not have pressed the invitation.

Arrius dismounted and handed the reins to Joric. "Since you two seem to get along so well, tie Ferox up, and if you have a handful of grain to give him, he'll at least tolerate you until it's gone."

As Joric led the horse to a water trough nearby, Arrius followed Ilya into the tavern removing his helmet before ducking under the low doorway. He saw immediately from the interior that it had been a private villa at one time. From first appearances, the previous owner had spared little expense in its construction. The spacious and partly-covered courtyard was filled with tables and benches instead of the traditional gardens and fountain common to a residential villa. It was still early in the day for any customers, and no one was present except a servant scrubbing the trestle tables and a huge man standing in a doorway across the courtyard. Arrius wondered if he might be Attorix. The man watched him suspiciously as he followed Ilya down the colonnaded walkway. They passed through a doorway into a corridor connecting on one side to a small dining chamber and the kitchen on the other. Another door at the end of the corridor, he guessed, provided access to her private rooms.

Wordlessly, she motioned for him to seat himself while she entered the kitchen. He heard her issuing instructions to someone followed by the rattle of cups and the banging of cupboards. She returned a moment later and sat down across from him. Soon a young, attractive woman entered carrying a wooden tray bearing a pitcher, two plain ceramic cups and a small loaf of bread. The woman placed the tray on the table then left silently. Although neither spoke as Ilya poured a small quantity of wine into each cup, Arrius did not feel the silence was uncomfortable. In fact, he was thinking that if neither one said very much, there was less likelihood of antagonizing each other and repeating the results of their last meeting. He watched as she picked up a knife and skillfully sliced the bread, admiring the delicacy of her hands, the serene expression on her face. She looked up and caught him staring at her. Both quickly looked away in embarrassment. He searched for something to say desperately wishing for a clever word that would assure her he was capable of some social grace even as he marveled at the effect she had on him. He reached for one of the cups and drank deeply to cover his confusion then he worried she would think he was just another Roman who drank too much.

Ilya spoke first. "It seems for two people who had much to say to each other before, we seem to have little to speak of now."

"I confess I was afraid of saying anything that might provoke you which is the last thing I want to do."

Her eyes warmed, and she returned the smile. "I thought Romans were afraid of nothing. Can it be I've been wrong?"

He laughed. "We're only afraid of the things we do not do well including failing to converse well with a beautiful woman."

Ilya felt her face flush at the compliment and regretted her propensity to blush so easily. She suppressed a sudden flash of irritation at the reference to her physical appearance and resisted an inclination to lash out at similar comments she found offensive. Why was it men seemed so preoccupied with how a woman looked and how uncaring they were concerning what a woman might consider important? She was positive if she gave in to her usual feelings on the subject, it would doom once and for all any possibility of reconciliation although why she wanted to be on friendly terms with him was beyond her understanding.

"Is it Centurion or Praefectus that I should address you by?"

"Praefectus is now my rank, but I prefer you call me Marcus."

"Then that is the name I will use. I suspect you've been quite busy since your arrival."

"I have and will likely continue to be so. There is much left to be done before I'm satisfied the garrison is prepared to perform according to my standards."

At first, she was ready to let his response go unchallenged but lost her initial resolve to avoid argumentative remarks.

"By performing, you mean ready to fight the local tribes?"

Arrius was immediately aware his innocent reply was about to sow the seeds for additional argument.

"I mean no such thing. Indeed, the last thing I wish is for any unrest. I would prefer a peaceful coexistence between Rome and the tribes. I've found there is less to be gained in war than peace."

She was intrigued by his reply. "That is a strange comment coming from a professional soldier. I thought you would relish the idea of fighting. Most men seem to."

He looked away and appeared to focus on some distant place and time. She was afraid she had said too much and regretted her impulse to say what she felt at the risk of offending him.

"I'm certain I felt that way at one time. In fact, I know that was true, but it seems a long time since I believed that. Perhaps it's because I've seen much of war. I would be content never to see a battlefield again, but if I must then I want my legionaries to be prepared."

His thoughtful expression and explanation surprised her. Perhaps this Roman was different from the rest. She contrasted his answer with Beldorach's obsession with making war on the Romans. She understood her cousin's hatred of the Romans, but when he wasn't fighting Romans, he was just as likely to raid the other tribes.

Joric entered the room and sat down next to his mother giving Arrius an opportunity to compare the two. As Ilya was pleasing to look at, Joric also was going to be a handsome man.

After silently staring at Arrius for a moment, Joric asked abruptly, "How did you get that scar on your face?"

The question provoked a stern rebuke from his mother.

"Joric, it's impolite to ask such a question." Although she privately wondered the same.

"It's all right. It was a long time ago when I was a young centurion in Parthia. If my helmet had not fallen off, the Parthian cavalryman would not have cut so deeply."

"Do you have other wounds?" Joric asked with disarming candor evoking another stern comment from Ilya.

"Joric, that's enough!"

Arrius was amused as much by the boy's forthright manner as his mother's obvious embarrassment.

"Too many, I'm afraid, and the cold weather reminds me that I wasn't as careful as I should have been."

"I think you must be a great warrior," Joric said in open admiration.

"No, Joric, I've known great warriors in my time, but, unfortunately, most of those are gone now."

"One day, I, too, will be a great warrior," the boy said, his eyes shining.

"There are more important things to do with your life than becoming a warrior."

"What is more important than winning honor and dying gloriously in battle?"

"There is no glory in death," he said more sharply than he intended. When he saw the surprised look on the boy's face, he softened the tone of his voice. "Joric, I'm certain when I was your age, I thought as you do. But now after so many years, I think living is preferable to dying." The crestfallen look on Joric's face caused him to add, "There is honor in being a warrior, but there is also hardship and going without the things that matter more than fighting battles such as having a fine son like you."

"Why don't you have a family? Decrius does."

"Joric, that is quite enough; it is rude to ask such things."

"I don't mind. I never found either the right woman or the circumstances for a family. In that, Decrius is most fortunate."

"I have no father. He was killed when I was too young to remember him. Mother said he was a warrior, and the Selgovi still talk of him."

Arrius watched Ilya's face go white. "Joric, go and finish chopping the wood, and when you've finished, I want you to help Attorix."

Joric stood up with a contrite look on his face. "I'm sorry, Mother." Then he cast a quick glance at Arrius. "One day may I ride your horse?"

"I'm certain Ferox would like that very much." His face wreathed in a smile, Joric disappeared through the door.

An awkward silence descended on the small room. Arrius saw Ilya staring out the small window, lips compressed, hands in her lap. He started to stand. "I must go."

Ilya turned to him and reached out a hand to restrain him, "Don't go. I apologize for my son's manners. He is young but should know better."

"Don't apologize. He's a fine boy who is merely inquisitive and proud of his father."

"I do not know who his father is." She said in a low voice.

Shocked into silence, he waited for her to elaborate. After a moment or two of continued silence, she lifted her head, drew a deep breath and looked at him, face devoid of color.

"I told Joric a long time ago about a father that never existed. It was easier to make up something than to tell him the truth that he was the result of being raped by Roman soldiers."

Arrius was stunned by her admission. It explained her hostility to Romans in general. Not knowing what else to say and regretting the circumstances that had caused the admission and her embarrassment, he said, "I'm sorry. You must find my presence unwelcome. I'll trouble you no more."

"It's no trouble. You're here at my invitation, and if I've embarrassed you then I'm sorry for that. Indeed, I have no idea why I told you. No one else here at Banna knows of it, and I would appreciate it if you would keep my secret. One day I will tell Joric when I think he's old enough to understand."

"I'll keep your secret."

"As you may have surmised from what Joric said, I was born into the Selgovan Tribe." She omitted the fact her father had been High Chieftain.

"Why did you come to Banna?"

Ilya hesitated, deliberating on just how much to tell him. She decided to limit her comments to the essentials. "I found it necessary to leave the tribe when Joric was born for reasons I will not go into. I came here because at the time I had nowhere else to go."

He knew there was more to the story than what she was saying. The fact she owned the tavern suggested she had enjoyed a status and wealth greater than an ordinary tribal member, but he elected not to probe.

"Then you joined the Brigantes Tribe?"

"I belong to no tribe, least of all the Brigantes. I remain here for Joric's sake. One day he'll have to decide who he is and what he will do then I will leave Banna and go far away where no one knows who I am."

"I've no doubt, thanks to you, when Joric is able to decide, he will choose well." He admired both her dedication to her son and her capacity to deal with adversity in practical terms when her clientele was primarily Roman. "You've done very well for him and have every right to be proud."

She looked closely at him searching his face to see if he really meant what he said. When she was convinced he did, she smiled gratefully.

"It hasn't been easy, but we've managed." She took a sip of wine and then studied him, a quizzical look on her face. "You're not at all what I expected. You're a soldier, but you do not talk like one. In fact, I wonder that you are a soldier at all."

"Recently, I've had occasion to think the same, but it seems very late in my life to dwell on the matter. As Joric will do one day, I chose what I would become. Perhaps Joric will choose more wisely than I did."

"Circumstances may give him fewer choices than he might wish."

Arrius pondered the strange remark, but it would be some time before he understood what she meant.

He decided he had better leave and reached for his helmet. This time she did not attempt to dissuade him. They exchanged a few perfunctory comments, both once again feeling awkward as they retraced their steps to the door. Outside, he found Joric rubbing the stallion's nose, and from the whickering noises the animal was making, the attention was welcome.

"It looks as if you made a friend, Joric."

"One day will you let me ride him?"

"I think that's possible, but only if your mother agrees."

"Joric rides like the wind. You and he will decide when the time is right, and my approval will not be necessary."

"Well, then that's settled. When there is less snow and the weather is better, Ferox and I will come back." He looked at Ilya. "That is if you permit."

"There is no need for you to wait until the winter passes. You are welcome here whenever you wish to come."

"As my duties permit, I would like that very much."

He gently kneed the stallion toward the stone bridge and the fort looming beyond. For the first time since leaving Judaea, he considered the possibility Fortuna had decided to favor him. Perhaps it would be appropriate, and wise, to overcome his usual skepticism regarding sacrifices to the gods and make a suitable offering. He was still thinking about it when he rode through the east gate.

As the praefectus rode past them, the guards wondered why he was smiling.

Historical Notes

The descriptions of the various Roman ranks, organizational positions, tactics and religious customs are a product of my research and the prolific material available on these subjects. The bibliography includes the references I drew most upon.

Much has been written about the Bar Kokhba rebellion in what is normally referred to as the second Jewish revolt. The first Jewish revolt from 66-70 CE was well-documented and described by Josephus, a Jewish general, who after having been captured by the Romans, became so Romanized he is reviled by Jews to this day. Unfortunately, there was no counterpart to either Josephus or Tacitus to provide a clear account of the Bar Kokhba rebellion, and Talmudic sources are at best conflicting and obscure.

Bar Kokhba whose real name was Shimeon Ben Kosiba (or Simeon Ben Kosziba) has been characterized as both a messianic and a military hero; the former resulted from the endorsement of Rabbi Aquiba (Akiva), one of the most prominent and influential religious leader of the time. The *nom de guerre,* Bar Kokhba, was, in fact, derived as described in the novel. Whether Bar Kokhba believed he was a messiah is something we will never know. That he was apparently a successful and charismatic military leader, at least for a time, cannot be disputed. He maintained the upper hand in Judaea for the better part of the first two years of the rebellion. It is generally accepted as historical fact that Bar Kokhba's followers were dedicated to the extent they cut off a finger signifying both loyalty to Bar Kokhba and solidarity to the Jewish cause.

Although the seeds of rebellion in Judaea never stopped germinating after the previous revolts, Hadrian's irrational and clumsy attempts to Hellenize a culture that abhorred fundamental Jewish tenets only focused more clearly the divide between the two cultures. Hadrian's inability to understand, much less tolerate, Jewish culture became a rallying cry for Jewish discontent. For example, the issue of circumcision that Jewish custom demanded and Hadrian's Hellenic orientation thought was tantamount to sacrilege of the human body was a significant basis for disagreement. The final spark that ignited the Jewish revolt and forged a common purpose for resisting Roman occupation was caused by the reconstruction of Jerusalem destroyed by the Romans in 70 CE. Hadrian intended to rename Jerusalem, Aeilia Capitolina (Aelia was his middle name) and Jupiter (Capitolina) the major Roman deity. In the process of the city's reconstruction, the remains of the Temple of Solomon were further weakened and subsequently crumbled; this became the ultimate rallying cry for a people absolutely fed up with Roman occupation.

Initially, the Romans were caught off guard when the uprising began, and the Jewish army enjoyed early success including the recapture of Jerusalem. There is speculation one Roman legion was destroyed or cashiered during this early period. The first Roman reinforcements sent to the region probably came from Syria and Egypt. The *Deiotariana* Legion stationed in Egypt was likely sent to Judaea somewhat earlier than I place it in the narrative. Its origin was as I described. That it was lost, for reasons unknown, sometime in 133 or 134 CE is the conclusion of most historians. The cause of its destruction because of battle or because it was disbanded for cowardice is not known. In the chronology of Roman history, the legion was never mentioned again after that time frame. There are conflicting reports Hadrian lost an additional legion in Judaea, but I was not able to verify which legion it was. By the end of the revolt, Hadrian may have had as many as seven legions in the province and surrounding region.

The slaughter and enslavement of the Jews was undertaken with a vengeance and brutality consistent with warfare of the day. There is little doubt Hadrian intended to provide an object lesson throughout the empire that rebellion against Rome would not be tolerated. I drew heavily on Josephus's detailed account of the previous rebellion to give some sense of the carnage practiced by both Romans and Jews.

The final Jewish stronghold was Beth Thera (Bather, and various other spellings) on a high ridge southwest of present day Jerusalem overlooking the Valley of Sorek. The Jews lived in caves underground. It is a testament to their resistance to the end how they mustered the numbers they did to make a final stand virtually beneath the Roman nose. How Bar Kokhba met his end is uncertain. It is generally accepted he had become a bitter disappointment to many Jews when they became convinced he was not the messiah after all. Some sources say he was killed by the Romans, others that his life ended at the hands of his own warriors.

There were no triumphs celebrated in Rome following the conclusion of the unpopular war. It seems there was a greater attempt to forget the war than to memorialize or commemorate its end. Three years after the revolt ended, Hadrian died at the age of 64 possibly of liver disease. By then he was an enfeebled, deranged man who turned on even his closest friends, of which he apparently had very few.

The route and length of time it took Arrius to travel to Britannia from Judaea is based on traditional Roman travel routes. Thanks to the research of Edward N. Luttwak, I made a reasonable estimate of how long it would have taken Arrius to reach Britannia during a fall sail across the Mediterranean and a winter march across France (Gaul) and Britannia.

In July of 2006, I traveled to the United Kingdom to see firsthand the places I was writing about. Rutupiae (Richborough, England north of Dover) where Arrius enters Britannia is not exactly the impressive gateway it once was. The Wantsum Channel separating the Isle of Thannet from the mainland is now very much silted up leaving the ruins of the Roman fort literally high and dry above the narrow Stour River. Nothing remains of the triumphal arch except a foundation now dominated by the low walls of a more modern Saxon fort built on the fort's original site. The Roman fort's defensive trenches are still visible, although the original walls of the fort were probably used in building the Saxon fort. The fort's west gate was a main arterial route that eventually reached Hadrian's Wall and the Antonine Wall farther north.

Eboracum (York) was the headquarters of the Ninth Legion and later the Sixth Legion, *Victrix* during the period of the novel. Unfortunately, the only remaining physical evidence can be found under York Minster Cathedral. Some of the foundations of the fort were found during 20th century excavations done to shore up the cathedral. There is an excellent museum beneath the main cathedral floor that includes a model of what the fort may have looked like based on the foundations uncovered.

The Sixth legion was responsible for the security of the northern frontier. The description of the mission of the Sixth and the role of the Roman auxilia described by Sextus Trebius is historically accurate. The wall was a "tripwire" manned by foreign troops from provinces across the breadth of the Roman Empire. It was the practice of the Roman Army to position non-Roman auxiliaries on the frontier. The legions were placed in rear positions to act as the main defense should hostilities break out. The wall itself was less a defensive position and more a means for population control and taxation. The Brigantes Tribe was one of the largest tribes dominating the central and northern regions. It would have made sense for the Romans to keep a close eye on this tribe as well as other tribes in the region south and north of the wall. The capitol settlement of the Briganti was only a short distance from Eboracum — a likely reason for the *Victrix* to be located there. Beldorach's attempts to stir up the Brigantes Tribe while a failure was realistic. The Briganti did revolt on at least two separate occasions. Early in his reign, Hadrian went to Britannia in 122 CE and presumably provided detailed guidance on where and how the Wall was to be constructed. Given the image of the hands-on individual Hadrian was known to be and his passion for architecture and building, it can be assumed he probably had definite ideas concerning how the wall would be built. It is for his widespread public works projects throughout the empire that he is best remembered apart from his destruction of the Judaean province.

Hadrian's reasons for constructing the wall are accurately described in the prologue by his instructions to Nepos and General Titurius. As he describes his monolithic project, Hadrian refers to a nearby turf and timber fort a short distance to the south and occasionally coincident where the wall was ultimately constructed. Agricola had similar forts built during his progress north into Caledonia (Scotland). The forts were later referred to as the Stanegate forts during the medieval period, a name still used today to differentiate this line of forts along Hadrian's Wall. While Agricola attempted to expand the Britannian frontier, Hadrian's objective was just the opposite.

Roman Military Rank and Structure

Auxilia (owks ilia): Auxiliary refers to the non-Roman forces that frequently manned the frontiers. In Britannia, legionaries from Tungria (northern Belgium) and Hispania (Spain) and many other Roman provinces garrisoned the forts along Hadrian's Wall. It was common practice during the empire to relocate indigenous troops to locations along the Roman frontiers in other than their own tribal lands. The latter provided further assurance against internal rebellion. The legions frequently remained behind the line of auxiliary forces as reinforcing elements to the frontier lines. This practice also left legionary forces available for vexillations to other parts of the empire where border incursion or local rebellions threatened or must be contained. There were three main elements of the *auxilia*: cavalry *ala* organized into *turmae* (troops), the infantry *cohortes* and the mixed cavalry and infantry called the *cohortes equitae*. Auxilia forces were either designated as *quingenaria* (500 strong) or *milaria* (1000 strong). Surprisingly, it was the cavalry *ala* that was considered the senior command over the infantry *cohortes* which in turn took precedence over the mixed cavalry and infantry unit when they were of similar size.

Ala (ah la; al aye-plural): Wing; refers to Roman cavalry. During the time of Julius Caesar and the republic, the Roman Army depended on foreign cavalry, placing its emphasis more on heavy and light infantry to win battles. Caesar's battle experience in Gaul taught him the importance of cavalry, and gradually the Romans began to place more importance in cavalry capabilities for reconnaissance patrols, skirmishing and flanking maneuvers. By the second and third centuries, the Roman army had completely embraced the use of cavalry and had become proficient in its use. The cavalry *alae* were the highest paid in comparison to the infantry units attesting to their increased value.

The auxilia cavalryman wore boots with spurs, a lighter cuirass and carried a longer sword. Their shields were considerably smaller and round instead of the rectangular, curved shield of the foot soldier. In addition to the sword that all cavalry wore, some were armed with small javelins or darts carried in a quiver attached to the saddle. Other cavalrymen carried longer spears that were not thrown but were used to jab downward.

The saddle during the period had four pommels which helped to maintain a firm seat since there were no stirrups. Stirrups were not used until sometime in the fourth or fifth century.

Centurion: The officer commanding a century (see below)

Century: A unit of 80 men and the basic unit of the Imperial legion; 60 centuries to a legion. The century was divided into ten *contubernia* with eight men assigned to each *contubernium*. Each *contubernium* shared a mule to carry their baggage, a tent in the field, a room or rooms in garrison and were allocated rations as a small unified mess.

Cohort: Six centuries – 480 men

Cornicularius (corn e cue lahr ius): Senior administrator of a military headquarters.

Decurion (decuriones pl) (day cur e on): An officer commanding a *turma* or cavalry troop.

Legion: Consisted of ten cohorts and approximately 5000 men commanded by a legatus legionis (general). The following are the legionary names and origins of the legions cited in the novel:

III Augusta Raised by Caesar Augustus

III Cyrenaica Named after the province where it was distinguished

III Galicia Formed from the veterans of Julius Caesar's Gallic legions

VI Ferrata (Ironsides) Formed by Julius Caesar

VI Victrix (Victorious) Pre-Augustan

X Fretensis Pre-Augustan

XX Valeria Victrix (Strong and Victorious) Title awarded after the defeat of Queen Boudica 60 BCE

XXII Deiotariana Raised by King Deiotarius of Galicia to assist Julius Caesar before integration into the Roman Army

Optio (optiones pl): A rank below centurion. The optio carried a knobbed staff and was generally positioned in the rear to prod legionaries who appeared to be ready to break ranks. Most likely they were equivalent to senior sergeants.

Praefectus Castrorum (Pray fech toose kah straw room): Camp prefect and a position usually accorded to an older senior centurion who had served successfully as a *primus pilus.* The position would place the incumbent next in line to assume command of a legion after the senior tribune.

Primi Ordines (prim e or din ays): The centurions of the first cohort and the senior centurion of each of the other nine cohorts.

Primi pilatus (pree me pee lah toose): Former primus pilus-senior centurion.

Primus pilus (pree moos pee loose): It literally means first file and was the form of address and title of the senior centurion commanding the first cohort (about 800 men) in a Roman Legion. In seniority, the primus pilus ranked only below the legion commander, the six tribunes and the *praefectus castrorum* (see above). The position was prestigious and the apex of a centurion's career.

Tribunus Laticlavius (tree bun oos lah tee clah vee oose): One of the six tribunes assigned to a legion and the senior tribune in the legion. He wore a cloak with a wide purple strip differentiating him from the narrow stripe worn by the junior tribunes. He was second in command to the legion commander. Tribunes were considered staff officers without direct command authority with the exception if the Tribunis Laticlavius when assumed command of the legion.

Glossary

Acceptum (ahk sep thoom): The amount of military pay receipted by a legionary when he was paid.

Ballista (ball is ta — ballistae pl): Catapults of one form or another. The large *ballista* or *onager* (mule) launched stones while the smaller *scorpiones* (scorpions) shot arrow-bolts.

Balteus (bal tay oose): The Roman military belt that more than any other item distinguished the legionary. Divestiture of the belt was considered a severe punishment and a disgrace.

Bracae (brack-eye): Leather trousers worn down to just below the knee.

Bucellata (boo si lahta): The hard-baked biscuit, much like hardtack, made from ground wheat mixed with water then baked.

Caliga (ae): (cah leg a; cah lee gye): The hobnailed boot-sandal all Roman officers and legionaries wore. They varied in thickness if not in basic design according to the weather and terrain. Somewhat open around the upper foot they were laced to mid-calf or higher, depending on the weather. In winter and cold regions, legionaries wore socks and wrapped their legs in felt or wool cloth for additional warmth. The Emperor Caligula derived his name from the time he was a small boy and spent much of his time around legionary barracks. Because of that, he was given the nickname "Little Boots."

Castigato (cah sti gahto): Corporal punishment as when a centurion would strike a legionary with his vine (vitis) stick.

Cornicines (car nee seens): Horn blowers.

Denarius, denarii (pl): The largest Roman coinage denomination. It is estimated the legionary foot soldier was paid about 180 denarii a year with the combined infantry and cavalry legionaries earning more. The cavalryman was the highest paid legionary. The centurions were at the top of the army pay-scale and depending on seniority, earned as much as five times the amount of an ordinary legionary. Legionary pay was withheld to pay for rations, equipment and fodder; therefore, it is impossible to say with any certitude precisely what the legionary had left for discretionary spending, but it is safe to assume it wasn't very much. Withholdings were even made for burial in the event the legionary died he would be assured of appropriate ceremonials and offerings in his behalf.

Dolubra(e) (doe loo bra — doe loo bray pl): Combined pick and axe

Fustuarium (foos twar e oom): A harsh sentence reserved for especially serious offenses such as sleeping on guard or cowardice. The condemned man was set upon with cudgels by members of the individual's own unit, probably his century. The punishment was occasionally administered to an entire unit including a legion when the charge was cowardice. In such cases, lots were drawn and every tenth man was condemned. The term "decimate'" refers to this practice. In most cases, the individual or individuals died from the brutal beating. If an individual somehow managed to survive (probably rare), he was summarily dismissed from the army in disgrace.

Gladius (glah dee oose): The short sword carried by officers and legionaries.

Imaginifer (emah gin e fur): The legionary who carried a representation of the emperor or deity.

Manus (mah noose): The image of an upraised hand, palm out, fingers joined affixed to a standard below the eagle and representing the oath each legionary took

Medicus (medi coose): Medical orderly.

Phelorae (fay lor eye): Military decorations worn on the cuirass or on a leather strap across a segmented corselet

Pilum (pee loom), pee la (pl): Although one generally thinks of the short sword, or gladius, as the weapon that most characterized the Roman legionary, it was the heavy javelin which defined the Roman Army. Slightly over six feet in length, it had a long pyramidal shaped point that took up almost a third of the total length of the weapon. The Roman Army depended on volleys of pila to deliver a punishing barrage before the front ranks charged. The metal shafts of each pilum were not tempered and bent easily on contact. The latter was an intended consequence and resulted in weighing down the shields of the opposing ranks allowing more lethal opportunity to wield the gladius at short range.

Praetorium (pry tor ium): The commander's quarters in a Roman fort.

Principia (prin sip ee ah): The headquarters building in a Roman fort.

Pugio (poo gee oh): The dagger each legionary wore on the *balteus* on the opposite side from the *gladius.* Centurions wore the dagger on the right side while the legionary wore his on the left.

Quaestor (kway eh stohr): Quartermaster in charge of stores and supplies for a legion or other military unit.

Sacellum (sahc el loom): The sacred shrine where the legion standards are stored.

Sacramentum (sahc rah men toom): The oath each legionary took to the emperor after recruitment and later during the empire to the legion commander he served to assure personal loyalty

Scutum (skoo toom): Shield (plural - **Scuta**)

Sesterce (ses ter see, sestercii -pl): A coin worth approximately a quarter of a denarius

Signifer (sig ni fuhr): Standard bearer

Tessera (tes er ah): A wooden tablet presumably covered by wax upon which was inscribed the daily password. The *tesseraius* was the officer responsible for carrying the tablets (*tesserae*) for each guard section for the four guard reliefs. Each guard section then passed it on to his replacement. In the morning, the tablets were recovered. If any were missing, the punishment could be extreme from death to dismissal depending on the circumstances.

Testudo (teh stu doh): A tight defensive formation named for the tortoise in which the inside ranks placed their shields over their heads while the outside ranks kept their shield facing outward. The formation provided protection from arrows and other missiles from above and the sides.

Torque (tor kwee): Military decoration worn around the neck

Vexillation (vex eel lat shun): A term used to describe a detachment to or from a legion. Typically, the Roman legions lost or received vexillations from other legions according to tactical or strategic requirements. The vexillation concept was more likely to have been exercised at the cohort level to maintain unit cohesion.

Via Principalis (wee ah prin se pahlis): One of the two main streets of a Roman fortress that bisected the *via praetoria*. Near the intersection of these two roads is where the headquarters or principia would be located.

Victrix (wik triks): Legion name meaning Victorius.

Vitis (wee tis): The distinctive twisted vine stick a centurion carried symbolizing his rank. It was also frequently used as an instrument for administering corporal punishment.

Place Names

Aelia Capitolina: Hadrian renamed Jerusalem after himself and Jupiter: Aelia was his middle name and Capitolina referred to Jupiter—both names were highly offensive to the Jewish people as was renaming Judaea, Palestina

Carthagae: Carthage.

Banna (Bah na): Birdoswald, England. In Latin Banna means tongue or spur and refers to the geography of its location at a sharp bend of the River Irthing.

Belgica (Bel ghee ka): Generally modern-day Belgium and part of northern Germany.

Britannia (Bree tah nee ah): England, Wales and Scotland.

Bravoniacum (Brah voh nah ki oom): Kirkby Thore, England, approximately 25 miles south of Birdoswald.

Burrium the town of Usk

Dacia (Datiae or Datia — Da-chee-ia): Extended over what is now the Carpathian-Danube region consisting roughly of Romania, parts of Hungary, Bulgaria, Yugoslavia and Moldavia.

Deva (Dew wah): Chester, England.

Durovernum (Duroh vehr noom): Canterbury, England.

Eboracum (Eh bor ah coom): York, England. The ruins of the headquarters of the former ninth and sixth legions lie under York Minister Cathedral and were discovered in the last century when the cathedral foundations were being repaired. They can be seen today via a self-guided tour of the crypt.

Fanum Cocidii (Fah num ko cee dee): Bewcastle, England, located 7-8 miles northwest of Birdoswald (Banna). The Latin name Shrine of Cocidius probably derives from the local Britannic god Cocidius who was variously associated with the forest and hunters but was also depicted in statues and stone etchings as a warrior. Fanum Cocidii was the only known Roman fortress named after a deity. It is possible Fanum Cocidii was a fortress used by local British tribes before the Romans arrived, and the Romans either adopted the existing name or coined it out of respect for the deity. The worship of Cocidius was widespread in Britannia and bore similarities to the Roman god Sylvanus, which may account for the Roman willingness to continue honoring and worshiping the deity.

Gaul: Generally encompassing modern day France including Belgium and Luxembourg.

Joppa: Jaffa now part of Tel Aviv.

Massilia (Ma seel e yah): The port of Marseille, France.

Parthian Empire: Encompassed the area generally including what is now Iran and Iraq

Portus Itius (Por tus Ee tee oose): Boulogne, France.

Puteoli (Poo tee oli): The Italian port of Pozzuoli in the bay of Naples.

Rutupiae (Rhu too pee-aye): Richborough, England, ten miles or so north of the town of Dover and about five miles south of Ramsgate.

Uxellodunum (Uck el lo doo noom): Stanwix, England, a suburb of Carlisle in northwest England. It is thought this was the probable location for the command headquarters for the entire wall defense. For command and control, this far western location may have been favored over a more central site simply based on the greater threat posed by the Novantae and Selgovae Tribes populating the west and central sections respectively. Positioning the largest cavalry unit on the wall at this location would have provided a rapid response in the event the far northern outposts were attacked. It also makes strategic sense for the Romans to locate a large body of cavalry here as a cavalry *ala* (wing) was traditionally used to screen the flanks of an attacking legion. Should the Romans launch an attack north of the wall, the cavalry wing would likely have been used to screen the western flank.

Bibliography:

Blair, PH. *Roman Britain and Early England 55 B.C. – A.D. 871*, W.W. Norton & Company, New York, London, 1966.

Bowman, A.K. *Life and Letters On the Roman Frontier*, the British Museum Press, London, 1994 and Routledge in the U.S. and Canada, 1998.

Burke, J. *Roman England*, W.W. Norton & Co., New York, London, 1983.

Caesar, Julius, *The Gallic War*, translated by H. J. Edwards, Loeb Classical Library, Harvard University Press, Cambridge, Massachusetts, 2004.

Cowan, R. *Roman Legionary 58 B.C. – A.D.* illustrated by A. McBride, Osprey Publishing, Botley, Oxford, UK, 2003.

Eban, Abba *Heritage, Civilization and the Jews*, Summit Books, Simon & Schuster, New York, 1984.

Goldsworthy, A.K *The Roman Army At War, 100 BC- AD 200*, Oxford University Press, 1996.

Harris, S., *Richborough and Reculver,* English Heritage, London, 2001.

Josephus, *The Jewish War*, translated by G.A. Williamson, Penguin Books, Ltd, London, 1981.

Luttwak, E. N. *The Grand Strategy of the Roman Empire From the First Century A.D to the Third*, The Johns Hopkins University Press, Baltimore and London, 1979.

Renatus, FlaviusVegetius *Roman Military*, translated by John Clarke 1767, Pavillion Press, Inc, Philadelphia, 2004.

Speller, E. *Following Hadrian,* Oxford University Press, Oxford, U.K. 2004

Tacitus, *The Agricola,* translated with an introduction by H. Mattingly (1948) and revised by S. A. Handford (1970), Penguin Books, London England, 1970.

Webster. G. *The Roman Imperial Army, of the First and Second Centuries A.D.*, University of Oklahoma Press, Norman Oklahoma, 1998.

Wilmott, T. *Birdoswald Roman Fort*, English Heritage, London 2005.

Don't miss ARRIUS Volume II, Legacy.

Coming from Moonshine Cove Publishing, LLC in 2018.

Read the first chapter beginning on the next page.

Chapter 1

Arrius was tired. The days had been long, and sleep was a luxury snatched a few hours at a time wherever he might be at the time. From past experience, he knew this was the critical period to transform the Tungrian cohort into some semblance of a fighting unit with the capability of doing more than performing guard duty. Fighting formations were practiced on the training field followed by century-size patrols conducted both south and north of the wall. At first Decrius and Rufus accompanied all patrols to ensure their recent battle experience was passed on to the legionaries who had not gone to Judaea. Arrius planned to accompany each cavalry troop at least once during overnight patrols to better assess their capabilities; the two he had ridden with so far proved their worth, and he was optimistic the remaining one would prove as proficient. In comparison to the infantry, the cavalry contingent at Banna was far more field-ready.

Unfortunately, it was with the majority of centurions he felt little change had taken place because of loyalty to Betto that still prevailed. Its effects were corrosive and left Arrius feeling uneasy key officers could not be depended on when put to the test. The indicators were manifested in the way many of the officers responded unenthusiastically to his orders, executing them correctly but with no indication or willingness to extend their efforts beyond what was ordered.

He kept waiting for Betto to say or do something egregious enough that would justify transferring him elsewhere; however, the centurion never allowed an opportunity to occur when either his competence or loyalty could be legitimately called into question. On the surface, Betto appeared to be the one officer who went out of his way to execute his orders quickly and thoroughly. He didn't trust Betto and thought it unlikely he ever would. Arrius realized it was simply a matter of time before one or the other would determine it was time to resolve their differences. Until then, he would keep his senior centurion under close observation.

Arrius was used to the harsh disciplinary measures and punishment common in the Roman Army; yet Betto's methods were as brutal as he had ever seen in the legions. The most severe measures at his disposal were used sparingly and selectively. On occasion, he had little choice but to impose severe penalties for serious offenses. The day before he had imposed the *fustuarium* on a legionary found sleeping on guard duty. The fact the legionary had been paid by another legionary to stand an extra relief was not sufficient to mitigate the sentence. He was now waiting for Antius Durio to notify him all legionaries not on guard had been assembled along the length of the via principalis to witness the punishment. The fustuarium would be carried out by the legionaries from the condemned man's century. The legionary who had paid the condemned man to take his shift would receive 50 lashes.

His thoughts were interrupted by the arrival of Antius Durio, the cohort's chief administrative officer who had a worried frown on his face.

"Praefectus, a messenger from Camboglanna has just arrived," referring to the fort ten miles to the west and midway between Banna and Uxellodonum. "General Arvinnius arrived there approximately an hour ago. He plans to remain a few hours at Camboglanna to inspect the garrison before coming to Banna. He plans to stay the night here before continuing his inspection of the eastern Wall. Do you want to postpone the punishment formation?"

"No, there's yet time, and the two legionaries are by now reconciled to their fate. Is the cohort assembled?"

"It is, Praefectus."

Arrius stood up and followed Durio through the headquarters, thinking over as he did the things that must be done to prepare for the legion commander's arrival. He estimated they would have an hour after Arvinnius's departure from Camboglanna to assemble the cavalry troop not on patrol and all centuries not on guard duty in parade formation and ready for inspection. Without knowing the general's preferences, he assumed he would be interested in those things with which any commander might be concerned. He would have liked another week to prepare, but at least the essential changes he wanted made had been accomplished.

Arrius mounted Ferox and walked the horse to the intersection of the fort's two main streets. He reined in the stallion and waited for the guard detail to bring the two prisoners forward. The legionaries flanking either side of the wide street linking the east and west gates stood silently waiting for the punishment to commence. The centurions were positioned at intervals to ensure only cudgels were used. The legionaries who were to carry out the sentence had been cautioned not to hold back out of sympathy or friendship. He had known a few rare occurrences where the condemned legionary had survived the gauntlet.

Arrius heard a commotion and the guard detail emerged from the doorway of the nearest barracks. The two men to receive punishment had been stripped to their linen underdrawers. He noted with approval that both men, ashen-faced, walked toward him without having to be dragged. The legionary to be flogged had his arms tied to a stout pole stretched across his shoulders.

Arrius said in a commanding voice, "Officers and legionaries of the Second Cohort, you are assembled here to witness the punishment of two men who failed in their duty to the cohort and to Rome." Then looking at the prisoners, he asked, "Does either of you ask for relief or clemency?"

The legionaries both chorused, "Yes!"

Arrius directed his attention to the ranks of legionaries. "A request for clemency has been requested. Didius is to receive 50 lashes. Should the punishment be reduced?"

A roar of approval echoed throughout the fort along with shouted numbers. "So be it, let the number of lashes be reduced to 25. Sitorix has been condemned to the fustuarium. Should the sentence be reduced to flogging?"

There was an angry uproar, a response that did not surprise him in the least. Sleeping on guard was possibly the worst offense known, as the lapse potentially jeopardized the entire unit. Even staunch friendships ended when such dereliction occurred.

"Guard detail, give Didius 25 lashes."

An optio stepped forward and uncoiled a whip. Two legionaries forced the prisoner to his knees and grasped each end of the pole to prevent the man from moving. For the first few blows, there was no sound to be heard except the hissing of the whip followed by a sharp smack as it hit bare flesh. By the time the fifth blow had landed, Didius could be heard grunting with each successive strike that soon gave way to a continuous moan. Arrius surveyed the faces of the legionaries nearest him. With the widespread inclination for gambling common in the legions and auxilia, he was certain there were wagers placed on how well the flogged man would bear up under the punishment. He saw Betto staring with rapt attention at the victim's bleeding back and was disgusted at the obvious enjoyment the centurion seemed to have watching the bloody spectacle.

By the time the last blow was delivered, it was apparent by the legionary's silence he was unconscious and remained so as the guards carried him to the infirmary. Arrius nodded to the optio, and Sitorix was escorted to the east gate. The ranks of legionaries remained silent as the condemned man walked unaided between his guards. Arrius had known a few men similarly condemned who lost their manhood, soiling themselves with fright and embarrassing all who bore witness. Shameful exhibitions were more often than not met with prolonged suffering. By contrast, the majority who accepted their fate bravely died quickly. It appeared Sitorix would meet his gods quickly.

Moments later there was a crescendo of noise as Sitorix commenced his run to the west gate. He went down first no more than ten paces from where he started. Arrius found himself silently urging the man to regain his feet. Surprisingly, he not only stood up but sprinted vigorously down the street, blood cascading down one side of his face from a glancing blow that left a flap of his scalp hanging down across his forehead. As the legionary approached the mid-point of the gauntlet, it was apparent he had already suffered extensively. The slower he went the more blows he received. He fell again nearly opposite where Arrius sat astride Ferox. For a moment it appeared he would not be able to get up. He saw one legionary administering blow after blow, the dull meaty sound of his cudgel making contact with flesh and bone loud enough to be heard over the shouting of the legionaries. Miraculously, Sitorix managed to stand and made off in a shambling gait, closer to a walk than a run. A few steps later, he fell for the last time. A dozen legionaries encircled the prone man and took turns administering the final blows.

Arrius immediately directed his attention to Antius Durio standing next to Ferox, the drama of the bloody punishment already dismissed from his mind.

"Signal the mile forts that General Arvinnius is conducting an inspection of the Wall. I will meet him at the western mile fort and escort him to Banna. Inform Betto and Durmius Lucillus they have two hours to prepare the legionaries, the barracks, stables and the fort in general for inspection. All cavalry and legionaries not on guard will stand formation inside the fort as soon as the western mile fort signals we've departed. Send a messenger to Seugethis to come to Banna with a troop. There's a possibility the general will go to Fanum Cocidii. If so, Seugethis will escort him there and back."

An hour later, Arrius exited the west gate under a leaden sky and cantered toward Banna's western most mile fort, stopping briefly at each of the signal towers and mile forts long enough to ensure all was in readiness in case Arvinnius decided to stop for a quick inspection. By the time he reached his destination, he was satisfied Arvinnius would find nothing amiss at Banna's western garrisons.